*continued . . .*

# *Smokeout*

"Hilariously over-the-top . . . with knowing wit and biting sarcasm."
—*Chicago Tribune*

"Pantsless legislators. Poison dart guns. Million-dollar bribes. Just another day at the Florida Legislature. If only the real world were as clear and as fun."
—*The Tampa Tribune*

"A hilarious political satire that reflects our blackest fears about the politicians we elect."
—*The New York Times Book Review*

"A baker's dozen of subplots converge in a wild and woolly finale that teeters on the edge of farce. But thanks to Date's animated characters, who are quirky without being cartoonish, and impeccable narrative timing, the fast-moving plot never veers out of control."
—*Publishers Weekly*

"Deftly plotted and seasoned with unforgettable characters . . . Carl Hiaasen may have an heir apparent."
—*The Providence Journal*

# Speed Week

"Good, twisted fun, cheerfully subversive. The Chamber of Commerce should hate it, which is the highest possible compliment for any Florida novel." —Carl Hiaasen

"Babes, bikers, and a bad-ass shark in Daytona Beach. I love it!" —Les Standiford

"Dark suspense and dark comedy. . . . This one has more turns than the Daytona 500." —*The Buffalo News*

"Date makes each attempted hit a humorous study in criminal incompetence . . . *Speed Week* is one book you'll be tempted to race through on a rainy spring afternoon." —*Chicago Tribune*

"Revels in the sleaze and greed of wacky nincompoops driven mad by the Florida sun." —*Kirkus Reviews*

"S. V. Date is a graduate of the Carl Hiaasen School of Florida Novel Writing, and *Speed Week* suggests he's among the star pupils. . . . His plot charges like one of those Daytona racers, and he has the warped sense of humor required to bring Daytona to tacky life. *Speed Week* is one swift little ride." —*St. Petersburg Times*

*Berkley Prime Crime titles by S. V. Date*

SPEED WEEK
SMOKEOUT
DEEP WATER

# Deep Water

## S. V. DATE

BERKLEY PRIME CRIME, NEW YORK

DEEP WATER

A Berkley Prime Crime Book / published by arrangement with the author

PRINTING HISTORY
G. P. Putnam's Sons hardcover edition / October 2001
Berkley Prime Crime mass-market edition / October 2002

Visit our website at
www.penguinputnam.com

ISBN: 0-425-18692-X

Berkley Prime Crime Books are published
by The Berkley Publishing Group,
a division of Penguin Putnam Inc.,
375 Hudson Street, New York, New York 10014.
The name BERKLEY PRIME CRIME and the
BERKLEY PRIME CRIME design
are trademarks belonging to Penguin Putnam Inc.

PRINTED IN THE UNITED STATES OF AMERICA

10  9  8  7  6  5  4  3  2  1

*For Aai and Baba*

*Many thanks,*

once again, to Neil Nyren for his navigational assistance; to Lauren Charlip for a sharp pair of eyes; to Marcia Gelbart for a reality check; to the *Palm Beach Post* for *not* being like the *Orlando Advocate*; to Orion and Rigel for keeping it, for the most part, below 100 decibels; and to Mary Beth, as always, for everything.

# prologue
## ...

The blue sea kayak glided silently through tea-colored water as Irlo "Bobby" King let the paddle rest against his chest. Somewhere in the thick morning mist, not so far ahead now, was the lone acacia tree that, according to his earlier reconnaissance, marked the southern boundary of Africaland.

Africaland, wedged between New Patagonia and Swamp Country, abutting the Untamed Arctic, and across the river from Golf, U.S.A., and, of primary significance to Irlo King, the site of all four deaths of Wild Dominion's much-ballyhooed rare and endangered species. For ten straight hours the previous day, from park opening to sunset, Irlo had ridden the Wild Dominion Safari Tram, over and over, breaking only for a zucchini-and-sprouts sandwich he'd smuggled past the turnstiles in a fanny pack. Ten straight hours of mind-numbing banter from the pith-helmeted "guide." Ten straight hours of Discovery Channel platitudes mixed with Whipple Corporation self-congratulatory propaganda, as he surreptitiously but painstakingly sketched a layout of the habitats of the dead animals vis-à-vis the Serenity River.

Fifty-six dollars and fifty cents, less the five percent

Florida resident discount, but including a usurious nine percent tourist tax, it had cost him. Nearly a full day's pay. But, as he kept reminding himself, it would be worth it. If his theory was correct, then sixty bucks to the devil himself would be worth it.

The gentle current began nudging the nose of the kayak downstream, and Irlo King dipped his double-ended oars, pulled awkwardly one way, then the other, until the boat pointed north again. Or at least what he thought was north, given the opacity of the mist. The fear began to nag him that he wouldn't be able to find it before the park opened, but then he calmed himself: If not today, then tomorrow. What was going on, Whipple would not be able to fix in a single day. No way.

With a deep, calming breath, he peered through the fog until, finally, not ten yards off, appeared the solitary acacia marking the end of the ingeniously landscaped fence that kept the carnivores of the savannah from feasting on llama and other South American delicacies.

He resumed paddling as quietly as he could, first stroking closer toward the Golf, U.S.A, side, then paralleling the riverbank just close enough to make out some detail on shore. Stealth was of the essence. An early-morning groundskeeper at the golf park, a Dominion trainer doing his rounds—either would have a radio with which to summon a Whipple sheriff's deputy. And that, he knew, would not be good. Definitely not good.

Eyes glued to the shore, he counted strokes as he paddled. He had estimated it was about three hundred yards beyond the border. Three football fields. The better part of a fairway in a developer's wet dream. Three hundred yards of upland scrub, slashed and carted off to make way for a nice, weed- and bug-free strip of overfertilized grass. Or even worse, three hundred yards of wetland, ditched and drained to round out yet another back nine.

With an effort, Irlo King unclenched his teeth and set his mind to the problem at hand. No point getting all worked up and losing his focus. The Southside Mall, Egret Chase, the River Bend Club: All were important projects, and all deserved his undivided attention, at the proper time. Just as Whipple Corporation deserved it now.

He kept counting his strokes, wondering if perhaps he could have missed it, when suddenly it appeared on the golf park bank: a thick black pipe, partially buried, running down into the murky water. He allowed himself a smile, then gracelessly turned the kayak across the river and pulled himself to the Dominion side. If it was there, it would be most readily apparent either right across from that pipe or just downstream.

He felt the riverbank through the floor of the kayak before he saw it, the fog was so thick, and decided he wasn't going to be able to see anything from the boat. He waded through the muck, dragging the boat up onto the dirt and weeds, before he reminded himself that he was now, on foot and unprotected by fence or moat or any other barrier, in Africaland, where a trainer had been mauled and partially eaten by a pride of lions just a month earlier.

He began walking, and almost immediately his mouth went dry and his heart began to race when he noticed a powdery, whitish residue on the pebbles at his feet. With eyes wide and fears of being consumed by carnivores at least temporarily at bay, Irlo moved up the bank, stooped at the waist, until finally he found a demarcation line marking the limit of the residue. He glanced back at the river, estimated a height difference of about one and a half feet, and immediately ran a couple of mental calculations to derive a water flow rate.

This time he allowed himself a full, ear-to-ear grin, buckteeth biting deep into his lower lip, eyes bright and distant. He could just see the size of the headlines as, finally, Whipple Corporation was confronted with a scandal even its storied public relations machine couldn't sweep under the rug.

From a pocket of his cargo pants he produced a gallon-size Ziploc bag, into which he collected as many pebbles, leaves, clumps of grass, and handfuls of silt as he could fit, all of it coated with the still-damp residue. Carefully pressing the seal together, he tucked the bag into the kayak, then from another pocket of his pants pulled out a half-dozen plastic vials. One by one, he filled each with river water, once more dreaming about his impending vengeance upon Whipple Corporation, nay, upon the entire Central Florida pro–strip mall, pro-sprawl ruling elite—

*SQUAWWWWK!!*

Irlo nearly fell face-first into the river, the noise so startled him, and his first instinct was flight. After all, he'd seen enough National Geographic specials—had even been to the real Africa once—to know that birds always sensed the approach of a predator, even before the prey. And then he stopped to consider the noise again, placed the sound as the defensive bark of a turkey vulture.

He blinked twice. Turkey vulture. Carrion eater. What carrion would there be in Africaland, where all the beasts got their London broils and porterhouses, extra rare, at the same time each day? Unless, of course, the rumor of the missing snow leopard was true. . . . And, no, not once in ten hours at the park the previous day, a total of seventeen tram rides, had he seen so much as the whiskers of the animal.

Inexorably drawn now, he moved along the bank in the direction of the noise, half wondering if he could have been mistaken about it being a turkey vulture, when through the mist appeared a gaggle of the birds, snapping and picking at a carcass in their midst.

It was the snow leopard.

Recently dead, too, Irlo surmised from its condition. One of the birds pecked at his hiking boot, and Irlo kicked it away disgustedly. They were foul creatures, perpetually covered with their own droppings, so that even a scratch would quickly become a raging infection.

He thought of the pebbles and the water, of the significance of their laboratory analysis, and compared it with the shock value of a dead, endangered Whipple animal, the fifth in as many months, and Irlo knew what he had to do. With a dead animal, it wouldn't be just headlines anymore, but satellite trucks. A great, big, long line of satellite trucks, parked end-to-end on the shoulder just outside Whipple property, with puffed-hair, heavily made-up TV babes breathlessly describing the unspeakable horror of yet another rare, endangered specimen, this time a cuddly snow leopard, barely more than a cub, dead at America's favorite theme park, and in the words of the massing protesters here: What *would* Waldo say?

Irlo kicked aside one bird, then another, ignored the pecks and scratches of two others as he moved in toward the dead cat. This was national now, not just Florida. The *New York Times*. The *Washington Post*. CNN. Hell, it was the stuff of Jay Leno jokes, so that even the *Orlando Advocate* would be forced to acknowledge it. He smiled at that thought as he scooped up the carcass over the protesting squawks and began staggering back toward his kayak.

Finally! The bastards weren't going to get away with it this time! All their cockamamie excuses about why none of the dead animals could possibly be *their* fault, how they were just as disappointed, dismayed, and so forth as the animal rights groups, how they had every confidence that their internal investigation would ultimately solve the mystery, without the well-intentioned but unnecessary meddling of outside organizations—all of the crap they'd gotten by with following the previous deaths simply wasn't going to fly this time.

Because this time he, and not Whipple, would be in charge of the necropsy, and the truth would not be denied. He jerked the deadweight of the animal higher as he walked, ignoring the decaying flesh's fetid odor as he imagined the airtight case the cat's remains gave him. Now, not only did he have evidence of Whipple's environmental carelessness, he had absolute, incontrovertible, made-for-TV proof, as well!

Another vulture pecked his ankle, replacing his vision of being interviewed by Ted Koppel with a white flash of pain. Irlo kicked at it angrily but connected only with feathers as the big bird squawked and hopped aside.

Where the hell was the kayak? He couldn't believe he'd walked that far in the first place. Or maybe the leopard's weight was starting to get to him. He estimated it was fifty or sixty pounds, spread across four feet of carcass, impossible to carry easily. Especially with a pack of angry scavengers picking at him. Which reminded him: Before the end of the day, he'd have to start on an antibiotic. Maybe Stephanie's husband could write him a scrip and save him some time.

He sneered at the thought of the man his ex-wife had married, but then decided he wasn't going to let even that diminish his triumph. Every cause, he supposed, needed those whose role seldom went beyond attending cocktail parties and writing checks.

At long last the kayak appeared out of the fog, and apprehension gripped his insides when he realized he could see it, even though it was still a good twenty or thirty yards away. The fog was starting to lift. He was running later than he'd planned. Way later.

He stood over the little boat, still holding the cat, and decided that the only way would be to drape it over the bow. He let its front paws dangle down into his seat, shoved off, and quickly climbed in. He paddled briskly, sacrificing stealth for speed, every once in a while waving the oar at a vulture that would swoop down.

He maneuvered to the middle of the river, but realized that even from there he could see both banks clearly. Meaning, he accepted with a gulp, that anyone on shore would be able to see *him* clearly as well. Well, a few more minutes and he was home free. He had to make it back down to where he'd pulled off the service road, just north of where the Serenity River passed the town's exclusive Founders' Estates neighborhood and entered Lake Serenity.

Five minutes to get the cat in the trunk, the kayak on the roof rack, and he was outta there. Five minutes to the Turnpike, an hour and a half to his pal at the veterinary school in Gainesville. He would use every minute of the drive on the cell phone to spread the word, get everyone organized, so that the moment they got the results from the necropsy and the water samples, they could start the media blitz.

He should call Armstrong, too, he decided, to get him to work his contacts. But first, before anyone else, he would call Stephanie about that prescription. She'd ask why he needed it, and he'd let slip a couple of details. Real nonchalant. Like it was no big deal. And by the end of the conversation, when the enormity of his achievement was clear, she'd know how badly she'd screwed up, dumping him as she had.

Another vulture flapped its wings at him as it snapped at the dead cat's body. Irlo awkwardly swung his oars at the bird again and immediately resumed stroking the water. Finally, he saw the clump of trees behind which he'd parked his car, and rhythmically pumped his arms from side to side. He was sweating heavily now, breathing hard, clenching his teeth against the stench of the carcass, which seemed to grow stronger by the minute. The birds had already picked the poor creature's eyes out, and its hollow sockets stared at him ghoulishly.

It would be nice to get the leopard safely in his trunk, where he no longer had to protect it from marauding birds or have its decaying face just inches away. Perhaps he would allow himself a stop at a motel on the way to Gainesville. Take a nice, hot shower. Maybe clean and dress his vulture bites. Put on clean clothes that didn't have snow leopard pus on them.

Sure, he told himself as he ground the kayak into the grassy bank and hopped out. What was a twenty-minute stop in the scheme of things? Surely the cat's condition wouldn't worsen appreciably because of a slight delay. He dragged the boat out of the water, patting his cargo pants pockets for his keys as he backed uphill toward where the Saab was hidden, decided he *would* stop on the way to Gainesville—

"Brought your own vultures, I see," a voice rang out. "Now, *that's* advance planning."

Irlo turned enough to see a pair of cowboy boots and green trousers, and that was the last thing he saw before the black sackcloth came down over his head.

# one

## ...

As he did every morning, Dickie Gillespie, mayor of Serenity, Florida, strode along the Promenade with supreme self-importance, nodding authoritatively at passersby, smugly acknowledging their apprehensive glances.

Part of his mystique was the warm-up suit. With its official Whipple logo—the stylized muskrat head superimposed with an embroidered, cursive *W*—the suit was among the gear available only to top executives. It was unavailable in stores—and therefore worth a small fortune on the black market for Whippleobelia. Gillespie made sure to wear a different color every day, a not-so-subtle reminder to the townsfolk of his pull with the company.

But most of the deference the commoners showed him, he knew, derived not from anything he wore, nor from his less-than-intimidating physical stature. It came from The Clipboard, and Dick Gillespie made sure to carry it with him everywhere.

The Clipboard, with its hundreds of pages of scheduled community chores, association rules, and up-to-date records of membership dues in the various clubs, was the enforcement mechanism behind the covenants agreed to by every homeowner, and Mayor Gillespie was the enforcer.

It was his affinity for that role, in fact, that got him the job as mayor. The shock of white hair and ruddy cheeks and disarming smile were all important as far as the quintessentially-quirky-but-warmhearted-small-town-mayor thing went, but Gillespie's reputation as the unforgiving casting director of Whipple World's various musical numbers, as someone willing to kick ass and take names—that was the sine qua non for the job.

A jogger appeared through the mist and waved cordially at Gillespie. He returned a half-smile. Then, after she had passed, he turned to watch her ass recede into the fog. It was, he had to admit, a fine ass. Considering the woman was the mother of two toddlers, it was a magnificent ass, and Gillespie felt himself salivating as the blue nylon running shorts jiggled away.

Quickly he turned to his clipboard and flipped through pages until he got to the M's. Debbie McMahon. Schoolteacher, taking time off to raise her kids. Husband an engineer at Lockheed. House on Charleston Lane in the Plantation neighborhood. Fully compliant. All community chores attended to. No demerits.

Gillespie grumbled and shut the clipboard. With some women, it was just never going to happen. He shrugged it off and started moving again. He wasn't going to get upset about it. Life was too short. Plus, women were like the monorail at Whipple World: There was always another Mrs. McMahon in another couple of minutes.

He power walked to the end of the Promenade, then across Front Street, down a block, and began his survey of the single-family homes in the Cornwall neighborhood, the "most" New Urban of the whole New Urban town, whatever the hell that meant. The Whipple Architectural Division had tried to brief him on the goals of the movement, in case he ever found himself in the position of having to explain it to the media. But Dickie Gillespie's eyes had kept glazing over, and ultimately the higher-ups decided it wasn't worth the effort. That it would be easier to just make certain that Gillespie never had to talk about New Urbanism, which was all fine and dandy by him. What the hell did he know or care about architecture and urban planning? His background was showgirls, and he was damned good at it.

Twenty years in Vegas, another dozen in Atlantic City, putting together the best revues in the business, and now in Florida in a quasiretirement. Sure, the shows were tamer than the things he could do at casino hotels, but what the hell? The winters were nicer and golfing a lot better. And the fringe benefits were every bit as good. Ever since he'd been tapped for Serenity mayor and given free rein to staff Town Hall however he pleased, the fringe benefits were downright fine.

He turned down Plymouth Street, began eyeing the two- and three-story, small-lot homes, each fronted by a flower bed cultivating species from the *Serenity Annuals* pamphlet, each accessorized with porch swings and planter boxes and mailboxes from the *Serenity Patterns* book. With a practiced eye he took in the details of each house, checking for nonconformity in a quick once-over, then moved on to the next. He came to a three-story tan Victorian that had, he saw, just installed a new picket fence. With a tape measure from his pants pocket he measured first the height of the fence, then the width of the gate, then grunted in disappointment. Fully compliant—no demerits. No demerits meant no fringe benefits for Dickie.

He glanced back at the houses he'd already checked with a scowl, wondering whether to go back with a more critical eye, then decided against it. He had to be at UPSVIL by eleven to cast the Millennial Revue—one hundred fifty new girls who had to be winnowed down to twenty.

Dick Gillespie considered those numbers and perked back up as he resumed his walking inspection, and had nearly walked the length of the street when he realized he hadn't seen anyone on any of the porches.

Quickly he flipped through the clipboard to the Cornwall neighborhood, found Plymouth Street, and, checking his watch to make sure of the date, determined which house had porch duty that morning and strolled back down the block. It was a white colonial with black shutters, a crab apple tree in the front yard, and, of most significance to Gillespie, no one on the front porch. He clucked disapprovingly and put a check mark against the name Anderson.

Another demerit. Another fine. He'd have to have another talk with them, remind the couple who'd had the shaggy lawn episode two weeks earlier and the peeling paint thing the previous month that one more demerit and they were gone, forfeiting any equity in their home, as per the sales contract. Gillespie allowed himself a smile as he considered his good fortune. The Andersons were among a good many house-rich, cash-poor Serenityites. He worked as a ride mechanic in the Enchanted Realm. She worked in the Golf, U.S.A., pro shop by day, served drinks at the Morty Muskrat Lounge at night. He recalled seeing her there in her uniform, how her legs seemed to stretch forever from spiked heels to the hem of her miniskirt.

Yessir, he'd have to have a little talk with Gail Anderson, maybe during one of her breaks at the Lounge. Explain to her again the dangers of racking up demerits in Serenity, maybe offer her a way to work off some of them in her off hours. Yessir, life was good.

He was wearing a wide smile at the thought of Mrs. Anderson in her Muskrat Lounge fishnets, making his way back to his own bungalow overlooking Lake Serenity, when he glanced up and noticed that the mist was finally clearing, and that he could see the town's water tower, decorated with the ubiquitous muskrat ears—and, this morning, also decorated with a giant yellow banner with red letters: "WWWS? FIX OUR HOMES!"

His good mood instantly gone, Mayor Gillespie reached for the cell phone in his pocket, dialed with one hand as he broke into a trot toward the water tower.

Lew Peters stared fixedly out the arched windows of Prince Charming's Palace, overlooking the Enchanted Realm, as he listened to the chief financial officer's weekly update on Whipple Corporation's overall health. He stared out the window rather than at the projection screen down the conference table, because his CFO always used a PowerPoint presentation to illustrate his talk. And PowerPoint was a product of the twerp.

"Overall, we're looking good for the third quarter," the CFO droned. "Attendance is up four percent from the same period last year at all four parks: here, California, Euro-Whipple, and Osaka Whipple. We're on track to break ground for Singapore Whipple by year's end. The network is dominating prime-time ratings. Consequently ad revenues are up nine percent. Whipple Records is—"

"Our market cap?" Lew Peters demanded.

The CFO sighed, thumbed his remote to move the presentation ahead a dozen frames. "As you can see, our stock's thirty-day rolling average is up a dollar nine from the beginning of the quarter. Unfortunately, Microsoft went up sixty cents. Because they have more total sh—"

"Bottom line, we're still behind them."

The CFO nodded, yes, and then began explaining why that ought not matter, that their return on investment was better, and how in just the past three years they had surpassed both AT&T and General Motors, which was nothing to sneeze at, and they were growing with selective moves into high-profit areas, and ultimately that strategy would reward. . . .

But Llewellyn J. Peters III had stopped listening. He hated Microsoft, and he hated even more the little twerp who ran it. Here he'd been for the past decade and a half, shrewdly building an empire from a tired old amusement park company, finding and enforcing efficiencies to let him earn the cover of *Forbes,* twice, and *BusinessWeek,* once, in the past year alone, not to mention a glowing Column One write-up in the *Wall Street Journal,* and at the end of the day, it didn't matter one stinking little bit. Wall Street still loved Microsoft more than it loved Whipple, and the twerp consistently had stayed tantalizingly ahead. Even worse, the little geek hadn't even broken a sweat doing it. No risky mergers, no bold strategies, no nothing. Just the same, find-other-people's-good-ideas-and-steal-them as he'd always done, and Wall Street treated him like some boy-genius conquering hero.

Well, fuck Wall Street. He had a five-year plan, and a ten-year plan, and a fifteen-year plan, and in the sixteenth year, there'd only be two corporations left worth owning. And then he'd take on the bastard, *mano a mano,* and kick his scrawny little ass, and *then* who'd be left standing?

Peters looked up, realized the room had been silent for some time, and nodded at the first vice president to his left. "Investments?"

"Yes, sir. We expect to have on the order of one point one, maybe one point two billion cash by the end of the fourth quarter. Approximately a third of that is necessary to complete the acquisition of Schylle Newspapers. Their second-quarter profit margin was twenty-nine percent, two points better than ours, but we think we can goose that up to thirty-three, thirty-four percent. As regards the remainder, we looked at the automakers, as you suggested, but the only lines that approach our profitability standards are the SUVs."

Peters grunted. "And I suppose Ford doesn't want to sell us just their Excursion and Expedition."

"Sir, those two vehicles account for a small fraction of total sales but make up nearly a quarter of total profits. So, no, sir, that's not likely. We looked into buying the entire company and closing down all but the sport utility lines, but their union contracts would make that prohibitive."

Peters grunted again. "Well, keep trying. They're making forty cents on the dollar on those damn things, and I can't think of one reason we shouldn't enjoy some of that."

"Sir, there's also come available a complete lot of gaming equipment. Brand new. An expansion deal fell through in Atlantic City, and now the contractor is unloading it below cost. Tables, machines, card shoes, chips, costumes for the waitresses. The whole suite. I realize it's not budgeted for this quarter, sir, but I think it represents a substantial savings—"

"How much?" Lew Peters demanded.

"Two point one million."

Peters stroked his authoritative chin for a few seconds, then nodded confidently. "Do it." He glanced at the next VP down the table. "Litigation?"

The company's chief lawyer cleared his throat and opened a manila folder. "Well, sir, we have sixty-four pending cases. Three injury claims from incidents in the parks, including that lady from Ohio who lost a toe in the Wicked Witch Tea Cups. Her attorney wanted her to hold out for five hundred grand, saying he could show negligence in the ride's design and so forth. But we were able to back-channel her with lifetime passes to all Whipple parks for herself and one-year passes for all her kids and grandkids. Two children, only five grandkids. We got off easy there."

Peters moved his wide mouth unhappily, as if eating something unpleasant. "Lifetime pass. How old is she?"

The lawyer glanced at his folder. "Fifty-seven, sir. She's five-three and weighs two-seventy. Our actuaries say she'll be lucky if she makes it to sixty."

Peters wobbled his head from side to side, considering. "Okay. Do it. But be careful with those lifetime passes. They ain't cheap. Now, what's going on with the day-care center thing?"

"WeeWuns School in Lake City. That," the lawyer flipped a page, "is one of the forty-seven trademark-infringement cases currently open. I'm glad you brought that up, sir. We've looked at their books, and they're telling the truth. If we insist on a quarter million, they'll have no choice but to declare bankruptcy and close down."

Peters glared silently, dark eyes flashing. The man hadn't even wanted to press the suit in the first place, despite the fact that the school had allowed its kindergartners to paint a hallway mural depicting fully a dozen different Whipple characters. Morty and Mindy Muskrat. Gordon Gopher. Billy the Baboon. Mongoose Mike. Kallie the Kangaroo. Wally Warthog. All of them and more, and not even a token attempt to get permission. Not that Whipple Corporation would have granted it, but that wasn't the point.

"You make it sound like a bad thing," Peters said finally. "I, on the other hand, see it as the perfect teachable moment for all the other little brats thinking about ripping us off."

The lawyer squirmed in his leather seat. "Yes, sir, but I was just concerned. . . . Well, the school has nearly a hundred students, preschool through kindergarten. That's a hundred sets of parents. If the school has to close, the local paper will certainly do a story. We might not come out looking too good, is all."

Peters brooded a silent minute. "Fine. You win. What are their assets?"

"Thirty-five thousand, seven hundred."

"Then settle for forty," Peters ordered. "And I want the mural down, understand? Not just painted over. Removed. Make the little plagiarists scrape it off with their fingernails, if they have to. Got it? Good. Who's next?" Peters glanced down at his agenda, then up at his next vice president. "Ah, Whipple Development Corp. My favorite. So how are things at America's Hometown this fine morning?"

The Vice President for Real Estate, cowed by a near-weekly harangue, kept his eyes on his report. "Serenity is fine, sir. Between forfeitures and loan collections and user fees, we are maintaining a $960,000 monthly positive cash flow. Combined with an amortized accounting of the federal—"

"We are *not* going to spread that out," Peters interrupted. "That was a one-time bump for your revenue, and that's how we're going to account for it."

The Vice President for Real Estate swallowed hard. "In that case, Serenity is on track for a third-quarter pretax profit of eleven percent. Which, I must point out, is two points higher than the industry standard for home mortgage financial services, which at this phase of the operation is essentially what we are."

Lew Peters drummed his fingers on the varnished conference table. Outside the window, a bright green, Mongoose Mike–themed gondola rose toward the fake-snow-covered fake Mont Blanc. "Yes, but you see, you're *not* any old home mortgage company, are you? You're a division of Whipple Corporation. And at Whipple Corporation, the target profit margin is twenty-seven percent, not eleven. So what action plan have you formulated to get you from where you are to where you need to be?"

Peters watched with disdain as the Real Estate VP shuffled some papers, finally cleared his throat. "As I suspected," Lew Peters said. "Fortunately, I *do* have an action plan. It is as follows. First, adjust the interest rate on all the loans upward three-quarters point—"

"Sir!" Even the vice president seemed stunned by his own outburst. "I mean, well, we just two months ago raised the rate a full point. Folks are gonna start to grumble. I mean, I don't think they ever believed an adjustable-rate mortgage meant it was going to double in just three years."

"Then they should have read the fine print," Lew Peters continued. "Perhaps now they will. Second: I seem to remember something from our Merchandising Department that we have about twelve hundred Jubilee Edition Gordon Gophers in a warehouse somewhere. If the Whipple-a-Month Club sends them out as a bonus selection, that should get rid of eleven hundred of them. Unless, of course, you have any objections?"

The vice president stopped scribbling notes, shrugged in defeat. "They just got Gordon Gophers four months ago. . . ."

"Well, now they shall have two." Peters interlaced his fingers and stretched his arms contentedly. "After all, they're all lucky enough to, quote, Live in Serenity, unquote. I should think they would be overjoyed to have a second Gordon Gopher. Finally, I would say a fifteen percent rate hike in electric, sewer, and water is long overdue, no? A little quick arithmetic says . . ." Peters closed his eyes for a second, "approximately $44,000 in additional revenues per month. Puts it just over a million a month on the plus side. Still not twenty-seven percent, but a nice round number just the same. Wouldn't you agree?"

The vice president forced a smile and nodded. Sure.

"Good. Human resources?"

A stern lady with a faint mustache kept her arms folded across her chest. "We continue to have problems with this Top of the World Club, sir. We caught two of the Enchanted Dancers sneaking out this morning."

Peters sighed with frustration. The tallest tower atop Prince Charming's Palace was the highest point in Whipple World, taller even than Mont Blanc in the Realm or the geodesic golf ball in UPSVIL. And at the very top was a sort of widow's walk, accessible by a concealed ladder, that had of late been littered with bits of foil wrappers and soiled with questionable stains.

"Damn homos," Peters muttered. "More trouble than they're worth."

"It's not just gays, sir," the Personnel Vice President said primly. "Heterosexual cast members as well seem to have trouble checking their libidos when it comes to the Top of the World Club."

"Well, we'll help them, then. Have the locks for the roof access doors changed. And put out a memo: Henceforth, open-air copulation on Whipple grounds, be it male-on-female, male-on-male, or any other combination, is a fire-able offense." Peters nodded severely, began straightening his papers. "Anything else?"

A nervous-looking vice president at the far end of the table raised his hand timidly, cleared his throat when Peters looked his way. "Sir, we're receiving a number of media requests to do a fifth-anniversary piece on Serenity. A couple of architecture magazines, the *New York Times Magazine,* and so forth. With the Jubilee coming up, they were wondering—"

"Fuck them," Peters declared. "Serenity is not the news. Our polar bears are the news. Tell them to write about our polar bears."

The Vice President for External Affairs bit his lip, then continued. "Sir, we've suggested just that. But not all of them are accepting it. Several have asked rather pointedly about the delay in Serenity's Phase II. And I'm afraid, sir, that one or two might try sneaking in without permission. You know, as tourists. That would require stepped-up sur-veillance, and even then we might not catch them. So I was thinking, if we offered an exclusive to a friendly outlet, it might take much of the pressure off."

Peters frowned, skeptical. "That's all it takes? The rest of them lose interest if someone else writes it first?"

"It's worked in the past, sir."

Peters closed his folder and passed it to a waiting sec-retary. "Great. Fine. Call Leahy with it. If that's all, we're adjourned."

He whisked the profit-and-loss statement for Whipple Pictures out of his briefcase while he waited for his vice presidents to clear the boardroom, then ducked into a hid-den passageway behind a bookcase. Still reading, he climbed a stone spiral staircase built into one of the Palace's corner towers and emerged in an alcove off the anteroom to his own suite, where he nodded to his receptionist and wandered in to his desk.

There he put down the Whipple Pictures financials and immediately saw the two memos at the top of his in-box. He scanned quickly, a scowl hardening as he read about the water tower incident.

He pushed the button on his intercom and began growling even before his secretary answered: "Get ahold of Albright. Have him meet me this afternoon on the walkthrough. Then call Burbank. The lazy bastards ought to be up by now, right?"

Led by one teacher, and followed by two more plus a parent volunteer and an assistant principal, the three second-grade classes from Orlando's Willow Run Elementary School trooped into the darkened viewing room and lined up in front of the railing overlooking the Untamed Arctic's showcase tableau.

Emma Whipple counted the little bodies as best she could, given their continued milling about, and marked the total on her clipboard. She directed the helmet-haired TV reporters and shaggy cameramen to opposite corners, then retreated to a folding chair at the back of the room to rub her bare arms for warmth and scribble notes for the press release she would write describing the events about to unfold.

Just beyond the railing was inch-thick plate glass, and on the other side of the glass was forty-degree "ocean" water washing up on a cave-pocked plateau covered with real ice, all of it expensively refrigerated to near-authentic temperatures. It was Whipple World's most ambitious exhibit yet, a true challenge for the company's crack Enchanteers, who, until then, had dealt with only the papier-mâché reality of the Realm and the relatively simpler Africa, Asia, and South America zones in the Dominion.

Bringing the subzero habitat of Baffin Island to subtropical Florida hadn't been easy. The entire 130-acre exhibit had to be enclosed in an insulated shell of marine-grade plywood, the interiors covered with painted canvas to keep visitors from noticing that it was actually ninety degrees outside under a steamy white sky, not ten degrees beneath a cobalt-blue one.

The project also had not been cheap. Even before the overruns, the last preconstruction estimate had been $14 million. Lew Peters had balked, even though the whole thing had been his idea, a way to take the fight directly to archenemy Sea World. Ultimately, of course, Peters had signed off, vowing to get it back in higher soda and ice cream prices, because it was integral to his plan to make Waldo Whipple World the sole tourist destination in all Central Florida.

Naturally, corners had been cut to save pennies. Half-inch plywood instead of three-quarter. A fifteen-foot-deep "ocean" instead of twenty-five. The entire exhibit repositioned adjacent to the Dominion's southern border, so it could share refrigeration pipes with Serenity's ice-skating rink. Untamed Arctic still had come in over $17 million and almost three months late.

The "soft" opening Emma had originally scheduled with Willow Run Elementary had to be postponed, once, twice, a total of four times. To the point where she had to bribe school administrators with free weekend All-Parks Passports if they went through the effort of once again collecting signed field-trip forms.

Which meant, Emma knew, a nasty memo from Lew Peters to her boss, who in turn would pass it along to her. She sighed in resignation. Peters saw freebies to the park not as low-cost goodwill, but lost profit. Such giveaways required permission from the division vice president—something Emma had failed to collect. The cost of the passes, therefore, would now be charged against her salary, and she began mentally tallying the damage and deciding how to cut her personal budget for the final two weeks of the month to avoid dipping into what was left of her savings.

A crescendo of children's voices brought her back to the present, to the viewing room packed with seven-year-olds. Another ten minutes and she could leave the chill of the Untamed Arctic and head over to Africaland to simultaneously thaw out and interview the "new" woman elephant trainer for a press release she had to get out the next morning.

She rubbed her arms again as she watched the second-graders start to lose their initial interest in the still-empty exhibit, hoped the trainers were also noticing this and would soon get the show on the road. After years of planning and two months of serious hype, this was it: the unveiling of Waldo Whipple World's newest inhabitants, the cuddly, lovable polar bear cubs, Snoball and Igloo.

Playful and rambunctious like all babies, and with a compelling backstory of having been orphaned and abandoned, then rescued from an iceberg found floating out Baffin Bay into the North Atlantic, Snoball and Igloo were poised to take the theme-park-going world by storm. The relentless Whipple marketing machine had already cranked out Snoball and Igloo T-shirts, sneakers, caps, coffee mugs, and toilet seats. The Whipple-of-the-Month Club had already commissioned ceramic Snoball and Igloo figurines. Whipple Videos was set to release "The Snoball and Igloo Story" at $29.95 a copy, $26.75 with Whipple Club membership.

All of it with the idea of cementing in the public's mind the association of arctic marine critters with Whipple, thus blunting Anheuser-Busch's five-year head start with *their* polar bears and easing the introduction of walruses in another year, dolphins in two years, and, three years out, a brand-new outdoor aquarium filled with Sea World's stock-in-trade: killer whales.

Ahead of her, a chant began among the second-graders: "Snoball! Igloo! Snoball! Igloo!" Little feet began stomping in time, little hands started pounding the plate glass that offered both underwater views of the "ocean" as well as aboveground views of the shore.

Emma glanced anxiously at the largest cave in the ice-covered "hillside," where hidden inside were the polar bears' cages. She started reaching for the cell phone clipped on the belt of her skirt to call the trainer's quarters, find out what the holdup was—when suddenly, out of the black hole came ambling first one ball of white fluff, then another.

The children broke into cheers and applause as the bears tried to stop on the ice, couldn't, and skidded into the water. The kids laughed uproariously, the camera crews dutifully recording the gaiety, and Emma smiled. Given Central Florida sensibilities, she could see that this was going to be the lead story at five-thirty, six, *and* eleven.

The bear cubs were still frolicking in the water, diving down deep, batting at the plate glass, wrestling with each other, when the arm of a trainer appeared from the cave, just long enough to toss a handful of Ball Park Franks, the Official Hot Dog of Waldo Whipple World, out onto the ice. In a flash, the bears popped out of the water and onto the ice ledge, the children hooting and laughing, and set upon the hot dogs, greedily snapping up a couple, then batting the others around on the ice, chasing after them, batting them some more, batting each other, growling cheerfully.

The children were eating it up, and Emma began composing in her head the press release she would blast-fax out to Florida newspapers, radio stations, and television stations later that afternoon: *Kids Welcome Hot-Dog Loving Cubs.* She would have to interview a child or two, maybe a teacher, then pick a quote off the preapproved Lew Peters list . . . when she noticed a flash of black in the "ocean," saw it rocket up toward the ice, saw it climb up and out of the water with its forepaws.

It was Sammy the Seal, whose birth in the adjoining Blue Ocean exhibit two months earlier had turned around a long string of negative news about unexplained animal deaths at the Dominion. She blinked, unable to remember Sammy's role in the soft opening's script, wondered if maybe the trainers had changed it without notifying her. And then she started getting a bad feeling in her belly.

Maybe it *wasn't* part of the script! Maybe the little guy had climbed up and over the low retaining wall surrounding his tank at Blue Ocean, just like the consultant had warned . . .

Sammy barked happily, started waddling toward Snoball and Igloo. The bear cubs glanced at each other for a moment before ambling at the seal, setting upon him, quickly tearing him limb from bloody limb.

Emma stared openmouthed at the carnage for a long moment, finally realized that except for the satisfied grunts of the feasting polar bear cubs, the observation room was deathly quiet. Finally she heard a child whimper. Then another. With angry glares for Emma, the teachers and assistant principal began herding their charges out the exit, some crying, some with thumbs in their mouths, most just stunned into a zombie-like silence.

On the ice tableau, a trainer wielding a forked stick was unsuccessfully trying to separate the cubs from the remnants of Sammy's carcass. With a long string of profanities heard by the last of the children, the trainer gave up and retreated to the "cave" containing the door to his office.

Emma sighed wearily. She would have to cancel with the elephant trainer yet again. Also everything else she was planning that afternoon. She gathered up her clipboard and headed for the exit. It was going to be a long day.

●　　●　　●

Ernest G. Warner sat at his computer terminal, idly let his fingers roll across the keys: *the quick brown fox kills the venal editor . . . the quick brown fox maims the cowardly reporter . . . the quick brown fox procures a quantity of plastic explosives and one night razes the venal, cowardly newspaper . . .*

Ernie Warner, at age thirty: an almost-winner of the Pulitzer Prize for his hard-hitting, take-no-prisoners environmental journalism. Ernie Warner, at age thirty-five: the managing editor for Florida's fastest-growing newspaper, challenging the *St. Petersburg Times* and the *Miami Herald* as the state's best. Ernie Warner, at age forty: a languishing former star, enjoying the money and the perks earned from his continued loyalty to the profitable-as-ever but now thoroughly embarrassing *Orlando Advocate,* a big-city daily that had become not only more shamelessly boosterish and incestuous than the smallest town rag, but, even more troubling to reporters as a class, as tightly wound as the worst corporate bank.

All employees were required to wear approved colored clothing every day except the fourth Friday of each month—a home office–approved "casual" day on which khakis were permitted. All window blinds had to be kept at a uniform, thirty-five-degree angle, as measured from a plumb line from ceiling to floor. All desks and cubicles were to be cleaned of all paper at the end of each workday. Employees were limited to two four-by-five photos at their work sites, to be displayed in Chicago-approved frames. No plants. No postcards. No campaign buttons or funny hats. To make sure the rules were followed, Chicago decided to make compliance with the neatness guidelines a standard of performance on employee evaluations, as important as meeting deadlines or accuracy.

Most of the quality reporters and editors—which is to say, most of Ernie's cohorts—had abandoned ship when the focus on good journalism got replaced by good Chamber of Commerce citizenship. The rest had bailed when the stupid edicts from Chicago began.

Not that it made any difference to the pooh-bahs. Freshly minted journalism school grads could meet their word-count quotas almost as well as seasoned pros, with a lot less complaining and for a lot less money.

Ernie erased all the subversive, brown-fox claptrap from his monitor and concentrated on finishing his story. It was a long front-page feature about the new-car dealership about to open in Seminole County—a guaranteed sixty columns a month of advertising, Leahy had enthused when he'd assigned him the story. Ten years earlier, Ernie would have flat-out refused to write such a thing and probably quit the paper. Five years earlier, he would have argued that such an article belonged in the Auto Section, not on the front page. Now he tried gamely to find the best adjectives to describe the "low-pressure sales staff" and the "sparkling, twenty-first-century showroom."

He stopped for a moment to wonder what in hell that meant, "twenty-first-century showroom." The picture showed cars parked in a big, glass-walled room. And that was different from a twentieth-century showroom . . . how? He sighed to himself and glanced at the clock on the wall. Four-fifteen. Another hour and forty-five minutes and he could escape the place for a solid fifteen hours. Escape in his forest-green Mercedes that still smelled new, with a nice, soothing Mozart sonata on the CD player for the ride home. Escape in the hot tub on his real California redwood deck . . .

He shook his head and typed "twenty-first-century showroom," when his assistant knocked at his door.

The boss needed him.


As usual, the television in the corner of Jack Leahy's office was tuned to the Financial News Channel. Jack buffed his fingernails while he watched.

"Hah! See that, Ernie? Ninety-one dollars a share! That's up two bucks today. Which means, by just sitting here, going out for my lunch, coming back and sitting here some more, I've made about . . . seventy-four thousand dollars. You know, that's still enough to buy a house in some parts of the country. Isn't capitalism wonderful?"

Ernie worked to contain his disdain. After all, Leahy wasn't the only one in the newsroom who knew exactly how much richer or poorer each rise and fall of company stock left him. He himself knew almost instinctively that a two-dollar gain meant his deferred compensation plan was suddenly eighteen grand fatter.

"You rang?" Ernie asked.

"Got a hot story for you."

"I await with bated breath."

Leahy flashed a smirk. "Oh, let's not be cynical. That's the last thing the world needs is another cynic. Skepticism? Sure, we need that, in our business. But cynicism? Uh-uh. No sir. Not here."

Ernie forced his lips into the semblance of a grin. "Gee, Jack! What is it?"

"That's better. Anyway, I just know you're gonna love it: You know it's been five years since Serenity opened?"

Ernie couldn't help groaning. He hated anniversary stories, and he flat-out loathed Whipple stories. The two intertwined would be a living hell.

"I was thinking," Jack Leahy continued, ignoring him, "a look-forward sort of piece: The second five years in America's premier planned community. Maybe: Urban Planning the Whipple Way. A Fairy Tale Come True."

Leahy looked up with his usual cheerful grin, and Ernie knew it was well past the stage where he might be able to talk him out of it. He studied the perfect suntan, the pleasant smile, the pale blond hair. He wondered in what life, on what planet, Jack Leahy could possibly have been a streetwise reporter and a crack, frontline editor, a man savvy and smart enough for Ernie once upon a time to have looked up to as a mentor.

"Why don't you just have the Whipple flacks write it and put my byline on it? It'll save everyone a lot of time."

"Ernie, Ernie, Ernie." Jack shook his head sadly and rose to primp before a mirror. "Do you know how your salary compares to the median reporter's here?"

Ernie shrugged, defeated. "More," he admitted.

"Five times more. You're earning an upper-management salary for a senior reporter's job. But you know what? I think you're worth every penny. Always have. You're my *go-to* guy. When there's only two and a half seconds left, and it's our ball at halfcourt, there's no one I'd rather have take that three-pointer. *You* the man!"

Ernie sighed dejectedly. Ever since the pro basketball franchise had come to town—Orlando's first and to date only big-league sports team—Leahy had become the insufferable white upper-middle-class hoops fan. Ernie had long ago given up trying to discourage him from talking like some fool sports announcer.

"When do you need it?" Ernie asked at last.

Jack Leahy grinned foolishly, put Ernie in a headlock, and squeezed. "See? I knew you'd come around. You're the *franchise,* man! And don't think Chicago hasn't noticed, if you know what I mean." He nodded at him seriously, then moved around and sat back at his desk. "Anyway, I was thinking your piece would make a swell anchor for our Jubilee package."

With his hands, Leahy started laying out the paper in the air in front of him: "Your story, stripped across six columns. Maybe Tommo's column down the left."

Ernie groaned inwardly. Tom "Tommo" Biaggo was the paper's insipid local columnist who'd yet to see, visit, or hear about something Whipple-related that he didn't immediately find need to orgasm over in print. "So his column would actually *touch* my story on the page?"

"Now, now, now. Team player, team player," Leahy

*tsk*ed. "Maybe an aerial shot of Serenity in the middle. We can call it 'Five years of Serenity.' Or something like that. Or even better, maybe somehow we can get a picture of those cute little bears on the front. Now, that's something I know our readers will eat right up. Remember, when we put them on the front page, back when Whipple got them, our single-copy sales spiked forty percent? Our focus group that week gave the bears picture and story an eighty-seven percent approval rating. That's almost as high as our coverage of the Ted Bundy execution. I just wish there was a way to put the little buggers on the front *every* day. Now I wonder if there isn't any sort of connection between the two, something we can use as a peg. . . ."

The more Leahy talked, the more Ernie realized what a total pain in the ass this assignment was going to be. He would have to find a way to weave cuddly polar bears, a fawning mention of the Whipple Institute, a respectful nod for the serious work at the Whipple BioGen Research Lab, a worshipful description of Whipple president Lew Peters, and a reverential history of Waldo Whipple himself all into a glowing, 2,000- or 2,500-word tribute to a place whose mere existence made his skin crawl. He glanced at Leahy's clock, told himself: one more hour. One more hour and he could leave all the stupidity behind for the rest of the day.

"Have the bears ever been in Serenity?" Leahy asked, still on the bears.

"If they haven't, I'm sure we could get Whipple to bring them out there for our photographers," Ernie deadpanned.

Leahy blinked twice, nodded thoughtfully. "You know what? I bet they just might, if we told them they were going to be the centerpiece for the page. And I know just the place: Founders Park, out by the lake. Maybe swinging on the swings with some of the neighborhood kids . . . You suppose bears know how to hang on to swings?"

Ernie shrugged helplessly.

"Well, anyway, see what you can do, bear-wise."

Ernie shrugged again and nodded weakly. He had no intention of asking anybody to do any such thing. He had learned long ago that when it came to idiotic suggestions from editors, a shrug and a noncommittal nod were the best response.

"I'm thinking of having an extra twenty thousand copies printed to be distributed free at the Jubilee. You know, kind of a souvenir issue for all the national and international media that will be there. Give ourselves a little exposure." Leahy picked up a putter leaning against the wall. With a toe he scattered a handful of golf balls on the carpet, then set a rimmed cup in their midst.

Ernie said, "If the Clean Team comes in right now, am I an accomplice to this unauthorized use of company floor space, or do you take the fall yourself?"

Leahy shot him a wry smile and missed another three-footer. "Cynicism versus skepticism, Ernie. Remember that."

Three shots later, there were still no balls in the cup, and Ernie forced himself to look away from his boss's ineptitude. Every month or so, he felt obliged to accept Jack's invitation to play a round at their gated subdivision's Jack Nicklaus–designed championship course. The pure displeasure of these outings usually provided him with three weeks' worth of excuses not to play again.

"You know, we really ought to hit the links soon," Leahy said. "It's been, what, a month?"

"So you want me to finish writing twenty-first-century dealership first? Or get right on Serenity?" Ernie asked quickly.

Jack Leahy paused to think about it. "I'd really like to get the dealership into the paper by the end of the month. Their grand opening is in August. How about if you start on Serenity tomorrow and finish writing the dealership story when you can? Speaking of which, how's the Mercedes?"

Ernie had started to move for the door when he turned

back with a sigh. Like it wasn't enough working with the man, and then living in the same exclusive neighborhood. He'd had to compound things further by agreeing to go car-shopping with him a few months earlier. Buying two cars at once, they had figured, would save them each an extra few thousand dollars. "The car's fine."

"It's not a car. It's a Mercedes. And it's not just fine. A Honda Civic is fine. A Chevy Corsica is fine. A Mercedes, my friend, is an exquisite piece of engineering. An infusion of art into the everyday," Leahy enthused. "I can't tell you how much I look forward to even short drives now."

As much as he hated to, Ernie found himself agreeing. As stupid as it sounded, his time each morning and each evening in his S500 had become a thing to savor.

Leahy clucked as he resumed hitting golf balls. "I hate to say I told you so, but you should have gotten the convertible. I've lost count of all the fine young female specimens who check me out at stoplights. I pretend not to notice, especially if Lynda's in the car. Don't need to get slapped, after all. But a good-looking, single guy like you . . ."

For a moment Ernie saw himself in Jack's cream-colored SL500, cruising top-down along A1A, his favorite part of the road, up in Flagler County where it paralleled the red sand beach on one side and coastal marsh on the other, a beautiful brunette beside him. No, a blonde. Maybe . . . one particular blonde. Maybe Stephanie. . . .

He shook himself free and reached for the door. "Thanks, but I like my car all the same. Good old-fashioned frame. Safer in a rollover, all that."

Leahy retrieved his golf balls and put them back in a jar on his credenza. "Whatever. But you get a hot date and need to borrow a one-hundred-percent guaranteed babe magnet, you just let me know."

Ernie once more made for the door.

"Oh, hey, hey, hey, before you go: Remember we have that Circulation Task Force meeting next week about that eighteen- to thirty-year-old male problem. You do remember, right? Market penetration fourteen percent? Sports came up with the idea of having Mountain Mathis cover City Hall as a way of luring those readers. I'm not sure about that. I'd think he'd need some pretty heavy editing."

Mountain Mathis was the Orlando Magic's seven-foot-two, three-hundred-pound center. The man could barely write his own name, Ernie knew. He had a seven-million-dollar house filled with arcade games and not a single book, according to a loving profile the paper had done sometime back.

"No, Jack, I don't think Mountain would be a good idea."

"I thought not," Jack Leahy agreed. "So what have you come up with?"

Ernie hadn't given the problem a second thought since Jack had appointed him to the committee a month earlier.

"Tits," he said.

Leahy blinked twice. "Excuse me?"

"Like in England," Ernie deadpanned as he opened the door. "Page Three girls. Birds of the day. Think about it."

Lew Peters walked, arms crossed, toward the end of Front Street to survey the new bandshell at the east edge of Portofino Square. He led his entourage through a buzz of activity, with some workmen laying brick pavers, others installing bulbs in the old-fashioned streetlights, and still others putting a second coat of white paint on wooden pilings along the lakefront seawall.

"The bleachers," his External Affairs Vice President pointed, "will go there. Capacity about two thousand. Folding chairs in front up to the foot of the bandshell, another thousand, and then families who want to set up blankets on the lawn can do that, too. I'm thinking we'll have four thousand of the five thousand residents in attendance."

Lew Peters scowled. "Why not the other thousand?"

The vice president tugged at his tie uncomfortably. "I suppose we could make it a requirement. I just thought it would be easier to generate applause if we had mainly those who wanted to be there. Plus, trust me, sir, this is not a big site. Four thousand plus all the tourists will *look* really crowded."

"Okay, fine. Four thousand. But let's make sure we take attendance. Keep a record of those who don't show up. Turn it over to Sheriff Albright for his files."

Ferret Albright said nothing as he followed Peters and the vice president along the Promenade, occasionally looking downward and back over his shoulder whenever they walked past a woman in high heels.

The vice president made a note on his clipboard. "Consider it done, sir," he murmured, then pointed left and right. "There and there will be the risers for the cameras. The satellite trucks can park on Front Street. And our production van will go right there."

Peters asked: "How many cameras?"

"So far seventy-four. Of those, fourteen will be broadcasting live. Another twenty-seven stations, mainly foreign, won't be here physically, but will be using our feed and doing live commentary from their home countries."

Lew Peters grunted and walked down to the waterfront, where tiny wavelets on the lake splashed against the concrete wall. In another week, the entire seawall was to be packed with boats tied stern-to, like they did in the real Portofino, and dressed out in full colors. It would be the biggest party the world had seen since Millennium Eve in Times Square. Headliner acts from morning until midnight, celebrities out the yin-yang, all to commemorate the twin anniversaries of Waldo Whipple World's Twenty-fifth and Serenity's Fifth. Actually, the two were four months, one week, and three days apart, but Peters had decided to roll them together for hype's sake into one glorious Whipple Jubilee that would also serve as the official ribbon-cutting for the latest profit center, the Chautauqua-like Whipple Institute.

"WBC will be here live all day," the vice president continued. "The anchors from the news division will take turns hosting. Oh, and they agreed to preempt championship figure skating in the afternoon and *Who Wants to Be Adopted by a Millionaire* that night."

"How gracious of them," Peters said. "Now I won't have to fire them. Sponsorships all set?"

The vice president flipped a page. "Yes, sir. Our corporate sponsors total one point three million. A couple of them asked again about hanging a banner, and I told them you said if they didn't stop complaining, you'd take their names out of the program, too. Our costs came in at just under eight hundred thousand instead of the original eight-fifty, thanks to your labor suggestion, so we'll see a profit of five hundred thousand."

"Excellent." Peters began walking back toward the bandshell, eyes closed as he calculated. "Five hundred thou return on outlays of two point one over seven months . . . Not too shabby, eh? Now if Serenity could generate those kinds of numbers consistently, we wouldn't have to be so hard on them, would we?"

The vice president muttered assent, then tapped his pen on the clipboard's final page. "I believe that's it, sir. As you suggested, the *Advocate* is doing a piece on Serenity's five-year anniversary as part of their Jubilee special edition for that morning. They asked permission to distribute copies here. I told them you wouldn't mind. . . ."

Peters grunted, his eyes squinting down the road, out beyond the edge of downtown where a work crew was erecting a Cyclone fence topped with barbed wire around the base of the water tower. "Sure, whatever. But tell Leahy that in light of the circumstances, we'll be wanting sixty percent of ad revenues, not the usual fifty. It is, after all, our goddamned Jubilee." Then he turned on Albright. "Mr. Sheriff."

Albright pulled his gaze off a miniskirted brunette in a pair of platform sandals and instantly moved to his boss's side. "Sir."

"Your forensics department—" Instantly, Peters's aristocratic nose crinkled unhappily and sniffed at the air. "Good God, man, what have you been in? You reek of dead cat."

Ferret Albright blinked, once more confounded by Peters's uncanny sense of smell. On his second week at Whipple World, Albright had reorganized his collection before work one morning. Hours later, Peters had told him he smelled like shoe leather.

"Snow leopard, sir," Albright answered.

Lew Peters narrowed his eyes and regarded his security chief severely. "This isn't some new fetish of yours, is it?" Then he raised a palm to forestall an answer. "Forget it. I don't want to know. Your forensics people, have they come to any conclusions yet regarding this morning's vandalism?"

Albright eyed the water tower up and down, once again nice and shiny and white and unadorned save for the muskrat ears. "No sir, not yet. The banner was six flat sheets taped together. No name brand, could have been purchased at any Wal-Mart in Central Florida. The lettering was spray paint. Nothing special about it, either. We're still trying to lift some hairs from the duct tape." He patted Peters on the shoulder. "Don't you worry about it, sir. We'll track down whoever did it."

Lew Peters unhappily regarded the spot on his polo shirt where Albright had touched him. "Sheriff, I *know* who did it, as do you. It was those Serenity Weathermen assholes."

"Serenity Underground, sir," Albright corrected.

"Whatever. Fucking vermin is what they are. Rodents. I don't need to tell you, Albright, that I expect not one peep out of them during the Jubilee. Not so much as a paper napkin with that stupid WWWS crap. Understand?"

Albright, eyes lowered, grunted.

"They are vermin, Mr. Albright. Your job is pest control. If you don't stay on top of them, they'll multiply uncontrollably." Lew Peters watched as the workmen held a branch against the electrified chain link until it burst into flames. "If you can't handle it, we may well need a new sheriff in town. Got that?"

With a blonde in wobbly stilettos in tow, Mayor Dickie Gillespie hustled through the deserted but still lighted Old Towne Square, across the shortcut through FutureWorld, skirted the moat for Prince Charming's Palace, and headed directly up the exit ramp into the unloading area for the Good World ride.

"Hey," the blonde complained through her chewing gum. "We're goin' the wroo-ong way, Mr. Gillespie. Says right they-uh: exit."

Gillespie ignored her and kept moving up the ramp. She had great legs, good tits, and not even a trace of the ridiculous Brooklyn accent in her singing voice. Which is to say she had cleared the first hurdles on the road to a mezzo-soprano slot Gillespie had in his Millennial Revue. There was only one audition left.

They reached the top of the ramp and came to a shallow slough filled with a line of empty boats that extended into a dark tunnel. He released her wrist to move behind a control console against the wall. She bent over to pull off one shoe and massage her foot. "For Goo-od's sake, Mr. Gillespie, if you'd a told me we were gonna run the whole way, I'd a taken my shoes oo-off!"

Dickie Gillespie grunted, studying the row of switches, and finally threw a series of white ones. The water in the slough began flowing, and a dim series of night-lights came on in the tunnel. And echoing through the tunnel came distant singing, noticeably out of phase between one side and the other: *"It's a world of sunshine, a world of fun . . ."*

Gillespie quickly dragged the blonde into the lead boat just as it began slipping down the tunnel. Impatiently he undid his Sansabelts and pulled them to his ankles, then watched with increasing interest as the blonde pulled her cotton blouse over her head and reached around her back to undo her bra.

"I swear to Goo-od I don't understand how come we just can't get a room," she complained as heavy white breasts burst free and settled on his knobby knees.

He pointed skyward and put a finger to his lips: "Listen!"

The boat emerged from the tunnel into a cavern filled with miniature landmarks from around the globe as tiny, animatronic puppets finished their refrain: *. . . a good world, yes it is! It's a good world, yes it is! It's a really good world!*

"Hear that? I've worked in this place seven years, and I can say with all sincerity, I *hate* this fuckin' song! But this night forward? When I hear it, I'm gonna remember this. Now, you want in the Millennial Revue or not?"

The puppets, after a short bridge, began again in a new key as the blonde bent to Dick Gillespie's boxer shorts, stopped, then reached into her mouth to remove her gum and began looking around the boat.

"*Now* what?" he demanded.

With an index finger she stuck the gum onto the boat's gunwale. "Savin' it for later."


Her eyes bleary from yet another fifteen-hour day, Emma Whipple put the finishing touches to the great Seal Dismemberment Cover-Up: a cover letter for the lifetime All-Parks Whipple World Passports for the reporters and camera crews who had filmed the debacle, and then oh-so-graciously turned over their videotape afterward. She had already sent out one-day tickets for all the children and their immediate families and one-month passes for the teachers and administrators of Willow Run Elementary. A grand total of $51,000 in graft.

At least, she thought sourly, she hadn't needed to argue the necessity of this one with her boss. The authorization letter had been waiting on her desk when she got back from the Dominion, along with the memo reminding her, in all capital letters, that under the terms of the visiting media members' credentials, all audio or video recordings of events on Whipple Corporation grounds were Whipple Corporation property, and unauthorized release would be considered actionable.

No such threats, of course, had been necessary. The reporters had salivated at the thought of the lifetime passes, face value $9,995, and had happily agreed that Sammy's demise was but a tragic accident, and surely there was no reason to ruin an otherwise perfect Grand Opening by mentioning it to anyone back at the station, let alone to the general public.

Emma took a long breath and blew it out slowly. Such had become her life. In the best light, she took Whipple's circumstances on any particular day and gave them the most favorable spin possible. In the worst light, she lied for a living.

A lackluster world's fair with blatantly commercial sponsorship had been sold as a forward-thinking, global showcase. A sixty-dollar-a-day zoo became a research center for threatened species. The careless slaughter of a baby seal became a nonevent.

It hadn't, of course, started out that way.

The great-niece of Waldo Emerson Whipple himself, Emma had come to work at Whipple World fresh out of college, starting in hotel management, moving to finance, then external affairs. She was the only Whipple child in her generation remotely drawn to the company, the rest of the relatives developing an interest only after Uncle Waldo died suddenly and distributed the entertainment empire in prorated pieces across his extended family.

The company declined precipitously for four years during the squabbling. Upgrades and renovations, indeed, all capital projects, were put on hold, then forgotten. Feature films didn't get made. The animation studio all but shut down. So when a management group led by consumer finance king Lew Peters promised to reorganize the company, to make it healthy again, Emma had inwardly cheered as her greedy relatives took their ill-gotten gains and handed over their pieces of their family legacy to a professional.

It took only a few months after the public offering for Emma to start reappraising Peters. Gone forever, she realized, was Uncle Waldo's at times eccentric emphasis on top-quality entertainment at the expense, if need be, of bigger profits. Instead, *everything* was driven by profits. Admission prices were raised once, sometimes twice a year, even as park staff was cut. Water fountains were eliminated while soda cups were shrunk and the prices, naturally, raised. And then, when the good times hit and the money started rolling in, Peters had gone on a buying spree of every undervalued company on Wall Street, regardless of its core business.

Uncle Waldo's little amusement park company now owned such things as Whitney Pharmaceuticals, World Broadcasting System, Fontaine Auto Auctions, Pace Communications, a raft of dot-coms, a big piece of Roper-Joyner Tobacco, a majority interest in a record studio known for its artists who liked to cuss, and controlling interest in the Southeast's biggest chain of pawnshops. The latest rumors included a secret takeover of a newspaper chain and a behind-the-scenes partnership with Las Vegas's second-biggest casino.

For the first year or two, Emma was treated with quiet respect when she reminded her bosses that her great-uncle had stood for family and quality first, a fair value second, and profits last. By the third and fourth years, deference became tolerance, and by the fifth, barely concealed impatience.

Over the past few years, she had come to accept that she wasn't going to change the way Peters ran things. She knew Peters would never dare to fire her—to oust the only remaining Whipple at the Whipple Corporation would generate far more bad press than it was worth—but she could see that her job would grow increasingly insignificant compared to her title. "Associate Vice President for External Affairs" was what her business card said. One of a team of flacks was what she was, responsible for press releases about Wild Dominion and Serenity.

When Uncle Waldo had been alive, she was being groomed for upper management, rotating through the divisions to learn the company through and through. That stopped abruptly when Peters brought in his own management team, and Emma was left to languish in the department she happened to be in at the time of Waldo's stroke.

At first, she had dreamed of a shareholder revolt: a grassroots uprising against Peters's mercenary, un-Waldolike worship of the bottom line. It eventually dawned on her that shareholders *liked* Peters's way of doing things, and she, not he, was out of touch. Merely embodying her uncle's dreams wasn't going to make them real. She realized she had waited too long to cut bait and move on.

Now, at age thirty-six, she was single, not even dating, and her biological clock echoed ever louder in her head. By year's end, she promised herself for the hundredth time, she would reevaluate, decide then where to go and what to do.

But until then, she would get Waldo Whipple World through the latest crisis brought about by Lew Peters's expansionary zeal. They had built a wild-animal park as big as the one in San Diego without any of the necessary but expensive wild-animal expertise on staff. They were now taking the first steps to challenge Sea World without any marine mammal expertise, or even any common sense. How else to explain an unsecure boundary between an Arctic ringed seal and its natural predator?

Emma cleared her head of such thoughts and returned to the cover letter. She gave it a final once-over and stuck the six copies in their individual overnight envelopes for delivery the following morning. She put all six envelopes in her out-basket and removed the one remaining item from her in-basket.

With a deep sigh, she began reading yet another necropsy on yet another dead Dominion animal, this time a snow leopard. Like the previous necropsies, this one, too, was essentially useless. No surprise, really, given that the forensics "vet" was really the chef at UPSVIL's Mongolian Village. He had taken a couple of veterinary courses in a community college once, and Peters didn't want to spend the money for a real animal pathologist.

The animal's carcass, it seemed, had washed up on the shore of the Serenity River, half eaten by vultures. Or perhaps an alligator. The vet-chef wasn't sure. Emma read through the meager report a second time, then set it down on her desk. She put her fingers to her keyboard and began, almost somnambulantly, to type a press release about the tragic death of Sorley the Snow Leopard—wholly natural and therefore not newsworthy. She attributed his demise to a condition he had before Whipple had acquired him. She reconsidered that for a minute, but put her queasiness aside. The necropsy, after all, hadn't specifically ruled such a thing out, and given its inconclusiveness, her theory seemed as good as any.

Following standard operating procedure for bad news, she postdated the release and put a sticky note on it indicating that it should be sent out Friday after 6 P.M.—late enough to miss Friday's newscasts and, she hoped, Saturday's papers. With any luck, it would not be noticed until Monday, when most media outlets would deem it too stale to mention at all.

She felt more than a little greasy, like she did each time her job forced her to cross the gray area between stretching the truth and flat-out lying, and decided she would take a nice hot bath when she got home. And then she remembered the date and groaned. It was her night for Promenade duty, and she was running late. Porch duty and downtown duty she didn't mind, but Promenade duty she couldn't abide. Her choices were jogging, which she hated, or walking the town's big, dumb, slobbering Labradors, which she hated even more.

She gathered up her purse and made for the door—when she noticed the sheet of paper in the output tray of her fax machine. She set down her purse and sat back down at her desk. She would definitely be late for Promenade duty, but at least she would be able to claim an excused tardiness.

With her eyes scanning the police report from the Whipple Sheriff's Office, her fingers began typing out another press release. A gray 1992 Saab had been found at the bottom of the retention pond in the middle of the cloverleaf of the Turnpike's exit for Serenity. No sign of the driver. Per standard operating procedure with this sort of item, Emma did not mention in the news release that it was the third such car found in the pond in as many months.

# two

**...**

The sun finally crept over the horizon, and Lew Peters elbowed the gangly, sullen-faced man beside him and pointed down the slight incline.

"There. See? This, Chorus Boy, is why we're here."

In the Serenity, née Wichkatuknee, floodplain, a thick white mist was visible in the low-lying areas, ending abruptly halfway upslope. The visual effect was that of a heavy river of fog flowing down into a wide lake.

Lenny Fizzogli stared unhappily into the valley and said nothing. He hated getting up before dawn. He hated when Peters called him Chorus Boy. More and more, he hated Peters.

"This time of year, the morning fog follows the contours of the land," Peters continued. "It's like looking at a life-size topographic map." He stopped to smirk at Lenny. "You *do* know what a topographic map is, don't you? They teach that to aspiring geologists at the University of Florida, do they not?"

Lenny kept his arms folded across his chest and still said nothing. Four years earlier he had embellished his educational training a tad on his job application, giving himself a master's in geology from UF. In fact, he had never even been to Gainesville. He had merely received a well-drilling certificate from the school's Food and Agriculture Sciences extension program in Yeehaw Junction.

He had wanted one of the landscape engineering jobs that Whipple was hiring for when it was planning Wild Dominion. He had made it to the interview when the chief designer realized Fizzogli didn't know his dolines from his fluvials and had Personnel investigate his background. Lenny had instead been referred to the Old Time Bears Extravaganza based on the junior high musicals he had listed on his résumé. With no other prospects outside lawn maintenance, Lenny had danced, in the costume of a bear drinking from a jug of whiskey, in the show's chorus.

For three years he had danced, constantly getting into fistfights with the predominantly gay chorus members who kept looking at him in the dressing room, before Peters had approached him with his proposition.

"Perhaps the mistake was mine. You are obviously a child of the video era, and here I was trying to communicate verbally. So here we are. Now I can *show* you what I want."

Lenny Fizzogli bristled. "I did what you told me. I drilled a bunch of wells."

And he had. Thirty-eight wells, in all. Twenty-two of them large-bore pipes totaling 13 million gallons a day, doubling Whipple's existing output. That hadn't been enough, so he'd gone even deeper, down into the artesian well to increase pressure and, therefore, the flow rate. So deep, in fact, that he'd gone down into the underlying salty layer, sending a torrent of the stuff into the Serenity River and turning it brackish.

"Yes, you did. No argument there. And now we have lots of good, salty water to replenish Africaland's watering holes. No wonder Simba went nuts and ate McGuire. Well, all that's water under the bridge, so to speak." Peters unrolled a large map on the hood of his Range Rover. With his finger he traced a blue line, then pointed at the tendrils of mist. "The Serenity River, connecting all the lakes on the south side of Orlando, Lake Toho and so forth . . . You did read Beckwith's report, right?"

Armand Beckwith had been Waldo Whipple's original geologist in the 1970s. The report in question was a massively thick study on the hydrology of the Serenity basin, filled with footnotes and charts and jargon words that Lenny had given up on after the executive summary, although the binder itself continued to reside on his dinette table. Lenny didn't bat an eye as he lied: "Yes."

Peters flashed him a skeptical look. "Well, as Dr. Beckwith found: approximately 60 million gallons a day into Lake Tohopekaliga. Yet no apparent outflow from Lake Toho? How can this be? Which is how the good doctor came to his conclusion about the cracks and fissures in the limestone, the underground river, and so on and so forth. Water disappearing into the ground up here," he jabbed a finger at the topographic map, "and coming out down here."

Lenny studied the map, at all the faint squiggly lines, at the dashed red lines someone had drawn parallel to and on either side of the Serenity River. He nodded slowly, knowingly, said nothing for a long while. He looked up to Peters staring at him.

"You don't understand one fucking word of this, do you? Well, probably just as well."

Lenny's ears burned. He could see where this was going. Back to the chorus line. Back to those homos staring at his ass, bumping into him as they got into their bear costumes, "accidentally" touching his dick, expecting him to like it . . . Well, goddamn it all, he *didn't* like it, not one tiny bit. He was straight, after all. Had slept with a woman, what, ten months earlier? A year, tops . . .

"I understand it good enough," Lenny Fizzogli declared. "You wanted more wells to get all the water running underground right now above ground instead."

"Very good," Peters said. "So take a good look. Where the fog is now? Those are the areas we need more pumping. More pumping, more water aboveground."

Lenny stared helplessly at the map again. One of those homos in particular, Brendan something, the one he had to beat the crap out of all those times . . . *God,* he hated him. Shiny white teeth, faggy blond hair. Man, if he had to go back to the Bears Extravaganza, he was going to have to beat the crap out of him again, just on general principles. . . .

His ears burned, but one of them also hurt, he realized. He looked up and saw that Lew Peters had grabbed hold of it to point his head out across the floodplain. "Those red dashes on the map correspond to that elevation there, right up to that long concrete wall just below the Whipple Institute. Got it? I'm not going to tell you again . . ."

The pain in his ear caused lights to flicker behind his eyes, began triggering fragments of memories from Beckwith's report about the Serenity floodplain . . . about his recommendation against building there because of the area's geological instability, because of the potential for sinkholes and other settling . . . because of his belief that too-rapid removal of groundwater could lead to a series of collapses, leading possibly to free flow from the Lake Toho system . . .

Lenny winced as he stared, head tilted to mitigate Peters's ear-pulling, out across the valley, at the town of Serenity laid out on the banks of the river, above it the walled compound of the Whipple Institute. "But if I keep drilling down there, couldn't that end up flooding the whole basin?"

Lew Peters scowled harder, torqued Lenny's ear another half-turn. "That, my wanna-be doctoral candidate in hydrogeology, is a question several pay grades above yours. I'm not paying you to hypothesize and plan, am I? I'm paying you to drill."

Peters finally released Lenny Fizzogli's ear, rolled up

the topographic map, opened the driver's door to the Range Rover, and climbed in. "I'll give you exactly two weeks to start showing me some progress. If you can't, well, I'm sure your boyfriends on the chorus line would love to have you back."

Lenny Fizzogli watched the Range Rover disappear down the dirt road toward Golf, U.S.A., glanced unhappily at the rolled-up map in his hands, and stared with narrowed eyes out across the valley.

Ernie Warner slipped into his dress shoes and stood straight to appraise himself in the mirror. Hair starting to cede more and more territory to the gray that had started at his temples, face starting to soften at his cheeks. Even the eyes seemed not as bright as they once were.

With a deep breath he let his hands begin the automatic motions on his tie, a nice, conservative striped blue today, best for making a neutral impression with a new source, according to the *Advocate* dress code. Around, through, around again, through again, and up and through a final time. A full Windsor, nice and symmetrical between the buttoned-down collar. Five mornings a week, fifty weeks a year, getting on twenty years . . . five thousand Windsor knots. He wondered if Chicago had an award for that, maybe an official Schylle tie tack or something.

Well, he couldn't complain. It wasn't like wearing a tie every morning and dealing with meetings and memos and the like was some special torture reserved for him. Millions of guys across the country did so each morning and trooped into work without feeling sorry for themselves. And yet . . .

Somehow, things were going to be different for him, he had thought, once upon a time. He had enrolled in the hometown school and gone to work for the hometown paper, but despite it all had harbored visions of something bigger. Of opening the paper's first Mexico City bureau, or even a Havana bureau someday. Of going out each day in short sleeves and a bush jacket and bringing the world back to his Central Florida readers in a clear and compelling way.

For the sake of all this he'd even kept his social life loose, shying away from any serious relationships for the ability to go, at a moment's notice, and get the story. He could remember his buddies' weddings he'd attended in his twenties and early thirties, could remember thinking to himself: The schmucks! Tying themselves down so young, when there was so much still out there.

Of course, that was all before the *Advocate* had shrunk down upon itself. Before it closed not only its one "foreign" bureau—the Latin American correspondency in Miami—but its Atlanta, Jacksonville, and Tallahassee bureaus, as well. Readers wanted more local news, the focus groups had said. And he, the fresh, young managing editor on the fast track, had helped give it to them. He personally had delivered the pink slips to a dozen veteran reporters in the state bureaus, and shuffled a dozen more into ridiculous jobs in the suburbs.

And so now, here he was, single and childless, his high school and college buddies watching their own kids start middle school, even, in some cases, high school. He pushed those thoughts from his mind and gritted his teeth for the coming day as he strolled across the bedroom suite, down the wide, curved staircase, and into the tiled foyer to retrieve his keys. The whole day, he would spend on Whipple property, and if that wasn't bad enough, he'd be accompanied the whole time by an actual Whipple descendant, an Emerson Whipple, to answer any and all of his questions about Serenity.

Well, he'd give the kid a break. It wasn't his fault he was a Whipple. Anyway, what was dumber: Gushing about how wonderful a planned community built by a theme park company was? Or listening to that drivel and then writing a magazine-length article about it?

Ernie was about to punch in the code to set the alarm when the various phones in the house began bleating and chirping. Ernie moved to the nearest one, in the kitchen, answered it, and felt something like electricity surge up and down his whole body.

It was Stephanie, and for a moment the vision of her in a white bikini top and cutoffs flashed through his brain. That was how she was dressed when he met her all those years back, when he was still the paper's environmental writer and she was a sea-turtle activist counting nests at Canaveral National Seashore. That was how he always envisioned her, on those fewer and fewer occasions each year that they spoke on the phone.

"I was hoping to catch you before you left for work."

Her voice was like honey. Soft and sweet enough to make any male crave more and more. "You got me. I was just walking out the door."

"Then I'll make it quick," she said. "It's about Bobby."

Ernie felt himself deflate. Of course it was about Bobby. When *wasn't* it about Bobby? Each time she called, he somehow managed to raise his hopes. Maybe the second husband, the orthodontist, hadn't worked out. Maybe she needed some consoling from an old friend—someone who really knew her.

And each time, it was instead about something for Irlo "Bobby" King, her first husband, a little dweeb who somehow had successfully competed against Ernie for her affections way back when. Bobby was holding a press conference the next morning to expose a corrupt developer. Bobby was organizing a petition drive to recall the mayor. Bobby was releasing a study that showed how polluted Orlando's lakes had become. She had ultimately left him for someone with a newer kitchen and a better retirement nest egg, but had continued working with him at his little Florida Earth Justice cell anyway.

"Come on, Steph. You know I can't get his stuff in the paper." The *Advocate* had for years relegated Bobby

King's growth management, pollution, and other Chamber of Commerce–unfriendly tirades to the back of the book, near the cosmetic surgery ads. Then King had exposed the *Advocate*'s in-house pollution scandal, how its old printing presses had leaked deadly trichloroethylene into the area's groundwater, via the community weekly, which had harped on it for all eleven weeks it took for Chicago to settle with the state for a seven-figure sum. "Besides, I'm not even the environmental writer anymore."

"It's not anything he's doing," Stephanie corrected. "It's that he's, well, gone."

Ernie checked his watch impatiently. "How so, gone?"

"Like not around," she said. "He was supposedly working on this mondo, huge, big-deal project. Something so big we'd have to hire someone to staff the office all week, there'd be so many national press calls. Anyway, he was going to explain it all last night at a special cell meeting he called. We all showed up, but he didn't. I tried him at his house, on his mobile. No answer. I even went over. Nothing."

On the first page of Ernie's otherwise blank notepad were the directions to Serenity's Portofino Square. A solid thirty-five-minute drive, and he was supposed to be there in twenty minutes. "Shoot, Steph, maybe he's sick or something."

"I told you, I checked his house."

"A new girlfriend, then."

"Bobby? I doubt it. Who has time, when the fate of the earth's in the balance? Anyway, he would have told me. Ernie, I'm just worried. It's not like him to miss a cell meeting, and definitely not a special one that he called. I'm thinking maybe he's in the hospital, or had a wreck or something."

Ernie sighed to himself . . . wondered if *he* were sick or went missing, if Stephanie would be worried about him. Probably not. "All right. I'll check with the Highway Patrol when I get a chance. Anything else?"

"Oh, thank you, Ernie," Stephanie cooed.

Despite himself, Ernie felt his insides melt. He waited, half expecting her to continue, maybe with some remark about how perhaps she'd made a mistake when she'd picked Bobby instead of him, and then Dr. Braces instead of Bobby. . . . But she said nothing more. "Sure," Ernie said finally, before venturing: "How are you doing?"

And Stephanie began a stream of small talk about tennis lessons and the Junior League and the garden club until Ernie, unable to reenter the conversation, simply took the cordless with him into the garage, and then into the Mercedes, and then started driving until her oh-so-sweet voice faded into silence.

# three

**...**

Emerson Whipple pointed across the lake at the south edge of town and rattled off another statistic about how many acres the company was committed to keeping in pristine condition. She was a few yards ahead, and moving as fast as she was when they began that morning. It was Emma Whipple actually, Ernie corrected himself. She preferred Emma.

And that one fact, that Emerson was not some snot-nosed Whipple heir in his twenties but instead a smart, attractive woman in her thirties, had been the sole bright spot of the day. Eighty-five degrees and climbing, and she had conducted the walking tour like a forced march, hitting one neighborhood and architectural style after another—an "overview," she called it, to be followed by intensive visits in the days to come.

"In fact we are dedicated to preserving 158,000 of Whipple World's 219,000 acres as natural habitat," Emma quoted. "I believe, as a matter of comparison, that that percentage is far higher than any municipality in Florida, according to the master plans on file in Tallahassee."

Ernie slowed as he walked, scribbled "158,000" and

"219,000" in his notebook, nearly full already and it was only two o'clock. He capped his pen again and, as casually as he could, wiped his forehead with his rolled-up sleeve. He was sweating like a pig. She, in contrast, seemed perfectly at ease despite medium heels, hose, knee-length navy skirt, and matching jacket.

He glanced up to see her waiting on him, and he pretended to scrutinize his notes. He already had enough to fill two magazine-length stories, all of it information she seemed to know off the top of her head.

"Any questions?" she asked.

He noticed a drop of sweat starting to roll down from his temple, tried to think of a nonchalant way to get it, finally gave up and dabbed it with his shoulder. "Yeah. I don't suppose there's any place air-conditioned in Serenity that needs visiting?"

Emma Whipple smiled, flashing a perfect set of small white teeth. "I'm so sorry. I was born and raised in Florida. I guess I don't even notice the heat anymore."

Ernie gave up all pretense of dignity and mopped his face, brow, and neck with his already damp sleeve. "I was born and raised in Orlando. There isn't a day when I don't notice it."

She squinted down the Promenade where it wound around the northern shore of the lake, then back toward the old-fashioned downtown, filled with boutiques and restaurants and antique stores. "Well, we could go back to the Water Reuse Center. It's nice and cold there."

His nose involuntarily clamped back up as he recalled the sewage plant's powerful aroma. A result of the experimental, BioGen-engineered bacterium used to break down all organic material within a matter of hours, the guide at the all-new, all-stainless-steel facility had explained. "I was thinking, actually, of an air-conditioned place that doesn't necessarily smell like, uh, well . . . like *effluent*."

Emma checked her watch. "Well, I'd hoped to finish the overview this afternoon so you could get out of here by five. We have a lot more to cover tomorrow, and I don't want to get behind—"

"I don't need to get out by five," Ernie offered. "If we took a break now, we could pick back up a little later, maybe when it starts cooling off a bit?"

"I just didn't want to keep you from your wife . . . or kids."

Ernie shook his head. "Don't have either."

She looked again toward downtown and smiled. "Olde Towne Ice Cream?"

At four-fifty for a single scoop, Old Towne Ice Cream was aimed directly at the tourist trade, as was, Ernie quickly deduced, pretty much every other merchant in the three-block "downtown." In fact, he had noticed, there was really nothing useful for purchase in all of Serenity. No grocery. No hardware store. No pharmacy.

That made sense, tourism-wise. Visitors for the day rarely needed a quart of milk or a new toilet valve, but he wondered where Serenity residents were supposed to go for such necessities. Kissimmee and its stores were a good twenty minutes away.

Not that he cared. All he had to do was get a good feel for the place and then spin a yarn about its creation, about the finally realized dream of Waldo Whipple himself, an old-fashioned community where neighbors cared about each other, where kids could walk to school, and so on and so forth. And cute polar bears. A utopian community where cute polar bears had once visited.

In the meantime, Emma Whipple had turned out not to be such bad duty, after all. Cute, with a small, turned-up nose and a face defined by just enough angles to make it remarkable, jet-black, professional-looking, medium-length hair, and a small, trim figure to boot. Upon taking their seats, she had at first prattled on about the roots of New Urbanism, and Whipple's attempts to get the most

prominent architects in the field to design the public build-
ings, but Ernie had ultimately turned the conversation to
the quality of the ice cream, and how, even as overheated
as he was, ice water on top of ice cream made his teeth tingle.

She had laughed again, an almost musical sound, and
Ernie began to wonder if she was single. She wore no ring,
but then he remembered reading somewhere that Whipple
had some bizarre jewelry policy. Or was that a facial hair
policy? Either way, no ring didn't say anything about a
steady boyfriend. And she was a source, anyway. He
oughtn't be trying to hit on her.

Ernie set down his spoon decisively. "The best five-
dollar butter pecan I've ever had," he announced.

Emma's brow furrowed a touch as she wiped her own
lips with a paper napkin. "Well, this *is* prime real estate,"
she said, nodding at the plate-glass window overlooking
the lake. "Lot of demand for stores on Front Street. That
drives up the rental values. You know how it goes."

"Sure." Ernie grinned. "And if residents can subsist on
Häagen-Dazs, Whipple Collectibles, and Swatch, I guess
they're home free."

Emma glanced at Ernie's notebook anxiously and drew
herself upright in the wrought-iron chair. "Oh, I don't think
that's fair. And Serenity is really no farther from groceries
and sundries than many of the exclusive, gated communities in the area. In fact, the average distance from Bay Estates, Wendleworth, and Egret Trace to the nearest grocery
store is twelve point nine miles. That's only three miles
closer than Serenity, six minutes by car at an average speed
of thirty miles per hour. In fact, a community satisfaction
survey we conducted last December showed that Serenity
residents were ninety-four percent, quote, very satisfied,
unquote, with the proximity of—"

"Emma," Ernie said, reaching out for her elbow. "It's
okay. I'm from the *Advocate*. I'm writing a puff piece."

He glanced at where his fingers still lay over her thin,

tanned arm. She had startled when he'd touched her, but then had moved her arm back into contact with his hand, he had noticed . . . or thought he had noticed. Maybe she hadn't moved it back at all. Maybe she was deeply offended that he'd even touched her in the first place. Quickly he drew his hand back.

Emma glanced at her arm, his hand, and then safely out the window before she came back with a smile. "I'm sorry. But you know, the national press does love to make fun of Serenity. The mere idea that Whipple might get involved in something like that . . . Well, I'm sorry."

"It's okay." Ernie shrugged. "It's my fault for having egged you on."

She returned to her ice cream and took a last bite of half-molten French vanilla, and for one, long, lascivious second, Ernie imagined what it would be like to kiss her at that moment, her lips, cool against his, warming as the effects of the ice cream disappeared, opening slightly, his arms around her, pulling her closer. . . .

He blinked to a half-smile, felt himself redden.

"I thought I'd lost you," she said.

"No, no. I was just, uh," he stalled, glanced at his notebook, "roughing out an outline in my head for this article. You know, figuring out what piece goes where. The general concept, the architecture, the state-of-the-art sewer plant."

Emma giggled. "By all means, mention the sewer plant. But you have to call it the Water Reuse Center." She laughed again. "Okay, off-the-record, I'll admit some of our euphemisms are a bit much. The school is an Integrated Learning Academy. The teachers there are Learning Leaders. Even the tourists who walk around and gawk are Visiting Guests."

"Sounds like our newsroom," Ernie offered. "We used to be a newspaper. Now we're a Multimedia Entertainment and News Source. I'm not a reporter anymore, but a Content Provider. The poor schmucks on the daily beats, like police or city hall, they have to file hourly updates of their stories for the Web page, and then go on camera to read their story out loud for the *Advocate*'s cable news station, and then file their story for the paper. But at least they're getting paid more, for all the extra work."

"Well, that's nice," Emma said. "That they're getting compensated for all their extra time."

Ernie snorted. "I was only kidding about that. In fact, in a sense, they're getting less. Throughout the boom of the nineties, we held our payroll increases to under two percent. The local cost of living grew at three and a half percent. The difference went into the profit margin."

"Sounds like a Lew Peters strategy," Emma mumbled, then looked up with eyes wide. "That's off the record, too! Don't you dare print that!"

Ernie waved his hand carelessly. "Don't worry about it. I'm here to help, not offend. You make money, we make money, everybody wins. It's the Jack Leahy way. This story, I wouldn't be surprised if we let Lew Peters himself proofread it before we run it." He frowned, remembering something. "By the way, those baby bears you all have . . ."

"Snoball and Igloo?" Emma's eyes narrowed in concern. "What about them?"

Ernie chose his words carefully, trying to minimize the stupidity of what he was about to say. "I don't suppose they've ever been to Serenity? Like on display or anything like that?"

Emma released the breath she'd been holding. "No. Why?"

"No reason." Ernie shrugged. Outside, a pair of sunburned midwesterners in floppy hats, Ohioans from the look of them, peered in through the window. "Uh-oh. A couple of Visiting Guests."

Emma pretended to stand up. "You want I should grab them for an interview?"

The floppy-hatted woman turned to the floppy-hatted

man and rubbed a green zinc-oxide paste onto his nose. "I think I'll pass," Ernie said slowly, then glanced back to his assigned escort. She was seriously pretty, he decided, noticing a small dimple on one cheek that he'd missed earlier. Perhaps after the story was all done and printed and there was no question of conflict of interest, he'd give her a call. And, in the meantime, perhaps Serenity was a subject that deserved longer hours of study than he'd originally planned.

"What I really need is to talk to residents," he announced. "About a half dozen or so, preferably real gung-ho schmucks who came here because they wanted to be around Morty and Mindy Muskrat. You know: All Whipple, All the Time."

Emma lowered her eyes and played with her spoon. "Real schmucks, huh? Hmmm. I know . . . why don't you start with this one?" She looked up with a sharp smile. "I live over in the Low Country neighborhood. Myrtle Street."

Ernie stared slack-jawed, his chances with Emma Whipple dissolving into the ether before his very eyes, and groaned audibly.


In a practiced slouch against the tunnel's wall, Ferret Albright took his afternoon break with one eye peering out a metal peephole drilled through one of the concrete blocks and opening out amid rocks and monkey grass.

The rocks and monkey grass were in a tree planter, and the tree planter was set in the asphalt at the entrance to the Good World ride in FairyLand. Ferret Albright had dibs on all the ground-level peepholes in the catacombs beneath the Enchanted Realm, and the one at the Good World ride was by far his favorite. The ride's peculiar demographics made it so. A disproportionate number of the riders were mothers with young children, typically the only adults who could be coerced into repeat trips through the singing puppets.

Through careful reconnaissance, Albright had determined which of the park's attractions had the highest percentage of young women visitors, and consequently made it clear to the other peephole purveyors that he expected priority access at all times, and that he was ready to abuse his authority, and bust some heads, or worse, if anyone got in his way. Not that he faced a whole lot of competition.

Unlike some of his perverted colleagues who fought over the peepholes in the women's bathrooms or, most popular of all, the women's changing room at the Roaring Cascades water slide, Ferret Albright cared only for ground-level peepholes. Ferret Albright was a foot man.

He didn't really know when it began, but guessed it was an early age. While his junior high classmates were clipping out the *Sports Illustrated* model in her infamous fishnet swimsuit, young Ferret had snipped and filed away the photo of her from the previous page, the one that showed both of her oh-so-perfect feet.

The predilection became a fixation a few years later when the very same model had wandered into the Burdines shoe department at the local mall, where a skinny, pimply Ferret had fitted her in a pair of spring pumps—and afterward pocketed the little nylon footsies she had worn while she tried them on.

Ultimately, his little hobby, as he liked to think of it, was professional lawman Ferret Albright's pride and downfall, both. His pride, because unlike the sickos who wanted to see Whipple World's female guests with their tops off or their pants down, Ferret was interested only in what women were freely revealing in flip-flops, sandals, and, most racy of all, those strappy heels that had become popular again. His downfall because it was his interest in women's feet that had finally lost him the reelection for Volusia County Sheriff three years earlier. He had survived a federal grand jury looking into his practice of stopping black and Hispanic drivers and confiscating their money on the pretext that it was drug proceeds, but he couldn't get past the scandal that erupted when a young, attractive civil-rights lawyer sued his department when Albright photographed her open-toed pumps with a Polaroid after pulling her over for a broken taillight. Volusia County voters had a pretty high tolerance for racial profiling, not so much for foot molesters.

Ferret had returned to retail shoes for a time, but kept getting fired by department stores from Tampa to Fort Myers to Pembroke Pines; inevitably, a female customer would wind up complaining about the excessive amount of fondling she had received from the salesman. As the sheriff of Waldo Whipple World, Albright had gone foot free for the first six months before finally giving in to his urges and setting up his own personal peepholes.

He couldn't help it. Any woman's foot made him feel a little warm, but a finely turned ankle in some high heels, the calf muscles stretched taut in that hypnotizing curve . . . well, that always made his lunch hour a success.

Albright moved his head slightly against the concrete to scan the line moving in front of the peephole, cursing softly as a branch of a fern waved in the wind and partially obstructed his view. Damned slacker groundskeepers. He'd have to take care of the plant himself, next time he was in the park.

The wind abated, the branch moved out of the way, and Ferret Albright resumed his survey of women's tennis shoes and flats amid children's legs and stroller wheels, and he began thinking about work, about the troubling reports that a Department of Environmental Protection cop car had been seen cruising Whipple Corporation land south of Serenity, about what he'd have to do about it, when the line moved forward a bit, and into view came a pair of expensive, tan feet in shiny, black, high-heeled Kenneth Cole sandals.

His breathing quickened as he let his eyes feast on the

carefully buffed heels, the stretched, sloping arch, the perfectly painted toes . . . and Ferret knew that this one was a keeper. With his left eye still peeping through, he reached with one hand to remove a worn nylon footsie from his back pocket, and with the other hand reached to an adjacent shelf, where a loaded Nikon camera awaited. Finally he pulled himself away from the peephole and slid the lens into the perfectly sized metal tube. Then, with footsie-clad hand, he grabbed hold of the remote-control shutter release, plunging down with his thumb until the motor drive had shot off the entire roll.

Ernie Warner drove in silence. No CD, no radio. Just the perfectly serene, luxury-car hum of his Mercedes as he simmered and stewed over how, with utterly no provocation, he had bollixed it up with the first decent lady he'd met in, what, months? No. More like years.

Perfectly easy conversation in a nice, harmless setting. Getting to know each other a little. Nothing too formal. And what does he do? Screw the whole thing up with good old sarcasm. Wasn't enough to just ask for interviews with some real residents. He had to get in a good dig, too. And, boy, was it a dandy. Real clever. Real, top-rate, *Tonight Show* stuff. She had cooled instantly and never really warmed up again. They had continued their walking "overview" of the town, and she had shaken his hand, told him she'd see him in the morning, and that was that.

Ah, fuck it, he thought, as he flew down the empty access road toward the Turnpike. Before he'd shown up that morning, he hadn't even known she'd existed. Surely it wouldn't be so hard getting over that. Of course he still had the problem of dealing with her professionally for the next three or four days. Of having her stand there, listening to him ask grown men and women who had a crush on the world's largest entertainment company about what, personally, they liked best about living in a town designed as a tourist attraction.

Well, he'd made his bed. Now he would lie in it. He began to wonder if maybe Leahy was right. Maybe somehow, somewhere, he'd slipped over the line between seeing both the lighter and darker sides of things to seeing only a dark side. Maybe it was no longer a reflection of the world he saw, but a reflection of himself. Maybe, he thought with a sigh, he would call Stephanie, see if perhaps her husband had one of his frequent out-of-town trips coming up and she'd like to come sit in his Jacuzzi with him again, for old times' sake. One last time, and then never again.

He let that thought sit there for a while. Steph still had no problem with him, or seemingly anyone else, for that matter, seeing her naked. She'd come over, strip down, hop into the redwood hot tub, then lecture him about how scarce redwood was, and how the timber companies were trying to buy enough members of Congress to let them cut the last of the trees down, and *then* where would they be?

By the third glass of wine, she'd stop chattering on about Wellington, the orthodontist husband, and Bobby, the environmentalist crusader husband. . . . Damn, he'd forgotten to ask around about him. He'd need to do that before he could call her, no getting around it. At least to the local cops, maybe the Highway Patrol. That way he could tell her the truth: Yes, he'd asked around. No, he hadn't learned anything. Then, at least he wouldn't have to lie to her as he conspired with her to commit adultery.

He opened and closed his mouth with distaste for the word. He hated to think of what he occasionally did with Stephanie as that. He had, after all, seen her first, before either of her husbands. He was on the verge of justifying things to himself when he noticed the flashing blue lights in his rearview mirror, glanced down at his speedometer, and groaned.

*Another* speeding ticket. The ticket itself he would

barely even notice, a couple hundred bucks, at most. But the delight his insurance company was taking in the combination of speeding tickets and big, new luxury car was starting to make distressing headway into his bank account. He pulled out his wallet for his license, tried to decide whether to try and talk the cop out of writing it or just resign himself to paying, when he glanced at the cop's face and squinted.

The cop half smiled, a big, serious face trying to be personable. "Come on, Ernie, it hasn't been *that* long."

The uniform was forest green, but not that of a sheriff's office. Ernie recognized the markings as that of a Department of Environmental Protection officer and smiled. "Tony?"

"Captain Armstrong, to you."

Ernie jumped out of the Mercedes to pump his hand. "Captain. Well, congratulations are in order."

Tony Armstrong shook his head. "No. My boss retired. I was promoted, and then they cut my staff to zero. I'm a chief without any Indians. You?"

It had been years since he'd seen his old friend. Six years, if Ernie was remembering right. Back then, Lieutenant Tony Armstrong of the DEP's Fifth Region had been one of his best sources, a steady stream of information about corporate polluters and illegal dredgers and the various others who would assault what was left of pristine Florida for fun and profit. And then Ernie had made his big jump up into management, at about the same time that the polluters and dredgers pooled their campaign contributions and got themselves a much more business-friendly DEP chief.

"Became a chief for a couple of years," Ernie summarized. "But my main job was to downsize the Indians. So I decided I didn't really want to be a chief after all."

Tony Armstrong offered the shrug of a fellow survivor, then nodded at Ernie to follow him to his cruiser. "I called your office, they said you'd be around here somewhere.

Perfect coincidence. I've been hanging around this part of the county for a couple weeks, too."

Despite being out of practice for years, Ernie felt a twinge of excitement when he saw the expanding cardboard file case on the front seat of the patrol car. Armstrong reached in and handed him the first manila folder, sat in the driver's seat as Ernie opened it and began reading.

It was a lab analysis of a series of well water samples taken from ranches, farms, and state park holdings in a wide swath south and west of Kissimmee. Every single reading showed elevated salinity, with the samples farthest north showing the highest levels.

"Saltwater intrusion," Ernie concluded.

"Exactly." Armstrong nodded. "With the problem diminishing the farther downslope you get."

Ernie flipped through the rest of the packet and then turned back to the cover page. "So Whipple Corporation is drawing too much water."

"Yup."

Tony Armstrong removed his eyeglasses, puffed a breath on each small oval lens, and polished them on his green knitted tie. They were, Ernie recalled, the same style Armstrong had worn for the dozen years he'd known him. The style Ernie used to kid him about endlessly, along with the nerdy shoes and wide-lapeled jackets he would wear out of uniform.

"By the way, have you noticed, Tony? Your frames are in fashion again," Ernie ribbed. "Think of all the money you saved! Another ten, twelve years, maybe wide lapels will make a comeback, too."

"Take a look," Tony Armstrong said, ignoring him, putting his glasses back on, "at the next packet in there. The surface water numbers."

Ernie turned dutifully to the next set of stapled sheets, deciding his old friend still hadn't developed much of a sense of humor regarding his own appearance. The lakes and streams just west of Whipple property, he saw, also had slightly elevated salinity. He blinked as he tried to remember what sort of rainfall year they'd had so far.

"Huh," he said at last as the truth finally dawned on him. "There's been plenty of rain . . . and yet we've got brackish water, in the middle of the state, nontidal. . . . What's going on, Tony?"

Armstrong grinned. "Good. So I have your attention finally? What's going on is that for some reason, the Serenity River is running brackish, and the runoff is affecting downslope waters."

Ernie flipped through the pages quickly. "What are the Serenity River samples showing?"

"That's a good question. I've requested permission to take some. They've denied it."

Ernie scoffed. "What do you need permission for? You're the state! Just go in and . . . Oh, right."

All Whipple Corporation property, Ernie remembered, was governed by the Central Highlands Improvement District, created specifically for Whipple in the early 1960s by the Florida Legislature and then enshrined in the Florida Constitution in 1968. The district's five-member board was, by law, appointed by the Whipple CEO.

"Oh, right," Armstrong agreed. "They contract for their own police and fire protection, they can build their own airport, without state approval, or set up their own power grid, or even build a nuclear power plant. They sure as hell don't have to let me monitor their environmental compliance. They do, though, have to follow the general laws of Florida. So if I can show they're violating water-quality laws, I can get a subpoena and bust 'em. I'm waiting on some water samples from a CI. If they show what I think they'll show, then I can leak you the whole kit and caboodle. You put it in the paper."

"Whoa, whoa, whoa, let's back that up: a CI? You've got a confidential informant getting you water samples?"

Ernie smiled at the thought. "Will he get to wear a ski mask in court, if he has to testify?"

"Go ahead and laugh. But I wanted water samples, and I'm going to get them, Lew Peters be damned. That's yours and mine and everybody else's river, by the way, up to mean high water. In case you've forgotten, now that you're a fancy schmancy," he glanced up at the S500, "overpaid . . . Anyway, you interested or not?"

Ernie finished perusing the packet, closed the file folder, and handed it back. "Sorry, Tonto, no can do."

Armstrong blinked, then followed Ernie as he walked back to his car. "Excuse me? I figured you'd be *drooling* over something like this. Ernie, it's *Whipple,* for God's sake! What's wrong with you?"

"What's wrong is that my paper just awarded Whipple its Corporate Citizen Gold Medal. Lew Peters was our Floridian of the Year." Ernie climbed into the driver's seat as Armstrong looked on in dismay. "The reason I'm out here at all, Tony? I'm doing a fluff feature about the Jubilee. Front page, stripped across six columns. My big challenge? Find a way to get cute polar bears in before paragraph four."

Tony Armstrong shook his head sadly. "I thought you were somebody I could count on, man."

Ernie stared out at the forest beside the road. It was neat slash pines, rank and file in perfect order. Although technically outside the Whipple World gates, it was still Whipple property. But because it was beyond what the public thought was Whipple, Peters had cut down all the old-growth long-leaf pines, for their timber value, not long after he'd taken over.

"Yeah, well, we got mortgages to pay." Ernie nodded at the walnut dashboard. "Car payments to make. I'm sorry I can't help. But look, once you get those water samples and officially charge the bastards with something, I'll do what I can to make sure we don't bury the story completely."

Armstrong looked at his feet. "Actually, I was hoping

an article might strengthen my hand. Maybe force my boss to authorize an enforcement action. He, uh, just happened to be among Whipple's Public Sector Best and Brightest last year. . . ."

"Don't tell me." Ernie started his engine. Even with his window open it barely made a sound. "One Month Passport?"

"*Lifetime* passport," Tony Armstrong said.

Ernie clipped his seat belt. "Then you know exactly what I'm talking about. I got a couple of names at the St. Pete paper might be able to help. They still do the occasional muckraking. Plus there's a columnist down in Miami who thinks Lew Peters is the Antichrist. You might want to try him. Otherwise, you're on your own, amigo. If you guys ever decide to give Whipple an award or something, let us know. We'll definitely want to cover that. But, listen, for old times' sake call me in a couple of days. Let me know what those water samples show, will you? Just for my personal curiosity?"

Tony forced a smile. "Sure, Ernie. I'll do that. Might even help you get some of that old outrage back. I'll call you."

Armstrong wiped his granny glasses clean a final time, adjusted the Smokey the Bear hat on his head, and headed back to his patrol car. Ernie watched him in his sideview mirror for a while, and then, with a sigh, put the car into gear.

# four

...

The uniformed sheriff's deputy yanked down yet another handbill, this time from a sapling elm, and shoved it into a bulging canvas sack before climbing back into his cruiser.

Emma Whipple pretended to ignore it, but out the corner of one eye glanced down Beaufort Way and saw a long line of beige handbills the deputy hadn't gotten to yet. She turned instead down Edisto Avenue, where the saplings seemed clear of any posted material.

"Again, on Edisto, we see the influences of the South Carolina Low Country. The deep porches, the high ceilings, the tongue-and-groove paneling. The Charleston look." She spoke in the modulated speech of the tour guide. Pleasant. Interested. Fully memorized. No need to deviate from the script. "On Kiawah Street, we have a couple of homes that are actual replicas of historic homes from the real Charleston."

To her right and behind her, Ernie Warner wrote something in his notebook, nodded, and said nothing. A half hour of walking so far in the cool morning, and he had said maybe a total of ten words. Which was just fine with

Emma. She'd picked a lightweight pantsuit that day and comfortable flats, and fully intended to walk his ass off.

His cut at Serenity and its residents wasn't the first she'd heard from visiting reporters about her home. Reporters as a group, she knew, seemed to take pleasure in putting others down. She'd come to accept that. And yet . . . his snide remark had stung deeply, far more than similar ones by writers from the *New York Times* and the *Washington Post*. Perhaps it was because even after announcing his intention to write a typical *Advocate* puff piece, he still hadn't been able to resist a poke. Like it was so blindingly obvious that only a total nitwit could live in any place as goofy as Serenity, and therefore ridiculing its residents ought to be acceptable in polite company. Kind of how making fun of Cleveland or Buffalo was okay.

She snuck a sidelong glance at him as he strode past one picket fence after another, walking along, looking smug, writing down little smart-alecky comments about everything he saw. Like right now, he was probably noting how every fence was the identical height, painted the identical off-white shade. The jerk.

"Right, this is your neighborhood, then. Isn't it? The Low Country?"

Emma flashed a frosty smile but said nothing, saw Ernie Warner's hopeful look dissolve into resignation, and she almost wavered into forgiveness. He was, after all, cute, in a nonthreatening, grown up sort of way. And it had been ages since she'd been with a man socially who wasn't either secretly gay or an aggressive corporate climber mistaking her for someone with a measure of clout within the company.

And then she thought again how Ernie had so easily and so cavalierly trashed the one dream her great-uncle had so fervently believed in, only to die before it could be completed. Well, screw Ernie Warner.

To the left, down Mount Pleasant Lane, she saw another deputy collecting leaflets from car windshields, so she turned right, quickly bringing them back to the lake and Founders Park, where she stopped before a weathered-looking granite monument.

"Our War Memorial," she said simply, almost starting to elaborate about how the names engraved in the stone were Serenity residents' grandfathers and great-grandfathers who had died in the First and Second World Wars.

But then she realized that unlike ordinary tourists who accepted the obelisk at face value, Ernie Warner had probably searched his database and found the seven-year-old article in an obscure Georgia weekly about Whipple Corporation's attempt to buy the local war memorial for fifty thousand dollars, and how a petition drive had eventually sent them packing despite the town council's hundred-thousand-dollar counteroffer. How Whipple had proceeded to commission a monument from scratch: half of the names ancestors of the first homesite buyers from the original sales lottery, the other half invented out of whole cloth.

Ernie Warner kneeled down to look at the names at the base of the monument, and Emma realized he would, if she didn't act quickly, see the name Martens Muskrat, the war hero grandfather of Morty, which one of the Enchanteers hadn't been able to resist slipping onto the list of names for the engravers. . . .

"Over there is our Enviroground. All wood and recycled plastics. The play surface is twenty inches of cypress chips over mulch, exceeding by fifty percent the recommendations of the American Society of Playground Engineers. A living example of Whipple's—"

And then she noticed the young mother and toddler in a heated discussion on the far side of the empty playground, the child escaping and running for the swing set, the mother chasing her down and yanking her away just as she stepped onto the cypress chips, scolding her as she carried her off. Emma puzzled over that for a moment, then noticed the big capital letters that someone had drawn in the wood chips.

Quickly she turned back toward town and started power walking. "We'll hit the Down East neighborhood next, and then Portofino Square."

Ernie Warner had not finished a decipherable word all morning. Each time he thought of something to jot down, she would take off again in forced march mode, leaving a few letters of scrawl in his notepad, incomplete, unconnected with anything else.

It didn't really matter. Four of five quotes from Emma, a few more from some "real people," background from stories in other papers, and that was pretty much all the research he'd need to whip together two thousand words of drivel. That, plus the damned polar bears.

With a sigh he followed behind her as she headed for yet another themed neighborhood. She was still pissed, no doubt about it. She hadn't said a word to him all morning that wasn't part of the official Serenity Tour Guide script. Small lots. Gabled roofs. New Urbanist, neighbor-oriented "front porch" communities. Whatever that meant.

It was okay. He'd been bad, and he'd serve his penance. He crossed a street, Bangor Avenue, and noticed yet another sheriff's car at the far end, the deputy out plucking handbills off a row of stake-supported maples. The third deputy he'd seen that morning collecting flyers. Or maybe it was just one deputy he'd seen three separate times. He'd never been close enough to get a good look at him. Or them.

The little flyers, though, were starting to intrigue him. Emma was clearly steering him away from them and he was beginning to wonder why. He thought he'd seen the headline on one before Emma had directed his attention elsewhere: "Serenityites Arise!" had been the exhortation. At the bottom had been the letters WWWS. The same letters he'd seen seemingly all over Serenity the past day and a half. In the playground wood chips, carved into a park bench, even on a small cardboard sign stuck in the hand of one of the animatronic geezers who sat and waved from the front porch of the model home by Serenity's main entrance.

He wondered if the letters held some sort of significance he was missing, if the constant cleanup effort was a function not of Whipple's well-known anal retentiveness, but rather of some strange kind of political repression. He had first assumed that the abbreviation had something to do with wrestling, that America's lowest comedy had infected even its Utopia. And then he remembered a feature he'd read in the religion section a couple of years back: W-W-J-D . . .

And suddenly he knew what WWWS meant, and he couldn't help but grin.

Emma was still ahead, walking briskly, narrating about rooflines and casement windows and attention to detail, when she stopped short. There in front of them on the sidewalk, in some kind of fluorescent orange paint, were the ubiquitous letters.

He watched her a moment as she glanced at him, then at the sidewalk, then at him. "What Would Waldo Say?" he asked finally. "Serenityites Arise? Serenity Underground?"

The cool indifference was gone now, replaced with poorly suppressed fluster. "High school kids," she said after a time. "You know, antiestablishment games. Normal, harmless graffiti." She cleared her throat and resumed walking. "Okay. Portofino Square, and then Town Hall."


To the untrained eye, the Department of Enviromental Protection patrol car looked pretty much like the Whipple Sheriff's cars. Same-model Crown Victoria. Same basic white-and-green color scheme. But Ferret Albright's was not an untrained eye, and to him the difference between his

own Crown Vic and the DEP car hidden in a clump of pal-
mettos off the narrow access road to Serenity's well fields
was blindingly obvious.

The DEP cruiser, like all vehicles of sworn police officers in the state, had blue flashers on its roof. His own car
had yellow flashers, and to Albright that distinction was
everything.

For once upon a time he'd been a *real* sheriff, with a
real uniform with real stars on his collar, and the ability to
arrest people, and all that stuff. Now, he knew, he was basically a rent-a-cop. True, he was better equipped, certainly
better paid than most sheriffs in the whole country, but that
couldn't change the fact of those stupid yellow flashers.

And all because of one, lousy, dead honor student.

The kid had been driving suspiciously, like the car was
stolen or something, and one of his deputies had rightfully
tried to pull it over. The kid had panicked or gotten distracted, and had run the Trans Am into a ditch. Whipple
lawyers had argued it was the kid's own fault, for not stopping. But the parents had asked why, if the, quote, sheriff's
deputies, unquote, at Whipple weren't real police, should
they be allowed to have sirens and blue flashing lights on
their vehicles? And in a rare dark moment in Whipple legal
history, the damned judge had agreed.

Within a week, every one of his department's cars had
to switch its rooftop bars from blue to amber. It didn't matter so much in the daytime—a Crown Vic was a Crown
Vic, and motorists still respected that. At nighttime,
though, as a tool of intimidation, his cruiser was now
worthless. In the rearview, the only things visible were
headlights and flashing yellow. He looked like a tow truck.
Who was going to pull over for a tow truck?

He pushed aside the unfairness of it all as he continued
his walkaround of the DEP car. It was empty, Albright
could see, and unlocked. He debated for a few moments
before approaching the passenger-side door, pulling his
sleeve over his fingers, and lifting the latch.

On the seat was an expandable cardboard file folder, on the floor, a vinyl computer case. With a final glance around, Albright sat on the edge of the seat and began riffing through the files, instantly seeing that, yes, the DEP man had been gathering information on Whipple property. He had begun to consider his options when he heard a voice ask him what he was doing.

Albright glanced up to see a large cop in DEP uniform, his right hand on his hip . . . a mere inches from his service pistol. He could see that the little strap securing the gun behind its butt had already been unsnapped.

Slowly, Albright answered the cop's uneasy smile with a relaxed grin. "Oh, *there* you are," he said, gradually standing. "I called and called. I guess you didn't hear me. I was, uh, wondering if you might have a coupla extra UTCs." The standard Florida traffic infraction form. "I'm clean out and was heading back to headquarters, when I noticed you here and thought I'd bum some off you."

It was a bald-faced lie, and Albright knew the cop wouldn't buy it. On the other hand, he knew that the cop knew that the DEP had no business snooping around Whipple without Albright's permission. It was a standoff of untruths.

The cop considered this, then bent past Albright into his cruiser, leaning toward the glove box, which is when Ferret Albright jumped on his back and threw his arm around his neck, carefully tucking the crook of his elbow against the man's Adam's apple like he'd read in the latest issue of *Law Enforcement Monthly,* and then squeezed for all he was worth as the cop thrashed about.


As in the four other houses he'd visited, the ceramic figurines got prominent display in an area all their own, in this case a specially built alcove in the foyer. There were Morty and Mindy Muskrat, Billy Baboon, Tobias the Tortoise, Mongoose Mike, and all the others. Thirty or forty in all, obviously freshly polished, not a speck of dust to be seen.

"My Whipple-of-the-Month Club collection," Mrs. Celeste explained conspiratorially. "I have *two* Gordon Gophers."

She did indeed, and had arranged the leering rodents like sentries at either end of the display. Ernie had no idea what to say to her, just as he'd found his natural interrogatory skills at a loss with the previous four homeowners. They were all so terribly nice, so well-meaning. That he could even consider ridiculing them for their harmless vice made him feel like a jerk.

"You sure do," he said finally.

"The second one came this morning. It was a bonus selection," she confided. "More lemonade? I have plenty."

Ernie examined his nearly empty tumbler. It was fresh, from real lemons, and he'd already downed two glasses. "No, thank you, ma'am. It was delicious, though."

"Well, if you change your mind, just holler. I make some fresh every mornin'. That and some nice sun tea."

She walked back into the parlor with the help of a four-pronged cane, waved Ernie and Emma to seats on the couch. At just a month shy of eighty-nine, she was Serenity's second-oldest resident, she had explained, and Ernie had noted. She had been born in Kentucky, spent most of her life in Georgia, and retired with her husband to Florida. After he died, she had used the insurance money to buy a Founders' Lot that she had won the right to purchase in the Serenity lottery.

He scanned the room, out of questions, taking in Mrs. Celeste's touch on the stock Whipple home. She had obviously hand-embroidered pillows on the couch, but had chosen, predictably, Whipple characters for her motif. On one wall was an official Enchanted Realm clock, and the home entertainment center was chock-full of Whipple videos and Whipple CDs.

"I'm a member of both Whipple Video and Whipple Music," she explained. "Just another perk of living here."

Ernie nodded absently, squinting to see the titles of three identical CDs in orange jewel cases. . . . Yup, sure enough, they were the latest effort by the suburban, white-boy rap group Krazy Klowne, whose song "Burn, Mutha-fucka, Burn!" had forced Whipple Records to pull the title off the shelves after the Baptists organized nationwide protests and threatened a boycott of all Whipple movies, television programs, and theme parks. It had been front-page news everywhere. Everywhere, Ernie recalled wryly, except at the *Orlando Advocate,* where it barely rated a two-paragraph brief the day of the million-copy recall.

He wondered how many members the Whipple Music Club had. He wondered if they had all received three "bonus selections" of Krazy Klowne CDs, or just the members who were lucky enough to "Live in Serenity." He almost asked, then caught himself as dear Mrs. Celeste leaned forward to offer more lemonade.

He lifted a hand politely, let his eyes roam over the room again. Mongoose Mike coasters on the table, a pair of "Elephant Prince" lamps on the end table.

"I guess I do have a lot of Whippleobelia," Mrs. Celeste said, watching him.

Ernie returned his gaze to her and tried to smile. "It's all very nice."

"Thank you. But it's nothing compared to my sister. She started collecting it when we were little girls, back when there was Morty Muskrat but there wasn't even a Mindy yet, let alone Gordon Gopher or Mongoose Mike." She reached over from her easy chair and laid a wrinkled hand on his. "You know, she lives in Serenity, too."

Ernie saw himself sitting in yet another parlor, his eyes glazing over at an even larger display of Whipple-related collectibles. He swallowed hard and forced another smile. "I'd love to see it. Is she home?"

Suddenly Mrs. Celeste and Emma Whipple traded a

strange look, and Mrs. Celeste began mumbling about her laundry, and no, actually, now that she thought about it, her sister, Marjeane was her name, well, she'd gone back to Kentucky for a couple of weeks to see the grandkids, and wouldn't you know it, she'd forgotten to give her a key, and—

Emma Whipple stood abruptly with an exaggerated glance at her watch. "My *goodness,* would you look at the time! Come on, Ernie, we don't want to keep Mayor Gillespie waiting."

In a cavernous airship hangar at UPSVIL's maintenance yard, Lew Peters only half listened to his foreman as he walked the length of the keel, casually casting an eye from the flat bottom that rested atop an array of hydraulic jacks, over the hull, and way up the tall superstructure to the tops of the smokestacks.

Those, he knew, were largely ornamental, with narrow flues running along the inside to vent the diesel exhaust from what originally had been the boiler room. He got to the massive paddle wheel at the stern and stopped. It was largely ornamental, as well. True, it would spin, but the locomotion provided therein was nothing compared to that generated by the twin, thirty-inch screws a couple of feet below the waterline.

From the tone of the man's voice beside him, he realized his foreman was asking a question. He mentally reran in his head the last fifteen or so words that he'd heard, decided he still had no idea what this fire hydrant of a man with the Popeye forearms was asking.

"What?" Peters said finally.

"Bottom paint," Popeye said. "Before we put her back in, she's gonna need a couple thousand gallons of bottom paint. Both the hull," he put a giant paw on one of the thick spokes of the paddle wheel, "and this. I know where we can get some of the good stuff, tributyl tin."

Peters screwed up his brow now. "That's what I thought you said. Why would we want some?"

"Fresh water, sixty-five- to eighty-five-degree range, I'm thinking three coats of tributyl tin will last three, four, maybe five years. Copper-based epoxy will get you two seasons, tops."

Lew Peters turned his eye upward again, up over the gold lettering, *Dixie Princess,* and then over the freshly painted white railings and overhangs. Five decks, completely gutted, then rebuilt to replace open seating for five hundred passengers with seventy-eight luxury suites, each with its own Jacuzzi bathtub and large-screen television. The low-rent cafeteria had been turned into a walnut-paneled dining room. And the very top deck, which had been an open observation area, was being lovingly restored to its original purpose.

"Cost difference?"

"Not much. Copper's about hundred bucks a gallon. Tin about ninety-five."

Lew Peters blinked quizzically. "Then what, pray tell, is the issue? Works better. Slightly cheaper. Why are you even asking me?"

Popeye crossed his arms across his barrel chest. "Tin's illegal as hell. It'll keep any slime from growing on the hull, but it'll also kill pretty much any fish in a quarter-mile radius, too. DEP will nail us with some nasty fines if they find out."

Peters sighed. He should have known. Popeye's last job had been at a boatyard on the toxin-rich St. Johns River in Jacksonville. "As far as I am aware, by state charter, the Central Highlands Improvement District and *only* the Central Highlands Improvement District is responsible for water-quality inspections on Whipple property surface water, no?" He smiled, turned the corner, and started walking up the starboard said. "In which case, it becomes a purely economic decision, does it not?"

The foreman shrugged, nodded, and continued his update on the progress of the renovations as they walked. Finally they finished a full circuit and Peters started slipping back into the sport coat he'd slung over his shoulder. "Looks good. She'll be ready for service by next autumn, I trust?"

"No problem." Popeye admired the boat's prow for a moment, then turned back to Peters. "Just one question. We're adding about ninety, ninety-five thousand pounds to the gross weight. The naval architect tells me that works out to about four feet higher on the waterline. That's no big deal, propulsion-wise. I assume she won't be entered in any sort of race."

Peters checked his watch impatiently. "Your assumption is correct. So your question is . . ."

"Four more feet gives her a draft of seven feet." Popeye frowned. "I thought somebody told me that when she goes back in, it'll be in Lake Serenity."

"That, too, is correct. And your question?"

"Well, Lake Serenity has a controlling depth of six feet. Sir, that water just isn't deep enough for the *Dixie Princess*."

Peters smiled, tugged at his monogrammed cuffs to pull them the requisite half inch beyond his coat sleeves, then clapped Popeye around the shoulders. "Don't you worry yourself. It will be soon enough."

The white-haired, red-cheeked gentleman with the jeans and string tie certainly looked the part of a small-town, cracker mayor. And the way he talked, like his mouth was full of marbles, Dick Gillespie definitely sounded like a small-town mayor.

And yet, something wasn't quite right.

"Folks'll do what they do. Ain't no ed'cation in the second kick of a mule, now," the mayor said, and then smiled wide.

Ernie smiled back, started to write down what he thought Gillespie had said, although he had no earthly idea why. Random, unconnected southernisms were all he was getting from the good mayor. Not that he needed anything at all. Whether Serenity was run by a polished professional or a country bumpkin was wholly irrelevant to his article.

"So do you think the connection with Whipple has helped the town, in terms of the property appraisals? I was thinking of the moderate-income housing in particular," he asked gamely.

The mayor leaned back in his chair, thinking, and then became distracted by another of his assistants who came in through the side door of his office and bent over to return a manila folder to the bottom drawer of a filing cabinet. Ernie became distracted too. This assistant was about five-feet-ten, blond, wore three-inch white heels and a white minidress slit entirely too high. He saw the flash of curved flesh near the top of her leg, and realized she was either wearing some kind of thong underwear or no underwear at all, and further realized that Mayor Gillespie had a perfect view from where he was sitting to know for certain, one way or the other.

From the other chair, Emma Whipple cleared her throat to bring her male companions back to reality, and the mayor grinned widely once more.

"Shoot, you know the ol' sayin': If you gonna need a friend, you better bring you dawg."

Ernie blinked, began to write down the aphorism in his notepad, then scratched it out in disgust. It began to occur to him that Dick Gillespie had not answered one substantive question about his town, either about its finances or its operation. He had asked about the experimental kindergarten-through-twelve school, and Gillespie had answered about the chickens coming home to roost. He had asked whether the property taxes were comparable to the surrounding area and Gillespie had gone on about the huntin' dog who'd always eat the downed quail instead of retrieve it.

Out the corner of his eye, he noticed a tall redhead in a microskirt and tight sweater vest totter in on spiky mules, bend over to open the same filing cabinet drawer, and pull out two folders. Ernie felt Emma's gaze on him and carefully kept his own eyes locked on the mayor, who without any shame tilted his head down for a better view.

Gillespie watched the girl leave through the side door, then threw his boots up onto the middle of his empty cherry desk. Ernie thought back through the half hour they had been there, and it dawned on him that he had not seen a single female employee in Gillespie's office who wasn't, one, young, two, beautiful, and, three, dressed in something absurdly skimpy.

In fact, now that he thought about it, he hadn't seen *any* Town Hall employees who didn't look like they'd just walked out of a Victoria's Secret catalog. The woman in the clerk's office, the cashier at the utilities desk, the receptionist outside Gillespie's office: every single one looked to be in her early twenties and was drop-dead gorgeous. What the hell kind of Town Hall was that? None that he'd ever been in before.

He glanced down at his notes, desperately trying to think of something else to ask Gillespie, anything at all, when the blonde returned with another file folder to the same bottom drawer and struck a butt-out pose as she bent down. Mayor Gillespie casually knocked a pencil off his desktop, then quickly pounced down to retrieve it, keeping his head down at ground level until the blonde finally stood upright, flashed them all a smile, and walked back out.

Ernie sat dumbstruck, half listening to Gillespie remark on a farmer and his prize bull with a twinkle in his eye, and suddenly he felt Emma Whipple dragging him by the arm.

"Well, thanks again, Mayor. I know you need to close up shop and get going." Emma Whipple led him through Gillespie's outer office, past the gauntlet of babes toward the front entrance. "If Mr. Warner has any more questions, I'll be sure to pass them along."

•   •   •

Ernie Warner strolled toward his Mercedes through the quickly darkening Down East neighborhood, past a row of New England bungalows, lighter than he'd felt in months. He'd scored major points with Emma Whipple, he knew, simply by refraining from being a pig.

She'd hustled him out of there, worried that somehow Mayor Gillespie's lechery might get prominent mention in his article, and he'd had yet another opportunity to explain, no, he was writing a puff piece for a paper that specialized in them, and given that Mayor Gillespie had refrained from actually yanking his trousers down and taking care of himself while ogling his office assistants, Mayor Gillespie would come off as a lovable, caring, and eminently quotable small-town southern mayor.

And, wonder of wonders, Emma Whipple had smiled at him! Not just a professional grin, but a warm smile of genuine affection that told him she was seriously reconsidering her anger over his calling all Serenity residents "schmucks." It was his restraint, he knew, that was figuring into that reevaluation. His ability to see an attractive, partially . . . no, *mostly* naked young woman and maintain his dignity and his focus.

He'd taken the opportunity of the slight thaw to ask, completely off the record, for his own personal amusement, how it was that Serenity's residents could have elected such a boor to the town's highest office.

"*Completely* off the record?" she had asked, and then had explained that Mayor Gillespie wasn't technically elected to anything as much as he was "cast" for that role by the Marketing Department. As in China or Cuba, he was pretty much the only candidate on the ballot.

Emboldened, Ernie had asked about a Town Hall populated entirely by young chippies, and Emma Whipple had allowed how Mayor Gillespie's day job was casting director for the various chorus shows at the Enchanted Realm and UPSVIL, giving him a bottomless pool of talent from which to hire.

"Plus nothing in Town Hall is real," she admitted. "Those girls are basically there for show. If a resident actually pays a real bill there, it gets passed along to Central Billing and gets processed there. Those filing cabinets? Mayor Gillespie only lets them use the bottom drawers . . . for obvious reasons."

She had thanked him again for not trying to expose all their warts. "Someday we, the citizens of Serenity, will have a real mayor and real self-government. We're just getting started, is all."

She had sounded so sincere, so determined, that Ernie had been honestly touched. More than touched. Encouraged. Here she was, leveling with him, sharing her frustrations and aspirations, which proved to him, without a shadow of a doubt, that he still had a chance with her! The very next day, in fact, he would mention dinner. Casually, nothing too formal, but, hey, if he was there that late anyway, and traffic on the Turnpike would be thick through the evening hours, and if she didn't have dinner plans . . .

He nodded to himself as he approached his car. Yes sir, tomorrow would be the day. Midafternoon. Or maybe late afternoon would be better, would sound a little less preplanned. Yeah, late afternoon, he would broach the question—

Without warning his world was spinning as he found himself cut off at the knees, pitched over, facedown in the earth.

"Not a single word," a low voice intoned ominously.

Ernie peeked up as best he could, and realized he was beneath one of the many perfectly chosen, perfectly situated, perfectly trimmed azalea hedges between lots. The alternative to a picket fence, as long as the homeowner promised to let it grow no taller than waist-high and to promptly cut down renegade offshoots.

And now, one of them was serving as the perfect hiding spot to roll tourists in Whipple's Utopia of Yesterday. How about that for a little irony in Leahy's Serenity center-piece? Mugged in Paradise . . .

His assailant had a knee planted in his back, and his hands wrapped around his wrists. Ernie wondered if he had a gun . . . wondered, perversely, whether Serenity had reg-ulations for its street criminals about how often they had to clean their firearms.

"Wallet's in the back, right pocket," Ernie mumbled helpfully through a mouthful of soil.

"Shhhhhh!" the mugger hissed. "There's somebody coming! Shut up or you're a dead man!"

Ernie watched glumly as two pair of feet became visible beneath the hedge, then disappeared. He realized both he and his mugger had been holding their breath. "Wallet's got about fifty bucks, three or four credit cards. I promise I won't call and cancel until tomorrow—"

"You Ernie Warner, right? Reporter?"

Ernie blinked. Things either were not as bad they seemed, or much, much worse. "Why do you ask?"

"Okay, listen up, and listen up good," the mugger whis-pered hoarsely. "The water table around here. It's falling like a rock. You got it? And Lew Peters *knows*! Ask your-self: Why such a big fancy sewer project? Where's that new main running to? Check it out!"

Ernie puzzled on the hydrological complaint for a mo-ment, wondered what exactly he was supposed to do about it, and was about to ask when the pressure in the small of his back suddenly disappeared. He looked up to see a stocky figure in jeans and a dark shirt limp rapidly into the gloom and around a corner.

A car engine cranked to life in the middle distance, and Ernie knew there was no point in pursuit.

One by one, Ferret Albright removed bound reports and stapled sheafs of paper from the accordion folder and sep-arated them into two piles on his desk. On the right were those items to be further investigated. On the left was everything to be incinerated. The left pile was much taller than the right.

He pulled out another set of papers, flipped through them, saw they were about salinity levels of various water bodies to the west of Whipple property. He'd already seen more than he cared to about salinity, and he quickly tossed the set onto the to-be-incinerated stack. He reached into the accordion folder, found that it was finally empty.

He put everything in the left-hand stack back into the folder, laid it on his desk, then reached to the floor to open the black computer case. It and the folder had been the only objects of a personal nature in the Crown Vic that he'd had to remove before pushing the car into the retention pond at the center of the Serenity exit cloverleaf. He'd then taken the precaution of having a deputy in scuba gear put a cable on the front bumper so it could be winched from the far shore until it was right smack in the middle of the pond, where the thick brown water was a good ten feet deep. Realistically, it wouldn't be found until a drought lowered the water level a good four or five feet. Chances were it would never be found at all.

That, of course, didn't address the fundamental problem that he had disappeared a cop. True, it wasn't an FBI man or even FDLE, but a mere enviro-cop. Still, the man was a sworn, state law enforcement officer, and eventually someone would likely come looking. They would have a tough time getting any answers, given that the Whipple Sheriff's Office, even though it was technically a security service, had sole constitutional authority in the matter. But cops tended to stick together, and if important enough ones started making noise . . .

Well, what was done was done, and he'd have to cross that bridge if and when he got to it. He plugged the laptop into a power strip beneath his desk and booted up the computer, watched it go through its virus scan and open up to the Outlook e-mail program. Albright bit his lip, considered the risks, then stood to disconnect the phone line from the fax machine behind his desk and plug it into the laptop instead. He hesitated another moment, then clicked on the "Receive Messages" button. Within seconds came a slew of new messages, the last one from the cop's boss.

He moved the cursor and clicked on the boldfaced line, immediately saw the letter open up on the bottom half of the screen, the two antecedent notes appearing directly below in italics. Ferret Albright read the notes, read them again, and then realized with a sly smile how he would solve the problem presented by Captain Tony Armstrong's disappearance. He moved the cursor to the "Reply" button and, mimicking the style of Armstrong's last note to his boss, typed a few lines, read them over . . . and hit "Send."

That was it. Over the next week, he would continue replying to Captain Armstrong's boss, and by week's end, when the messages stopped, no one would have any reason at all to come snooping around Albright's neck of the woods.

He allowed himself a satisfied smile, watched as the message confirmation line flashed briefly, and then reached to move the cursor upward to read through the previous e-mails, when, with a gentle chime, up popped one of Outlook's ubiquitous appointment book reminders for Captain Armstrong for that evening: "Call EW."

Albright leaned back in his chair, let the initials mull around in his head for a while . . . EW, EW. He knew an EW. . . . And suddenly he felt the stroke of intuition hit him in the chest, like a locomotive. EW . . . He *did* know who EW was. . . . He thought of the shapely legs he'd never seen above the knees, the tan arms he'd never seen in anything sleeveless. Worst of all, the supple, perfectly sized feet he'd never seen below the ankle.

Emerson Whipple. Always professional Emma Whipple. No sandals, no slingbacks, no mules. Only prim, proper flats. At best, medium-heeled pumps. That and a smile that said she barely noticed his existence. The bitch.

He bet she was just flawless, too. The second toe just slightly longer than the big toe, all the others shorter in even, descending order. No corns or calluses. Heels buffed down to smooth skin.

He felt himself getting warm and fuzzy just thinking about her and forced himself to settle down and work things through. Tony Armstrong had been in touch with Emma Whipple. Well, technically he didn't know that. He had *intended* to contact her. Well, technically he didn't know that, either. Technically he knew that Armstrong had intended to contact someone with the initials EW.

But who else at Whipple World would that be other than Emma Whipple? He'd never trusted her, and he knew Lew Peters felt the same way. Still, she *was* the Old Man's niece, the only real Whipple left at Whipple Corporation. He would need more evidence than some initials in a dead eco-cop's appointment book before he could go to Peters.

It was her, though, and he knew it. And soon enough, he would be able to prove it. And when he did, he would get the assignment of disposing of her. And he would do so, loyally, but not before he had a chance to examine her fully, from ankle to toe.

Ferret Albright smiled at the prospect, then dialed Personnel and ordered up a full dossier.

Lying on his belly on his unmade bed, Lenny Fizzogli focused on the open textbook before him but found he couldn't concentrate.

The subject matter was dense enough on its own: the limestone and sandstone strata of subterranean Central Florida, flow rates and pressures of saturated layers, the evolution of a hydrological system through time.

Lenny Fizzogli would have had trouble following it under optimum conditions. And there, in the bachelor's dormitory in the backstage Cast Ghetto, with the nightly orgy getting going in the rooms on either side, Lenny Fiz-zogli labored under circumstances far from optimum.

The walls were paper-thin, typically cheap, Peters-era Whipple construction, and he could hear everything going on in his neighbors' rooms. On the one side was Jorge, who, with his weight lifting, always had his pick of the new hires. Every narrow-shouldered, lispy little pansy to come along, you could bet would wind up with Jorge soon enough.

And on the other side was Marc. Marc, with the baby face and the smooth skin and nice ass and . . . whoa, whoa, whoa! Nice *ass*? He shook his head angrily. That's *not* what he meant. None of those homos had a nice ass, as far as he was concerned. What he meant was, if Marc's ass were on a girl, it would probably be nice, is all.

He forced himself back to his text, to a section about how cracks and fissures are created in the shale and lime-stone layers, and the implications for deep groundwater and potential mixing with surface water. When he got through that book, *The Hydrogeology of Florida,* there were three others, with the promising titles *Groundwater: A Field Guide; Limestone and You,* and *The Wet Earth: Subterranean Streams of Our Time.*

The bastard Lew Peters, Lenny Fizzogli decided, was definitely putting the screws to him. No doubt he'd figured out Fizzogli's stretch on his résumé had been even bigger than he'd originally assumed. Yes, he'd worked at a water drilling company, but as a hand, not a crew chief, as he had claimed. Well, screw him. He'd show him, just like all the other pompous assholes who'd always lifted their noses when they found out he'd dropped out after the ninth grade.

Screw them all. He'd get this done and earn the reward Peters had promised. Move up and out of the damned fag-got flophouse, for one, and into a decent place. Get a new Ford three-quarter ton like he'd always wanted, with pin-stripes, fog lights, electric windows, the works.

He wondered where he should live. A place out by the beach would be nice, maybe one of those high-rises in Daytona. Then he could go park his truck right there on the sand, and chicks would walk by, check it out, and he'd invite them in, and he'd have a sound system. . . .

Maybe Marc could come out sometime, too, to visit, maybe have a beer, a backrub. In fact, he wondered who Marc was with right now. It seemed kind of quiet on that side—

He shook his head violently. What was *wrong* with him? When he finally left the Fag Motel, he wasn't ever going to see any of his gay housemates again. Not Jorge, not Marc, not any of them. Which is just how he wanted it. After all, wasn't that why he'd beat the crap out of so many of them? Because they kept coming on to him, without any encouragement whatsoever on his part? Okay, sure, there was that one time in the showers, but big, fucking hairy deal! It could've happened to anyone. It didn't make him gay. Fuck that, and fuck anyone who said it did.

Impatiently he flipped some more pages, got to a section about underground streams collapsing, decided this was a section worth paying attention to, and, with finger following along on the page, read as closely as he could. When caves and tunnels collapsed underground, a sinkhole was formed at the surface, thereby completely altering the surface flow, as well.

Such changes could take centuries, or not happen at all, Lenny Fizzogli read, but gradual changes in local groundwater levels affected the underground system's stability. He painstakingly converted what he read into regular speech, then nodded to himself. That was what Peters was getting at! The son of a bitch wanted to lower the water table and trigger a collapse in the Serenity basin! God only knew why, but what else could it be? Why else could he want all those wells drilled in an area that his own geologist had warned was unstable?

Lenny Fizzogli nodded to himself again, began reading

some more, about natural processes that could replumb an area's hydrology. Floods. Droughts. Earthquakes. He licked his lips, flicked long brown hair out of his blue eyes, and went back over the last part again. Earthquakes.

And he recalled some of the sideline work he'd helped with under the table back at Progress Water Systems. Clearing away annoying mangrove thickets so rich people could see the water from their waterfront homes. Gouging cuts through solid coral so waterfront homeowners could get their boats in and out. Leveling small hills to make driveways to rich people's houses more approachable. In every project, the tool of choice had been dynamite, although on occasion something more exotic had been available.

He remembered the earsplitting blast, the rush of warm air past his face. Most of all he remembered how the very earth would tremble beneath him. Lenny Fizzogli glanced back down at *The Hydrogeology of Florida*, at the single word in boldface announcing the start of a new subchapter: "Earthquakes."

And then he grinned. Lew Peters wanted a collapse of the Serenity basin? Then, by God, that's what Lew Peters was going to get.

# five

### •••

Ernie kept the phone pressed between his shoulder and ear as he began a rough outline for his puff piece, starting with the Dream of a Visionary, and leading to New Urbanism, leading to A Piece of Serenity in Our Backyard. He tried to figure out where to possibly work the polar bears in, but finally wound up doodling on his pad.

He was on hold with DEP headquarters in Tallahassee, trying to sweet talk the receptionist of the law enforcement director into telling him how he could get in touch with his old friend, Tony Armstrong, who was supposed to have called him days ago, but instead seemed to have disappeared off the face of the earth. He didn't want to talk to the director himself. He knew DEP had a strict, all-press-calls-through-the-press-office policy, and the press office had a consistent policy of ignoring all press calls. He hated to even try Tallahassee, for fear of getting Armstrong in trouble, but he didn't know what else to do. He kept getting answering machines at both home and work numbers, and got no response at all from the pager.

He drew a little polar bear beside his first subhead,

then gave it a pair of giant muskrat ears. Then he found himself writing out Emma's name in a variety of scripts. Annoyed with himself, he scribbled over the doodling and Emma's names and was drawing a series of solid lines beneath the mess when the elevator music in his ear went away.

"Sir? Sorry to keep you on hold for so long."

"That's all right," Ernie said as graciously as he could. "Just getting some work done. Any word?"

"Actually, Captain Armstrong's been checking in daily via e-mail."

Ernie blinked, wrote "e-mail" and an exclamation point on his notebook. "Did he say where he was?"

The receptionist hesitated. "I'm sorry, who did you say you were again?"

"Just an old friend. We were supposed to go fishing over the weekend. I got a new trolling motor I've been dying to use, and Tony said he'd picked up a couple of lures. . . ."

Ernie held his breath as the receptionist considered this.

"Weeeell. . . . I suppose it can't hurt to tell you this: He was in Lake Wales yesterday, and just outside Sebring this morning."

"Sebring? Are you sure?"

"That's what my boss said; I can let you talk to him."

Ernie quickly backpedaled. "No, no. That's all right. I, uh . . . Well, I guess I'm fishing by myself. Listen, thank you so much for all your help."

He stared at the handset after setting it back in its cradle, blinking rapidly as he thought. Sebring. Lake Wales. A good hundred miles south of Whipple World. Well, the watershed *did* continue south, clear into the Everglades. He supposed he could be sampling surface water down there. . . . Still, it wasn't like Tony not to call after saying he would.

It was odd. Combined with the equally complete disappearance of Bobby King, it was damned odd. Odd to the second power. He had finally got around to checking with the Highway Patrol, but they had no incident report with any King—Bobby, Irlo, or otherwise. Same with the area hospitals.

He shook his head, then checked his watch, realized he was running late again, and grabbed his notebook as he pushed back his dining room chair.

Emma was already at the agreed-upon spot in front of the quaint brick firehouse when Ernie caught her eye. She smiled, a genuine, glad-to-see-you smile, he noticed, and both his heartbeat and his step quickened.

Yessir, his faux pas about the intellectual capacity of Serenity's residents had been completely forgiven. He'd been given a clean slate with her, and he wasn't going to blow it a second time. She was wearing a skirt this morning, off-white this time and, it seemed . . . a tad shorter than the one she'd worn the first time they'd met.

Was it really shorter? And if so, was that some sort of signal? Like she'd be receptive to an offer of, say, dinner? He kept walking toward her, decided not to read anything into her choice of wardrobe. The shoes, after all, were the same style as those she'd worn the day before, and the blouse just as high around the neck. It could very well be that her skirt was shorter this morning because that's what her hand happened to fall upon when it came time to get dressed.

No, he wasn't going to read anything into it. He would stay calm. Friendly but not effusive. Cordial but not gushing. And at the end of the day, after a good, solid seven or eight hours of showing just how professional and interested he could be, he'd ever-so-casually ask her to dinner. She'd say yes—why not? And away they'd go, and he'd break the ice with the story about the weird guy dragging him into the bushes and telling him about the water table conspiracy. And she'd laugh and flash those perfect white teeth.

And panic gripped him: What if she didn't think the water table guy was funny? What if she thought it was him going off on the weirdos who lived in Serenity again? What if, and his hands began to sweat, she didn't even say yes to dinner?

Which was when, out the corner of his eye, he saw the young mother's bag of groceries split open.

Just ten yards away, down an alley behind a two-story Victorian, cans of soup, boxes of crackers, and a half-dozen oranges spilled onto the pavement. From the back seat of her car a baby cried, and she left the food on the ground to retrieve the child.

Automatically Ernie turned down the alley toward the old Toyota, waved toward Emma's shout, and quickly began rounding up zwieback toast, Campbell's chicken noodle, and big yellow California navels back into the torn paper sack.

"Thank you so much," the mother said, her arms full of car seat and grocery bags.

"It's nothing, ma'am."

He got his arms around the bundle of food and started following the lady and her still-crying baby up the rear steps of her house, held open the screen door with his shoulder as she unlocked the deadbolt, and was about to follow her in when he felt a hand on his elbow.

"Here," said Emma Whipple, slightly short of breath from her brief run. "I'll take those."

Ernie resisted, shook his elbow free, and started through the door. "No, I've got it."

"No, no. Let me," Emma insisted. "We've got a tight schedule."

"It'll only take a second. Besides, whether I take these in or you do it, we lose the same amount of time, right?"

He turned, but now the doorway was blocked by the

young mother, who had her baby on one shoulder and was trying to grab the food away from Ernie.

"Oh! I didn't realize you were a reporter!" Her eyes were wide and flashing between Ernie and Emma. "Here, let me—"

"Really, ma'am, this is ridiculous. I'll just set these down on your kitchen table—"

"No!" Emma shouted. "Don't go in!"

But Ernie was already in, and with his mouth hanging open was studying the home-building disaster that was the young mother's kitchen. Cracks radiated from the light fixture in the ceiling, running all the way to warped, badly painted molding. One wall seemed to cant inward, while another was obviously leaning outward. The ceramic tile on the counters was smeared with cement in some spots, chipped and loose in others. The cabinet beneath the sink oozed brown liquid that ran into a series of sponges arranged like a dam on the hardwood floor, which, Ernie noticed, itself was marred with uneven gaps between the boards.

The workmanship was so thoroughly bad that it was downright cheerful in its complete disregard for flush edges and right angles. Ernie almost reverently placed the groceries down on the maple kitchen island, watched in amazement as the oranges, seemingly possessed by some malevolent spirit, began rolling off the edge and onto the floor.

"You can't just leave them on the table," the mother explained. Both she and her baby were crying, the baby in long wails, she in shameful sobs. "You've got to put something heavy in front of them."

Ernie watched as the oranges continued rolling right out of the kitchen, gathering speed in the long hallway past the living room and finally stopping against the front door. He looked up to see Emma holding her head in her hands through a long sigh.

"Come on. Let's let Mrs. Marcus get Doreen down for

her nap." She took his hand and started pulling him toward the back door.

Ernie glanced back at the still-weeping Mrs. Marcus, tried to think of something to say, finally gave up with an I'm-sorry-to-have-bothered-you shrug, and followed Emma back into the sunshine.


"I really believed in this place."

Emma Whipple gazed out the bay window of her sitting room onto the empty lots of Phase II. "Uncle Waldo did, too. The Enchanted Realm, that was just an amusement park. He knew that. A nice, *clean,* amusement park, where parents didn't have to worry about whether the rides were safe or the carnies had prison records, sure, but an amusement park nonetheless. So then there was UPSVIL. But that kind of morphed into something else, something less than what he'd wanted. So finally there was going to be Serenity. And that was going to be his legacy."

Ernie sat on an overstuffed divan, holding an empty water glass. They had walked the three blocks to her house in silence. When she finally began talking, it had been a confession of sorts, and he got the sense it was something she'd been wanting to say for some time. He nodded sincerely, even though she wasn't looking his way.

"A real town, was what he wanted. No souvenir claptrap, no tourists, no Whipple kitsch at all. Just an old-fashioned town built on old-fashioned values but with the latest technology and eco-friendly principles. The best of the old combined with the most promising of the new. And so he got the plans laid out, and then he died. And then we got Lew Peters. So now we have," she waved a hand out the window, "this."

And it began to dawn on Ernie that Emma Whipple

was not just talking about Mrs. Marcus's disaster of a homestead, but about . . .

"Hold on, time-out," he interrupted. "So you're saying that poor woman's house is *not* an isolated incident? Just how many of the houses in this town are like that?"

"Well, they're not all that bad." Emma turned from the window with a sigh. "Of course, a few are even worse."

Ernie blinked, trying to imagine, short of a house actually literally falling apart around its occupant, how anything could be worse. He said nothing.

"How many? Well, we currently have one thousand six occupied units. A dozen, including this one, are on the approved list for media visits. Four hundred twenty-three are generally okay, but better kept out of the public eye. That leaves five hundred seventy-one that are like Nina Marcus's. More or less."

Ernie shook his head, slack-jawed. "Six hundred houses in that kind of condition? Why hasn't somebody done something? Why hasn't anybody sued?"

Emma picked at her fingernails. "Have you ever heard of the F-scale?"

Ernie squinted into the distance, remembering. "Something from psych class, I think. Right?"

"It's a measure of a person's propensity to accept an authoritarian existence. Everyone who entered the Serenity lottery filled out a lengthy questionnaire about their likes and preferences and so forth. They were told it was to build neighborhoods that reflected the tastes of the residents, but in reality it was a psychological profile. Only those applicants who exceeded a certain F-scale score were put into the lottery. And those people are by their very nature less likely to ask questions or cause trouble. You know the kind: the sort of person who doesn't complain about getting a sandwich with mayo when they'd asked for it without mayo?

"So far it's worked pretty well. For example, you remember that whole Krazy Klowne fiasco?" Emma asked.

"Well, Peters had the brainstorm of forcing recalled copies of that CD on every Serenity resident."

Ernie nodded. "Ahaaa. Things become clearer."

"I thought I saw you looking at Mrs. Celeste's music collection," Emma continued. "Can you just see her cranking up 'Burn, Muthafucka, Burn' on her stereo? Anyway, even if people were completely pissed off about the condition of their houses, it's not like they can sue. It was in the sales contract they signed. Any disputes have to be decided by a mediator appointed by a committee appointed by the mayor."

"And so Mayor Sex Maniac's committee gets to deal with the complaints—"

"Actually, the mayor hasn't gotten around to appointing the dispute-resolution committee yet. Actually, from what I understand, he has no intention of ever appointing one." Emma looked down again. "As per orders."

Ernie thought for a moment, shook his head. "Okay, they can't sue, and aren't psychologically inclined to sue in the first place. But how in hell did you guys end up with more than half the houses in such sorry shape to begin with?"

And Emma sighed again, then began the unpublished history of Serenity, starting with Lew Peters's insistence that the community generate as much profit as the theme parks or the movie studio. She explained about the high cost of skilled labor amid Central Florida's general building boom, and how Mexican tomato pickers from the migrant camps of Immokalee provided a less expensive alternative.

"What do tomato pickers know about home construction?" Ernie interrupted.

Emma shrugged. "Evidently not much. Anyway, it wasn't just tomato pickers. It was sugarcane cutters, too." And she explained Peters's decision to get rid of the Mexicans with a sweeping INS raid after they demanded a thirty percent, or fifty-cents-an-hour, raise. He replaced them with Haitians from the Glades cane fields, who agreed to work for half the Mexicans' original rate. "With these and a few other cost-cutting measures, the construction phase of Serenity was able to return twenty-two cents on the dollar. Even that, though, netted out to seventeen million dollars less than if the money had been invested in another theme park, for example."

Ernie couldn't help a snigger at the *Advocate*-esque greed. "Sounds like another bunch of pinhead managers I know. Seventeen million less. Seventeen million on what, a project totaling several hundred million? In a year when your profits will top three billion?"

"Mind the millions, and the billions take care of themselves. Lew Peters's motto." Emma bit her lip a moment, pondering something, then decided to plunge ahead, now that she'd started. "Anyway, you forget Peters's real reason for approving Serenity."

"I thought it was to show how a New Urban town could really work. Get back to a neighbor-based, instead of a car-based, community. That sort of stuff."

"That was Uncle Waldo's reason. Lew Peters went ahead with it because Whipple World needed a new sewer plant, and sewer plants are expensive, but there happened to be available that year those federal grants for wastewater plants, but only for bona-fide residential communities. . . ."

Ernie snapped his fingers, recalling yet another story buried by Jack Leahy. "Two hundred million. Whipple Corporation snagged all the grant money for Florida. I remember. Fifteen low-income housing projects around the state, down the tubes, all so Whipple could build more hotels and bring in more tourists. We played that story in two paragraphs, somewhere near the legal notices. I think we ran the company press release verbatim. We even used the suggested headline."

Emma Whipple, who had written that press release, cleared her throat. "Anyway, one hundred ninety-seven million federal dollars. More than enough to offset the seventeen-million-dollar profit shortfall in the construction phase. That was then. Now all Peters sees in Serenity is an eleven percent return, less than half of the company's other divisions."

Ernie took a deep breath, slowly evaluating the past hour. Emma's yarn had awakened long-dormant instincts. Deadened parts of his brain began recalling the tantalizing excitement he'd once been able to feel when he came across a potentially explosive story. The risk of not moving fast enough, and losing it to a competitor or TV. The thrill of seeing it stripped across the front page. The glow, afterward, of accomplishing something that could well spur change for the better.

He took another deep breath and pushed those old feelings back into their closet. Outside, the once-clear sky had sprouted puffy clouds that seemed to grow taller before his eyes. The rains would come early that day, or maybe even twice, if the clouds rebuilt quickly enough after the first set of storms. He set his empty glass on an end table.

"We should get going, if we want to see the Georgian Revival neighborhood before it rains."

Emma looked up, stunned. "Haven't you been listening? I'm *giving* you a blockbuster here. Just don't use my name."

Ernie studied Emma's floor shamefully. Her oak slats were of top quality, and joined together expertly. Neither tomato pickers nor sugarcane cutters, it was clear, had ever set foot in this house. "That type of article," he began, eyes still downcast, "I'm not really in the business of doing anymore. Maybe the *New York Times* or somebody like that—"

*"No!"* Emma shouted. "I can't get the *Times* in here. They're too negative. Plus you're *here.* You've done all the research. You *saw* how those oranges rolled clear the length of her house." She stared at him a long moment. "Come on, Ernie. You've done this kind of article before.

That one about the sewage discharges—that won a Pulitzer, didn't it?"

His shoes, he noticed, were getting scuffed. He would need to polish them. Either that or risk failing a Clean Team inspection back at the office. "Pulitzer finalist," Ernie explained. "There was a big hurricane hit Miami that year. Bad timing on my part." He glanced up to a plaintive look, dropped his eyes to his shoes again. "You don't understand, Emma. We honest to God don't write that kind of article anymore. My last story was a fluff feature about a new-car dealership. After my fluff feature on Serenity, I'll get another fluff feature. Probably about a new strip mall or something. Point is, Jack Leahy is simply not going to trash Waldo Whipple World. It's not going to happen."

Emma took another deep breath. "Okay, how about this. Don't write an investigative story. Write a human-interest piece: the great-niece of Waldo Whipple in a public feud with the company that bears his name." She waited for Ernie's look of amazement. "That's right. Go ahead, *use* my name. Uncle Waldo would've wanted it that way. This place is never going to change unless this gets out, and it's high time it did. Your seeing Mrs. Marcus's house was just what this town needed."

Ernie said nothing for a long while, then: "Peters will fire you."

"Probably, yes. But when this story gets out, the residents will feel like they've got the world's attention, and they'll take it on their own from there. Your article will empower them. Peters will be forced to make this town right."

Her eyes burned brightly, and Ernie found himself enchanted. Before he'd merely been attracted to her, charmed by her. Now he was in awe. She was smart, pretty, funny, and had guts to boot. And here he was, making excuses about how he didn't even have the balls to write a hard-hitting story anymore.

"Okay," he said after a time. "If you're willing to put your job, your whole future on the line for the good fight, the least I can do is make an attempt to chronicle it for posterity." He nodded again, this time with more conviction. "I'll go and sell this to my boss. I can't make any promises—"

"I don't expect you to."

The sky outside was rapidly darkening, and Ernie made his way to the front door. Leahy would want to know about the bears, if they could get the bears into the lead. If they could get a picture of the bears in Serenity, preferably including some children, for the front page. And instead he was going to tell him that Serenity was a fraud. A front created for the sole purpose of scamming federal money for a sewage plant.

"Well, let me go run this up the flagpole at the afternoon news meeting, see if anybody shoots," he said glumly.

"Your enthusiasm is contagious."

He glanced up to her smile, and he sucked it up to return one. He remembered again how he'd planned to finish the day with a casual, how-about-dinner? Then he thought about how he was soon going to have to explain how he had tried, but he just wasn't going to be able to help her. No, he wasn't going to ask about dinner. He wasn't worthy. "Well, I guess I'll see you Monday. Let you know how your story idea was received."

She reached out for his bare forearm, below his rolled-up sleeve, and he felt the hairs on his neck tingle. "You know, Ernie, I couldn't help but notice these last few days that for someone who's grown up in Orlando, you know surprisingly little about Whipple World."

Her hand was still on his arm, and he found that he was holding his breath. It was the feeling of being outside in a thunderstorm, the moment before a nearby lightning strike. What was she asking about? Oh yeah, not knowing anything about the park.

"How about we remedy that situation. Tomorrow? If you're not busy? The Realm, the Utopian Prototype Showcase Village, the Wild Dominion. The works. What do you say? Not as reporter and flack, but just regular tourists?"

She'd released his arm, he noticed, and he finally took a breath. Then he realized she was asking him . . . for a date! He looked at her, speechless.

"I can get free passes," she said. "Or . . . I guess that's probably against your paper's ethics policy, huh?"

"We repealed our ethics policy years ago." She was really asking him out, it dawned on him. She wanted to see him socially. "Now, the freebies reporters get on their beats are counted on as part of the compensation package. We use it as an excuse to hold salaries down."

"So is that a yes?"

Yes, the skirt was shorter than what she'd worn the other day, he decided. He watched her gather a loose strand of hair and tuck it behind an ear, then flash a smile with those perfect teeth and that perfect little dimple. No, he wasn't worthy, but he was for some reason being rewarded anyway.

"What time?"

The only thing between Dick Gillespie and an evening with his top candidate for a new Enchanted Acrobat team member was a stack of seven, maybe eight hundred e-mails on his desk, and the mayor flew through them at breakneck speed.

She was a honey, this one. A raven-haired, Far Eastern little darling. And a real acrobat, to boot. An honest-to-God little contortionist. Dick Gillespie smiled to himself, even as the other half of his brain processed page after page of electronic messages to and from Serenity's thousand households. Every house was wired, that was part of the sales pitch, but, thank God, not every house used their computer. Others used it sparingly—maybe an e-mail or two a week. Those homes made up for the five or six dozen residents who were absolute e-mail fanatics, writing dozens, even hundreds of e-mails per day.

Every single one was copied by the Webmaster, and thereupon landed on Mayor Gillespie's desk for his once-over, a chore he had originally thought might be fun, even titillating, but which he had grown to loathe. Because for every piece of tawdry computer sex he had happened upon, there were literally dozens of mind-numbing narrations of Sunday's picnic, or the family reunion in Tennessee, or Billy's report card. One old coot, Old Mavis Henry, belonged to some fucking recipe club, and received and sent the things by the dozens. One memorable afternoon, he had gone through eighty-four recipes for peach cobbler. Eighty-four. Why in hell should there be eighty-four different ways of making the same dessert?

He shook his head to regain his focus. What the fuck. It was his job, and he would do it. That's why it was called work. If it was fun, they wouldn't be paying him. He scanned a note from a Ron Kleinman to someone who appeared to be his brother, ostensibly about gardening. Dick Gillespie thought he sensed a whiff of sarcasm about Serenity's Shrubbery Guidelines in Kleinman's phrase "if I can get the hydrangeas past the plant Nazis . . ."

He twitched his upper lip, considering it. On one hand, if they rounded up all the residents who made some kind of derogatory crack about Serenity, they'd be left with a ghost town. On the other, Ron Kleinman's wife was a delicious little number he wouldn't mind getting a piece of sometime. He put the e-mail in the "subversive" stack and, with a glance at the wall clock, resumed his work.

Two more hours until his acrobatic Japanese honey. And boy, did he have an audition for her. It would truly be a night to remember, one for the record books, he thought with a leer. The only downside was how he would possi-

bly top it. Well, he would think of something. He always
did.

He flipped a whole stack of Mrs. Henry's spice cake
recipes onto the discard pile. The old bat needed a life.
Maybe some old geezer to throw her over the back of the
couch every now and again. Give her something to think
about other than stinkin' recipes—

Dick Gillespie blinked twice as he started the next e-
mail on the stack, then slowly broke into a wide grin. Pay
dirt. There was the familiar list of thirteen recipients, the
cryptic reference to J25 and the schedule of events being
"as they had talked about before." He read through it
again, then a third time, and decided it quite clearly
crossed the line between subversive and seditious.

He picked up the phone and dialed Sheriff Albright's
extension.


Ernie Warner balanced precariously on the back two legs
of the conference room chair. Too far forward, and the
chair would slam all four legs onto the floor. Too far backward, and he'd go crashing skull-first into the wall behind
him.

The exercise gave him something to do as he sat, numb
from the neck up in the *Orlando Advocate*'s evening news
meeting. He'd forgotten just how mindlessly stupid they
had become in the Era of Tidy Desks and Bigger Profits,
and he tried hard to ignore the explanations behind the
stories and the "logic" behind their ultimate placement.

He'd driven back downtown with the fantastic theory
that he would be able to talk the sloppy construction story
into the paper as a People Feature, just as Emma had suggested, and thereby win her respect and her heart. And
then, after whatever dust settled that needed to settle, he
could become openly involved with her. Hell, one day, if
things worked out, they could even get married. Why not?
Leahy's wife worked for the pro basketball team's PR

firm. The metro editor's boyfriend was the flack at city hall. The *Advocate* was nothing if not married to the community.

But then Ernie had gone to the five o'clock meeting—and returned to reality with a vengeance. The managing editor, a skinny woman who kept seven cats, each of them named after a character from *Melrose Place,* announced the results of that day's focus group: The story about the local Lottery winner ranked first, followed by an explainer about what stores would be in the new mall in MetroWest, and then a feature about a cat that got lost on a family outing to Tampa yet, remarkably, managed to find its way home. The daily horoscopes and the TV Best Bets would round out the front page, as they had for two years since The Strategic Marketing Plan found them to be the highest-interest items among the paper's dwindling readers.

"And we have TV versions of all three? Yes?" Jack Leahy asked.

He was referring to the paper's in-house cable television station, for which reporters were forced to write 150-word versions of their articles and, after getting primed with pancake makeup, read them to the TV camera that dominated the newsroom.

"Done," the expensive, Broadcast Content consultant replied.

Ernie groaned inwardly. The Orlando-Land TV was hands down the most hated element of the new order among the rank and file. Two extra hours of work a night, on average, with zero extra compensation. Not to mention the heart of the matter: Newspaper reporters had by and large made an active decision *not* to become television reporters. They thought TV was insipid and silly. Yet now they were having it foisted upon them anyway by a blown-dry consultant from Chicago who made four times the average newsroom salary.

He tuned out again, as the Living Well editor proceeded to explain his section-front offering for Sunday: "How to Make Time to Watch All Those Programs We Tape on Our VCRs"—a typical *Advocate* feature. The previous week it had been "How to Choose a Pedicurist," which had followed "How to Buy a New Couch."

The banal reality of his situation sank back in, and Ernie started growing more and more depressed about his prospects. Of *course* the paper wasn't going to say anything negative about Whipple World, even if it *was* a Whipple saying it. In the previous year, the paper had written exactly one critical story, for the purpose of entering a contest, and that had only been after commissioning a poll to determine readers' least popular people or groups. The readers had ranked gay, child-molesting pornographers at the bottom of the list, so the *Advocate* had responded with a hard-hitting series finding that gay, child-molesting pornographers were bad people.

"Ernie? Mr. Warner?"

Ernie realized the room's eyes were on him.

"Glad to have you back," Jack Leahy said with an easy smile. "How's the Serenity Jubilee coming?"

Ernie surveyed the expectant looks around the room, then took a deep breath. "Fine. No problems. It's just, well, I think we might have a line on a pretty decent exclusive. It seems that over half the homes there have some pretty serious construction flaws. Walls and floors not square. Bad tile work. Just generally awful workmanship. . . ."

The faces around the table stared at him slack-mouthed, like he was cursing a blue streak in church. Jack Leahy's face was set in a hard grimace. This was clearly the wrong place and the wrong time, he realized. It wasn't the other editors. They would react whichever way Leahy reacted. But here, among everybody, Leahy was reacting badly. He would need to sell this to him privately first.

"But that's another story for another time," Ernie mumbled. "As far as the Jubilee goes, we're all set."

Leahy nodded. "Good. Then we're finished. We're adjourned. Go forth and do good work! Ernie, if you could come with me."

Ernie followed him across the plush, blue newsroom carpeting, past the set for Orlando-Land television where a specially hired, red-lipsticked blond anchor was breathlessly explaining about the latest Lottery winner, and into Leahy's glassed-off enclosure. Leahy shut the door and closed the blinds.

Ernie thought about remarking on that fact, especially in regards to the No-Adjusting-the-Angle-of-the-Blinds rule, but decided against it. He didn't need another cynicism-versus-skepticism lecture. Besides, he needed to butter Leahy up, not piss him off.

"Listen, about those construction problems—"

"Now, Ernie. You've been here long enough to know our policy on confrontational journalism. That doesn't mean we never print negative stories. Hell, I still love a nice, sexy murder now and again, so long as it doesn't scare people or make them think Orlando's not a nice place to live. But that us-against-them stuff . . ." Jack Leahy shook his head. "Let those elitist papers up in New York and Philly do that nonsense. We're a part of this community, not its constant critic. Plus, having bought a brand-new house yourself, you of all people should understand the pressures a builder is under, and how hard it is to put up a house without at least a *couple* of little nits."

Ernie listened to the words dejectedly. He'd known coming in that this more than likely would be Jack Leahy's position. He saw himself the next morning, at Emma's doorstep, having to explain to her the bad news . . . and he decided to take another shot at it.

"Jack, you don't understand. I'm not talking a missing wall plate or some scuffed linoleum. I mean this lady's house was crooked. Literally. You set an orange on the floor, it rolls clear across to the other end."

Jack Leahy removed his key chain from his pocket and

unlocked the bottom drawer of his desk. "This lady, has she filed a lawsuit?"

Ernie sighed. "No. But that's another thing. This whole town, they're so—"

"All right, then. If she'd filed a lawsuit, said all these things in a sworn deposition, we might take a look then. But I'm not going to slander our Corporate Citizen of the Year based on some wild charges. Anyway . . ." Jack Leahy reached into his drawer and lifted out a stack of tabloid newspapers. "The other day? When you mentioned about British newspapers? I stood there, wondering: What the heck is he talking about? So I went to that store on I-Drive that sells all the foreign papers?"

Jack Leahy let out a low whistle and flipped open the top newspaper to page three, where a buxom bleached blonde wearing a bikini bottom and a sultry look leered back at them. "Ernie, call me sheltered, but I had *no* idea!" He flipped to the next paper in the stack, then the next. "Bird of the Day, they call it. I should say so."

Ernie blinked at Leahy, then at the topless photos, then back at Leahy, wondering how such a total dork could have risen so high in any one lifetime.

"Quite a concept. And I commend you for thinking of it. Something like this would really grab that male eighteen-to-thirty market." He chuckled to himself. "Grab 'em where it counts, I might add. The only thing is, obviously, there's no way we're going to get away with naked breasts on this side of the Atlantic. Not with all the Baptists in our circulation area. But then I got to thinking: *Surely* no one could object to a girl in a bikini. We could have a different girl each week. Bird of the Week. A contest, like those English papers have. And then I thought: Why go outside the paper at all? We got plenty of attractive young girls right here in Editorial. And Circulation? Advertising?"

He gave another whistle. "I tell you, completely off the record, I wouldn't mind seeing that receptionist in Classifieds in a bikini top. Anyway, one of two ways we could approach this. One, we could offer a bonus to each girl who appears—say, five hundred bucks. The other, more cost-effective way is just to make it a condition of their employment. Once a year, they have to appear in Bird of the Week. Although I wonder if that might not be construed as a sexual harassment–type thing. . . . I should probably run it past Legal. Anyway, what do you think?"

Ernie just stood there for a few moments, stunned, vacillating between rage and shame. Finally he shook his head and headed for the door, defeated. "It was a fucking joke, Jack. I was only joking."

Below him passed the topiary garden across the plaza from Prince Charming's Palace, the Wicked Witch Tea Cups, the Solar System Cafeteria . . . all of it from a vantage point that, literally, made the blood rush to his motorcycle-helmeted head. With great effort Dickie Gillespie craned his upper body upward, to where his ankles were securely strapped to the metal seat mounts of a red, Billy Baboon gondola on the Mont Blanc Skyway.

"We ain't got all night, Suki!" he shouted, then let himself dangle straight down again.

He wore a white biker helmet that said "Wild Thang!" and a striped cotton polo shirt, but was naked from the waist down, or, given his orientation, waist up. His limp member drooped unnaturally, brushing against the gray hair sprouting from his belly button as the gondola continued slowly a hundred feet above the deserted theme park.

A black-haired head peeked over the edge, appraised the distance to the ground, and then disappeared back into the gondola. "Mister Girrespie, I doan' know! Rook verry dangerous," Suki said.

"That's why," Dick Gillespie said impatiently, "you've got the helmet. Now, put it on and get moving. Come on, or we're gonna be at the Wild Dominion before we know it."

Above him, Suki slowly, grudgingly, put on the motorcycle helmet and peeked over the edge again. Gillespie glanced up and clapped his hands. "Let's go! Chop, chop! You want to be an Enchanted Acrobat or not?"

Glum-faced, Suki, nude but for her helmet, crawled headfirst slowly down his legs to position herself, then latched on. Dick Gillespie shut his eyes, let his arms dangle earthward, and let out a deep sigh.

# six

## ...

The first thing Ernie thought when Emma opened her door was that she was naked.

He stood there motionless, mouth partially open, even as her expression changed from a warm smile to a look of concern. "What's wrong?"

She wasn't really naked, he slowly realized. It was just the high-necked blouse, jacket, panty hose, and shoes that she normally wore but wasn't now that produced that effect. Instead she had on a skimpy white tank top, red shorts, and red, strappy sandals with thick wooden heels and white beads. The sandals in particular had him transfixed, and he looked up suddenly, embarrassed.

"Uh . . . nothing," he said.

She turned one foot to the side, then the other. "I know. I'm breaking my own rule about doing the theme parks. Wear comfortable shoes, I always tell people. But you know, I've had these for a year and haven't worn them even once. So what the hell. You ready to go?"

Ernie thought for half a moment about the news he had to break, then snuck another glance at her shapely calves, then decided the bad news could wait. "Let's do it."

And like the tourists Emma said they should be, they did, starting with UPSVIL, where they visited the Good Neighbor pavilion, sponsored by France; the Pristine Oceans, sponsored by Exxon; and Share!, the newest high-tech exhibit sponsored by Microsoft, featuring a brief history of the Windows operating system and an IMAX screen–sized Bill Gates explaining in a nasal whine that what was good for Microsoft was good for not just America, but the whole world.

They emerged back into the sunshine, leaned on a railing overlooking a clear, chlorinated lake that fronted the International Pavilion Parade.

"I know what you're thinking," Emma said. "You're wondering why ostensibly rational humans would stand in line for a half hour in order to watch a commercial by a giant chemical company. Or why Joe and Jane Smith from Des Moines save all year, or even two years, and then blow it all to take Billy and Susie to see a miniature Windsor Castle and Leaning Tower of Pisa when they could go to Europe for less money and see the real thing."

Actually, Ernie had been wondering whether Emma was wearing a bra beneath her tank top, and whether it was worth the risk of getting caught to try and peek in her armholes. "I was thinking nothing of the kind," he said, truthfully.

"Well, I wouldn't be offended if you did. Like I told you, I don't think this place turned out like Uncle Waldo had hoped. Why don't we take the monorail over to the Enchanted Realm? That's always been my favorite."

Once there, Ernie found he was no longer just tolerating his surroundings for the sake of Emma's company, but was actually admiring the wholesome fun of the Runaway Mine Car, the Possessed Plantation, even the Wicked Witch Tea Cups. He had been to the Enchanted Realm exactly once, twenty-three years earlier, not long after it first opened, and to the other parks only as part of the required *Advocate* senior management luncheons.

"A Whipple virgin," Emma had declared him, and then blushed as she realized the alternate connotation.

He, too, had immediately realized the words' more literal meaning, and it almost emboldened him into a risqué remark before he pulled back. More and more he had found himself trading casual touches with her—taking her hand to help her off a ride, brushing against bare shoulder, bumping knees—and he wondered if she intended things to head in the direction he hoped they were heading.

Then, on the Kilimanjaro Plunge, a ride he didn't realize until they were boarding required front and back seating rather than side by side, he found himself directly behind her, with no comfortable place to put his arms other than around her waist. And so he did.

And she didn't object—in fact, as the car began its steep initial ascent, she even wiggled backward until she was against his chest, whispering up into his ear that this was the ride, if he remembered, where the park photographer had been taking pictures of riders to sell them souvenirs, and young women had started lifting their tops and flashing their boobs at the appropriate time, to ruin the photos' souvenir value, and so the photographer had ended up putting all the boob shots on the Internet.

And Ernie couldn't help himself, asked: "You don't happen to remember the Web address . . . ?"

She elbowed him sharply in the ribs, and he responded with a tickle under her arms, and they were holding hands like schoolkids for the rest of the ride.

Lunch at the Solar System Cafeteria in FutureLand, and afterward they found themselves across from the Good World, with Emma leaning, pulling him into the line, and Ernie resisting for all he was worth. "Please, *please,* don't make me go on that thing!"

"You haven't had an Enchanted Realm experience unless you've been on Good World," she insisted. "Come on this with me, and I'll go on the Rescue Helicopters again with you."

Ernie considered this and relented, but soon began grumbling that he could already hear that damned song, even from outside. Emma entwined her arm in his, drew close.

"What's it going to take for you to quit your whining and enjoy this ride?"

He saw himself sitting back in the stupid boat as it started down the tunnel, the insane puppets going through their mechanized movements, singing, over and over and over. And then he saw Emma leaning him back, unbuttoning his shirt, kissing him on his throat, moving down his chest, moving down some more . . .

He became aware that she was studying him with narrowed eyes.

"What?" she asked. "What are you scheming?"

He said earnestly: "You don't want to know."

She studied him some more, then sighed. "Please don't tell me it's the Good World blow job fantasy." She shook her head. "Men really are all the same, aren't they."

Ferret Albright shifted his weight to his left leg again, traded left eye for right at the peephole, and resumed his survey. He was at his favorite station, soothing the frustrations of his day to that point with a little R&R.

Already he'd seen countless slides and wedges, dozens of pairs of thongs, and six pairs of strappy, spiky sandals. The sights were a nice diversion, but that still didn't let him forget the fact that thus far, his theory about Ms. Emerson Whipple had drawn a complete blank. He'd read and reread the personnel file but could find nothing particularly incriminating. He'd scanned her e-mail from the backup tapes off the Whipple server, and again, nothing. Basically she did her job, and based on a random surveillance brief from a year back, little else.

Still, EW. He was certain that couldn't be a mere coincidence. The cop had been getting tips about salinity problems on Whipple property. He must have been getting them from someone inside Whipple. And who was better situated than the chief of corporate communications?

And so it was that morning he'd decided to be more direct. If the DEP man had left a trace of his contacts with her, then surely she would have a similar trail of her communications with him. Not long after dawn he had slipped into her darkened office in Serenity with a master key and, flashlight between his teeth, started going through her files. And it was some time later that he'd nearly had a coronary when he suddenly heard a key rattling in the lock. He'd dove beneath the desk just before the light had come on and she'd strolled in to grab something off her credenza.

He had remained frozen probably five seconds too long after she'd flipped off the light and locked the door behind her—five seconds too late to get a look at the car of the man who had accompanied her into the office. A date, from the sound of things. She was collecting a visitor's pass for him, asking him whether he minded driving, where he'd like to have lunch.

Which meant, obviously, that the year-old surveillance report that indicated a solitary existence was no longer accurate. And that presented a problem. A loner who didn't date was easier to disappear than someone in any sort of romantic relationship. Now he'd need to figure out who this man was and determine what his response might be if his girlfriend were to go missing—if, that is, he could even prove a link between her and the DEP guy.

Albright sighed wearily. Like he needed another complication. On top of the Emma Whipple problem, by Monday he also had to come up with a plan to deal more aggressively with the Serenity Underground, what with the Jubilee approaching and Lew Peters getting progressively antsier. Rumor was, and it seemed to be backed up by that damn e-mail Gillespie had come up with, that the troublemakers were indeed plotting something for Jubilee

Day. Which meant, of course, that he'd been right when he'd recommended six months earlier to pursue the exter-mination option. Peters, on Gillespie's advice, had instead approved the idea of sending a message with selected disappearances.

Too subtle, he'd warned. A better message would be to eliminate them entirely. But had they listened? Of course not. Why would they? After all, he'd merely been in real law enforcement. What would he know about subversive gangs and how to deal with them?

A pair of tanned, shapely ankles moved into viewed, and Ferret Albright twisted his neck just so in order to get a good view—only to snort in disbelief when a child's stroller pushed in between his peephole and the feet, blocking his sight line. Happened every time, he fumed. Fucking strollers. Always getting in his way. Why in hell couldn't these women leave their brats at home for a change?

Several months earlier he had thought up a way to arrange a stroller queue parallel to and on the opposite side of his peepholes from the existing queues at his favorite rides. Adults would walk in one line and the view-obstructing strollers could proceed down the other. He'd abandoned the idea when he came to the conclusion that there was no plausible public-safety justification for such a thing, and he'd be left explaining his unusual pre-occupation.

He sighed bitterly. It wasn't fair. Peters had basically signed off on the peepholes in the women's bathrooms and changing rooms when they'd been brought to his attention. What message was the man trying to send? Voyeurism of his female guests' breasts and genitalia was okay, but a foot fetish, well, that was too weird?

Well, screw that, too. He shifted back to his right foot and left eye, and then he saw something that took his breath away: There, immediately in front him, were a pair of simply stunning feet—possibly the most gorgeous feet he had ever seen since the swimsuit model had come to his shoe store way back when.

A perfect arch, a strong but delicate ankle rising to sculpted calves, graceful toes, all bundled up in an incredibly sexy pair of red sandals with three rows of tantalizing white beads over each instep. He stared with growing lust. The color, too, was perfect: on the pale side, but a healthy pink, not yellow, complexion. Like they were normally kept in pumps and he was being treated to a rare public display.

With one hand he reached for the Nikon on the shelf, slid the autofocus lens into the metal tube, and, with a deep breath, pushed down with his thumb to set the motor drive whirring.


On the Mont Blanc Skyway, Ernie noticed the blemish on the metal's bright red finish right after the gondola car had passed through the concrete-and-stucco Kilimanjaro and back into the afternoon sunlight. He bent down and read the words scratched into the paint in capital letters: "DICKIE SCORED HERE."

He glanced up at Emma, who shrugged helplessly. "What can I say? I guess our crack cleanup crew missed that." She surveyed FairyLand as it passed below them, the lines for the rides dwindling as dinnertime approached. "You laugh, but that sort of thing really bugged Uncle Waldo. Graffiti. He wanted every visitor to see this place as fresh and clean as the day it opened. I think it came from taking his own kids to an amusement park when they were young, and getting just totally disgusted with the litter and the general low-rent attitude. That's what drove him to build this place."

They were the only two in a car big enough for six, yet they sat beside each other, touching lightly at the hips and shoulders. "His kids, I gather, weren't as taken by his credo as he was?"

"They liked the money all right. They liked it so much they sold out the first chance they had. Which is why you're able to read 'Dickie Scored Here' right now. In Uncle Waldo's time, they would have inspected this car top to bottom before park opening, and sent it to the repair shed. Now Lew Peters is squeezing maintenance and groundskeeping. Too much fat, he says."

Ernie gazed out from the gondola, Whipple property in every hazy direction as far as the eye could see. Golf, U.S.A., UPSVIL, Whipple Studios Florida. Directly ahead of them, at the downhill terminus of the Skyway, was Wild Dominion, with Serenity just beyond. Then he made the mistake of looking straight down—and immediately his vertigo kicked in.

He pulled away from the edge and took a deep breath. "Whoa."

"What's the matter?"

"Heights," he said simply.

"Oh, I love heights," she said, peering over the side. "Every September I go out west, to the Rockies or the Sierras. Two weeks of intense rock-climbing. Someday I'm going to climb El Capitan."

He stared at her blankly. "You're kidding."

"Uh-uh," she said, and shook her head. "It's not that hard, technically. It's just *really* tall."

Ernie glanced over the edge again, pulled away again. "So anyway. If Peters has taken the fun out of working here, then why do you stay?"

She shrugged. "Maybe Peters will try to sell off the theme parks and a white knight will buy them up. Maybe Peters will have a heart attack. Maybe Peters will get eaten by wild animals. Who knows?" She blew out a long sigh. "I don't know. I've asked myself that many times. But you're one to talk. Look at you, Mr. Pulitzer Finalist, why do *you* stay?"

He stared for a long moment at her bare legs, stretched across the car to the opposite seat. She had taken off her pretty but painful sandals for the ride, and her toes gripped the plastic bench. There was no getting around it. He had to tell her.

"I ask myself the same question. Speaking of which, I have some bad news about that story you wanted me to do, about the sloppy construction."

"I know."

"He wants a lawsuit. If there's a formal, sworn lawsuit, we can write a story."

"I kinda figured, when you didn't say anything this morning, it would be something like that." She squeezed his hand. "Don't worry about it. It'll work out."

Ernie shrugged glumly, felt her fingers lying lazily against his palm, found her eyes locked on his own before he consciously looked away at the same instant she did, and he knew that she, too, had realized the moment had lasted perhaps a second too long.

Ernie cleared his throat uncomfortably as Emma busied herself strapping her feet back into her sandals. "Well, I guess I ought to go see these polar bear cubs that Leahy's so high on."

Emma answered with a blank look.

"You know, Iceball and Fluff, or whatever their names are. Leahy insists I get them in the Serenity story, preferably in the first eight inches, before the jump. I told you: He wanted me to ask if they'd ever been in Serenity, maybe get a picture of them posing with some of the town's kids."

She laughed, adjusting her heel straps. "Sounds like your boss and mine ought to have a zoology lesson together. Lew Peters originally wanted to put the cubs in the petting zoo. We had to bring in a special arctic mammals consultant, explain to him that polar bears are the most aggressive, most deadly land animal in the world, period. Stronger, faster, and meaner even than grizzly bears. Peters relented only after Risk Management told him how much a wrongful-death suit for an eaten kid would cost." She held her legs out straight to study her feet. "Listen, I hope you've been adequately enthralled by my sexy shoes, because I'm *never* wearing them again. God, these stupid beads are torture!"

The gondola began its descent into the Wild Dominion terminus, and Ernie looked out across the ersatz Serengeti. "Why would you have to *bring in* a polar bear person? Wouldn't your trainer have that kind of expertise?"

Emma pulled out her compact to freshen her lipstick. "Wild Dominion Dirty Secret Number One: We didn't hire any actual experts, per se. They were all too expensive and already had good jobs in Washington and San Diego and places like that. So we hired from within. Our polar bear trainer used to sell pretzels in the Enchanted Realm. Which leads me to Wild Dominion Dirty Secret Number Two. That story about how Snoball and Igloo were orphans rescued off an iceberg? All bullshit. They're orphans, all right, but they were orphaned right here.

"Pretzel man apparently did some outside reading to prep for his new job, decided he needed to establish dominance over mama bear. So he brought a pressure-treated two-by-four from Home Depot, whacked her upside the head. Killed her instantly." She put away her mirror as the gondola drew into the station. "Anyway, we can't see the bears. Their exhibit's broken. Some problem with the refrigeration or something."

They stepped off the gondola when the pith-helmeted attendant opened the door for them. "No bears?" Ernie complained. "That's my reason for existence! How am I going to write about the damned bears if I can't see them?"

Emma shrugged. "I can show you a video of them. One of those when-animals-go-bad sort of things."

"What?"

She tugged him toward the entrance to the Wild Dominion Safari Tram. "It's a long story."

●　　　●　　　●

Roscoe Sembler dragged the second steel cage out onto the melting slush, threw it open, and turned with a scowl to find his charges.

It would be a long night, with a lot of scut work he hated under the best of circumstances, and these sure as hell were not the best of circumstances. He had tickets to a World Wrestling Federation extravaganza—Tommy "The Dork" Loomis versus Holmes "Hard Time" Johnson, the feature bout—and what would he be doing instead? Shoveling bear shit.

The goddamned, cheap-ass refrigeration unit beneath the Untamed Arctic exhibit was on the fritz again. Small wonder, considering they'd let a bunch of dumb-ass Haitians build the damned thing. Couldn't even talk English, most of them, yet there they were, putting together Lew Peters's latest high-tech masterpiece.

He had to get the animals into the cages, no small feat in itself, then load them up onto the flatbed and take them down the connecting tunnel to the Serenity Ice Rink, then come back and clean up the mess they'd left behind so that when they melted off the rest of the ice, the workmen wouldn't have to wade around in soggy bear turds.

Why refrigeration workmen should qualify for such special treatment was beyond him. After all, bear turds were his life. If he could deal with a few hundred dark lumps now and again, so could everybody else.

He blew out a sharp whistle and glared at the diorama until two white heads poked up from behind a "snowdrift" at the far end of the exhibit.

"Snowshit! Ig-face! In your cages! Now!"

Roscoe pointed at the cages, to reinforce his command. The bear cubs ignored him, continued wrestling with each other as they tumbled down the slope and into the "sea" before scrambling back out and shaking dry like Labradors.

"Stupid fucking bears," he grumbled as he pulled a

package of Ball Park Franks from his pocket, threw two of them out at the cubs. "Bears! Hot dogs, you dumb shits!"

Snoball and Igloo ambled after the wieners, snapped at them, and then decided to bat them around the ice instead. Roscoe groaned and stalked off to retrieve them, holding each bear off with a long, forked pole while he bent to the ice to pick up the frankfurter. "It's not play time, it's get-in-your-goddamned-cage time. Now move!"

As he held off Snoball with the stick and bent for a hot dog, Igloo circled around back and without warning slashed at his hand with a paw.

Roscoe stood, staring at the gashes in his hand, at how they were starting to redden with blood, and thought: Fanfucking-tastic. Hours in the infirmary, stitches, then back to the bear turds. . . . No way would he make even the final round of Hard Time's title defense now.

"Motherfucking bear!" Roscoe howled, then let out a sharp kick at Igloo, who took it in the belly and bowled over backward.

Enraged, Snoball charged from behind and knocked the cursing Roscoe onto the slush, then pounced on the work boot that had so assaulted his brother with furious paws and teeth, gnashing at Roscoe's ankle until with a spray of blood it finally severed and the booted foot was free.

Roscoe watched, openmouthed but unable to scream, as the bear cubs began batting their new chew toy around the ice. Then his world started to darken as shock set in.

The *beep-beep-beep*ing began as they were climbing the steps to Emma's front porch under a rapidly darkening sky, and Ernie couldn't help groaning.

"Yours or mine?" Emma asked, opening her purse.

"Yours." He shook his head. "I don't believe this."

"Oh, it's not all that bad. Besides, I said coffee. Remember? 'Would you like to come in for some coffee?' Not: 'Would you like to come in and get laid?' "

The word jarred Ernie, who started to dissemble, claim that the thought had never even crossed his mind, when Emma gave him a quick peck on the lips, then lifted her pager and thumbed a button to light up the display.

"Uh-oh. It's a 911. Major catastrophe." She gave him another peck and started back down the steps. "I've got to run. This could take a while."

"What is it?"

She pulled out her key ring and fingered her house key. "Don't know. But last time I got a 911, the black rhino had been found dead in the Dominion. The time before that, some guy had gotten drunk in UPSVIL, tried to swim across Lake Friendship, and got sucked down into the intake for the fountain. Whatever it is, it's going to take a while to come up with a good cover story to whitewash it. But here. Here's the key to my house. Make yourself comfortable. . . ."

He sighed heavily and pushed the key back at her. "I better not. It would probably be better if . . . Well, I've got some things to take care of at home, anyway. Maybe we could just do something tomorrow? Dinner?"

Emma put the key back in her purse. "Tell you what. Brunch. Right here. I'll cook." She started around back to her car. "Thanks. For today, I mean. I had fun."

"Me too," Ernie said bravely, realizing the evening, just like that, had ended.

"Tomorrow, then. Okay?"

She gave his hand a final squeeze and drew away, leaving him to push through the gate of her picket fence and down the block to where he'd parked the Mercedes. As he walked, he couldn't help humming to himself. Despite the abrupt finish, he really had no business complaining about his luck. She liked him, no doubt about it, and the fact that he was a worthless coward working for a worthless cowardly newspaper didn't matter a lick.

The hum turned into a whistle as he approached the car. Yessir, it had been a good day, all things considered.

Smart, beautiful, sassy. A good person. Emma. He even loved the name. Emma. A bit old-fashioned, but what the hell. Emma Whipple. Emma Whipple Warner.

He was reaching for his keys, wondering whether Whipple Warner would take a hyphen or not, when his world suddenly went black, he felt himself wrestled to the ground, and he heard a voice close in his ear: "Do not struggle, Mr. Warner, and you will not be harmed."

It was two men, at least, Ernie decided, and some sort of cloth bag over his head. He thought the voice sounded like the one that'd warned him about the dropping water table, although he couldn't be sure. He was about to ask, when a car pulled up beside them and he was hustled into the back seat, where a pair of hands fastened his seat belt. Two other belts clicked before the car peeled out. He rode in silence, his safety-conscious captors on either side, as the car turned left, then right, then left again, slowed, made another right, and stopped.

The whole thing had lasted no more than four minutes, and the car had never approached highway speed. They were still in Serenity.

The seat belt was removed and he was walked up a few steps, down a short hall, then down a flight of stairs. A basement. He was pushed down onto a hard seat, and four arms held him there.

"Got him, Earl," said a man.

Water Table Man for certain, Ernie decided after hearing the voice again.

"Goddamn it," a voice replied. "I'm not telling you again, Seis. No names!"

Any remaining fear Ernie had right then evaporated, replaced with something resembling amusement.

Beside him, Water Table Man cleared his throat. "As you requested, Subcommander Zero. We brought the *periodista.*"

"Very good, Subcommander Seis. Tres? Any problems? Witnesses?"

"None," the guy on his other arm reported.

"Excellent."

It was all Ernie could do to keep from laughing. He strained to memorize the exchange so he could write it down verbatim.

"Mr. Warner," the man named Earl but called Zero intoned solemnly. "Any idea who we are and why you are here?"

Ernie moved his head to get a fold of sackcloth out of his mouth. "You're members of the Serenity Underground, and you want press coverage?"

A murmur went up in the room. Beside him, Subcommander Seis said, "See? He's good. I told you."

"Then how come he hasn't tried to see anything outside the Official Tour?" someone asked.

"He has," Seis defended. "He saw Nina Marcus's house. Remember?"

"Then how come we haven't read a word about it in that rag of his?"

"That's enough," Zero said. "A brief history, Mr. Warner. You are correct. We are indeed the Serenity Underground. And your visit with us tonight should serve as ample proof that we're *not* a group of attention-seeking teens."

"*Heck* no!" a voice piped up.

"We are a group of Serenity homeowners," Zero continued, "who, quite frankly, Mr. Warner, are mad as hell and aren't going to take it anymore, if you get my drift. We were sold a bill of goods, moving here. We were promised Whipple quality. And so we bought in. Come to find out not only did we not buy quality, we also don't have any of the consumer protections every other homeowner in this state has! Whipple runs everything. Mayor Dick is a Whipple stooge. The Grievance Committee, which has yet to meet, are all Lew Peters appointees. We finally read our sales contracts, to take legal action, and guess what: right there in the fine print, we can't even do that! We're screwed, Mr. Warner, and no one gives a damn."

"What Would Waldo Say," Ernie said.

"That's right, Mr. Warner. What *Would* Waldo Say? That's all we have. The rightness of our cause. And our question is: What are you going to do about it? You saw Mrs. Marcus's house. We'll show you a hundred more, if you want. We'll get you pictures. We'll actually rip out door frames and tiles, examples of what we're talking about. But can you, Mr. Warner, get any of this into that corporate toady newspaper of yours?"

Ernie sighed. It was going to come back to that. "Well, I can see y'all have already noticed, we're not exactly the *New York Times*. We don't really do that kind of article."

A groan went up from around the room. "See?" a voice cried. "I told you this guy would be a waste of time!"

Ernie shook his head to loosen the bag. "You know, it would really help if you guys took this sack off my head."

"Why?" the voice behind him asked. "So you can rat us out easier to Lew Peters?"

"We have in our business what's known as 'off the record.' It's when I promise not to use your name or any other identifying characteristic that would get you in trouble," Ernie offered.

The room broke into squabbling for a while, until Zero called for order. "I don't believe there exists the level of trust for that to happen—yet. However, if you can get into your newspaper mention of tomorrow's event, you might win over some confidence."

"Why?" Ernie asked, his interest piqued. "What's happening tomorrow?"

"Noon, tomorrow. Be sure to be in town and outside. You'll see." Zero hit a gavel of some sort. "Unless there's anything else, we're adjourned."

The two subcommanders on either side pulled him up by his armpits and started leading him toward the staircase. Ernie stopped, turned toward where he thought Zero might be: "What happens then? Say I do get whatever it is you're doing into the paper? Then what? How do I get hold of you?"

"Don't you worry about it. We'll get hold of you," Zero said. "Noon tomorrow, Mr. Warner."

On the ride back to where his Mercedes was parked, Ernie turned to the side where Subcommander Seis sat and said through the sack, "Don't worry about the other day. In the bushes. I didn't get a look at your face."

Seis just grunted.

Ernie thought again of that encounter, of the way the man had limped hurriedly away afterward. "I did notice your limp, though," Ernie said. "Old football injury?"

"Nam," Seis said.

Ernie nodded empathetically. "Shrapnel?"

"Don't I wish," Seis scoffed. "Slipped getting off the plane in Saigon. It was rainy and the stairs were wet. Got a steel pin the size of a penlight battery holding it together. It's in the shape of a T, and the bone healed around it. Still can't go through an airport without getting searched."

"At least it kept you out of the jungle," Ernie offered.

"Wasn't going to the jungle. I was an accountant. On the General Staff." The car stopped, and Seis pulled Ernie out. "Here you go, champ. Safe and sound."

The car peeled out again, and by the time Ernie had freed the cord tied loosely around his neck and got the sack off, Seis, Tres, and the unnumbered driver were out of sight.

The flashlight tucked between chin and chest, Lenny Fizzogli lay on his belly to lower the pipe bomb on some string down the fissure in the rocks, where a small branch of the Upper Serenity River seemed to appear out of nowhere.

According to Armand Beckwith's thesis, the river's feeder springs were constrained by narrow tunnels that limited the amount of water that could flow through. If those narrow openings were somehow widened, Lenny Fizzogli had reasoned, then that should increase the amount of water passing through, and therefore the amount of water in the Lower Serenity, thereby increasing the water level of Lake Serenity.

And how better to open up a narrow passageway than with half a stick of dynamite, sealed up nice and tight in a waterproof casing, with an underwater fuse and timer?

Lenny Fizzogli let out string until he felt the package hit bottom, then coiled up the line and tossed it into the pool. He got up and moved downstream, to where a sliver of the clear creek connected with the muddy main stream. He'd found the spot only after hours of searching through the scrub, getting eaten alive by no-see-ums that didn't seem fazed in the least by his bug repellent, getting more and more ticked off by Lew Peters's unreasonable deadlines.

Two weeks to come up with an action plan. What bullshit! As long as Fizzogli got the job done by the end of the year, as he'd promised, what possible difference did it make to Peters whether it was six weeks or six months?

Well, he'd look on the bright side. No matter how big a pain this job was, all this reading and research and hiking around in the damp, bug-infested woods, it was still better than what he had been doing. Yes sir, no doubt about it. A bad day playing hydrogeologist beat a good day on the Old Time Bears Extravaganza anytime.

No more of those asinine lyrics—*I ain't really got a care, Since I'm an Ol' Time Bear!*—no more hot, stupid bear costume, no more working with a bunch of damn homos every day, and having to shower with them afterward, have them looking at him all the time.

Although, he had to admit, he'd never had as many back rubs as he'd had since moving into the Fag Motel. That part wasn't so bad. Especially the back rubs Marc gave, how afterward, he'd . . .

All right, so living next door to Marc wasn't so bad, and

if people thought he was gay because he enjoyed that, so be it. As long as they understood that he reserved the right to beat the living crap out of anyone who said so out loud, he could live with that. And really: gay, straight, bi. What the hell difference did it make to anybody what kind of human contact somebody enjoyed? Who were they to judge—

A sudden boom and subsequent rumble interrupted his philosophical musings. Too late he glanced at his watch, realized he'd forgotten to set the stopwatch to see how it compared to the timer he'd used inside the pipe bomb.

Shaking his head, he shone his flashlight at the water running at his feet, thought for a moment it seemed to be moving along faster since the explosion. Excitement started to grow as he walked back to the little pool where the water bubbled up. If this worked, then he'd have the money Peters had promised in no time! That truck was as good as his!

But then he got back to where he'd dropped the pipe bomb and saw . . . nothing different. Not a thing. Water still flowed lazily out, rippling as it flowed into a wide circle before converging into a relatively narrow creek bed.

His bomb hadn't done a damn thing!

Disgusted, Lenny Fizzogli heaved his knapsack full of supplies over both shoulders and started making his way back to the road.

# seven
...

In the bottom of one of her rarely used stainless saucepans hanging above the stove, Emma Whipple glanced again at the reflection of Ernie Warner. He was still staring at her backside.

She smiled inwardly. She had thrown on a pair of jogging shorts and a tank top that morning, not realizing the effect it would have on her new boyfriend, who acted like he'd never before seen a woman in such skimpy attire.

He was, she could tell, infatuated. And that was fine. She was interested, too. But between interest and a serious significant other was a lot of legwork, and she wasn't going to repeat the mistake of skipping it. Who exactly was he? And why, if he was as wonderful as he seemed, was he still available at age forty?

It occurred to her that he could ask himself the exact same question of her: Why, if she wasn't some deranged *Fatal Attraction* type, wasn't she safely married with kids already? She stirred the scrambled eggs, then reached for a pepper mill to grind some fresh. "So you had a story to tell me? Something after I was called in . . ."

Ernie blinked his eyes to snap out of his ass-admiring

reverie. She had welcomed him at the door with a peck on the cheek, and immediately his heart and hormones had raced into overdrive, tempered only by his sense that she could very well be the One, and that any rash actions now could screw things up for good.

He sipped his coffee and stretched his legs, then casually announced, "I was kidnapped."

He nodded once to her skeptical look. "Yup, kidnapped right here in River City, just outside your picket fence. Black hood over the face, car pulling up, disorienting drive around town, the works. May as well have been Beirut. Or Bogotá."

"Seriously?" she asked, stirring the eggs.

"Oh, they were thoughtful enough to fasten my seat belt for me as we drove. Vicious desperadoes to be sure, but *safe* vicious desperadoes."

Emma turned to him with hands on her hips and brow furrowed. "You're making this up."

"I am a journalist, dedicated to the truth. I couldn't do such a thing." He sipped from his coffee. "We drove around for a while, then went to the house of Subcommander Zero. At least I think it was his house."

"*Sub*commander?" Emma took the eggs off the stove.

"I never got a chance to ask. At one point they let slip that his real name was Earl."

"The Serenity Underground!" Emma exclaimed, dishing out eggs scrambled with sautéed peppers and onions. "Earl Zimmacker is the leader of that. He's a retired autoworker from Flint. He's a good guy."

"You *know* him?" He tasted his eggs after she had sat down. "Hey . . . these are delicious! And the coffee's great, too."

"Why, thank you. Flattery, by the way, will get you far. So yeah, I know Earl. He used to be the ringleader of about a dozen people who kept taking their complaints to the Town Council meetings. I guess they finally realized that wasn't going to have any effect whatsoever and stopped showing up. Not too long afterward, we started seeing the

Serenity Underground flyers. Like I said, he's a nice guy. And you *know* I think they have a legitimate beef. They just haven't been terribly media-savvy yet."

"Well, they may be improving on that front. If nothing else, last night was a really good publicity stunt." Ernie chewed on a piece of toast for a moment. "So, your turn. What was so important that you got called away on a Saturday night?"

Emma sighed, shook her head. "This has to be completely on background."

"Naturally. Hey, you're talking with the *Orlando Advocate*. All the News Local Business Leaders Think Is Fit to Print."

She finished her bite and set down her fork. "Remember how I was telling you how our polar bear trainer killed Snoball and Igloo's mother? Well, the little cubs got their revenge."

Ernie froze, his orange juice glass halfway to his lips. "They ate him?"

"Not completely. It seemed like they were more interested in playing than eating."

Ernie shook his head reverently. "That is so cool. What a perfect story! God, sometimes I *wish* I worked for a real newspaper."

Emma dabbed at her lips with a paper napkin, set her chin on clasped hands. "So why don't you? You appear capable. You seem not to have any . . . entanglements in the area. What's holding you back?"

He set down his silverware and studied her eyes. She had crossed her legs under the table, and he was aware that her toes—intentionally or unintentionally, he couldn't be sure—were grazing his calf. He realized the discussion had suddenly become more serious.

"I could ask you the same question," he said finally.

"I have the feeling we'd both pretty much have the same answer." She laid her hand on his. "Am I right?"

Ernie lifted his eyebrows, recalling the exact moment,

years earlier, when he'd for the first time neutered a story without even a small fight. He'd still been managing editor, and his City Hall reporter had uncovered a minor bid-rigging scandal involving a low-level Republican operative. The county GOP boss had called Leahy. Leahy had called Ernie. Ernie had killed the story. He'd been tired, and couldn't face the thought of yet another drawn-out argument followed by yet another capitulation.

"I'd like to tell myself that it's something important, something noble. Loyalty. An idea that maybe, just maybe, if I stay long enough, I can make things better. Although I suppose, in reality, I think it's more about comfort. Comfortable job. Comfortable house. Comfortable car. What's that principle of physics? Inertia? A body at rest remains at rest . . ."

"Unless acted on by an external force," Emma finished, stroking his palm with a finger. "So am I going to be your external force?"

Ernie swallowed. "Am I going to be yours?"

She merely looked at him, saying nothing, studying him, for a moment licking her lips as if searching for the right words—when the kitchen clock began to chime, and Ernie looked up with a groan.

"What?" Emma asked, blinking in confusion.

"It's noon."

"And . . . so?"

"The subcommanders. They told me they were planning some event today. At noon. They told me to be outside."

"An event? Huh. They mainly leaflet the neighborhoods. Although last week they strung a banner off the water tower. That lasted all of about fifteen minutes before Ferret Albright's goons cut it down. Where did they say they were doing it?"

He shook his head, struggling to his feet. "They didn't. They just said be outside."

She took his hand and led him to the front door. "Okay,

let's go see their stunt. Plus it'll be nice to have some company while I put in my porch time. I'm a little in the hole, on account of working late last week."

Ernie pushed the screen door open for her and sat beside her on a cushioned swing. "Porch time?"

"Don't ask." Emma glanced up and down the street. "Okay. Here we are. Outside. Now what?"

He squinted in one direction, then the other, then shrugged. "Beats me. They said be outside. Noon. Maybe they meant downtown? By the amphitheater?"

"Shhh . . . listen." Emma tucked a strand of hair behind an ear and cocked her head. "Hear that?"

Ernie heard a low drone, quickly sprang off the porch and down the stairs onto the front lawn. "Look!"

Above them, finishing a capital *W* that took up nearly a quarter of the sky, was a red single-engine biplane. It circled around back to the top and began another downward line. Another *W*.

"Now, *that's* pretty bold." Ernie laughed. "The goons won't be able to cut that down, will they?"

Emma watched in awe as the plane started the third *W,* then heard a new noise. She squinted off in the distance, finally made out the approaching helicopter. The Whipple Sheriff's Department helicopter. "I wouldn't be too sure about that," she said.

The green-and-white helicopter charged straight at the biplane, which flew off halfway through the *S,* leaving behind a lowercase *C,* the bottom of the *C* stretching out toward the horizon. The helicopter broke off chase as the plane disappeared, then returned to the skywriter's handiwork and repeatedly flew through the smoke from all angles, until not one trace of a letter remained, only a fuzzy white cloud in an otherwise blue sky.

Emma turned to Ernie, mouth open. "Wow."

Ernie squeezed her shoulder, checked his pocket for his keys, and strode toward his car. "I've gotta go."

•    •    •

Head back against the top of the couch, eyes focused on some point in space an indeterminate distance beyond the square ceiling tiles, Ernie reflected on the frailty of human dreams. The sheriff's helicopter, its work done, had no sooner headed back to its base than Ernie had known, in a flash of inspiration, how to irretrievably sneak Serenity's dark underbelly onto the front page of the *Advocate* and, thereby, all the papers of Florida and then the whole nation:

A "brite."

Newspaper slang for a short feature, meant to liven up an otherwise dreary page devoted to misdeeds. Something light, to draw out a chuckle from the reader. The *Advocate* under Jack Leahy absolutely adored brites, sometimes putting three, even four of them on the front page.

Ernie had visualized it as it was happening: angry homeowners, resorting to skywriting their protests after all other avenues of redress had failed, only to be squashed by Whipple's image-conscious machine. That, in and of itself, was funny. Stick in a nice, laconic quote from Subcommander Zero, a no comment from Whipple sheriff Ferret Albright, and he had a three-hundred-word gem he could, on his own, with no upper-management review thanks to it being a weekend, slip into Monday's paper.

And it would be a gem that simply *begged* for a string of follow-ups the next day. Who exactly were the Serenity Underground? What exactly did they want? Why was Whipple Corporation so intent on silencing them? Who was Subcommander Zero? Why did he call himself that?

Wonderful follow-ups, indeed. And if the *Advocate* didn't do them, well then the Associated Press, the *St. Petersburg Times,* the *Miami Herald,* the *Palm Beach Post,* and pretty soon everyone else in the world would. And the *Advocate* would have no choice but to follow suit.

He had raced downtown to the office, composing the story in his head as he drove, certain he could bully the Sunday page designer into giving him an eight-inch "containable" on the front, no jump, and Leahy wouldn't be the wiser until he saw it in print the next day.

He burst into the newsroom, rushed to the A-desk—only to find Jack Leahy himself seated at the big pagination computer screen, reviewing the second part of his pet three-day series on Central Florida's top-rated Realtors. Leahy had been surprised but delighted to see him, even as Ernie gamely started pitching his idea, and then beckoned Ernie into his office, where he'd immediately taken a personal call. From his wife, it seemed, reminding him to pick up her cleaning on the way home.

Ernie half listened to Leahy's end of the conversation while he considered his options. He could, he supposed, leak what happened to the AP reporter in town. But she would want attribution, which neither he nor Emma could provide. Albright would certainly deny everything. He could check air traffic control at Orlando International, see if they'd noticed anything on radar. But he knew from previous experience that such low-altitude flights wouldn't necessarily show up on their scopes unless the aircraft were using transponders.

He sighed heavily. Emma had to go back into the office that evening, to attend to the Great Polar Bear Trainer Cover-Up. He had sacrificed an afternoon with her for this opportunity, which now was lost, unless he could somehow manage to persuade—

"Sorry to make you wait. You know how wives are. Actually, come to think of it, I suppose you don't." Jack Leahy rubbed his hands together. "Now, you were saying? A near midair collision over Serenity?"

Ernie glanced down from the ceiling to Jack's smiling, tanned face and perfect dental work. "I guess you could call it that. I told you: That protest group? The Serenity Underground? They hired a skywriting plane. The Whipple Sheriff's helicopter flew right at it, chased it off."

Jack Leahy stroked his chin. "How close did they come? What's the FAA rule on approach distance? A thousand feet, or something like that, right? Would you say they came closer than a thousand feet?"

Ernie shrugged helplessly. "I don't know, Jack. I didn't see this as a flight-rules–violation type story. I saw it as a *funny* story. A brite."

"Funny? What's funny about it?" Jack Leahy shook his head. "Maybe if the FAA opens an investigation. We might want to look into it then. Until then . . . were any of the TV stations there?"

"I didn't see any," Ernie said glumly, thought: Perhaps I can tip one of *them* off. . . .

"Well, then, like I said. I just don't see it." Jack Leahy opened a cabinet in his credenza and pulled out a large portfolio. "You know, Ernie, if you spent as much energy building Whipple up, instead of trying to tear them down, I think you could really make that breakthrough you're· looking for. In your writing I mean. Don't get me wrong. You're good. Darn good, in fact. It's just that, well, you have to get through all this negative energy."

Ernie sighed again. He'd been through this lecture . . . how many times in recent years? He couldn't even recall. Jack had gone to some Schylle management retreat with obstacle courses and ropes and had come back spouting a load of New Age crap about Positive Energy and Synergy and Opportunities of Excellence. Near as Ernie could tell, they were all euphemisms for increasing workload while decreasing costs. Reporters would work harder so there could be fewer of them and thereby boost Schylle's shareholder dividend for the umpteenth straight quarter.

And to think he'd abandoned a day with Emma Whipple for this. Instead she'd kissed him and sent him off to battle. Her gallant knight, fighting for truth and justice. Getting his butt kicked yet again—

"I'm glad you happened in, though. That idea of yours? That Bird of the Week thing? I wanted to show you how well that's turning out. I wanted to run something past you, too."

Jack Leahy displayed a stack of pasted-up flats. Each had a quarter-page, head-and-torso photo of a good-looking young woman in a micro bikini top. Her name was in italicized text underneath, followed by the department each girl worked in and a brief description of her job. The overline read: "The *Advocate* Angels."

Ernie flipped through, saw the courts reporter, the tourism reporter, the pro baseball columnist—even the new clerk on the City Desk, who was barely out of high school. He glanced up, mouth open.

"I don't believe this! What did you threaten them with?"

Jack Leahy *tsk*ed disapprovingly. "Now, Ernie. Why do you always assume the worst of me? I told you. I put up a five-hundred-dollar bonus."

"That's it? Five hundred bucks?" Ernie stabbed a finger at the photo of the courthouse reporter, an outspoken feminist and easily the newsroom's sexiest lady. "You got Toni Welch to take her clothes off for five hundred dollars?"

Leahy shrugged. "Carrot and stick, Ernie. Carrot and stick. That's always been my management style."

"Okay. So the stick was . . . ?"

Jack Leahy shrugged once more. "It was made a performance standard for their job description."

Ernie shook his head. "You're sick, you know that? You're making a mockery of this profession. You—"

Jack Leahy held up a hand. "Please. There's no need to be sanctimonious. It's like on the TV news. You don't see them hiring *ugly* girls, do you? And male viewers, when they watch, they look at them, and they . . ."

"Imagine them naked," Ernie finished.

Leahy snapped his tanned fingers. "Exactly. My point exactly. And along those lines," Leahy carefully uncovered a second stack of page dummies, "I wanted your opinion, but not if you're going to sit up on your high horse about this."

Ernie looked at the new stack, then did a double take.

There, on the pasted-up pages, ready for the camera room, was Toni Welch again, only this time she wasn't even wearing a bikini top, but instead had one arm wrapped around her chest, *Sports Illustrated* Swimsuit Issue style.

"Tell me," Jack Leahy said. "You think this goes too far? For a family newspaper, I mean."

Ernie shook his head in disgust, started for the door.

"Pout if you want, Ernie. Wait till you see the numbers. Our focus group showed a potential eighty-four percent penetration in our target market, with a permanent loss of only four percent in the rest of our readership. Bottom line: It works!" Leahy shouted through the closing door. "Don't forget! This was *your* idea!"

Ferret Albright had his cowboy boots up on a plain steel desk, and was thumbing through a depressingly nonincriminating dossier on Emerson "Emma" Whipple, when his prisoner came to.

He was sitting on the concrete floor when he shook his head, groaned, and began complaining about a headache. Only then did he notice that his arms were chained to iron rings set in the wall.

"You can't be serious." The prisoner squinted across the dim, windowless room at Ferret Albright. "A dungeon? At your Sheriff Station? Does Lew Peters know?"

Ferret Albright closed the manilla folder and set it on the desktop. "Your head hurts because of the chloroform. An occasional side effect. As to your present whereabouts, well, you'll see soon enough."

The prisoner put on a defiant look and glared at his captor. "Okay. If you want to see Whipple Corporation lose a ten-gazillion-dollar false-imprisonment lawsuit, then you go ahead and keep me chained here. Otherwise I suggest you get your ass up and let me go this instant."

Ferret Albright put his feet on the floor and sat up straight, calmly opened another folder on the desk, and pretended to read for a moment. "Commander Seis, right? Oh, I'm sorry. *Sub*commander Seis. Whatever the fuck that means." He glanced up at his prisoner. "Why don't you tell me about the J25 plans?"

Subcommander Seis shifted uncomfortably. "I don't know what you're talking about."

"That skywriting thing. Was that part of the Big Plan?" Ferret Albright clasped his hands together on the desk, as he'd seen an interrogator do once in a spy movie, and smiled. "Or was that just random, run-of-the-mill troublemaking? Like the banner on the water tower?"

Ferret Albright removed from the folder a printout of the e-mail that Mayor Gillespie had sent his way and read it aloud, then tucked it back in the folder.

Subcommander Seis slouched against the wall, defeated. Then he finally noticed the aroma of the place. He sniffed the air and made a face. "Where the hell are we? Smells like shit."

Ferret Albright laughed genially. "Son, you're in Waldo Whipple World. Not even the shit stinks here. Besides, we don't call it shit. We call it effluent. Clean enough to drink. You'll be seeing for yourself soon enough. But for now, why don't you tell me the real names of all the new *sub*commanders? I'm thinking any recruits you may have enlisted since, say, February?"

Ernie strode up the stairs, checked the numbers on the house a final time, and rang the doorbell.

A week earlier, what he was about to do would have been unthinkable. A year earlier, unimaginable. And ten years ago, simply beyond the pale of anything a self-respecting newspaperman could do.

But that was then. That was before Jack Leahy had completely lost his sensibilities. It had taken Ernie a full day to calm down from his latest run-in with his boss. He'd needed a full two days before he could explain to Emma what had happened, and it was in the talking it out with her on the phone that he'd decided that, okay, maybe he couldn't get the Serenity Underground into the *Orlando Advocate,* but that didn't mean he couldn't do *something*.

With Emma working long hours on publicity preparations for the Jubilee, Ernie took it upon himself to track down Earl Zimmacker. And after two days of scoping out his house, he finally saw what he was waiting for: a dozen middle-aged men trooping up to the front door, alone and in pairs, wordlessly gaining admittance.

Ernie rang the bell a second time, and a woman in a brown pantsuit opened the door for him. Mrs. Zimmacker, he decided.

"Hi, I'm with the *Advocate.* I'm here for the Underground meeting."

Mrs. Zimmacker looked at him suspiciously.

"I was here the other night?" Ernie explained. "You remember. I had the bag over my head? They told me about the skywriting stunt?"

Mrs. Zimmacker pursed her lips, opened the door to let him pass, then directed him to the staircase leading down to the basement. Ernie thanked her and descended the steps, noticing now how the handrail was unevenly stained, the paint on the wall seemed streaky, and the risers themselves creaked with his weight.

Earl and the rest of his subcommanders stopped talking when they heard his approach and went into a wide-eyed panic when they saw his face.

"Christ, it's him!" one of them shouted, grabbing his papers and cramming them up his shirt.

Others jumped up from their chairs and bumped into one another in their attempt to hide. At the front of the room, Earl Zimmacker instructed his troops to stay calm and, above all else, not say a word about the other night.

Ernie raised his arms and cleared his throat. "Everyone, please. I'm not here about the other night."

The scrambling around stopped, and Ernie surveyed the

faces, noticed that the one who'd jumped him in the bushes, the one with the limp, Subcommander Seis, didn't seem to be among them.

"Why *are* you here, then?" one of them asked.

"I'm here to help you get your message out."

A different one, tall with nerdy horn-rims, scoffed. "Then how come you didn't write about our message the other day? And how Whipple's jackbooted thugs stomped on our right to free expression?"

"I *did* write about it. I just couldn't get my paper to run it," Ernie said defensively. "That's what I came to talk to you about. I don't think you're ever going to get the *Advocate* or any other local media to break your story. They're all just too deeply in bed with Whipple."

The faces of the men fell, as if he'd confirmed their worst fear.

"But," he continued, "I'm just guessing that you guys don't particularly care whether the local press covers you if you can get your message out nationally. Am I right?"

The subcommanders looked to their leader for guidance, and Earl Zimmacker cleared his throat with authority. "Just what is it that you're proposing, Mr. Warner?"

"Sunday is the Jubilee. Live network television, international media. You can't ask for a bigger forum. And if there's one thing that's certain about Lew Peters, it's that he'll do whatever it takes to avoid bad press. Remember Krazy Klowne? The company yanked more than a million copies of that CD off the shelves. It cost them a fortune. But they did it, because not doing it meant taking a PR beating. If you guys get your message out during the Jubilee, you're pretty much guaranteed that Peters will make you whole."

Earl Zimmacker shifted his feet uncomfortably. "We're well aware of the Jubilee's potential, and made big plans accordingly. That is, we thought we had. Only thing is, Subcommander Seis, who was our Jubilee Action Chairman . . . well, he had a family emergency he had to tend to. Anyway, upshot is we're kind of in disarray."

"Well, what was he planning?" Ernie asked.

"We were going to leaflet the place, aerially," one of the other subcommanders piped up. "He was going to get a plane and dump the messages on the audience during the dedication ceremony. Except, because of the skywriting fiasco the other day, now our pilot's refusing to work the Jubilee. He heard Whipple was planning a cordon around its airspace. Seis said he was working on a fallback plan, but I don't know what it was."

"Can't anyone call him?" Ernie asked, then saw how the subcommanders dropped their eyes in shame. "What?"

Earl Zimmacker gave a long sigh. "Truth is, Mr. Warner, we're not sure about Seis. He supposedly went to Fargo, North Dakota, to take care of his sick mother. But he didn't tell anyone when he would be back or what the fallback plan was or anything. So we're kind of worried."

There was an awkward silence, and then another subcommander finished in a Mississippi drawl: "We're kinda worried, Mr. Warner, that ol' *Say-ez* went AWOL on us. We think Whipple either scared him off, or bought him off, or—who knows what? Something."

"He won't be the first," another one offered. "In the past six months we've lost Cinco and Trece. Sick family, job transfer. Never a good explanation. And now Seis."

Ernie shook his head impatiently. "Okay, Seis can't coordinate Jubilee. Fine. Point is, *somebody* has to. This is too good an opportunity to pass up." Around him, downcast heads began perking up. "Come on, guys! A chance like this doesn't come along every day!"

At the front of the room, Earl Zimmacker, Subcommander Zero, wordlessly polled his comrades, then turned back to Ernie. "Okay, Mr. Warner. You're the media expert. How do you suggest we get their attention?"

All eyes on him, Ernie stepped forward and began: "Okay, here's what's got to happen. There are going to be a hundred TV cameras there, half of them broadcasting live. What you need is some way to get past Whipple security and get their attention. And at least at first, it's got to look harmless. . . ."

At the New Age classroom-without-walls, Serenity Integrated Learning Academy, Mayor Dickie Gillespie sat in the front row of the school's auditorium, watching a frumpy, middle-aged lady wring her hands and recite the "Out, damned spot!" scene from *Macbeth* and growing ever more sorry that he'd agreed to audition the finalists for the drama teacher opening.

He was on applicant number eight of ten. None of them, in his opinion, worth a damn as an actor. That wouldn't have been so bad if even one or two of the candidates had some of the qualities Dickie Gillespie looked for in his hires. But no. Of the four female finalists, he'd now seen three, including the size eighteen Lady Macbeth, and not a one was worth even a second glance.

He would have to ask his secretary do some extra bottom-drawer filing when he got back to Town Hall, in order to make up.

Dick Gillespie listened with half an ear—*All the perfumes of Arabia will not sweeten this little hand. Oh, oh, oh!*—as he perused the next finalist's folder. Chris Gaston, he read. Age twenty-eight. From Quebec. Played ice hockey at high school and college, where he majored in film and drama. Taught at Toledo South High in Ohio, where he'd left six months earlier.

Another guy. Great. Dick Gillespie wondered what kind of a moron the school principal was, for one, permitting six of ten finalists for the job to be male, and two, not having a single babe among those women who did make it. What in hell kind of applicant pool was that?

He realized that the Fat Lady Macbeth was finished, and looked up with a forced smile to thank her and call in the next one. Two more, and he was out of there. Back to Town Hall and his lovelies. Pick one of the finalists at random—did it really matter who directed the stupid school play each semester?—and be done with it. No more volunteering for civic duties. That was *not* part of his job description, and he was damned—

He glanced up to see a stunning brown-eyed beauty in miniskirt and high heels at the front of the stage, smiling at him. He did a double take, then checked his folder again. Aha! Chris was *Christine,* not Christopher. He looked back up, incredulous. "You played college ice hockey?"

Chris Gaston flashed another smile, a perfect, bright, white, toothpaste-ad smile. "The first woman in the whole province."

Dick Gillespie was intrigued. An athletic little minx . . . He asked, "And what did you get out of that experience?"

Chris Gaston shrugged. "A lot of bruises. A couple of cracked ribs. Oh, and dentures." She tugged at her magazine-perfect teeth. "These come out."

Now Dickie Gillespie was really intrigued. "You know, we've got an ice rink right here in Serenity."

Chris Gaston asked, "Really?"

Subcommander Seis's real name was Harry Spunkmeyer, Ernie learned from a phone call to Emma. Given that and an approximate age from his own observation, he was able to get a street address and date of birth from the state's Division of Highway Safety and Motor Vehicles. And given those two things, he ordered a full dossier from a company called InstaTrak, which compiled all the public records available electronically anywhere in the country, including information given to would-be creditors through the years.

That report in hand, Ernie saw that Harry Spunkmeyer was born in Frankfort, Kentucky, married at age eighteen, earned a bachelor's degree in accounting, served four years in the U.S. Army, discharged honorably, with a rank of first lieutenant, after which he earned a master's degree in geology and went to work for the Missouri state transportation department. He became a widower at age forty-eight, at which point he sold their house in Cape Girardeau and bought a Founders' Lot at Serenity for $198,000. He owned a 1993 Cadillac Coupe de Ville, with a present value of approximately $4,500.

His mother's maiden name was Thelma Bergstrom, and she was born in Decatur, Illinois. She had lived in Knoxville, where she married George Spunkmeyer at age seventeen, and then, for various lengths of time, lived in Frankfort; Charleston, South Carolina; Athens, Georgia; Pensacola, Florida; and Galveston, Texas.

At no time, according to the public records at Ernie's disposal, had Thelma Spunkmeyer, née Bergstrom, ever lived in Fargo, North Dakota. A check of Fargo's public utilities and property rolls showed neither a Thelma Spunkmeyer nor a Thelma Bergstrom. Not now, not for the past decade.

Ernie called all the nursing homes in and around Fargo, just to make sure, but there was no such resident. He put the phone down after talking to the last nursing home in a hundred-mile radius of Fargo, thought for a minute, then called Emma at her office to see if she knew the real names of Subcommanders Cinco and Trece.

At the next Serenity Underground meeting, Ernie was let in without comment and took his seat in Earl Zimmacker's basement, just like one of the subcommanders. He waited until Earl had finished the treasurer's report and asked if there was any new business before raising his hand.

"These defections you guys have had. How well did you know them?"

Subcommander Quatro, a design architect and head of recruitment, crossed his arms defensively. "Well, I'll grant you that our attrition rate has been a bit high of late," he said. "But nothing out of the ordinary for a clandestine action group, I imagine."

Ernie bit his lip to keep from grinning. "I don't mean any disrespect here, but last night I got the real names of those subcommanders who've walked. You know where I got them? Whipple Public Affairs. They seem to have quite a roster."

Every face in the room stared at him in horror. "*All* of us?" Subcommander Doce, a Serenity Academy learning leader, asked.

"No, not all of you, for whatever that's worth. But you've got a bigger problem," Ernie said. "Seis? He doesn't really have a sick mother in North Dakota. Near as I can tell, he doesn't have any relatives there at all, sick or well. And Trece wasn't really transferred to Saskatchewan. And Cinco didn't really move to Maine."

Earl blinked at him grimly. "So what are you saying? They're traitors? I can't believe that. I'd trust Seis with my life."

The thought had occurred to Ernie, but he kept it to himself. If Emma had access to the names, then it clearly wasn't a terribly big secret. The question was *how* they were getting such good information, if not through an informant. He looked up to the light fixtures, noticed a telephone on a side table, wondered if Ferret Albright would stoop to a listening device. Then he saw the shining new personal computer on the desk at the back.

"Y'all aren't using the town's computer system, are you?"

Earl Zimmacker scoffed. "We weren't born yesterday, Mr. Warner." He nodded with authority. "We all subscribe to Infinity Online. We send out notices, announce meetings, that sort of stuff, via e-mail."

Ernie groaned, shook his head. "Infinity? So I guess you guys missed the news last year? Infinity was bought out by Nexstar Communications. Nexstar, a wholly owned subsidiary of Whipple?"

The subcommanders sat stunned for a moment, then started murmuring disconsolately until Earl Zimmacker banged his gavel on his table. "Okay. What's done is done. That can't be helped. From now on, no more e-mails. Anything else, Mr. Warner?"

Ernie thought for a moment. "Not really. Except whatever plans Seis and the others might have been involved in for the Jubilee? Assume Albright knows them. If I were you, I'd plan something entirely different."

The gray-haired widow stared at Ernie with furrowed brow and narrowed eyes. Despite Emma's presence, despite his promise not to use her name or identify her in any way, she wanted no part of any newspaper article, not even one with the potential of finally, at long last, making Whipple Corporation fix her leaking pipes and replaster her cracked walls.

Ernie stared at the empty notepad page beneath the date and time notation he'd made in the corner and tried to think of how to ask his question a different way. Neighbors of Subcommanders Cinco and Trece had also started out tight-lipped, but had eventually cooperated at the prospect of salvaging their property values. Old Mrs. Duncan, so far, hadn't said a useful word.

"The others who disappeared," Ernie paged back through his notebook, "were making noises about suing Whipple, or in some other way going public with their grievances."

Subcommander Cinco, the retired teacher who'd supposedly returned to Maine, had been fed up with the Morty Muskrat–centered curriculum at the Serenity Integrated Learning Academy, and had been talking about writing an article for a national teachers' magazine, according to one of his neighbors. Subcommander Trece, who supposedly had been transferred to Canada, had been so frustrated about the problems with his own house that he had actually approached a number of residents about a class-action lawsuit. In both instances, the men had simply disappeared one day. Eventually, word of their respective moves filtered back to the neighborhood, although Ernie had not been able to find anyone who had actually spoken to his or her vanished neighbor.

It was that completeness of the disappearances that had nagged Ernie from the first. For men to move away without a word, and then, a week or so later, for their belongings to be crated up and loaded into moving vans and their houses to be put on the market and sold . . .

Mrs. Duncan said nothing, so Ernie continued: "Did Mr. Spunkmeyer do or say *anything* indicating he was considering taking some sort of action about his house?"

Mrs. Duncan shook her head and shrugged, then glanced suspiciously at Emma. "Never said nothing to me. Of course, even if he had, I would'na been interested. I'm perfectly happy with the quality of my house." She forced a smile. "And of my life here in Serenity generally."

Ernie traded glances with Emma, then said, "Mrs. Duncan, please. You can trust her. She's trying to help. After all, if your family name was being sullied by a greedy corporation, wouldn't you want to do something?"

Still Mrs. Duncan seemed unconvinced. Ernie pointedly put his pen and notepad back in his pocket. "Mrs. Duncan, please. Look." He held both open hands in the air. "I'm not even going to write any of this down, okay? He was your next-door neighbor. Word is he's taking care of his mother in North Dakota. Except that his mother doesn't live in North Dakota. In fact, I found out today that she died three years ago. So you tell me: Why would Harry up and leave like he did and then lie about it? Does that seem like him?"

Mrs. Duncan's expression softened, and Ernie realized he was very close.

"Was there anything?" he repeated. "Anything at all?"

Mrs. Duncan took a deep breath. "Water."

And Ernie remembered the whispered tip in the bushes. "Water? You mean about the water table dropping?"

Mrs. Duncan shrugged. "Never did completely understand that. All I know is water. He was very concerned about water."

Ernie stroked his chin, wished for the hundredth time he'd pressed Harry Spunkmeyer for more details when he'd had the opportunity. "Did he used to hang around the river?" Ernie asked on a hunch.

"No. Not the river," Mrs. Duncan said, shaking her head. "The playground."

Emma sat on the Gordon Gopher–shaped swing, gently swaying backward and forward while Ernie paced around the Morty Muskrat slide. The sky had darkened past evening shades and was now pure black, with the brightest stars shining through the haze of light created by the theme parks to the north.

"Beautiful night, huh?" Emma leaned back and kicked her feet to swing higher. "You know you can see the Enchanted Realm fireworks from here? Enchantment in the Sky. They'll be doing them in another hour or so."

Ernie moved to the Billy Baboon jungle gym, squatted, then began digging down into the cypress chips that made up the playground surface.

Emma watched him for a minute, finally asked, "What are you doing?"

Ernie dug through six inches of chips before he hit the sandy soil ubiquitous to much of Central Florida. "Water. The man's a geologist by training. He tips me off to a problem with the water table, right? Yet he's hanging around a playground." Ernie refilled his hole with the mulch, wiped his hands on his pants, and stood. "Why?"

"Beats me." Emma kicked off her shoes and swung even higher. "Why don't you come here and swing with me?"

Ernie watched her arc back and forth for a minute, then

turned to study the big plastic tunnels that snaked through the jungle gym. "Can't. I'll get seasick."

"Seasick?"

"You heard me." Ernie knelt before one of the tunnels and tugged at its anchoring system. "I don't suppose the names Tony Armstrong or Irlo King mean anything to you."

Emma shook her head. "No. Should they?"

"I guess not. One's a DEP officer." Ernie resumed digging through wood chips. "The other's an enviro-nut. Both were supposedly snooping around Whipple. Now one's down in Hendry County and won't return my calls, and the other's disappeared off the face of the earth. It's totally out of character for both."

"Well, I doubt they were ever actually here. It's Whipple policy not to allow either the DEP or any sort of activist on property. Hey, do you seriously get seasick on a swing?" Emma pumped ever harder. "I've never heard that before. You mean even as a kid it made you seasick? Or only now, as an adult?"

Ernie ignored her and kept digging, this time kept going when he hit soil.

"Ernie, you can't fight their battle for them. And besides, if your editor wasn't willing to print a story about the Whipple air force chasing off a skywriting plane, what are the chances he'll print an article about Whipple's groundwater?"

"It's Seis's disappearance that bugs me." Ernie scooped another handful of earth onto a growing mound. "The others I never met, so I really can't say. But Seis . . . I just can't believe he'd sell out to Whipple."

"Oh, you should," Emma said authoritatively. "People do it all the time. You'd be amazed how little it takes. A one-year All-Parks Passport is the going rate. And if there really *was* something wrong with the groundwater, I'm sure Lew Peters would be more than willing to dip into his slush fund to take care of old Harry."

Ernie stopped digging for a minute, watched Emma swing into the sky, then back to earth and up again, her cotton skirt flying in the breeze. His first time with Emma in days, and instead of picking up where they'd left off on the weekend, he was dragging her around town playing detective. He watched as she pointed her toes skyward at the top of her arc and sighed. Harry Spunkmeyer, formerly Subcommander Seis of the Serenity Underground, was now a millionaire somewhere, living off his hush money. It was as simple as that.

And yet . . . something refused to fit. Harry Spunkmeyer was a malcontent, but most of Serenity's residents were malcontents, and rightfully so. If Lew Peters was ready to pay off somebody for threatening a lawsuit or going to the media, then eventually he'd have to pay off everybody. And that would cost a lot more than simply having built Serenity right in the first place.

"Why does the average, disillusioned Serenity homeowner not write a letter to the editor of the *New York Times* about their beef?" Ernie asked.

Emma answered, still swinging. "One, they're not completely disillusioned. They still want to believe in the Whipple magic, that ultimately Whipple will do them right. And two, they know that Lew Peters never loses. His vindictiveness is legendary. They all signed these awful contracts preventing them from suing by making them pick up all the legal costs of both sides, regardless of outcome. They know that Peters will bankrupt them if they make a fuss."

Ernie recalled the fear evident in Mrs. Duncan's face. "And that's it? They're not scared? As in physically scared?"

Emma thought about that. "Well, there are the rumors among the conspiracy theorists. You know: Ferret Albright's got a secret dungeon somewhere. Ferret Albright gets rid of dissenters by feeding them to the alligators. Ferret Albright gets rid of the bodies by dissolving them in acid. Ferret Albright's a sexual deviant—"

"Ferret Albright *is* a sexual deviant," Ernie said. "Just because the *Advocate* won't print negative stories doesn't mean its staff doesn't know about them."

"All right, so he's a little weird. Point is, these things are like urban legends. They get started, and embellished, and after a while, nobody really believes them."

Ernie considered this. "Okay, for the sake of argument, all the former subcommanders were bought off by Whipple. All three of them, including Seis. How come you haven't heard anything about it? Even though the known list of Serenity Underground members was made available to you?"

"That's because," Emma said, pumping ever higher, "Lew Peters has an interest in making sure I don't inadvertently arrange media interviews with known subversives. What interest does he have in even a single extra person knowing how much money he's shelling out to keep those subversives quiet?"

Ernie thought about that as he lifted a handful of sandy dirt and let it slip back through his fingers onto the ground. Finally he said, "Hmmph," and resumed digging. "By the way, you remember that time you told me this playground had twenty inches of mulch on it? You guys barely have a fourth of that. Six inches."

"It's all right. We hardly ever have any real children using it, anyway." Emma blinked as she considered what she'd just said. "Which is weird, given how many children live in this town."

"One day last week, on our walking tour, I saw this little girl run over here to play and her mom dragged her off and read her the riot act," Ernie recalled. "I thought that was a little strange, too. . . . Hello . . . look at this!"

Emma slowed her swinging to peer in his direction. "What?"

Ernie lifted out a handful of pea gravel, packed tight with a reddish-brown clay. "This. Less than three inches below the mulch. This is not a natural soil for this area."

"Meaning . . ."

"Meaning," Ernie continued, rolling the gravel around in one hand, "somebody put this here. It's like fill. Although, as fill goes, it's kind of expensive. It's almost like a subbase for roadways or something. But this playground's nowhere near a road—"

"Aahhhh!" Emma shouted, then dug her heels into the cypress chips to stop the swing. She stared at Ernie open-mouthed.

"Yes?" Ernie prompted.

Emma stood, turned slowly around in a circle. "This whole place . . . it's all different."

Ernie looked around too, and then back at her. "Different from what?"

"The swings . . ." She put her hand on one of the vinyl swing chains, sat back down. "They used to go the other way, facing the lake. I remember, because I went on them a few months back, and I thought to myself, if I just sat the other way, I could watch the fireworks at the Enchanted Realm. But *now* look how they are!"

Ernie looked. They were arranged facing the bandshell, so that the arc of the swing was parallel to the shoreline, not perpendicular to it. "Are you sure?"

"Positive. And look at the slide. It used to run toward the lake, too. And now it runs the other way. And also, it's on the wrong side of the swings. It used to be on the left."

Ernie scratched his head, walked over to the four-by-four supports for the swing set, and tried to lift it. It refused to budge or even shake. Ernie leaned against the post, silently surveyed the playground for a minute.

"So why would they want to change it around?" he asked finally.

Mayor Dickie Gillespie lay buck naked at center ice, the flags hanging downward from the rafters of the Serenity Ice Castle drifting in and out of focus, thinking: If this is what it's like to have a woman with no teeth, then maybe growing old won't be so bad after all. . . .

Abruptly, the partially nude woman lying perpendicular to Mayor Dick over the Serenity Fighting Chipmunks logo lifted her head slightly and complained, "Mmm mips ahh fhee-ing."

Mayor Dick glanced down in annoyance and blinked. "What?"

Chris Gaston leaned to one side and slid her dentures into her mouth. "My tits are freezing!" she repeated.

He glared at her for a moment. "You want to teach acting, right? Act like they're not!" he ordered. "Besides. You're Canadian. You should be used to it."

Mayor Dick laid his head back down on the ice as Chris Gaston put her teeth back in their little plastic case and returned to her task.

Then she gasped in horror and scrambled to her knees, for ambling toward her from the north goal were, she was quite certain, two frisky polar bear cubs. She got to her feet, ran toward the boards, and tumbled over into the visitors' bench— just as Dickie Gillespie opened his eyes in time to see one of the bear cubs swipe at his crotch.

His scream reverberated through the Ice Castle while Snoball and Igloo happily batted their new toy across the blue line toward the south goal.

Dora Minor was in her early thirties, attractive but still working to get her prechildbirth figure back, and bleary-eyed at the late hour Ernie and Emma knocked.

The house was one street in from downtown but, Ernie noticed, had a line of sight on the playground from the second-story windows. The second Dora Minor opened the door, Ernie knew she was indeed the same woman they'd seen hustle her little girl off the playground that morning. He proceeded to assure her that in no way would she get in any sort of trouble for talking to them, and in no way would her name be used in an article.

Dora Minor hesitated for a long minute, peered anxiously over their shoulders for late-night joggers or sheriff's cars, then allowed them in and led them to her kitchen table.

"We're sorry to bother you so late," Ernie said after they had sat down to cups of decaf.

"That's all right. I was going to wait up for my husband," Mrs. Minor said, stirring her coffee. "He works a full shift at the Realm, then a second one at UPSVIL so we can afford this place. Perfect, isn't it? We're working day and night so we can live in a new house with moldy ceilings in a town where my little girl can't even use the playground."

Ernie and Emma traded glances. "That's why we're here, Mrs. Minor," he said. "Can you tell us why?"

Dora Minor studied them both a final time. "Promise you won't use my name?"

"You have our word," Emma said. "Waldo Whipple was my great-uncle. I feel awful about what's been done in his name and want to do what I can to make it right."

Dora Minor's face softened. "What would Waldo say?" Then her smile disappeared and she leaned forward. "It was about three, three and a half months ago. I'd just gotten Britney down for the night and had lain down myself. Mike wasn't due home for hours, and I thought I'd get a nap because I was fighting a cold.

"Anyway, I had just put my head down when I heard this rumbling outside. There was a good moon that night, and I was able to see the playground quite clearly—and it was disappearing."

"Excuse me. Disappearing?" Emma asked.

"Sinking. There was this hole in the ground, and it was just swallowing up the entire playground. Swing set, jungle gym, everything. I looked around, but I couldn't see anyone on the street or looking from the windows or anything. But a couple of minutes later a sheriff's car stopped on Front Street, and within ten minutes, a whole bunch of Town Maintenance vehicles had shown up. They had three big dump trucks, and they filled that hole right back up, and a steamroller packed it all down. Then another crew came in with playground equipment and put up a brand-new one, all before morning."

Ernie and Emma listened, spellbound, until Dora Minor had finished. "Except they didn't put it back up the same way," Emma said. "They got it turned ninety degrees, didn't they?"

Dora Minor nodded. "You noticed that too, huh? Not many people did. Yeah, they put it facing the other direction. Not that it makes a difference. Knowing what could happen, there's no way I'm taking my child there ever again. None of the moms are. Just like we avoid Founders' Estates."

"Founders' Estates?" Emma asked, then suddenly recalled how work on two of the million-dollar homes there had been set back months for unknown reasons. "Oh my God! You mean those two lots that had those problems with the foundations—"

"Yup," Dora Minor said. "Gone. Except there weren't just two lots. There were six." She rattled off the addresses from memory. "We moms avoid those streets like the plague. No telling when the ground might open up again."

Emma and Ernie crouched down behind a thicket, swatting mosquitoes and watching the side entrance to Serenity's gleaming new Water Reuse Center.

Emma scratched at her ankles, then shifted her weight to lean closer to Ernie's ear. "Explain to me again why we're here? What sinkholes have to do with the sewer plant?"

Ernie slapped at his neck, then scratched furiously. "I'm not sure. Sinkholes happen when the water table drops—that I know. The question now is why. Why is the water table dropping? We've had plenty of rain. There really aren't any major new housing developments on this aquifer."

A mosquito flew into Emma's ear, and she shook her head to get it out. "Okay. So once again: What does all that have to do with the new sewage plant?"

"I don't know," Ernie conceded. "Seis mentioned the water table, and then he mentioned the sewage plant, that first night he tackled me in the bushes. I thought about it, and it just seems the whole thing is somehow tied to this place. Your new, expensive sewage-treatment plant. The thing got finished eight months ago. The sinkholes started happening seven months ago. The Underground subcommanders started disappearing six months ago. On top of all that, my DEP friend was looking into salinity levels in the Serenity River before he went AWOL on me. I don't know, but everything keeps coming back to water."

Emma stared at the building glumly. "Well, let it never be said I'm a whiny date. I'm sure years from now this will seem funny, but right now, I've got to tell you . . . there! He's coming out again!"

From the side door of the white building emerged a uniformed security guard. He reached down behind a bush for a softball-sized rock, which he placed on the threshold. Then he gently let the heavy metal door swing back against the stone, allowing it to remain slightly ajar.

"Why doesn't he just open it with his key?" Ernie whispered.

"The side door can't be unlocked with a key. Only the front door. And if he goes in or out that way, he goes past the security camera."

The guard walked to the front of the building and sat on a low retaining wall, then pulled out a pack of cigarettes and a lighter. Ernie pushed the button on his watch to start the timer, nudged Emma, and they scampered, bent at the waist, to the side door, opening it just enough to slide in before letting it fall back against the rock.

Emma glanced around the cavernous room, at the tile floor and the stainless-steel holding tank, at the empty control booth above, and whispered, "Okay, we have twelve minutes. Let's go."

Ernie started walking around the edge of the giant vat, waving a hand beneath his nose. "Smells like a sewage plant, all right."

"What did you expect? An English garden?"

"No. Just a hunch I had . . . one that looks like it didn't

pan out. My DEP friend? Tony Armstrong? I ran into him about a week, ten days ago. Anyway, he was looking into elevated salinity levels downstream of Lake Serenity. So earlier today I started thinking: What if it really wasn't a state-of-the-art wastewater-treatment plant? What if it was just an old-fashioned sludge plant and they were diluting it with brackish water way down from the Floridan aquifer? That would cost just a small fraction of that two-hundred-million-dollar grant, and the company could pocket the rest."

He stared down into the murky liquid with fingers pinching his nose, then looked around on the floor until he spotted a small twig that had been tracked in from the outside. He bent for it and tossed it into the vat. Immediately the water around it began to froth.

"Jesus . . . would you look at that!"

Before their eyes, the twig diminished in size, until it disappeared entirely. The water stopped hissing. "Wow," Emma said. "I guess that would be the genetically engineered aggressive bacteria. I'd never seen them in action before."

Ernie looked around the room with a frown. "Well, so much for my theory of this place not being a Level Three plant. I guess we should get out of here." He checked his watch. "We have eight minutes before the night watchman gets back."

They started for the door, passing an indentation in the vat wall where a glass window showed a collection of debris halfway filling a mesh basket.

"What's that?" Emma asked, stopping.

Ernie stepped closer. "Huh. This must be where all the nonbiodegradable stuff that accidentally goes down the drain winds up." He studied the control panel over the bin, pressed a green button labeled "Rinse." The basket rose out of the vat on mechanical arms, and nozzles began dousing the contents with a spray of water. "If your earring goes down the drain, this is where it'll end up. Of course, in most treatment plants, you know the number-one item showing up in these bins? Condoms."

Emma stood on tiptoe to look over his shoulder. "Thanks for sharing. Shouldn't we get out of here?"

"We have another few minutes. Anyway, don't you want to see what your neighbors are flushing down their johns?"

The water stopped spraying, and Ernie peered into the clothes-hamper-sized bin. "Every so often they have to empty this out, to keep this stuff from gumming up the works. See all that sand? From kids rinsing their feet in the tub instead of outside. I'm surprised Lew Peters hasn't cracked down on that." He noticed a glint in the basket and reached in. "Look what else somebody lost down the drain."

He handed her a small ring, and Emma turned it over in her hands, fingered the raised numbers that made up the design. "One. Four. Three. Huh. I wonder what that stands for."

Ernie took the ring back. "It's an 'I love you' ring. One-four-three. The number of letters in each of the words. Some lighthouses used to flash that sequence." He flipped the ring over, then back. "You know what? I know somebody who has one of these. His ex-wife gave it to him years ago. He still wears it around his neck on a little chain. As a matter of fact, he's one of the guys I asked you about. The environmental activist who was supposedly working—"

"Look at that!" Emma reached into the basket and picked out an oblong metal disk, about the size of a half dollar but three times as thick. At one edge were two slots and the remnants of some hard plastic tubing. "I wonder what . . . Oh!"

Ernie saw the look of curiosity on Emma's face turn to one of revulsion. "What?"

"Don't you know what this is? Ernie, this is a pacemaker!"

"Pacemaker."

"A *pacemaker*. You know. It makes a heart beat regularly." Emma breathed in sharply. "Ernie, only one person in Serenity has ever had a pacemaker. Old Man Wilson. He moved out four months ago, all of a sudden, without telling anybody. . . ."

Ernie stared at the object in her hand with a sinking feeling in his gut. "Emma, you don't *know* it's a pacemaker, and even if it is, you don't know whose—"

"And you want to know what he said at the Town Council meeting, three nights before he disappeared? He said he wanted his leaky roof fixed, and told Mayor Dick that his nephew was a producer at *60 Minutes* in New York, and how would Mayor Dick like Mike Wallace crawling up his ass?"

Emma leaned over the basket and started sifting through the contents as Ernie nervously checked his watch. "Emma, that guy's going to be back any minute—"

"Look. A pair of eyeglasses."

She lifted them up to the fluorescent tubes overhead, and Ernie saw that the polycarbonate lenses had been eaten by the bacteria, leaving only the gunmetal-gray frames—small, oval frames that had once been old-fashioned but now were in style again.

"What's wrong?" Emma asked.

Ernie reached out to the stainless steel retaining wall to support himself. "Those glasses. They're Tony Armstrong's glasses. He's had them for years."

"Your friend? The one from DEP?" Emma thought for a moment. "I thought you said he was down in Hendry County. . . . So how did his glasses end up in here? Oh, my God, Ernie! That other friend of yours, the one with the I-love-you ring? He didn't happen to drive a Saab, did he?"

Ernie blinked, stared at the ring, then at Emma. "A gray one. How did you know that?"

Emma took a deep breath. "Because they pulled it from the retention pond out by the Turnpike about a week ago. Everyone just assumed it was another dumb tourist, taking the cloverleaf too fast. . . ."

Ernie pushed down the nausea in his belly, gritted his teeth and pulled himself back to the wire basket, ran his fingers through the gravel and sand and paper clips and the occasional piece of disposal-mangled silverware, and came across a peculiar, T-shaped piece of shiny metal rod.

He held it close to his eyes, turned it over and over—and then he knew what it was.

"What is that?" Emma asked, although her tone made it clear that she didn't really want to know.

"This . . . this is the pin that used to hold together Sub-commander Seis's knee. The one he mangled in Vietnam." He looked up to see her face frozen in disbelief, glanced at his wrist to check his watch. "Come on. We better get out of here before cigarette man comes back."

# eight

### ...

Emma Whipple sat, arms crossed and face glum, at her kitchen table as Ernie kept the phone to his ear, on hold. On the table between them were the pacemaker, the surgical pin, and the eyeglasses frame. Not a one, they had determined already, bore any useful identifying marks. Not a serial number among them.

"Yes?" Ernie said into the receiver. "Right. It would have been in Saigon, I would guess. . . . Oh, I see. . . . Yeah, I was afraid of that. Okay, well, thanks for trying."

He set the phone in its cradle on the wall and sat back down. "I guess you heard."

Emma took a long, deep breath and blew it out. "No records?"

Ernie shook his head. "Nothing. Some pieces they bought ready-made, some they fabricated locally. Either way, they no longer have the documents. I guess I can't blame them. It's been almost forty years. Who could have guessed somebody would need to identify a soldier by a piece of metal put in his knee that long ago?"

"Poor man." Emma shuddered, rubbed her bare arms.

"You think he was already dead? Or that they threw him in . . ."

Ernie lifted the T-shaped bit of metal and examined it for the hundredth time that morning, then stared across the table at Emma. She had dark circles under her eyes, as did he. Neither had slept since they got back from the sewage plant, instead hitting the computer to research as much as they could about Army hospitals, I-love-you rings, pacemakers, and Smythe Optical, a now-defunct eyeglass maker from New Hampshire.

"I don't know," he said after a time.

"But they really did kill him, didn't they?" she persisted.

Ernie nodded wearily. "Yeah. I think they did. And your Mr. Wilson. And my old buddy Bobby King. And Tony Armstrong. And probably those other Underground subcommanders, too. Our only problem's proving it."

"What's so hard about proving that? How else did Homer Wilson's pacemaker end up in the water-treatment vat if he wasn't thrown in?"

Ernie put his hands palm down on the table and sighed. "Okay. Let me play devil's advocate. One, we can't prove it belonged to Homer Wilson without a unique serial number or something like that. Ditto with the ring. Service Merchandise sells a hundred of those a month in Florida alone. No serial numbers. Nothing. Ditto with the glasses. Two, without proving the pacemaker was Mr. Wilson's, we can't prove he's dead, or even that he's not where Dick Gillespie says he is: back in New York somewhere. Three, and this is our biggest problem, guess who has sole jurisdiction to investigate all crimes, including murder, on Whipple property?"

Emma stared blankly out her kitchen window at another perfect Central Florida summer morning. It was, she thought, a perfect crime for the perfect town. Troublemakers, disliked by the company, disappeared by company henchmen, and the only ones who could investigate were company cops. And then they would ask her, the company flack, to put a pretty face on it. She swallowed her disgust and took another deep breath. "And no one in any of the outside police agencies can look into it unless Ferret Albright asks for help. Right?"

"As per the Florida Constitution, 1968 revisions."

Emma nodded. "Okay, so it comes back to the *Advocate*. We need to get this in the newspaper."

Ernie scoffed. "Sure. Let's just take our evidence over there right now. Let our crack photo staff take some pictures of Mr. Wilson's telltale pacemaker."

"Come on, Ernie. You said it yourself: Leahy doesn't care about consumer scams or corruption, but he can't help himself if it's a good murder. Right?"

"Right. A good *murder*," Ernie said. "We can't even prove these people are dead. And even if we *could* prove that they're dead, we don't know who killed them, exactly. We'd need to be able to show who killed these people and why."

Emma bit her lip for a long moment. "All right. You need a smoking gun? Let's go find one. Tonight. After the parks close."

Ernie blinked. "You serious?"

"Lew Peters is a details man with an instinct for profit margin. Everything he does, he does after carefully deciding how to maximize return. With him, nothing is an accident. Harry Spunkmeyer was killed for a reason, and we're going to find out what it was." She sat up straight in her chair. "You with me? Or against me?"

Ernie smiled in admiration. "With you. Although I don't know how we're supposed to get in. Isn't his suite on the top floor of Prince Charming's Palace? I'd heard it was impenetrable."

"You leave that to me."

Hand in hand, Ernie and Emma walked along a dimly lit tunnel, every so often crossing a side tunnel that branched off to the right or left. On the wall next to it would be the name, stenciled in spray paint, of a restaurant or a ride in a particular "land" of the Enchanted Realm. They had dropped underground a short ways after climbing a stone wall to enter the park, from the kitchen of the Olde Time Burger Shoppe on Morty Muskrat Mall, right next door to the Plaza of Presidents.

The tunnels, Emma had explained, were Great-Uncle Waldo's way of allowing all the necessary but unappealing activities of an amusement park—emptying trash cans and restocking soda dispensers—to take place out of sight of the paying guests. Plus, she had conceded, Waldo just plain liked the idea of secret passages. Always had, from the days of reading Hardy Boys adventures in his youth.

They had waited until midnight, well past the time when janitor crews were deployed all around the park to clean rest rooms and mop floors. It gave them the advantage, in all likelihood, of not being seen by anyone else. It gave them the disadvantage, in the event they *were* seen, of having no good explanation to account for themselves, and Ernie thought he could hear his own hammering heart echoing in the narrow, concrete-block passage.

She tugged him down a side tunnel, nearly dark, then up a stone spiral staircase lit every twenty feet or so with bare bulbs tucked into "torches" mounted on the wall. It was right out of some Bela Lugosi horror picture.

"I don't believe this," he said.

"I told you. He was really into secret passageways. Wait till you see the next part." She reached a wide landing and pushed on a concrete block with considerable effort. Slowly, the whole section of wall pivoted open, and they stepped through into a library. She pushed on a floor-to-ceiling bookshelf and the whole thing swung closed.

Ernie shook his head. "Amazing."

"Isn't it? Come on. It's right around the corner."

He followed her across the small room and into the anteroom of an office. The far wall had a series of medieval-shaped arch windows with metal frames. "So we're in Prince Charming's Palace now?"

"Yup. Top floor. From the windows you can see downtown Orlando on a clear day. We're just one key away. . . ." Emma went to a closed door and dug into her pocket, pulled out a key, and only then looked closely at the doorknob. "Uh-oh."

Ernie's heart sank. It had been too easy. The moat around the castle had a functioning drawbridge, which was ceremoniously closed every night just after the fireworks, according to the gee-whiz profile of the bridge-tender that Jack Leahy had ordered up a couple of years back. Emma's tunnel had taken them beneath the moat and up into the Palace without incident, everything going according to plan—right up until her "Uh-oh."

"Uh-oh what?" he asked wearily.

"The lock. He's added a deadbolt, and I have a feeling . . ." She inserted the key into the slot and tried futilely to turn it. "Just as I thought. The skeleton key doesn't work. Darn it all."

Ernie bent to the doorjamb, jiggled the knob, tried shaking the door, but found it wouldn't give even a hair. It was solid oak, costing a thousand dollars, easily, and feeling like it weighed a thousand pounds. "I don't think we're getting past this," he said finally.

"What?" Emma bent to study the lock. "So that's it?"

He fingered the deadbolt slot, then ran his hand down the door all the way to the bottom. "These aren't pickable. That's why burglars don't like them. There are no springs. You need a key or some pretty specialized tools, neither of which we have. It would take a battering ram and five or six huge cops to knock it open. But then he'd figure out pretty easily that someone had broken in." He turned to her and rubbed her shoulders. "Well, we knew it was a long shot. Come on. Let's get out of here."

Emma crossed her arms and set her jaw. "He's not beating us that easily." She glanced around the room, settling on the arched windows, and nodded. "I know. Come look at this."

Ernie moved to the casement-style window and looked. There was a hand crank that opened the window in and out. Emma put her palm on the glass. "Watch." As she pushed, the crank began slowly spinning and the window opened outward into the gloom. "See that?"

He peered out the open window at the narrow ledge that ran the length of the building, then down eight stories into the black moat, then back at Emma. "You're not serious. . . ."

"I most certainly am."

"Have you lost your mind? Emma, that thing's not even a foot wide!"

"It's exactly seven and one quarter inches. And only twelve feet to the first window in Lew Peters's inner office. I know, because I've done it before."

Ernie looked incredulously out the window again, then back at Emma. "*You* did it before? When?"

"When I was ten years old. Don't ask me why, but I got it in my head that I should."

"And what happened?" he asked, shaking his head.

"I got grounded for a month is what happened. Point is, Ernie, I can do it. I'm a pretty good rock climber. I'm not scared of heights. The wall of the castle is nice and rough, plenty of fingerholds. Once I get to the window, all I have to do is get my trusty nail file in the crack and pry it open. Then I'll let you in the door."

He looked down at the moat again and felt his head begin to spin. Quickly he shut his eyes and pulled his head back inside. "Okay. *I'll* do it."

Emma gently stroked his face. "My poor, chivalrous Ernie. My poor, chivalrous, acrophobic Ernie." She slipped the strap of her purse over her head and shoulder so it lay flat against her hip and, before he could stop her, climbed up on the sill and out the window. "See you in a second."

Ernie opened his eyes to find her gone, stuck his head back out the window to see her inching down the ledge and into the night. "Emma!" he hissed, closing his eyes against the height. "Get back here!"

Emma was pressed against the castle wall, moving steadily away. "In another second, I'll be halfway." She took another step, the toes of her black flats pushed against the faux rock wall, then moved her hands one at a time sideways. "See, I'm past halfway now. Now I'm actually closer to the other win—ahhh!"

He snapped his eyes open and his heart nearly stopped. She had caught herself with her elbows, but one leg still dangled down into thin air.

"Emma!"

Slowly she pulled one hand up the rock wall, then the other, ever so carefully lifted the dangling leg upward until bare toes found the ledge, and crept to the front of it. "I'm all right. My shoe slipped. I think it fell down into the moat."

"Emma, *you* almost fell into the moat! Please, please, *pleaaaase* be careful."

Carefully, her body pressed against the wall, she bent her left knee backward until her foot was at hand level, then pulled off the remaining shoe, struggled to find the pocket of her walking shorts.

"For God's sake, Emma, just drop it!"

"Are you kidding? These are Rangonis. From Italy. They cost three hundred and eighty dollars a pair. I'm *not* about to throw another hundred-ninety dollars into that filthy water."

Finally she got the pointy end of the shoe into the pocket and crammed it in. Then she resumed her traverse, one step and one hand at a time. Ernie happened to glance downward, emitted a low moan, and shut his eyes tight again.

She was going to fall, and it would be all his fault. Her life had been fine and dandy until he'd come along with his brilliant ideas. For years he'd wanted to make a heroic comeback in his journalistic career, and had manipulated her into helping him ... manipulated her into falling eighty feet to her death—

The hand on his shoulder about gave him heart failure, and he nearly yelled out as a palm pushed onto his mouth. Emma's palm, he realized with amazement. He turned to see the door to Lew Peters's office standing wide open.

"You coming in or not?" Emma asked.

"You got in!"

"Of course I got in. Weren't you watching?"

The inner office included a credenza, a huge desk, and several oak cabinets. Each was stuffed to the gills with file folders, and Emma and Ernie quickly divided up the search and set to it. Ernie got the desk, which seemed to contain summaries of all of Whipple Corporation's finances.

He paged through balance sheet after balance sheet for the last quarter, quickly understood the reason why Serenity's homeowners were never going to get their roofs repaired or their walls patched. "Wow. You know what the average profit margin for one of the theme parks is? Almost thirty percent. Compared to eleven percent for Serenity. No wonder the greedy bastard keeps cutting corners."

Emma closed one folder, tucked it back into a filing cabinet, and pulled out another. "Back in Uncle Waldo's day, the theme parks turned a seventeen percent profit. That was considered more than enough. You seen anything over there regarding a Project Full House?"

Ernie thought a moment. "Yeah. As a matter of fact, I have. It's something in the works, but the projected profit margin is almost fifty percent, if that makes any sense." He paged backward through the files until he found it. "Here. Assuming an average occupancy rate of seventy percent, the projected profit in the first year is forty-six percent, with capital costs amortized over ten years. After that, the profit margin becomes sixty-two to sixty-seven percent. Does that make any sense?"

Emma pulled a sheet from her folder. "You ever heard of the *Dixie Princess*?"

"Yeah. The biggest Mississippi riverboat every built. I remember reading about it in the *Wall Street Journal*. It was auctioned off a couple of years back. Some Canadian company. Manitoba something, right?"

"Manitoba Metals," Emma said. "A shell company owned by Whipple. Lew Peters bought the *Dixie Princess*, is refurbishing her at the old airship hangar by UPSVIL. And you're never going to guess where he plans to run her: Lake Serenity!"


Ferret Albright strode briskly over the bricked path through the predawn stillness. It was the only time of day he didn't mind being in the Enchanted Realm, when it was completely empty save for one of his occasional deputies on patrol.

Some of his men didn't mind security work in the park during operating hours, but he couldn't for the life of him understand it. Lew Peters had continued Waldo Whipple's dictum that uniformed police not be part of the Whipple "experience," so his officers had to wear the bulky, heavy costumes of Whipple characters for hours on end. Talk about demeaning. What the hell was the point of being a policeman if you couldn't wear a uniform and people weren't afraid of you?

Although, among his more sex-crazed guys, the word was you could pretty much get away with grabbing anything you wanted on a young woman—if you happened to be dressed as Gordon Gopher or Billy Baboon posing with her for a picture.

He personally couldn't see the thrill. What, after all, kind of feel could you cop when your hand was covered in a heavy, furry glove? Did that even count?

It took all kinds to make a world, he decided. Still, he personally was not about to begrudge any man his own pleasure, particularly after the ever-so-successful day he'd had. Finally, it seemed, he had found some decent evidence against Emma Whipple. He personally had arranged and overseen surveillance, and it had proven fruitful.

She had played hooky, staying home the whole day with her new man friend, and *what* a man friend it had turned out to be! He had noticed the *Orlando Advocate* parking decal on the car from across the road, leading him to stroll down a block and get the license number with a pair of binoculars.

The tag had come back to an Ernest Warner, which a computer search had identified as the paper's managing editor and a former investigative reporter. All of which confirmed his suspicions of Ms. Whipple: She had been getting information from the DEP man and passing it along to Warner, who no doubt was preparing some kind of exposé. Soon, he'd lay all this out for Peters, and the old man would be thrilled.

It was only later, after he had abandoned surveillance for the evening with Warner's Mercedes still parked in front of Emma Whipple's house, that it occurred to him that Ernest Warner's initials were also EW, and it was just as likely that Armstrong had been feeding his info directly to Warner. In which case, his suspicion of Emma Whipple had been based on an entirely incorrect supposition.

Well, no matter, he'd told himself. However he'd gotten to Emma Whipple's treachery, he'd surely been correct about it. How else to explain her collusion with a newspaperman—a newspaperman known for his environmental-writing awards?

He thought of a troubling possible answer to that himself as he walked through the Enchanted Realm: that Emma Whipple and Ernest Warner were sharing a purely personal relationship, having nothing to do with Whipple World or its various and sundry warts. The EW on Armstrong's computer might have referred to neither Warner nor Whipple, but to someone else entirely. To this point, he still had not conclusively proven anything.

Ferret Albright brooded about that as he walked, then brushed it aside. Surely Peters would want to be safe rather than sorry, and would authorize the disappearance of Emma Whipple—and possibly Ernest Warner, too.

He turned the corner past the Plaza of Presidents toward FairyLand, glanced up at the moated Prince Charming's Palace as he passed. As usual, every window in the fortress was lighted a soft yellow, another carryover from the rules of Waldo Whipple, who thought the castle looked too menacing at night when it was completely dark. He had heard, though, that one of Lew Peters's bean counters had done the math and figured out how much electricity could be saved if the lights were extinguished at park closing time. It was therefore only a matter of time before Prince Charming's Palace went dark at night.

Not that he cared. As far as he was concerned, the castle served no useful purpose. It had only one "scenic outlook," and that was from behind one of the urinals in the men's bathroom. Sort of a dick-level view, for the truly sick voyeurs among the forty percent or so of the Whipple employees who swung that way.

Presently he was at the entrance to the Good World ride, and he knelt before the little concrete planter in which was hidden his personal favorite peephole and removed from his pocket a pair of gardening shears. He shifted his position to match the line of sight from the peephole and quickly identified the offending fern. He opened the safety catch on the shears and started snipping.

"Lake Serenity is barely six feet deep." Ernie had crawled over to where Emma sat and read over her shoulder. "A boat like the *Dixie Princess* has to draw at least seven, maybe eight."

Emma put a finger in the air, fished for another file. "And I bet that's where Project Deep Water comes in. . . . I know I saw it somewhere. . . . Ah! Here." She pulled it from the drawer, opened the first item in it, a thirty-year-old executive summary from a geologist named Armand Beckwith. "Huh. It looks like this guy was Uncle Waldo's consultant. Look at this: 'The Weechkatuknee Valley has an average elevation of seventeen feet above mean sea level, compared to the twenty-nine-foot elevation of Lake Tohopekaliga to the east. Therein lies the ultimate unsuitability of the Valley as a site for any improvement—'"

She flipped a page: "'— as the current borders of Lake Weechkatuknee are a geological accident. Figure 1 shows the ultimate boundaries of the lake when natural processes open full flow from Lake Toho to Lake Weechkatuknee, creating an ultimate elevation for both lakes of twenty-seven feet above mean sea level.'"

Ernie and Emma stared at each other in silence until finally Emma spoke: "Peters built Serenity someplace he knew full well would eventually be ten feet under water."

"For the purpose of snagging that two-hundred-million federal grant for his sewage-treatment plant," Ernie added. "And when the lake does reach its ultimate height, he's going to run the *Dixie Princess* on it."

"Doing something that returns forty-six cents on the dollar," Emma continued.

Her eyes brightened, and she and Ernie said it together: "A casino."

They sat quietly, thinking about it, and Emma's brow furrowed. "Only, I thought casinos were illegal in Florida."

"They are. In Florida. But Whipple's not Florida, remember? It's basically its own country. The state Constitution even says so. The Central Highlands Improvement District solely determines what's allowable and not allowable on its navigable waters. I'll bet if you could check their minutes, they passed some sort of gaming exemption on Lake Serenity in the past few months."

"Okay, let's assume they did. Is he going to get this gambling boat ready and then just wait for the flow from Lake Toho to open up?" She pointed at Armand Beckwith's report. "It says right here that the natural processes could take upwards of fifty, even a hundred years to complete."

Ernie took the report in his hands, flipped a page, and pointed to a new section: "Unless there's a drought or some other condition that radically lowers the water table." He nodded his head, then began flipping through the Project Deep Water folder until something caught his eye. "Such as, for example, drilling all these new wells," he said, pointing at a piece of paper. "In which case, according to the good Dr. Beckwith, we're looking at a potential catastrophic collapse. . . . Aren't those the words he used? Catastrophic collapse? So we're talking, what, a flash flood putting Serenity under ten feet of water? Depending on the time of day it happens, possibly drowning five thousand residents?"

Emma read that section of Beckwith's report again, then looked around them at the various files they had gone through, then rubbed the goose bumps from her arms. "You have it now, don't you? You have your blockbuster article that even Jack Leahy can't resist: Lew Peters wants to drown Serenity to make billions from a floating casino."

Emma stood at the little photocopier on Lew Peters's credenza, feeding through the pages Ernie handed her. Ernie stood beside her, pulling documents from a particular folder, then replacing them in the same order in that folder before moving on to the next one.

Wordlessly they worked, until finally Ernie had replaced every folder back in the drawer from which it came and Emma had collated her photocopies and stuffed them into a manila envelope they had taken from a supply closet. Carefully they arranged everything back the way they remembered it when they'd come in, then studied the room closely. Outside, the sky was starting to lighten with the dawn.

"We need to get out of here." Ernie's eyes roamed a final time over the framed pictures of himself that Lew Peters kept on his polished mahogany desk. Lew Peters playing golf. Lew Peters at Aspen. Lew Peters at a Republican fund-raiser. They had not touched anything on his desk at all. Or had they? He shook himself from the trance. "Come on. The first shift will be coming to work soon."

"One last look," Emma said. "What's different about how we're leaving this place?"

Ernie shrugged impatiently. "We've taken about two hundred sheets of copy paper from an already open ream in the supply room. That and one envelope. No way is anyone going to notice. That's it. Now let's go."

"We still didn't find any solid proof of them killing Subcommander Seis, or any of the others," she pointed out.

"Doesn't matter. We found out *why* they would want to silence him, and that's far more important. Now I can print that he was warning the *Advocate* about an alarming drop in the water table, and was investigating the sudden appearance of sinkholes in the area when he disappeared. In the next sentence I reveal Lew Peters's secret plans to increase the lake level and build a casino and: Boom! There's the story. Let *them* prove they didn't have anything to do with the disappearances."

Emma nodded, handed Ernie the envelope and, from a pocket of her shorts, her remaining shoe. "Here. I'll meet you in the outer room."

He imagined her on that ledge again and tugged at her arm. "Come on. Let's just go."

She pulled free and pushed him out of Lew Peters's inner office. "After all the trouble we've taken to not leave a trace in here? You think he won't notice that his deadbolt isn't locked? Come on. This is a guy who, every morning, compares our market capitalization to Microsoft's. See if he's caught up to Bill Gates. Now go on."

She pushed him out and closed and bolted the door. Ernie unhappily moved to the window, opening it in time to see Emma emerge onto the ledge, straighten, and slowly push Lew Peters's window shut.

Ernie swallowed hard, forced himself to look down. It was quickly getting lighter, and he could see quite clearly the workings of the drawbridge, the dark water of the moat—and, floating on top, a tiny, black object. Emma's shoe. The hundred-and-ninety-dollar shoe. He wondered if, after they got out of Prince Charming's Palace, he wouldn't be able to retrieve it for her. Sort of prove his masculinity. Okay, so he was scared of heights, but dammit, he *could* get things out of a stupid old moat!

He searched the ground in the vicinity of the Palace for a pole of some sort, looking farther and farther afield—which is how he noticed the cop. Even in the gray predawn light, it was clear the guy was wearing a green sheriff's uniform—and heading straight for the castle.

"Emma!" he whispered hoarsely.

"I'm almost there," she said. "Just a few more steps."

"Emma, it's a cop!"

Emma froze, pushed herself hard against the stone wall. "Are you sure?"

The man was strolling casually, head down, hands in his pocket. He was just passing the Wicked Witch Tea Cups, getting ever closer. No doubt about it now. Definitely a sheriff's uniform. "Positive. He's not looking up, though. Come on, hurry!"

She hesitated, began moving again . . . closer . . . within a couple of feet . . . close enough to touch, when, eighty feet down and not a hundred yards away, the cop glanced up, and Ernie thought he could actually see his eyes get wide as one hand reached down for his gun.

•   •   •

Ferret Albright at first couldn't believe what he was seeing.

Something on Prince Charming's Palace. No, not something: some*one*! He reached to unsnap his holster as he broke into a jog, the gardening shears falling from his pocket and clattering on the brick pathway.

"Freeze! Police!" he shouted, getting the gun up, just in time to see the figure disappear, bare legs pointed skyward, into the window.

He stopped running, blinked, looked again. The window was closed. The castle was locked down tight. The drawbridge was up.

Had he really seen someone? He'd been daydreaming about the woman he'd seen over the weekend, the one with the pretty feet and the oh-so-sexy sandals with the little white beads, when he'd glanced up to see . . . someone on the ledge? A woman? A woman with bare legs? A *naked* woman? He squinted and stared at the window some more, now from directly beneath it.

No. He'd been seeing things. He'd been *wanting* to see the woman in the red sandals, and he'd imagined it. That's all. No big deal. Wouldn't be the first time. He grinned to himself, feeling his pockets for the garden clippers when he recalled he'd heard them fall to the ground. He turned to look back for them—when he did a double take and leaned down over the little stone wall into the moat.

Floating in the water was a woman's shoe. From the looks of it, an expensive one. He craned his neck directly up and looked again at the window where the bare legs had disappeared, then back down at the moat.

Then he reached for his radio and pushed the transmit button: "All units, all units. Signal twenty-four. Secure the Realm. BOLO for Caucasian female. Height approximately five-six, weight approximately one hundred ten. Age unknown. Subject possibly," and he felt his heart skip a beat, "barefoot."

• • •

Arm in arm they strolled, casual as can be, tourist tacky in matching Morty and Mindy Muskrat T-shirts, shorts, visors and flip-flops, skirting the Mongoose Mike section of the parking lot on their way to the service road where they'd left the Mercedes. Just another couple enjoying their honeymoon at Waldo Whipple World, getting in an early-morning walk prior to their all-included breakfast at one of the resort hotels.

"How much farther?" Ernie asked, glancing nervously at the three sheriff's cars staking out the main entrance to the Realm.

They had used one of Uncle Waldo's original tunnels, now fallen into disuse, from Prince Charming's Palace, beneath the Fantastic Raceway and the Backwaters Adventure and up at the west edge of the park, where they'd popped into a boutique long enough to outfit themselves in tourist regalia before hopping the wall.

"Another quarter mile or so," Emma said. "How do you want to do this?"

Ernie thought for a moment. He was exhausted but not sleepy, running on some sort of hi-test adrenaline. His brain was in a tizzy, going through the countless ways to organize what he knew already would be a prizewinner. Every paper in the country, the whole world even, would pick it up. How could they not? It had everything. Greed. Corruption. Murder.

Even a Chamber of Commerce toady like Leahy would have to see that. Even his go-along-to-get-along approach to community journalism would be overcome by a surefire Pulitzer, the paper's very first.

"I'll drop you off at your place, then I'll go home and sit in front of my computer until it's done. I'll bet by now Leahy is so freaked out about where my puff piece is, he's commissioned somebody else to call up my notes from the system to slap together something for tomorrow's paper, just in case."

Emma nodded, then frowned. "That deputy who saw us. You think anything will come of it?"

"I don't see how it could. First off, won't they assume we had something to do with that top-of-the-Realm thing you told me about?"

"Top of the World Club, yeah. Probably." She frowned again. "But what if they don't?"

Ernie shrugged. "If they don't, well, so what? What can they prove? We didn't take anything from his office. We even wiped up our fingerprints. If they want to get totally paranoid with hair and fiber specialists, well, the story will be out by then."

"And you're sure Leahy will print it?"

"Well . . . actually, no," Ernie allowed. "I'd like to think so. I'd like to think that deep down, *way* down, Leahy's still a newsman. But what I'll do is this: I'll tell him that if he doesn't run it, I personally will sell it to the *St. Petersburg Times* and the *Miami Herald* in time for tomorrow's editions. I think maybe once he understands that one way or another the story is definitely going to see the light of day, Leahy might decide that he may as well have it first."

They approached the Mercedes and Ernie pushed a button on his key ring to pop the door locks. He put the shopping bag full of his clothes and the purloined envelope in the trunk, then opened the passenger door for Emma.

"How's your knee?" he asked, nodding at the blood-smeared scrape she'd acquired when Ernie had yanked her through the window and onto the floor.

She bent to examine it, poked it tenderly with a finger, and stood. "I'll live." She nestled closer to him and put her arms around his neck. "You think you could kiss it and make it better?"

The idea bounced around his brain for a few long seconds, gathering steam . . . and then he shook himself out of it, moaning softly. "Emma, you don't know how tempting that sounds, as tired as I am—"

Emma kissed him quickly and slid into the car. "I'm

sorry I even mentioned it. You need to write this. Besides, I need to go into the office, too. There's supposedly some rumor that Mayor Dick had a sex-change operation that needs to be quashed." She saw Ernie's raised eyebrows and shrugged. "I don't know. Frankly? I'm pretty sure I don't want to either."

And then she closed her eyes for the short ride back to Serenity.

Ferret Albright followed briskly behind his boss, the proper two paces back and one to the right as they moved down the long corridor toward Lew Peters's suite. He had just finished explaining that morning's incident about the Palace interloper, massaging a few details here and there, such as how she'd managed to escape . . . and what, exactly, Albright had been doing in the park at that hour in the first place.

He had also boiled down to as clinical a description as he could manage an image that had been burned indelibly into his mind: long legs, tipped with a pair of gorgeous feet, flying, toes pointed, in through the window of Peters's outer office.

Actually, the prurient value of what he had seen notwithstanding, the incident had become a damned nuisance. Because it involved his suite, Peters had insisted on a full investigation—forcing Ferret Albright to pull valuable manpower away from the probe that he really wanted to move on: the Emma Whipple/Ernest Warner link. He had planned dual surveillance, perhaps a wiretap or two, with the idea of going to Peters by the end of the day, asking his permission to bring Ms. Whipple in for a little questioning. Instead he was wasting his time with common trespassers.

"So your conclusion is that your perpetrator, or your perp, as you people like to call them, is a Whipple Corporation employee trying, despite our prohibitions, to gain membership to the Top of the World Club." Lew Peters read Albright's report as he walked, flipping pages. "Was she climbing down from the roof?"

Albright realized suddenly that Peters was speaking to him. "Sir?"

Lew Peters stopped and turned, slapped Albright's chest with the slim folder. "Let me try again, in English: Did you see her climbing down from the roof?" He read the confusion on his security chief's face. "The roof. Of the castle. That *is* the location of the tryst that qualifies for membership, is it not? I ask because I'm curious as to how you're so certain she's a sex fiend, as opposed to, say, a spy from Sea World or Universal trying to sneak a look at our expansion plans. If she was climbing down from the roof, that would indicate to me she was indeed a Top of the World devotee."

Albright stumbled over that last word, ultimately decided it didn't matter what it meant. The more important consideration: *Had* she been climbing down from the roof? He couldn't honestly recall. He only remembered her being on the ledge. That and being barefoot. But if he admitted he didn't know, Peters would blow a gasket, and in the process lose the confidence Albright was counting on to get the go-ahead for action on the Emma Whipple problem.

"Yes," he said finally.

Lew Peters grunted. "But you didn't see her companion. So there's no way of telling whether she was gay or straight."

Albright blinked. He hadn't even thought of that. What if she *was* a lesbian? What would that make *him,* lusting after her feet?

"Not that it matters. Gay or straight, this exhibitionist shit has got to end. If they get away with it on top of Prince Charming's Palace, next thing you know they'll be doing it on the Kilimanjaro Plunge. And what would Uncle Bob and Aunt Ethel from Rapid City say about that?" He handed Albright's report back to him. "You said you might have one useful clue, yes?"

The shoe! Ferret Albright thought with growing excitement. An expensive Italian flat made of supple calfskin, hand stitched and oiled. It was just sitting there on his desk, waiting for his ministrations.

Albright affected a bored shrug. "She dropped it when she saw me."

"Good. I trust you will use your—how shall I put it—*special* expertise in those matters to track her down, as well as her lover, whatever the gender. Then fire them both. Make it a big, hairy deal among the cast. Make it clear this Top of the World nonsense is finished. Got it?"

Albright nodded and turned as Lew Peters pulled his key chain from a pocket and unlocked the door to his inner office.

"Just a minute," Peters said, sniffing the air.

Albright turned back toward his boss, who paused, blinked, looked closely at the door, then walked slowly to his desk, studying walls, desktop . . .

"Sir?" Albright asked.

Peters shook his head, sat in his chair, breathed deeply. "I smell . . . I smell shampoo. Not mine, not my secretary's. It's a woman's shampoo." He glanced down at his drawers, opened them, began going through his files as Albright watched silently from the doorway. "It looks the same. . . . And still I get the sense somebody's been through here. . . ."

Peters shut the drawer, let his eyes wander the room again, finally settled on the copy machine atop the credenza.

Albright edged into the room, squinting with curiosity as Peters walked to his copier, opened a side panel, and flipped open the top of the machine, revealing a tiny counter tucked beside the toner cartridge. Peters read the figure, pulled open a drawer in the credenza, and removed a small notebook. He blew out a low hiss through his teeth.

"Top of the World Club, eh, Mr. Sheriff? Just a couple of horny employees?" He closed the panel on the copy machine and turned toward Albright with arms crossed. "This woman. Find her. Recycle her. She will have with her, or will have knowledge as to the whereabouts of, one hundred and ninety-seven photocopies. Find them, and recycle them as well. Understood?"

Albright blinked, suddenly realizing the import of it all, and nodded.

"Today, Mr. Sheriff. This minute. I want this at the top of your agenda until it is completed. I want progress reports hourly. Now, get a move on."

Albright stood ramrod straight, snapped off a salute, and turned on his heels for the door.

Lenny Fizzogli gazed with pride at the lump of iron creating the deep depression in his mattress. Three feet long, a solid fifteen inches in diameter. The biggest damn pipe bomb the Internet—the whole world, for that matter—had ever seen.

The problem last time around, he had decided, was a lack of *oomph*. Standard-size pipe, standard, run-of-the-mill dynamite, standard bomb. Enough to blow up a bus station bathroom or maybe a car, but certainly not enough for any real landscaping.

That's when the first part of his brainstorm had struck: use large-bore, well-water pipe instead of the regular, household PVC. Why not? The wider the pipe, the more explosive would fit in it, the bigger, the more powerful the blast. He had plenty left over from the earlier phases of his project, along with end caps that screwed on for a nice, watertight fit.

He had just started loading it up with gunpowder when Brainstorm Part II hit: If gunpowder could make a moderate-to-powerful bomb, what would some *real* explosive do?

A nightlong search of the Internet had been pretty productive, with lots of stuff about Semtex and C4 and the inevitable, cheaper knockoffs out there, along with tables about blast energy and storage and handling hints. The only thing missing had been any really useful information about *where* somebody with a need for such material could acquire it.

Which was when the third and final phase of his brainstorm had come: Why not find somebody, right at Waldo Whipple World, with firsthand experience?

With that goal in mind he'd headed off for UPSVIL, only to discover that Libya did not sponsor a pavilion. Nor did Hezbollah. He had stalked the International Pavilion Parade until a recent news blurb he had seen connected with the exhibit in front of his eyes: the Basque region of Spain. Sure enough, the fellow manning the booth had referred him to the stockroom, where a shepherd on a work visa from Bilbao had happily called home to get him what he needed for the price of a phone card and a fifty-dollar commission.

And thus before him now was his masterpiece: a dull, rust-brown color, and backbreakingly heavy, to be sure, but a masterpiece nonetheless. He had gone back through Dr. Armand Beckwith's treatise and had determined the exact point where his device would be most effective, as well. A shallow pool five miles north of Golf, U.S.A., just adjacent to the spring that widened to become the main branch of the Upper Serenity River.

It had been Armand Beckwith's hypothesis that it was just upslope of that little pool where the waters of the Lake Tohopekaliga basin trickled through to feed the Serenity system. Eventually, after the inevitable processes of erosion through the decades, that trickle would naturally become a torrent until the water levels between the two bodies had equalized.

And that was where Lenny Fizzogli and his Water Level Equalizing Device came in. He thought with a grin: Afterward, he ought to market his invention, maybe even to the Army Corps and big land developers. Call it the Fizzogli WLED, Mark II. True, it wasn't really a second-generation model, but what the hell. Mark II just sounded so cool.

Now, if only he could think of a way to get it where it needed to be without getting a hernia. Getting it out of the truck and into the water wouldn't be that hard. He could manage that by himself, but getting it out of the dorm, out into the parking lot, and then up into the bed of the truck, that was going to be a ball-breaker.

He scowled in silence for a moment, finally became aware of the *tha-thump, tha-thump* reverberating through the walls. It was his gay housemates, blasting their Euro-fag music already, and it wasn't even noon. He blinked and brightened. His gay housemates! Of course! Half were queens, but the other half would *die* to show off their muscles!

Lenny Fizzogli opened his door, stepped into the hall and cupped his hands around his mouth: "I bet not *one* of you homos can dead-lift two hundred pounds!"

With a final furtive glance back at the last green, Earl Zimmacker cast his eyes downward at the tee and started the slow process of lining up his club.

"So we're set for tomorrow?" he murmured. "Nueve?"

Walt Littlefield, seventh-grade Language Arts Learning Leader and junior varsity baseball coach at the Serenity Integrated Learning Academy, kept a casual watch down the thirteenth fairway—north, his assigned direction. They had played half the round in silence, watching for lurking spies, checking the benches and flags and cups of the Town Course for listening devices. Finally, on the back nine, Zero had decided they could safely confer.

"The pitching machine is at my house," Nueve reported. "We're moving it down to the boat tonight."

"And the eggs?"

Nueve kept his eyes peeled to the north, whispered over his shoulder. "Got half of 'em filled. We'll do the other half early tomorrow morning."

Zero bent to remove and reinsert his tee into the grass. "Red and black?" He had read somewhere that those were the most popular revolutionary colors. "We should have red and black."

"We ran out of black," Nueve reported. "We're doing the rest in blue."

Zero frowned. "Red and blue? I don't know—"

"It's a midnight blue. Almost black."

Zero grunted and whacked the ball down the fairway, then traded places with Cuatro at the east side of the tee. "All right. Midnight blue. I guess it's only a diversion, anyway. The exact colors don't matter that much. What about the cover?"

Cuatro bent to tee up his Titleist. "It's done. Fresh tank of propane for the grill, all set up on the bow. You think two thousand dogs will be enough?"

Zero thought about it a moment. "Crowd should start gathering by oh-nine-hundred, we're set for ten-fifteen. Yeah. Two thousand ought to be more than enough. What kind did you get?"

"Ball Parks," Cuatro said unhappily. "But I had to. Any other brand, and we'd have gotten hassled for sure by the gendarmes."

Zero nodded agreement and turned to the man watching south, Veintiuno his most trusted remaining lieutenant. "Entry team?"

Veintiuno kept an unblinking eye back toward the twelfth green. Veintiuno was the youngest of the Underground members and, as a veteran of Army Special Forces training, was a natural for the key role in Zero's new, more aggressive J25 Mark II. "Entry team is set."

"You found someone with TV know-how?" Zero asked.

"My neighbor. Used to be a producer for a UHF station in Kansas. He says he can handle it."

Zero mulled that over for a minute. "You're sure he's safe? He's not a Whipple informant in disguise?" Ernie Warner's call explaining his find at the sewer plant had at first rattled him, then made him all the more determined and all the more cautious. "We can't be taking any chances."

Veintiuno squinted at an old man in a tam-o'-shanter bending over a putt on the green behind them. "With all due respect, Zero, if we didn't want to take any chances, we'd still be sitting on our couches admiring our latest ceramic Billy Baboon. This guy's plumbing leaked. It washed away the plaster in his ceiling and rotted the wood floor. Now you can see up from his kitchen into his upstairs bathroom. Don't you worry, he's with us a hundred percent."

Zero nodded once more and led his foursome to the golf cart. "Point well taken, Veintiuno, point well taken. Tell him, if he wants, he can tentatively be number Veinticinco, until we can ratify him at the next meeting. All right, it looks like we're as set as we're going to be. I don't have to tell you fellas what's at stake here. If we pull this off, we get all the attention we could ask for. If something goes wrong, there's a real chance we get returned to the food chain pronto, if Ernie Warner's correct."

They rode in silence down the fairway for a while, until Zero asked: "Should we head on back? Or keep playing?"

Veintiuno put a hand on Zero's shoulder. "That old guy playing behind us. I've never seen him before. We better keep going, in case he's watching us."

Zero murmured assent, stopped the cart, and the subcommanders piled out to find their balls.

With the black Rangoni on his desk, Ferret Albright flipped pages through the fifth and final volume of his photo album, carefully looking for a match. Each photo had a time and date stamp, which, when cross-referenced to credit-card receipts from admission tickets, could at least give him a starting point.

But despite all the high heels, leather sandals, plastic flip-flops, wedges, slides—a veritable parade of footwear and female feet in his personal collection—he had not one photo of a pair of black flats. He knew it ought not surprise him. He took pictures of sexy shoes, not practical shoes, no matter how stylish.

He got to the last photo on the last page, the pair of feet in the red sandals with the white beads, and Ferret Albright made a slight cooing noise before he shut the album and turned his attention to the shoe on his desk. Silently, he once more admired the classic lines. The way the upper was cut, there was obviously a good deal of cleavage visible between big toe and second toe, perhaps even between second toe and third toe.

He was already warmed up from the photo album, and the thought got him going again, and with a glance at the closed door leading to his outer office, he pushed the shoe to his face and inhaled deeply. With eyes pressed shut he savored the aromas that mingled in his nostrils: the most recent, musky tang of moat water. The still-present odor of newly tanned leather. And, in between, the delicious sweat from a beautiful woman's foot. Not just any beautiful woman, he reminded himself, but an industrial spy with the audacity to climb along a narrow ledge to gain access to secret documents. Oh, how he was going to love that interrogation. . . .

With an effort, he put the thought out of his head, stood with the shoe in one hand and his most recent catalog of high-end Italian imports for the mass market in the other, and headed down the corridor toward the crime lab.

He couldn't help smiling. Lew Peters wanted the documents back. All hundred and however many pages of them. Well, how was he possibly going to manage something like that? *Surely* he would need the woman's cooperation, maybe a few hours in his interview room. Or maybe a few days, sitting there, chained to his wall, without any shoes or socks.

Once more he found his pulse racing, and he took a deep breath to calm himself as he turned the knob to the Data Analysis Unit. He nodded to the pimple-faced geek at the keyboard of a big, twenty-one-inch monitor, who quickly clicked the mouse to make the giant image of a nude lesbian poolside orgy disappear.

Ferret Albright rolled his eyes and set the catalog on the table. "I need you to call up one of the credit-card databases."

The kid typed a few keystrokes and sat up expectantly. "What are we looking for?"

Ferret Albright studied the shoe a final time, inside and out, allowed himself to enjoy the scent without being too obvious about it. "Call up all purchases of a Rangoni Oste in the last, say, eighteen months, in a hundred-mile radius of Orlando. Size seven and a half, medium. Color: black."

The tech typed, clicked, typed a little more, and then waited. Finally the screen went blank and then came up with a neat table, sorted by date. "Two hundred seventy-three hits."

Ferret Albright squinted at the screen, scowled. "How about if you cross-reference that with Whipple employees?"

The kid nodded, typed and clicked a little bit, and sat back to wait. This time the screen was blank barely a second before coming back. "Four hits."

Albright scanned the names: Gilbart, Marsha; Hooper, Lynn; Norton, Helena; Whipple, Emerson.

Albright blinked, and blinked again before rereading the screen. Then he broke into an open-mouthed grin.

He'd been right! He'd been right all along! Son of a bitch. . . . Which meant, he realized with a frown, that she and her boyfriend must have left her house barely minutes after he abandoned his surveillance. *Damn* it all! He could have caught her red-handed, in the act. But how could he possibly have known they were about to sneak into the park after midnight and break into the boss's office? The lights in her house had been out for hours. . . .

Well, no matter.

He had her now. Now he'd have a complete package of information to use in his interrogation session. And a real Whipple, no less. A thrill shot through him; it would be like having a shot at real royalty—real royalty with gorgeous feet, to boot!

He picked up his catalog and shoe and headed for the door. "That's all I needed. You can get back to your porn now."

# nine

...

His eyes shut, his head back on the fluffy down pillow on Jack Leahy's silk-upholstered sofa, Ernie Warner felt himself drifting between semiconsciousness and an oh-so-tempting deep sleep.

All day he had sat at his home computer, stacks of the pilfered Whipple documents spread around him, his hand-lettered timeline propped up at the base of the monitor, and typed. In a zone he hadn't experienced in years, he had felt verbs and supporting facts and transitions flow from his fingertips, through the plastic keys, and onto the screen. Word after word, inch after inch, hour after hour, he had worked, until, finally, he had glanced up, realized it was past nine o'clock and that he was starving.

It was only as he reread what he'd written, munching on a cold-cut sandwich, that he saw with a sense of awe what he had done. A full eighty column inches, enough to fill three quarters of an entire broadsheet page with type, and every bit of it a gem. Quickly he had run it through spellcheck before calling his boss at home and telling him that he had good news and bad news. The bad news was that they had to tear up the front page for the next day. The good news was that they finally had an honest-to-God contender for the Big Prize. The one that started with a P.

He had driven the six blocks to Leahy's house, handed him a printout of the story and the packet of photocopies, and then had collapsed on the living room couch.

"This is quite a yarn."

Ernie half opened his eyes. A five-bladed fan, suspended from the cathedral ceiling from a long pole, spun silently overhead. Each blade was made of teak and looked recently oiled. The hardwood floor was polished to a sheen, and the throw rug in front of the hearth looked like a real oriental. He had to give Leahy credit: He had married a woman with taste.

"Thanks," Ernie said finally, and rolled his head to watch gas-fed flames leap behind the glass fireplace screen. "Jack, I can't help but notice you have a fire going *and* the air-conditioning on full blast."

"Lynda says it's foolish to have a fireplace in Florida if it doesn't get used." Leahy flipped the last page and set the stapled packet on the end table beside his recliner. "That story really is something."

"Thanks," Ernie repeated, then squinted suspiciously at his boss. "You're not thinking of cutting it, are you? I mean, I know twenty-five hundred words is on the long side, but it's an important story, wouldn't you agree? Remember, by way of comparison, when Whipple announced their Colossal Canyon ride? We gave them three quarters of the front page, and that was a damned *leak,* for Christ's sake!"

Jack Leahy made a steeple of his fingertips. "Now, Ernie, there's no need for profanity. I, uh . . . Just when were you hoping to run this piece?"

Ernie blinked and sat up. "Tomorrow! We yank the fluff piece and replace it with this. Insofar as this is *news* and we are still technically a *news*paper, right?"

Jack Leahy gathered up the packet, began reading it anew from the top as he walked his living room floor.

"You, uh, happen to see what happened with our stock today?"

Ernie groaned, let himself fall back into the couch. "No. Pray tell what? Jack, listen: I know we haven't done this kind of story in a while, and you might be a little worried about it. But you're going to have to trust me. It's *there*. This stuff is authen—"

"Schylle stock closed up seventeen and three-eighths, almost twenty percent, on a rumor that the company is the target of a takeover."

"Authentic," Ernie continued. "Every bit of it. Think of it: *Whipple* literally sinking America's Utopia of Yesterday so it can get into casino *gambling*! Using the home-rule authority our pinhead legislators gave them! On top of all that, we've got evidence of several extremely suspicious deaths. Murders, to be blunt about it, including those of two personal friends of mine." He raised a hand to quell the inevitable protest. "Now, I know what you're about to say: A pair of eyeglass frames and a metal pin do not a murder prove. Fair enough. But a pacemaker? Come on, Jack. That's not the sort of thing you take out on your own to put in new batteries, is it? The sort of thing that could accidentally fall into the toilet on you. Not to mention that cockamamie drilling they're doing, and the hundreds, even *thousands* of people who could potentially drown in a flash flood, if Lake Toho breaks loose in the middle of the n—"

"Aren't you at all curious about the purchaser of Schylle Incorporated? About who your new employer is?"

Ernie fell silent, finally making sense of the words his boss had been uttering. Slowly he felt the room start to sway as his stomach shrank into a hard ball.

"Word is the offer Monday is going to be one hundred and thirty dollars a share. A hundred and thirty, Ernie. This is something that benefits all of us, everyone at the *Advocate* who participates in the stock program. You, for instance. You have what, nine thousand? Ten thousand shares? That works out to a cool three hundred grand profit. Now think: What could you do with a spare three hundred K?"

Jack Leahy fingered the stack of paper in his hand nervously, licking his lips. Right then, Ernie knew.

"Oh, my God, Jack. . . . You guys sold us to Whipple Corporation, didn't you?" Suddenly he recalled the memo he'd glossed over in one of Peters's folders, one labeled "Project Megaphone," about increasing Whipple's presence in the print media. "Jack, how could you? How the hell can we even pretend to be an independent voice if we're owned by Central Florida's biggest employer?"

Jack Leahy put on his best Chamber of Commerce grin. "Oh, we'll remain plenty independent. Don't you worry about that. It'll just mean that, in certain areas, we might have to be a little more sensitive—"

Ernie buried his head in his hands. "You're not going to run it, are you?"

Jack Leahy said nothing for a while, shaking his head, then tapped at the top page of Ernie's story. "Look at it from my point of view, Ernie. As of Monday, I'll be a full vice president of Whipple Corp." He chuckled weakly. "Now, you must admit, printing something like this— well, it's hardly the sort of first impression you want to make with a new boss."

"Okay, fine." Ernie sat up straight with a deep breath. "Give it to me. I'll sell it to the AP or the *New York Times.* In fact, I'll *give* it to the AP and the *Times.* It's that important."

Leahy chuckled again. "Ernie, it's not like you're a freelancer. This was researched and written on *Advocate* time—"

"I quit," Ernie said, for a moment startling himself but then feeling a strange exhilaration. "There, I said it. I should have said it years ago, I think. I quit. I quit, in fact, as of two weeks ago. I'll send back last week's paycheck. Now give me back my story."

Jack Leahy stared at his star writer for a long moment, then glanced down at the packet. "Before I can do that, I need to ask: The documentation upon which this is based. It was divulged freely by Whipple Corporation?"

Ernie blinked, openmouthed, and then realized where Leahy was heading. "I got it from a Whipple employee, Jack. Now give it all back."

Leahy began strolling back across the floor. "This employee. He . . . or *she*," he looked up wryly for a second, "he or she had full access to these records? Or did he or she obtain them in an unauthorized manner?"

For just a second Ernie considered a wisecrack. That yes, Lew Peters had in fact given Emma permission to break into his office from a six-inch-wide ledge outside an eighty-foot-high window. He bit back the temptation and reached his hand out. "The documents are authentic, Jack. The documents speak for themselves. That's always been the litmus test in journalism when the public interest is involved. Look at the Pentagon Papers. Those were stolen. The *Times* printed them anyway."

Jack Leahy pursed his lips and nodded, continued walking away from Ernie. "True. But on the other hand, *Times* editors weren't in the direct employ of the Defense Department, were they?" He kept walking until he was in front of the hearth. "I, in contrast, am a senior executive for the corporation from whom this property was illegally taken. It is therefore my responsibility to my supervisor and my fiduciary responsibility to the shareholders—"

Ernie finally realized that Jack's right hand was opening the glass fireplace screen. With a yell, he dove across the room, grabbing Leahy around the neck and dragging him down onto the oriental.

"Ernie, take your hands off me this minute."

"Give me my fucking story, Jack."

They wrestled for a time on the rug, Ernie grabbing hold of the clipped packet of papers, losing them, grabbing them back, fending off Leahy's hands, until finally, in desperation, he wound back an arm and let loose a punch. It connected with Jack Leahy's jaw, and the older man lay on the rug, stunned.

Immediately Ernie backed off. "Oh, Jack, I'm *so* sorry! I didn't mean—"

"Mister, boy will you ever regret that. You may consider yourself fired, effective immediately. If you ever show up on *Advocate* property again, I'll have you arrested. Now, that packet of papers in your hands is Whipple property, and I demand that you turn it over this instant!"

Ernie stood, papers in hand, and the finality of what had happened sank in. He had flat-out told his boss no to a direct order. Had wrestled with him over it. Had slugged him, in fact. There would be no going back and editing away his transgressions.

Yet the more he thought about it, the better he felt. He had the story of a lifetime in his hands, and neither Jack Leahy nor anybody else could stop him. He blinked and realized that Jack Leahy was still berating him.

"You hear me, Ernie? Don't think for a minute our former friendship is going to get you out of this. I always knew you were a swell-headed prima donna. Mr. Fancy-Pants *Pulitzer Finalist*. Think the sun doesn't rise in the east unless you write about it. Well, are you ever in for a lesson, Buster Brown." He snorted, his prone body convulsing in laughter. "Huh! Mr. *Pulitzer Finalist* thought he didn't like Schylle's bean counters? Wait till Whipple takes over. Lew Peters is going to make Chicago look like a charity—hey, where do you think you're going? Ernie! I'm going to count to three, and by the time I get to two, I expect to see those documents in my hands. One . . ."

"No." Ernie said, and opened the front door.

"Two . . ."

The freedom coursed through him, filled his lungs. He felt empowered, in command. He decided he liked it, then turned back to face his former boss. Jack Leahy still lay on the rug, as if to preserve the evidence of his ex-employee's insubordination.

"Ernie, darn it, enough's enough. Now, I know you're upset. I can see how things got out of hand. I know you must be feeling terrible about hitting me, and—"

The laugh just bubbled out of him, and Ernie made no attempt to stop it. "As a matter of fact, Jack? I don't feel terrible at all. I feel pretty damn good, in fact." He reached into his pocket for the keys to the Mercedes. "In fact, remember when you made me write that stupid, blow-job feature about that new mall? Seminole Town Centre? Centre with an R-E? Let's just say we're even."

Jack Leahy scrambled up and over to the door in time to see Ernie start his engine and pull away from the curb. He took several deep breaths, then went to his study to find Lew Peters's home phone number.

Emma Whipple was brushing her hair when the car pulled up in front of her house, and she knew immediately it was Ernie.

She smiled to herself, checked her lipstick in the mirror, fluffed her hair, and headed for the staircase. He had said it would be at least eleven o'clock before he finished the always-grueling editing process with his boss, and sure enough, eleven-fifteen it was.

All day she'd swung from boundless euphoria over what was about to happen to an enervating dread. Within twelve hours, first Orlando, then the whole planet would know what a fraud the company that bore her family name had become, a prospect that brought both relief and shame. More than once she'd wondered if there wasn't another way, of perhaps taking what they'd found privately to Lew Peters, quietly forcing his departure.

And then she would remember the gruesome artifacts from the sewer plant and their only possible explanation, and a cold shudder would run up her spine. True, the eyeglasses proved little. But the surgical pin and the pace-maker? Someone at Serenity was taking image conscious-ness to unthinkable extremes, and it required a suspension of disbelief to think Whipple senior management could be wholly ignorant of what was going on.

Well, either way, there was no turning back now. Once the media had something, it was pointless trying to get it back. It was done, and she was glad for it, not least be-cause of the sense of purpose it had seemed to bring back to Ernie.

Ernie.

Such a funny name, really. *Ernie*. Although, she sup-posed, it was no funnier than *Emma*. Who would have guessed a month ago? Of course, who would have guessed a month ago that she would crawl along the top-story ledge of Prince Charming's Palace to snoop around in Lew Peters's office?

She smiled again as she closed off a messy guest bed-room and started down the staircase. No one could have guessed, least of all her. And tomorrow morning, it would all be out, and she and Ernie could begin a normal dating life like any normal couple.

"Coming!" she called as the doorbell rang. Instinc-tively her hands went to tie off the thin cotton robe she wore over her shorty silk nightgown . . . and then she de-cided: No, I *want* this to be the first thing he sees when I open the door.

She twisted the deadbolt, turned the knob—and the smile froze on her face.

"Good evening, Miss Whipple. We hope we're not in-truding."

It was a glowering Lew Peters, and behind his shoul-ders a leering Ferret Albright. Emma recovered, quickly wrapped the robe tightly about her and knotted it. "What do you want?" she asked coolly.

From the pocket of his sport coat, Lew Peters removed

a woman's shoe. A Rangoni, she saw at once. Her Rangoni. He held it before his eyes, a prize specimen.

"We were wondering. Would you mind, terribly, trying this on for us?"

Emma decided her best chance was to bluff, and bluff loud: "*Excuse* me? Have you *lost* your minds?"

Lew Peters grinned, barely lifting the corners of his thin mouth. He offered the shoe again. "May we? Look. If it doesn't fit, we'll apologize and be on our way. In the words of a famous American, if the shoe does not fit, we must acquit."

Emma held her ground in the doorway, gauging the look on Lew Peters's face. She decided to bluff even louder. "Okay. I've heard about enough. Get the fuck off my property, sir. This is still America, you know, even in Serenity." His face did not flinch even the slightest. "Okay, that's it. I'm shutting the door and calling the cops."

"No need," Lew Peters said, pushing the door open against Emma's weight. "I brought one with me. Sheriff? Detain her, please."

Emma struggled but to no avail, as the heavier and stronger Ferret Albright held her down, duct-taped her mouth closed and her hands behind her back, then threw her over his shoulder in a fireman's carry up the stairs and onto the landing.

Lew Peters scouted out the rooms, opened a door, and looked in disapprovingly. "After the attention to detail we give to your home, this is how you repay us? Upstairs, room two of the Tidewater is *supposed* to be a sewing room or a study. Not a guest bedroom. If you wanted a guest bedroom, you had the opportunity to buy one of the other models. Suggested floor plans are drawn for a reason, Miss Whipple."

He shut the door and led Albright into the master bedroom, where he pulled a chair out in front of the bed and motioned him to put her in it. Then he kneeled down with shoe in hand and grabbed her ankle. Emma watched in disbelief as Lew Peters slid her right foot into the Rangoni while, beside her, Ferret Albright looked on with envy.

"Well, well, well. It appears we've found our Cinderella, after all. Good detective work, Sheriff."

Albright puffed with pride. "I bet I can find that other shoe, Mr. Peters. At three hundred and seventy-four dollars a pair, I'll bet she hung on to it."

Lew Peters nodded, and Albright disappeared into her walk-in closet. Peters stood and crossed his arms. "By the way, I'm missing one hundred and ninety-seven pages of proprietary documents. You don't happen to know where I might find them, do you?"

Emma squirmed against her bonds, made a complaining noise in her throat until Lew Peters smiled and pulled the duct tape off her mouth.

"Sorry. Forgot. Now, then—those hundred and ninety-seven pages?"

She wiggled her jaw, considered screaming, decided against it. As thin as the walls were, she was unlikely to attract anyone's attention before Albright gagged her again. She decided to continue the bluff strategy: "I don't know what the fuck you guys are talking about!" she said.

Peters *tsk*ed softly. "Such language. Is that any way for Cinderella to speak to her Prince Charming?"

"Found it!" Ferret Albright announced from the closet entrance.

Sure enough, he had found the matching Rangoni, the one that hadn't fallen into the moat. Both she and Lew Peters stared at it, then at each other.

"Huh," Peters said after a time. "Then I suppose the reason you were out on that ledge was to . . . climb to the roof and join the Top of the World Club? Miss Whipple! I *am* appalled. You know the company has strictly forbidden that organization." He grinned at her, then clapped his hands. "Okay. Enough. Where are my goddamned papers?"

She stared at him in silent defiance, until Ferret Albright piped up from behind them. "Should I, uh, persuade her to talk?"

Lew Peters studied her with narrowed eyes. "Let's just take her to the Reuse Center, perhaps give her a little demonstration. . . . Maybe that'll loosen her tongue a tad."

Emma's eyes widened, first with shock that her and Ernie's suspicions of murder were correct, then with amazement that Lew Peters personally was behind it— and finally with the terrible realization that they planned to do her in the same way.

Ferret Albright stepped forward, the matching Rangoni in hand. "You want I should put her other shoe on?"

Lew Peters glanced at him, saw his fixation with Emma's remaining bare foot, and sighed. "By all means."

Ferret Albright sat at Emma's feet, lovingly took her heel in hand—and noticed something beneath her bed. He bent forward, blinked, and withdrew a pair of strappy red sandals with hard white beads running over the top. Ferret Albright stared at them silently, reverently, then at Emma's feet, then at the sandals again, until, feverishly, he yanked the Rangonis off and started strapping on the sandals.

Emma watched him with growing revulsion, then looked up at Lew Peters. He shook his head sadly and offered a shrug. "So my security chief is a foot fondler. What can I say?"

With ever-increasing crankiness, Snoball and Igloo dove off the bench at the hinged door in the hockey rink's penalty box, climbed back onto the bench, and with high-pitched squeals, dove off yet again.

They had already tried climbing the high Plexiglas walls, but to no avail. Their claws simply couldn't get a grip on the stuff, and they would fall down with moans of

frustration and anger. The door, they vaguely remembered, was how they'd entered their new enclosure, not
long after the human had pointed a long stick at them and
they suddenly had become so drowsy.

It had been many days since they'd had a decent
meal—about two-thirds of their late trainer—back when
they were still in their regular cave. Since they'd been
moved to the new cave, they'd had nothing. Well, Igloo
had finally eaten the hot dog they'd been playing with a
day or so ago, but other than that, nothing, and they were
ravenous. Thirsty, too. They had long ago finished the
bowls of water that had been left for them, and since then
had not seen a single human. Not since all the commotion
that started when they'd taken the hot dog from that one
pink one who'd been lying on the ice.

Snoball stopped diving for a moment and, with hind
legs on the bench, stretched across the gap to put his front
paws on the top of the ledge from where the Plexiglas rose
another four feet. Through the now scratched panel he
could see ice. He could certainly smell it, and his parched
lips smacked at the thought of sticking his snout down and
lapping up the nice, cold, goodness. . . .

He sniffed the air, but still couldn't detect any trace of
a human, and with another roar he threw himself at the
door again.


With a final shove, Lenny Fizzogli moved the heavy
length of pipe through a patch of soft dirt and onto the flat
boulder at the water's edge.

He lay down on the rock beside his bomb for a minute
to catch his breath, thinking through the checklist in his
head. Arm the bomb, set the timer, seal it up, then roll it
off the boulder and into the spring. Simple. And then cross
his fingers that it worked. . . .

Again he fantasized about the truck he would buy with
the money Lew Peters had promised. The chrome

bumpers, the extra-high suspension. Just the thing to meet babes on Daytona Beach, the ones with the sexy thongs and cool tattoos.

After this, never again would he have to drive around an old heap with no air-conditioning. Never again would he have to live surrounded by guys whose theme song was "YMCA." He could have sex with real chicks, not just guys who liked to dress up.

Although, truth be told, and he'd be loath to admit this to his high school buddies, guys who liked to dress up weren't necessarily *all* bad. That evening, for instance. He'd gotten Helmut and Franz, two of the new tenors in the Bavarian Revue, to help him lug his device down to his truck, only to have them demand $100 bucks each afterward. He'd told them he didn't have it, and they said they'd take it in services. He'd thought: What the hell. One last time wasn't going to kill him. And when it was done, he was surprised that he hadn't really minded it that much. Had actually—and he'd *never* admit this to his old buddies—even *enjoyed* it.

He thought about that, looking up at the stars, swatting the occasional mosquito that penetrated his bug spray. Well . . . If it came to it, and living in Daytona with the chicks didn't work out, he supposed he could always move back to the Fag Motel. Either way, he would keep the nice truck. That would serve to impress anyone, girls and guys alike.

Lenny Fizzogli stretched his arms up over his head and let out a long, luxurious yawn. The encounter with Helmut and Franz had worn him out more than he'd thought. He looked up and patted his bomb, then felt his eyes droop shut. He fought it for a moment, then relented. A nap would do him good. The bomb could wait a few minutes.

He tucked his hands under his head, rolled over on his side, and was asleep within moments.

• • •

Emma sat in the back seat of the sheriff's cruiser with Lew Peters while Ferret Albright went into the sewer plant and sent the night watchman home.

They had replaced the gag before leaving her house as well as winding duct tape around her ankles, and it had started to dawn on her that Lew Peters might not even bother trying to negotiate with her before tossing her in.

She tried to wiggle her fingers against the tape binding her wrists, but it was no use. The tape was high-quality cloth, and wrapped in several layers. With a sinking feeling, she realized that her best chance of getting away had come and gone, way back when they first came to her door. She could have run for it, screaming as she went to wake up the neighbors.

Even that, she knew, wouldn't have guaranteed her escape. She'd have been in bare feet and a robe, and even if Ferret Albright hadn't caught her, he could have simply pulled out his gun and shot her, and then used the authority of his office to cover it up.

"Finally," Lew Peters said, peering out the window at the returning sheriff.

Emma pushed thoughts of her missed opportunity out of her head. It was gone, and dwelling on it would do no good. She was outmuscled, for all intents and purposes a political dissident in a foreign police state. The only thing she had going for her was those documents. Lew Peters was clearly worried about them. She had to figure out a way to take advantage of that.

She thought about it as Ferret Albright opened the rear door and threw her over his shoulder to march back into the sewer plant. She thought about it as he sat her up on a table across from the stainless-steel vat. She thought about it as Lew Peters stepped in front of her and stripped the tape off her mouth.

She decided she would tell the truth.

"Are you ready to talk?" Lew Peters asked.

Heart pounding, she struggled to keep her lips from quivering, to maintain a look of defiance.

"No? Fine by me." Peters turned to Albright. "Take her metal. I noticed a ring on her right hand. Also her earrings. And that necklace."

Ferret Albright started removing her jewelry—to keep it from winding up in the vat's debris basket, Emma realized with horror. Lew Peters didn't care about the stolen documents at all! He was just going to throw her in!

"Don't you want to know where your hundred and ninety-seven pages are?" she asked, voice breaking.

Lew Peters shrugged. "I did. I don't particularly anymore. When we're done here, the sheriff and his deputies will have ample time to search your home and your office. Don't worry. They'll turn up."

"I doubt it," Emma said with a confidence she didn't feel. "Unless he has the power to illegally search newsrooms outside Serenity boundaries like he does private homes within them."

Now Lew Peters's forehead registered a single crease of concern. "News*rooms*?"

"You got it," Emma said, emboldened. "As we speak, the *Orlando Advocate* is laying out tomorrow's front page featuring your plans to flood Serenity and bring in casino gambling, as well as the highly suspicious disappearances of a number of community gadflies, including a sworn state police officer, *and* the fact that remnants from their bodies have turned up in Whipple's state-of-the-art wastewater treatment plant. . . ." She thought feverishly, decided a little embellishment couldn't hurt: "Remnants, by the way, that an independent laboratory analysis *confirmed* were from Harry Spunkmeyer, Homer Wilson—"

"That's it? Just the *Advocate*?"

A pang of anxiety shot through her. This wasn't the reaction she'd hoped for. "The *Advocate* ought to be enough—for a start. AP will see it, and the local TV. By the time the Jubilee kicks off, CNN will be cutting in live—"

Lew Peters let out a short chortle. "Silly woman. When you were going through my desk, didn't you notice a file labeled 'Project Megaphone'?" He turned to Ferret Albright. "Sheriff, is she all ready?"

Emma remembered the name, remembered not paying too much attention to what was in it.

Ferret Albright studied the collection of jewelry in his hand, then scanned Emma top to bottom, lingering with a long sigh on her soon-to-be-recycled toes. "I think so, boss."

"Project Megaphone, my dear Miss Whipple, is our latest acquisition. For the past year we've quietly been buying up the stock of a certain newspaper chain. I'll give you three guesses which one. Monday morning we announce the deal. If you were going to be around Monday morning, you'd have been in charge of drafting the press release." Lew Peters dragged Ferret Albright by the ear and put him squarely in front of Emma. "Then look again, Einstein. Those sandals you've got such a hard-on for. What are those beads, ceramic? Glass? Would you say those would be organic . . . or inorganic?"

Albright looked at the sandals again, remembered the first time he'd seen her in them, from his peephole beneath the Good World ride. He shifted his legs uncomfortably, feeling himself getting aroused despite the rough hand pinching his ear.

"I've told you once, I've told you a thousand times. Nothing goes in that vat that wasn't at one time part of a living thing. Now take those off of her. I'll tell you what. I'll even let you keep them, sort of a souvenir."

Emma, still stung by Lew Peters's revelation, struggled for something, anything: "Just because you bought Schylle Incorporated, you think you can control what the *Advocate* prints? You ever heard of editorial independence? My friend . . . I mean, the reporter who did this story, if you think he's just going to roll over—"

Peters snorted loudly. "Oh, please. We've basically owned Jack Leahy for years. Now that we've formalized the relationship, you can be sure he'll handle the matter as any good officer of Whipple Corp. should. The way your great-uncle would have wanted."

"How dare you!" Emma shouted. "You think Uncle Waldo would have condoned the kind of stuff you've done? You think Uncle Waldo ever had his henchmen murder somebody? You ought to be ashamed of yourself! What the . . ."

She felt a tickling on her toes, looked down to see Ferret Albright stroking her feet with a hand that appeared to be covered in a nylon footsie. He was groping and fondling, his face close enough that she could feel his hot breath on her skin. "You *sick* bastard! Get *away* from me!"

And she coiled and straightened her legs ferociously, kicking Ferret Albright squarely on the chin.

The blow caught him off guard and off balance, sent him sprawling back against the wall of the vat—for a long, teetering moment onto the lip—and finally, seemingly in slow motion, into the vat of foul-smelling brown liquid with a soft splash.

Stunned and wide-eyed, Ferret Albright stood, scrambled to the edge, put a hand on the edge, tried to raise a leg, and then let out a shriek that gave Emma goose bumps. Already she could see the bacteria at work, dissolving his uniform, turning his skin a fiery red—

Ferret Albright shrieked again, called out, his eyes bulging and bleeding, his red, raw hand outstretched toward Lew Peters: "*Heeeeeeelllll—*"

But Lew Peters didn't help, instead backed away from the vat, his face twisted up in disgust and horror, until finally, blessedly, Ferret Albright stopped shouting and sank into the muck. When his body rose again, it was visibly fizzing, the skin completely gone and the flesh underneath dissolving away.

Lew Peters turned his head away, held his nose. "Well! I really didn't need to see *that*. Did you?" He let loose a shudder as the remnants of Ferret Albright's body sank a final time. "Enough to give you the willies. . . . I guess I'll be needing a new sheriff now. No matter."

He stared at Emma up and down, and Emma stared back.

"I don't suppose you're going to jump into that vat by yourself, are you?"

Emma said nothing, and Lew Peters finally forced a grin. "A joke. To bring a little levity to the situation, is all." He took off his jacket, laid it on the table beside Emma, and began rolling up his shirtsleeves. "I guess this blows my plausible deniability all to hell. But you know what? At the end of the day? The buck stops here."

He reached to lift Emma off the table when a high-pitched warble started coming from his jacket. "*Somebody* give me a break," he groaned, setting her back down and digging the tiny phone from his jacket pocket. "Excuse me a moment. . . . Yeah? Oh, it's you. Listen, I'm glad you called. One of your reporters, I think his name is Warner, has in his possession some documents that belong to me. . . . You know about it already? Good. . . . Tell me you're not serious. . . ."

Lew Peters glanced angrily at Emma, then returned his attention to the phone. "You understand, Jack, that this could negatively impact your performance review?" He listened for a minute longer with a sigh. "I expect nothing less."

He hung up, stared at the phone for a moment, than looked up to Emma. "Slight change of plans."

•   •   •

Ernie drove through the night in a stunned daze, wandering slowly back toward his house, although what he do once he arrived there, he had no earthly idea.

She was gone. They had taken her. He was sure of it.

That's where he had gone, after storming out of Leahy's house, to plot an alternate strategy. The wire services, or maybe even local television, in time for the morning newscasts, now that the *Advocate* was out of the question.

He had called from his car but got the answering machine, and that had given him the first twinge of concern. She would have been anxiously awaiting his phone call, he knew. Still, it was certainly plausible that she could have gone to take a shower or something. . . .

As the minutes passed and she still didn't call back, though, that rationalization grew ever weaker, until finally, by the time he rolled up to her house, he knew even before he found the door unlocked that something was wrong.

Immediately he'd gone upstairs, and there, by her bed, was her pair of black Rangoni flats. Both of them, including the one that had fallen into the moat, and he knew exactly what had happened.

He left at once, on the fear that Albright's deputies were bound to be looking for him. He drove back home, for want of anyplace else to go. The police were not going to step on Albright's turf without his express permission—permission he was not going to give. And anyway, what could he tell the cops, even if they were willing to listen? That his girlfriend had left her house without locking her door?

He turned onto Blue Heron Way, around one curve, then the other—which is when he saw the Jeep with the Egret Trace logo parked in front of his house, and the uniformed security guard messing with his front-door handle.

Ernie burst from his car, yelling as he sprinted across a half-acre of Bermuda grass and over a row of azaleas, and confronted the guard as he prepared to tack a "FORE-CLOSED" notice on the front door.

"The fuck do you think you're doing?" Ernie shouted.

"You Mr. Warner?"

"Yes! What the fuck do you think you're doing?"

"Sir, you're to come with me to the office and sign some paperwork."

"What are you talking about?" Ernie demanded. He put his key in his lock, but found when he tried to turn it that it wouldn't budge. "What have you done to my lock?"

"If you'll just come with me—"

"And what the hell is this *foreclosed* bullshit? I've never been late on a mortgage payment in my life!"

The guard stepped from one foot to the other but held his ground. "According to the Association treasurer, sir, you've missed the last three payments. Association rules are quite clear. The Association, as registered agent for the lender, shall institute foreclosure proceedings after two consecutive missed payments."

Ernie's head spun. How the hell could such a thing have happened? He'd never, *ever* missed a payment, mortgage or otherwise . . . and then he recalled a bit of idle chatter from Jack Leahy in some past conversation, a complaint about how much of his time was taken up with their homeowners' association.

He grabbed the hapless guard's lapels and fixed him with a hateful glare. "Let me guess. The Association treasurer is Jack Leahy, right?"

The guard blinked and shrugged. "Well, yeah. What does that have to do with—"

And that's when Ernie heard the whine of a hydraulic pump, turned toward the road to see the tow truck he had noticed but ignored when he'd arrived. It was now parked in back of his Mercedes, the driver standing at the controls and ready to winch.

"God*damn* it!" Ernie shouted, releasing the security guard and sprinting back across the sod to his car, in the front seat of which, he remembered suddenly, were the stolen Serenity papers. "Let *go* of it, damn you!"

"Repo man," the tow truck driver advised. "Stay away. Just doin' my job."

Ernie ignored him, ran to the driver's side door, key ring at the ready, jumped in, and cranked the engine. He threw the gearshift into drive and gunned it—only to hear the wheels spin in the air. He gunned it again, but it was no use. He was going to have to go outside, physically confront the man, and figure out the controls to get his car down.

Hitting Leahy was one thing. He was bigger than Leahy, and his blow was completely unexpected. The repo man was both taller and wider, and, in his line of work, no doubt accustomed to threats of violence. But he was going to need his car, so he had no choice—and then he remembered the extra feature the salesman thought was so wonderful but which Ernie had figured he would never actually use, there seldom being very much snow in Central Florida.

He reached for a switch on the dash, flicked it to go from rear-wheel drive to all-wheel drive, bit his lip, and hit the gas again.

This time the Mercedes lurched forward, bursting free of the tow bar and straps and slamming hard to the pavement. Ernie sat there a moment, jostled but, he decided, otherwise okay, and wondered what on the car he had just broken. He looked in his sideview mirror at the tow truck, saw the driver climb out of the cab, crowbar in hand, and decided that whatever had broken could wait. He floored the accelerator and the car surged forward, making an unhealthy scraping noise but otherwise seemingly unaffected.

Ernie drove fast until he had gotten past the gates of Egret Trace, then more slowly as he tried to reassess. In his house was the computer with the Serenity exposé. He hadn't put it on disk, instead sending it directly to the *Advocate* typesetting system via e-mail. Which meant the only copies of the story and, more important, the Serenity papers, were sitting there next to him in an untidy heap.

Which meant the first thing he had to do was make photocopies. The dashboard clock said quarter after midnight. Where in suburban Orlando late on a Saturday night could he get copies? Probably nowhere. He would need to go to the university campus. There was sure to be a Kinko's or something nearby.

He turned at the next light, Sand Lake Road, to begin making his way toward Oviedo, when his car phone rang.

*Emma* was his first thought—but he knew the second he shouted her name into the phone that it wasn't. Even with both parties on cell phones, Ernie immediately recognized his former boss.

"You son of a bitch," he began. "I can't fucking believe what you did! Late on my mortgage? You asshole! And forget all that for a second. That story you're too cowardly to run? Well, now they've taken Emma! Don't start with me about proof, okay? She's gone and I know they've got her—"

"Miss Whipple," Jack Leahy finally interrupted, "is the reason I called."

There followed an uncomfortable silence, Jack Leahy's discomfiture and Ernie's disbelief hanging heavily over the airwaves.

"Calling about Emma," Ernie said at last. "Let me get this straight: *You* know where she is? How?"

Jack Leahy paused again, then said, "Ernie, I'm calling on behalf of our new publisher. . . . He . . . I mean *we* have a proposition to offer you. Emma is in the custody of, uh, Whipple authorities, as, well, of course, they have every right to exercise such on Whipple property, as provided by the Central Highlands Development Act of 1967, codified in the constitutional . . . Well, anyway, I believe that Mr. Peters would be willing to, uh, drop all prosecution of Miss Whipple if you turned over those stolen documents in your possession."

Ernie drove with one hand, in a daze now and slowing down. Cars honked behind him, then passed angrily on the left. "Jack, are you with Lew Peters now?"

"Um . . . yes."

"And you're with Emma, too?"

"Well . . . yes, as a matter of fact."

Ernie pulled off the road into a deserted strip-mall parking lot. "Is she okay?"

Jack Leahy laughed his trademark everything-is-going-to-be-fine laugh, the one that years earlier had come out in response to the question of whether the recession meant there would be layoffs in the newsroom. Ernie immediately felt his gut tighten.

"Of course she is," Jack Leahy said, and Ernie knew he was lying. "We're all civilized adults here, Ernie. Look, Ernie: Mr. Peters just wants his property back, and all will be forgiven. Emma's release for the papers. Just the four of us. No security. No police."

Ernie stared blankly across the parking lot. In the closed storefront were Whipple T-shirts, Whipple hats, Whipple collectibles. In the middle of the parking lot was a kiosk: film processing and discount Whipple tickets.

"When and where?" he asked.

"Mr. Peters says thirty minutes. . . . He says in front of Prince Charming's Palace in the Enchanted Realm. By the drawbridge. He says you're, uh, quite familiar with the area and should have no trouble finding it. . . . And we'll leave the leftmost gate at the main entrance unlocked. Ernie? Are you listening?"

Ernie blinked, checked the dashboard clock, and then looked out toward the street to gauge exactly where he was. "I heard you. Thirty minutes is going to be tight for me."

"Mr. Peters says he knows. He says he doesn't want

you stopping at one of the copy shops near campus. If you're not there in thirty minutes, the deal's off, and Emma is, uh, prosecuted to the fullest extent of the law."

Ernie heard muffled instructions over the phone, then Jack Leahy's voice again.

"Ernie? You haven't made any additional copies of that, uh, material, have you?"

Ernie sighed, wishing he had taken Emma's suggestion on the way to her house and stopped to run off fifteen or twenty sets. He'd been in a hurry, and had insisted they wouldn't need them.

"No," he said meekly, lacking even the energy to lie.

"Good," Jack Leahy said. "Then we'll see you in a half hour."

Ernie parked the Mercedes in the roadside bushes a couple of hundred yards down from the big, multispired, canvas awning that sheltered the ticket booths, then walked the rest of the way.

He wasn't sure why. Yes, he had the nagging suspicion that Ferret Albright's goons were lurking in the woodwork, ready to jump out at an agreed-upon signal, and that they would certainly impound any car they found in the parking lot. But he also knew that if Lew Peters intended to break his word, he could simply have the deputies surround him at Prince Charming's Palace.

In fact, he realized as he spun the turnstile in front of the leftmost entry gate, he was basically walking into a trap. He had no guarantee that Emma would be there, yet he *did* have with him the stolen documents.

What in hell was he thinking?

He should have left them in his car—no, he should have hidden them somewhere, and then told Peters and Leahy he would reveal the location the instant he and Emma were safely off Whipple property. He checked his watch, wondered if there was still time, decided there wasn't. Leahy had said a half hour. It was now twenty-five minutes.

He gritted his teeth and kept walking through the darkened park, his footfall echoing on the brick pavers. He kept squinting into the closed-up shops on Morty Muskrat Mall, behind the trees in their concrete planters, but he saw no one, and he tried to calm himself.

After all, Jack Leahy had assured him that Emma was safe, and that the only thing she had to fear was prosecution. Now, Jack Leahy was a lot of things, but murderer was not among them. Surely he had nothing to do with the disappearances, the disposing of bodies in the sewer plant. For that matter, he really had no conclusive proof that Lew Peters had anything to do with them, either. It could easily have been Ferret Albright, or some deputies in his office, carrying out an overzealous rogue enforcement of company rules.

He nodded to himself as he walked, trying to convince himself. Sure, sort of an out-of-control death squad, doing things without any direction from anyone in authority, doing things that just happened to coincide with the secret plans of the CEO—the CEO who was such a detail-oriented micromanager that he had personally approved all the floor plans for all the Serenity home models. . . .

Ernie swallowed hard and kept walking, occasionally glancing over his shoulder, still seeing nobody. Ahead was Prince Charming's Palace, looming tall against the dark sky, its windows lit from ground floor to battlements. It was *way* up there, on a little narrow ledge, that Emma had risked her life—how long ago had it been? Christ. Not even a full day. The previous night. The second of three he had gone without sleep, and suddenly the exhaustion hit him.

He was tired. He was sleepy. He should've just written the damned puff piece and left it at that. None of this had to be happening. He and Emma could have been in bed right now, together and safe.

And the deaths of Subcommander Seis, and Old Man Wilson, and Tony Armstrong would have gone unsolved and unpunished, he reminded himself. Of course, after he turned over the documents in exchange for Emma's freedom, the deaths would still go unsolved and unpunished.

Ernie checked his watch again and stopped at the arranged spot. He was a minute late.

The drawbridge remained up and closed. Behind him, the Wicked Witch Tea Cups and Kallie's Kalliope both stood empty and silent. Overhead, the bare cables of the Mont Blanc Skyway stretched off to the horizon, the gondolas stowed for the night in the sheds.

Nobody. He was all alone. He checked his watch again, getting more anxious. He was a minute late. A single minute. Surely they wouldn't have left after just one minute. . . .

From the left he heard a soft clacking of women's heels, and his heart stopped. There was Emma in a white robe, her hands behind her back, flanked by Lew Peters and the ever-grinning Jack Leahy. The noise, he realized, was from her sexy red sandals. The ones she hated.

"Emma!"

Emma sighed wearily. "Oh, Ernie. You shouldn't have come."

"Let her go," Ernie demanded.

"My papers," Lew Peters said flatly.

Emma said, "No, Ernie! Don't give them to him!"

"Come on, Ernie," Jack Leahy said. "Just give him the documents."

"Emma first," Ernie insisted. "Let her go."

Jack Leahy glanced at Lew Peters, then at Ernie, then nodded decisively. "Tell you what. We'll do it at the same time." He led Emma toward Ernie as Ernie removed from his shirt a manila envelope. Leahy let go of Emma's arm and grasped the envelope simultaneously. "There, that wasn't so bad, was it?" He winked at Ernie. "You owe me, buddy."

Ernie ignored him, hugged Emma briefly and immediately set to work on the duct tape binding her wrists. "Are you okay? What did they do?"

"Oh, Ernie . . ." She struggled through a sigh that threatened to become a sob. "I killed the sheriff."

"What?" Ernie asked.

"What?" Jack Leahy echoed.

Lew Peters said nothing, grunted as he sifted through the papers in the packet. "Is this everything?" he asked finally.

Ernie said, "All hundred and ninety-seven pages. Count them if you want."

Emma tugged at his sleeve, asked softly, "Did you run off a set?"

"Yes. Did you?" Lew Peters asked, as he put the papers back in the envelope and shut the clasp. "Well?"

Ernie glowered at him, pulled Emma closer. "No, I did not. Like I promised. Now, I've kept my end of the agreement, and if you'll excuse us, we'll be going."

Jack Leahy rubbed his hands together. "There. That wasn't so bad, was it? See, Ernie? I told you everything would work out just fine. You're still fired, of course. But no hard feelings, right?"

Ernie said nothing as he and Emma started walking toward the park entrance. They barely got past Lew Peters and Jack Leahy, Leahy prattling on about the synergy between Orlando's top tourist attraction and its top content provider, when Peters nodded sharply at the Wicked Witch Teacups.

Instantly a pair of uniformed deputies emerged from two of the cups, while another three appeared from behind the Billy Baboon River Adventure entrance, and still others came out from various other hiding places. Slowly they advanced on Ernie and Emma, forming a semicircle blocking their path to the park entrance.

"What is this?" Ernie turned a hateful glare at Lew Peters. "You got your damn papers back! Charges would be dropped, you said!"

Lew Peters gave him a malicious grin. "They were dropped. For the breaking and entering. However, there's still the matter of the trespass."

Emma leaned to whisper in Ernie's ear. "I know a way out. Come on. . . ."

"Trespassing? You've got to be kidding!" Ernie screamed.

Jack Leahy turned to Lew Peters with an appeasing look: "We did say *all* charges, Mr. Peters. And really, if we're going to drop breaking and entry, which is a felony, it doesn't make a whole lot of sense, if you ask me, to pursue the misdemeanor—"

"Actually, I can't recall ever asking you. Thank you just the same." Lew Peters raised a hand to the closest of the deputies. "Captain Minton? Please detain these two."

Now Emma pulled at Ernie's arm and broke into a run away from the guards. "There's no reasoning with him! Let's go!"

Ernie glanced over his shoulder, saw the deputies were walking faster but not running. "Where? Where are we going?"

"There's a tunnel that runs to the Good World ride," Emma said, clacking along in her high-heeled sandals. "If we can get down in there, we're home free."


Behind them, the captain had stopped beside Lew Peters as the rest of his men remained in pursuit. Lew Peters watched Emma and Ernie for a while, finally sighed. "Ah, the sight of a woman running in heels. Makes you believe in God again, huh, Jack?"

Jack Leahy, perplexed, nodded anyway.

"The perimeter is sealed off, correct, Captain?" Peters asked.

"Yes, sir. Also all the access tunnels, as you requested."

Lew Peters nodded contentedly. "Good. Then at any moment we should hear—"

He was interrupted by a scream, and through the gloom they saw Ernie and Emma confront a guard at the entrance to the Good World ride. Ernie struggled with him, but then Emma launched a kick to the groin, heel pointed outward, that dropped him with a low moan.

Lew Peters winced, watching the two run off in a different direction, toward the towering, out-of-all-proportion Mont Blanc that rose from the center of ThrillWorld. "Those damned shoes of hers. Lethal." He turned toward Captain Minton. "Okay. Enough of this. Have your men take them in."

Captain Minton saluted, then spoke into the radio on his shoulder as he trotted off toward the action.

"And no guns!" Lew Peters shouted. "The park opens in a few hours. We don't have time to be steam-cleaning any bloodstains."

Jack Leahy glanced up, looking for a trace of humor in Peters's face but finding none, and then finally swallowed hard and fell in silently behind his new boss.

Already, two green-uniformed deputies had come to the aid of the fallen one at the Good World ride, and more and more kept emerging from every entrance point to Uncle Waldo's tunnel network.

"Now what?" Ernie asked, looking over his shoulder.

"This way," Emma said, and began tugging in a new direction, running across an open courtyard, around a tall row of hedges that separated ThrillWorld from Klondike Kountry, toward the Sutter's Shack restaurant and souvenir shop. "One last chance. . . ."

They saw the fat deputy emerge from the store at the same time, immediately stopping in their tracks. On all sides were slowly advancing deputies, most of them walking with necks bent and talking into their shoulder radios.

"I can try a bluff," Ernie panted. "Tell them I sent a set of copies to my lawyer—"

"They'll never buy it," Emma muttered, scanning all around them, until her eyes settled on the entrance to the Mont Blanc Skyway. "Come on!"

They ran over a patch of lawn, over a park bench, and under the chains of the maze for the queue, until finally they were running up a long, spiraling ramp that wound around the concrete-and-plaster "mountain," occasionally passing portals out onto ThrillWorld.

"Did you see them?" Emma asked.

"Umm," Ernie grunted, struggling for air now. "It looks like they're forming a perimeter around the mountain. Is there a tunnel entrance here?"

Emma shook her head. "Gondola."

A ripple of fear went through Ernie as he remembered how high up the cables ran, but he pushed it down. The alternative was a pack of armed goons prepared to throw them into a vat of carnivorous microbes. He'd deal with the height.

He swallowed hard, still panting. "How much more?"

"Almost there."

They passed another portal, and Ernie could clearly see the lights of Orlando on the horizon. He avoided looking down, swallowed again, and set his mind to the immediate task: right foot, left foot, right foot . . . until finally they were at the gondola landing, a large room with one side open to the sky, a dozen gondolas painted the colors of various Whipple characters stacked against the opposite wall.

Emma opened the metal gate and rushed to the control room while Ernie studied the overhead mechanism. The heavy cable came in, wound around a large wheel, and went back out. Each gondola arm, however, hooked up and over not the cable, but a separate feeder track.

He squinted upward, saw that each arm had a series of wheels that rolled along the track, but that a spring-loaded clamp was positioned so when the gondola was moved over the Skyway cable, the clamp would snap closed onto the thick steel wire.

"Dammit, Ernie!" Emma wailed. "I forgot! When they upgraded this ride, they moved the control room to the bottom end, down in the Dominion. There's no way to start the stupid thing from up here!"

Ernie stepped over the safety chain to the ledge of the landing. A hundred feet down, a couple of the deputies pointed up at him. Then he saw a flash of dark green through a portal halfway up the mountain. "We need an alternate plan, fast. They're on their way up."

Emma stood beneath the cable. "If only we could find a rope, we could throw it over and slide out of here."

"Wouldn't work. The rope would fray before we got a hundred yards." Ernie squinted some more at the gondola mechanism. "But I think . . . if we could just wedge that clamp open, then the gondola would roll right down the cable, wouldn't it?"

Emma moved beside him. "Where?"

He pointed at the steel arm, the heavy springs that would push the clamp closed once the gondola was moved off the track that ran along the perimeter of the passenger-loading area.

"Right!" she exclaimed suddenly. "I get it! And I know just the thing." She bent to remove one sandal, then the other, and strapped them together, heels outward. "There. Two-and-a-half-inch heels. That should do it, right?"

Ernie examined the bound-together blocks of leather-covered wood that made up the heels, then the cable. The heels were at least a half-inch taller than the cable was wide. "It should, yeah . . . if the heels don't crush."

"For what I paid for these, they sure as hell better not." She climbed up the outside of a green gondola, one decorated with a cross-eyed Mongoose Mike. "Here, help me up."

Ernie pushed up as she climbed atop the carriage, then

handed her the shoes, which she slid into the slot between the clamp pads. "Like this?"

"Can you strap them in place?"

Emma undid one sandal strap, wound it around and through one of the clamp struts, then buckled it shut. "How about that?"

"Won't know until we slide it over the cable. Come on down and help me."

She climbed back down, the straps of her robe momentarily tangling in the works, and Ernie happened to glance upward at the opportune moment.

"Whoa! You're not wearing underwear!"

Emma freed herself and got back to the ground. "Oh, grow up. I was kidnapped from my house as I was going to sleep, for Pete's sake. Now what do we need to do to get out of here?"

Ernie heard approaching voices from the ramp and snapped himself back to reality. "Help me push."

Together they pushed the gondola around the loading area, right up to where the overhead track merged with the Skyway cable, and with a heave shoved the heavy car onto the cable. It rolled easily, the clamp unable to close down on the cable because of Emma's sandals.

"*Yes!* It worked!" Ernie shouted, then glanced back at the top of the ramp to see the first green-shirt emerge. "Uh-oh. Get in!"

Emma scrambled in, left the door open as Ernie pushed the gondola, the deputies behind him shouting for him to freeze, faster and faster toward the edge of the landing, and with just a step remaining lunged for the open door, stumbled, and—

"Ernie!" Emma gasped.

The car rolled down the cable, swaying slightly, and Ernie grasped the edge of the gondola door frame with his fingers, his legs swinging freely out over thin air, a hundred feet over the brick pavers of ThrillWorld. He concentrated on his grip, felt his fingernails starting to lose traction on the steel—and then he made the mistake of looking down.

The car was passing high over the Wicked Witch Teacups, gaining speed, deputies on the ground aiming upward with their guns, when the vertigo overcame him, and he began to feel light-headed.

"Ernie!" Emma screamed again, and this time she grabbed his wrists. "Pull!"

He looked up to see her face peering over the edge. "Let go . . . we'll both fall. . . ."

"No, we won't! I've got my feet hooked onto the bench. But you're going to have to help me. . . . *Pull!*"

And he closed his eyes and pulled, inch by inch, until eventually his face and then his elbows were on solid metal, and then his chest—and finally his legs. Emma rolled him inside, pushed the door shut with one foot.

He took one deep breath after another, counted ten in his head, then twenty. "Thank you," he said finally. "That would have been bad."

Emma stood, looked over the edge of the car as it flew over the pond separating FairyLand from FutureLand. "They're following us," she said, pointing behind them. "Huh. There's a bunch of deputies in that gondola car, but they don't seem to be moving."

Ernie groaned and stood, still shaky, and squinted back through the slowly brightening gloom. "I bet I know what happened. They probably didn't realize we had to jam that clamp open. They just pushed a car over onto the cable, and as soon as it did, the clamp fastened on tight. They're stuck. They can't even try again, because they've blocked the path. There's no way they can follow us!"

Emma turned to face where they were headed, down the slight grade toward the Wild Dominion. "Yeah—unless they turn the ride on."

Without warning, the lights on the cable towers came on and they heard the faint humming of motors.

"Like they just did now," she said, then stopped to

think. "But they won't catch us! They can only go as fast as the cable. We're rolling over the cable, so we're still going faster."

Ernie peered forward at the quickly approaching tower. "Yes, which means we'll get to the bottom all that much quicker. Which is where they're waiting for us. . . ." He glanced at her. "They must be, right? Where else could they have turned the ride on?"

She stood beside him and took his arm glumly. "Dammit all, you're right. Which means the only possible escape is for us to jump out of this thing. So we have our choice: Either we can fall a hundred feet to our deaths, or be thrown kicking and screaming into a vat of flesh-eating bacteria." She squeezed his hand. "Unless . . . I know! Where did you park?"

"By the front entrance—"

"Perfect! Ernie, we've got to jump!"

He looked down at the quickly passing ground, then back at her. "Have you lost your mind? We're not jumping."

Emma nodded her head and pointed. "Oh, yes we are, and we've got to get ready. Look!"

Ernie looked. Ahead, and approaching fast, was the big, trademark awning over the ticket booths by the front entrance, its multiple support poles giving it the appearance of a winter mountainscape. "We can't jump into that! We'll impale ourselves on those damn poles!"

But Emma was already reaching over the door to undo the latch from the outside. "Look at it this way: It's the only chance we've got. Plus there's a lot more canvas between poles than there are poles. The odds are clearly in our favor."

Ernie glanced out the open door, felt his head go light. "It's got to be a hundred feet down. . . ."

Emma wrapped him in her arms and gently moved him closer to the doorway. "We've come down at least twenty feet from the start of the ride, so that's eighty feet. Then the awning's a good twenty feet off the ground, so it can't be any more than sixty. Now, come *on*!"

The gondola slid every closer, and Ernie gritted his teeth and moved to the edge. "Well, if it's only sixty . . ."

"That's the spirit. Now hold my hand, and we'll jump together."

The awning sped closer, for some reason looking smaller and smaller as a landing site, Ernie thought, its peaks over the metal support poles appearing sharper and more numerous. His vertigo threatened a return, and he bit his tongue to distract himself. He bit hard, until he thought he tasted blood.

"We need to take into account our forward speed," he muttered. "Or we could end up jumping right over it onto the pavement."

"So we need to jump earlier than we think? Right? Okay." Emma interlaced her fingers with his, squeezed tight as the awning loomed closer. A pair of deputies guarded the front entrance from inside the park, but none seemed to be on the outside. "Okay, on the count of three. One . . ."

The path of the gondola was going to take them over the sharpest spire, Ernie decided.

"Two . . ."

He wondered how much it would hurt to have a pointed steel pole enter his body through, say, his groin, and exit through his chest. Probably a lot. Well, he probably should have thought of that before he decided to take on the world's largest provider of wholesome family entertainment.

"Three!"

Ernie sucked it up and jumped with both feet, and then the world began spinning, tumbling, the gondola grew smaller, its door flapping as it swayed, the parking lot came nearer, and Emma's robe and nightgown blew upward, he noticed with interest—at least, he decided, his final sight would be a happy one—until the tallest,

sharpest, meanest-looking metal-tipped spire approached
and passed harmlessly and they landed with a soft *whum-
mmp* on a trampoline of canvas. They bounced up once,
landed again, and this time two of the poles gave way,
slowly collapsing and setting them gently on the pavement in front of the ticket booths.

Ernie stood, breathing triumphantly, solid ground once
more beneath his feet. "I don't believe it!"

Behind them, on the other side of the gates, deputies
were shouting and running, and Emma stood and grabbed
his hand. "Which way to your car?"


Jack Leahy took a couple of running steps every so often
to keep up with Lew Peters's long strides, waiting for the
perfect moment to interject with the gentle reminder he
was crafting in his head, about how, since they had recovered the stolen material, and since Ernie Warner was now
a *former* employee and therefore easily labeled as a *dis-
gruntled* former employee who could not be believed,
didn't it make sense to just let him and the girl go?

He had, in fact, received precisely this sort of training
at a Schylle company retreat a few summers back: the art
of discrediting a former employee and thereby reducing
costs of litigation and potentially negative publicity.

Besides, further persecution of the pair might just
make them sympathetic enough for a television reporter
or even, God forbid, *Columbia Journalism Review* to do a
big piece on them. He nodded to himself decisively. Yes,
this was good advice, and he, as a soon-to-be loyal officer
of Whipple Corporation, had a sworn duty to bring it to
the attention of his supervisor.

They strode toward the Realm's entrance, Lew Peters
still silently brooding. He had nearly chewed the head off
his sheriff's captain when Ernie and Emma had escaped
on a Skyway gondola, and then had come close to striking
the man when he'd learned some fifteen minutes later that

the gondola had arrived at the Dominion station empty, and that the pair had managed to jump onto the ticket booth awning at the front entrance and from there to Ernie's waiting Mercedes.

He would have to pick his opportunity carefully, at just the right moment, to temper the man's anger rather than draw it on himself. They went through the revolving exit gate and then Lew Peters stopped in front of the two cars, the sheriff's cruiser he had come in and Jack Leahy's SL500 convertible.

"Your car or mine?" Lew Peters snapped.

Jack Leahy gulped, realized that the moment had been chosen for him. He cleared his throat cautiously. "Say, Lew, I was just thinking . . . maybe it might be better all around to just let them go? I mean, the very most you can charge them with is breaking and entering and larceny, and I'm just imagining them going to trial and getting up on the stand and testifying about escaping down the gondola. I think the media would eat that up. In fact, a trial would give them precisely the exposure they're—"

Peters glared at him with unconcealed venom, and Leahy quickly changed tack: "Either car would be a fine choice. Yours, of course, has the lights and siren and everything, but mine would probably be more comfortable and, quite frankly, faster. I mean, the acceleration in the five hundred series really is a thing of beauty. You hardly even realize you're moving. . . ."

"Okay, yours." Lew Peters reached into the trunk of the Crown Victoria, removed a small duffel bag, and climbed into the Mercedes's passenger seat. "Drive."

Jack Leahy started down the road toward the Turnpike, where the sheriff's deputies had set up a roadblock half a mile inside the Whipple World entrance, and cleared his throat once more. "Lew, I mean, Mr. Peters, I strongly recommend that we—"

"Shut up and drive."

Jack Leahy shut up and drove, and within a couple of

miles came to a gathering of sheriff's deputies, some in green-and-white cruisers, some in zebra-striped Land Rovers, all stopped on the road. Jack Leahy pulled up beside Captain Minton, who came and stood before his boss with head hanging.

"Well?" Lew Peters said.

"They, uh, got away, sir."

"They got off Whipple property?"

"No, sir." Captain Minton pointed his long flashlight, cop-style, with his palm downward, at the side of the road, at a break in the tall fence and the tire tracks that ran through it. "They went in there, sir. Into the Dominion."

Lew Peters nodded. "Great. And how many men did you send in after them?"

Captain Minton looked at his shoes again. "Well, none, sir. I told them, but they refused. See this section of the fence? Well, that's Africaland on the other side. And remember, Simba and his pride ate McGuire just last month. There was a certain reluctance to go in after them."

Lew Peters's eyes narrowed to slits as he stared, and Jack Leahy thought he would burst a blood vessel in his brain. He frowned, hoping it wouldn't leak out all over his leather seats. Then he licked his lips, preparing himself to offer advice on putting up a helicopter to track Ernie's car inside the animal park.

"Captain Minton," Lew Peters began. "Let me make sure I understand you. There's a certain . . . *reluctance* to go in after them?"

Captain Minton nodded solemnly. "Yes, sir. You remember. How Simba ate McGuire's head and arms, then disemboweled him and left him for the buzzards?" He shuddered at the thought. "Well, no one wants to risk—"

"*Captain* Minton! You and your men are security officers, are you not? It's your *job* to take risks!"

"Not from lions, sir. No one ever said anything about lions when I took the job."

"Well, I'm telling you now. I'm going to count to ten,

and I want you and every officer here inside that fence by the time I get there, or you can find yourself new jobs."

Captain Minton gulped but said nothing, and Lew Peters glared in silence for a long, long moment. Jack Leahy finally cleared his throat softly. "Mr. Peters, perhaps if we put up a heli—"

"Ten!" Peters announced. "Minton, you and everyone in this detail are as of this moment fired. Insubordination. No severance pay. Now get off my property. Leahy? Drive!"

Jack Leahy blinked. "Sir? Into there?"

"Your star reporter is driving a five-hundred-series Mercedes, is he not? Isn't yours as good as his?"

Leahy looked protectively at his hood ornament, then glanced at one of the Land Rovers parked nearby. "Why don't we take one of those? I mean, after all, they're specifically *built* to go off road—"

"Stop wasting time and drive!" Lew Peters screamed, opening the black duffel bag in his lap and pulling out a large machine pistol. "Now, you want to start off with Whipple with some nice stock options? Or a pink slip?"

Jack Leahy gulped nervously as Lew Peters slipped in an ammunition clip and racked the first round, then put his car into low gear and turned off the road and through the hole in the fence.


Through a small break in the branches, Ernie watched as the strengthening rays of the sun started to burn off the wisps of mist that hung over the grassy flatlands all the way down to the river. They had driven, Emma guiding, over Africaland's "savannah," toward a stand of trees, then backed into a clump of bushes to hide.

Beside him, Emma was curled up in the tan leather seat, trying to catch a few minutes of rest. Ernie tried to recall having a real night's sleep, what it felt like, and decided he couldn't remember. He'd lost track of how many nights in a row now they'd been up and about. It felt like a zillion.

He took a deep breath and stared blankly at the distant river. Soon, one way or the other, it would be done. Mid-morning, noon, latest, it would have to play itself out. They couldn't hide there forever. The Dominion would be opening shortly and, down in Serenity, the Jubilee festivities were set to start within the hour.

Now that it was light, they would come in with teams of Land Rovers, and his only chance would be to outrun them. Like a Thompson's gazelle, he would have to zig and zag across the grass, around the trees, back out through the fence they'd punched through on their way in, and then make a beeline to the Enchanted Realm parking lot and its protective throngs of tourists.

Which made it imperative that they stay hidden until the park opened. They needed as many tourists on Whipple property as possible to discourage the use of deadly force. The more wide-eyed kids in Muskrat ears were around as potential witnesses, the more likely they were to get out alive.

"Time is it?" Emma murmured, shifting her position.

Ernie gazed at her and, despite everything, felt an animal arousal. "Half past seven."

"Another hour and a half." She opened her eyes, frowned. "What are you staring at?"

He couldn't hide a smile. "You looked like one of those James Bond babes. Nightgown. Heels. No underwear."

She returned the smile and took his hand. "I don't know whether I should be flattered or alarmed. That you can be thinking like that in a situation like this."

Ernie put on a steely look and gazed impassively out the windshield. "Survival. We're talking the most elemental instincts, here. Flight from predators. Procreation."

"Thank you, Marlon Perkins." She straightened her robe and retied the knot. "Tell you what, you get us out of here, we'll go to a hotel, have a nice meal, and then we can see about the procreation part. Deal?"

He smiled again and squeezed her hand tightly, peered out through her window to see if the Dominion Safari Tram had started to run yet. "Deal. I thought we'd wait for the parks to open, give ourselves some tourists to act as wit—"

And the breath was knocked out of him as the car slammed up onto its right wheels, hung there a moment, then fell back heavily to the ground. "What the . . ."

Emma saw it first through his window: the giant gray head, the single yellowed horn on its nose, the blind fury in its black eyes. She screamed as the animal backed up through the scrub, lowered its head to charge again.

Ernie froze for just a fraction of a second before cranking the ignition and gunning the Mercedes out of its hidey-hole.

Jack Leahy just knew the bumpy ground was at the very least ruining his alignment and more than likely damaging his suspension, and was wondering whether Lew Peters would allow as a business expense whatever repairs were needed—when the other Mercedes burst out of a clump of bushes just ahead.

"There!" Lew Peters yelled, lifting his gun to rest the barrel on the top of the door. "Hurry!"

Leahy sped up, gritting his teeth against the knocks his poor roadster was taking, against the increasingly likely possibility that Peters was actually going to shoot at Ernie and the girl, when he first felt the ground thunder and next saw the giant beast lower its head at his car on an intercept trajectory. Leahy screamed just as his convertible was slammed broadside and knocked momentarily up on its left wheels.

"Drive! Drive!" Lew Peters yelled.

Leahy replied, "Shoot it! Shoot it!"

"Drive, you moron!"

Jack Leahy screamed again as the rhino pawed the dirt, then lowered its massive head and started galloping at his car once more. Leahy stepped on the gas in time to get the body of the car out of the way, but not in time to save the rear bumper from the beast's horn.

Leahy watched in dismay in the rearview mirror as the animal shook the plastic bumper off its horn, then proceeded to trample it. "Do you know how much a new bumper for a Mercedes costs? Why didn't you shoot it?"

Lew Peters snorted. "Do you have any idea what that animal costs? Do you know what it takes in bribes to even *find* an animal like that? That animal is worth more than you and your car together."

"I bet there's a huge dent where he rammed me, too," Jack Leahy pouted.

"Your whining grows tiresome." Lew Peters squinted into the sun, then pulled at Leahy's shirt. "There! Hurry up, they're getting away!"


Ernie drove the car over the veldt's bumps and potholes with a death grip on the wheel and his jaw frozen in determination. Beside him, Emma turned to look for Leahy and Peters.

"Damn! They're after us again." She turned back around and put her hands on the dash. "Look out!"

Ernie swerved, seeing the watering hole at the last instant, and found himself headed down a shallow gully, going faster and faster. Finally the foliage cleared, and he saw the plywood wall at the bottom of the hill.

"Uh-oh. . . ."

He tried braking, but it was too late, and the Mercedes burst through the thin facade and into a building with white floors and a blue ceiling and a swimming pool with a glass barrier and viewing area just beyond. It was, he realized, the still-broken Untamed Arctic exhibit.

"Terrific," he groaned. "Now what?"

Emma tugged at his sleeve and pointed at the last cave in the bears' habitat, the largest and seemingly the deepest of the three. "No, this is good. Drive in there!"

Ernie furrowed his brow. "Into that?"

"Hurry!" Emma insisted.

He took his foot off the brake pedal, flipped his lights on, and drove into the cave, which he quickly realized was a ramp leading down a dark tunnel. "Ah . . . now I remember. Serenity, right? The skating rink?"

"Exactly," Emma nodded. "And from there, if we can get out to the bandshell, hopefully there'll be a crowd there for us to get lost in."

Ernie drove slowly, his headlights providing the only illumination through the blackness. A couple of times already he had scraped the side of the tunnel with a fender, and he was afraid any more bumps would bend the fender in on the tire, jamming it so it couldn't turn or even popping it. Either way they'd be screwed.

"It's another half a mile, I think," Emma said. "Although it's hard to say, without any landmarks—"

"Uh-oh. . . ."

"Uh-oh what?"

He glanced in the rearview mirror again. "Thought I saw headlights. Yup. Headlights behind us."

Ernie stepped on the accelerator, now bumping the sides of the tunnel regularly, until suddenly it widened, opened onto a cavernous building.

"Slow down! Stop!" Emma yelled—too late.

The Mercedes barreled into the skating rink boards, knocking open the gate used by the Zamboni, and spinning and sliding across the ice. Around and around they spun, Ernie and Emma wailing in unison as the battered car slid clear down the length of the rink and finally stopped, its rear end in the hockey goal.

Ernie sat there a moment, still holding his breath, afraid to let go of the steering wheel. "You all right?"

Emma nodded, her own hands clutching the door handle and the side of her seat. "Yes. But we need to hurry. That opening's the only way off the ice. Turn left right there, and then I'll go open that roll-up door. From there it's only half a mile to the band—"

"Too late," Ernie said, watching the convertible, cream-colored Mercedes that drove slowly onto the ice and stopped, blocking their path.

In the passenger seat, Lew Peters inspected an object in his hands. Then he opened the car door wielding a pistol.

Lenny Fizzogli cursed as he struggled with his giant pipe bomb. It was morning, hours later than he'd planned, thanks to his having fallen into such a deep sleep. He had woken up stiff, with painful cricks in his neck, back, and shoulders, thanks to his having slept so long on a boulder.

As soon as he finished, he was going to find a hot shower, maybe get one of the boys at the Fag Motel to do his back for him. A couple of them were actual chiropractors, or so they claimed. He frankly didn't care, as long as they worked their magic.

With sweat streaming from his brow, he put his weight into it and finally got the giant bomb onto the lip of the rock. He stopped, flicked the timer start button just as the Basque shepherd had taught him, then gave the bomb a final shove into the water. He watched with satisfaction as it tumbled and sank into the pool, down into the grotto that, according to Armand Beckwith's surveys, was the principal outlet for Lake Tohopekaliga several miles to the east.

When it disappeared from sight, he stood, removed his sneakers and socks, then his jeans, too, and waded out into a shallow part of the pond just downstream. From there he could watch and feel the current directly, to see how it was affected by his replumbing. If everything worked as he hoped, the flow would increase considerably, with twice, three times, maybe even four times as much water running into Lake Serenity, enough for the river to start rising in its banks and, soon, spread well beyond them.

He checked his watch, realized he'd once again forgotten to set the stopwatch function when he'd started the timer. Oh well. It would be another minute or two. Not much more than that. After he was sure more water was actually flowing, he would hurry on down to the Jubilee celebration, camera in hand, and take a picture of the water level at the municipal dock, so as to document to Mr. Peters's satisfaction how it was rising and how he therefore had fulfilled his obligations and could he please get his money now?

Check in hand, it was down to Kissimmee Chevrolet to place his order for his custom truck. And from there a quick stop at the Fag Motel to see if Monty the chiropractor was there for a quick adjustment. Or maybe, he thought, rolling his head around on his stiff neck, he would hit the Fag Motel *before* the dealership. After all, they were ordering it anyway, so a delay of a few hours on a Saturday really wasn't going to make much difference. For that matter, an order placed Saturday probably wouldn't get processed until Monday, earliest. Which meant he really didn't have to go to the dealership at all. Which meant that after his session with Monty, he could go see what Helmut and Franz were up to, see if maybe they wanted to go help him pick out his truck. . . .

He felt a twinge of shame as he realized that his first choice of companionship during this all-important excursion wasn't a woman but, rather, two large homosexual men. Two large homosexual men who'd pretty much had their way with him the previous evening. He had become—there was no longer any denying it—precisely what for so many years he had loathed.

It was this thought tormenting his psyche when the sand and muck beneath his feet rumbled and water erupted from the pool with a tremendous splash. A smile came to his lips as he felt the current increase dramatically. *Yes!* Just like he'd planned! Just like he'd figured out, all by himself. He couldn't wait to show that bastard Mr. Peters. Show what someone without a fancy college education could manage by simply putting their mind to it—when without warning a giant hole formed in the water just yards away.

Lenny Fizzogli watched, mouth hanging open, as the water from the pool now rushed madly into the void, which, with a sudden rumble, lengthened even farther downstream. It was a sinkhole, he realized as the current grew stronger still, now threatening to knock him over and drag him down. Or maybe a chain of sinkholes, rapidly forming in the path of the Serenity, now that so much groundwater had been allowed to surface so suddenly.

In a panic, he struggled against the stream toward the bank. Too much explosive, he realized. Instead of merely widening the opening for the underwater source, he had set off some kind of cataclysmic chain reaction, with the entire riverbed collapsing from the weight of the new water.

He slogged against the rushing torrent, more and more of it splashing down his throat, when the ground finally dissolved from beneath him, and the current sucked him down into the maelstrom.

On shore, the crowd was starting to migrate toward the bandshell as Subcommander Zero continued serving up hot dogs from the aft deck of *Gone Fishin'*, his twenty-six-foot pontoon boat that, like every other vessel tied up to the downtown seawall, was festooned with tangerine and aqua, the Official Colors of Whipple's Jubilee.

He squirted mustard and ketchup onto another wiener, wrapped it in a napkin, and handed it to a rotund man in a

Morty Muskrat T-shirt and Billy Baboon ball cap, then checked his watch. It was almost time.

A few yards away, on the foredeck, Subcommander Nueve was hidden beneath a tangerine tarp, crouching beside a fully fueled gas generator, the Serenity Integrated Learning Academy's pitching machine, and a laundry basket full of plastic Easter eggs, each partially filled with red or midnight blue paint.

Subcommander Veintiuno would be preparing the strike force to approach the TV trailer in exactly eleven minutes, at which point Zero would slip his mooring lines and maneuver to a spot across from the bandshell and start lobbing the paint bombs onto the stage, thereby creating the diversion the strike force would need to take the trailer and replace the commemorative Whipple Jubilee video with one of their own featuring extensive documentary footage of their various grievances.

Timing was crucial. He knew Albright would waste little time putting the sheriff's boat in the water after them. The moment the Underground's video began streaming on the bandshell's Jumbotron, he would have to hightail it out of there, running the boat downstream to where he'd already positioned a getaway car.

His boat, he knew, was just one of many things he was about to lose forever if their strike failed. They would likely be hunted down and arrested. Then, after the media hordes had left that evening, they would be summarily disposed of, just like their fallen comrades.

Zero set his jaw and with a pair of steel tongs pulled another hot dog off the grill. Failure, therefore, was not an option. He handed the frankfurter to yet another muskrat-attired tourist while sneaking a peek at his watch. Five more minutes.

He saw that a Whipple corporate toady had taken the stage to a round of applause, which served to draw away the remaining handful of potential hot dog customers. Zero set down the tongs, wiped his hands on his Gordon

Gopher apron, and moved to the stern cleats holding the dock lines to prepare slipknots for a hasty departure.

And it was there, bent close to the deck, that he heard a distant rumbling before watching his and every other boat tied to the seawall strain against its upstream line. He scratched his head and stood, watching as leaves and other floating debris began moving ever more quickly down-current.

At the south end of the ice, Ernie Warner opened the door of the Mercedes and stood, arms crossed, eyes locked on the driver of the Mercedes at the north end. Jack Leahy dropped his gaze. He had known Ernie since they were both young men—Jack, still idealistic city editor, Ernie, a cub reporter, fresh out of school. Good times and bad, into middle age. And now, his new boss was going to march right up to Ernie and shoot him.

Somewhere, something resembling guilt bubbled to the surface, and he unhappily looked up to find Ernie's eyes still focused on him.

"When we're done here, I need you to run me over to the bandshell. I'm on in fifteen minutes. Then hurry on back and guard the entrance until some deputies get here." Lew Peters thought a moment, then set the gun on the passenger seat while he removed his jacket. "I better leave this here. In case any blood splatters."

From across the rink, Ernie Warner shouted: "Jack! The gun! Grab it!"

For a moment, both Leahy and Lew Peters glanced at the weapon, then at each other.

"Jack! What's the matter with you? He wants to kill us!"

Lew Peters still had one arm tangled in his sleeve. "Well, Jack? You have something to say?"

Jack Leahy quickly looked away from the weapon so as not to seem disloyal. At the same time, though, gunning down Ernie and his girlfriend in cold blood . . . well, it *did* seem a bit much.

He cleared his throat softly. "Well, uh, sir. I was just thinking, you know, maybe Ernie has a point. I mean, golly, an uncharitable view of what you, I mean *we* . . . an uncharitable view of what we're doing might even call it murder."

Peters finished folding his jacket onto the back seat, then picked up the gun and expertly racked it. "And that's different from what *we've* been doing for all these years . . . how?"

Peters started walking, had just stepped across the blue line toward Ernie's car when the whole building shuddered.

Jack Leahy, Ernie, and Lew Peters all stood still, knees bent, eyes scanning the building, when the ground shook again, this time cracking the ice down through the neutral zone and buckling the boards—and that was the break Snoball and Igloo had been waiting for as they tumbled through the disintegrated penalty box and sprawled out onto the ice, immediately seeing food standing beside a large, green metal box. They growled ferociously and ambled across the ice, stopping momentarily to lap at it, and then perking up at the screams emanating from within the box.

By the time they looked up, Ernie had climbed back into the car, locked the doors, and had his fingers on the ignition key . . . just as water began rushing in through the collapsed walls.

Emma squeezed Ernie's forearm until it hurt, as the ice in the rink broke into two large chunks, a green Mercedes sedan on one, a beige Mercedes convertible on the other, both of which began floating on the floodwaters out the gaping hole where the northwest wall of the Serenity Ice Castle used to be, down the rushing river toward Lake Serenity.

And through it all, pounding on hood, windshield, and

roof of the green Mercedes were a pair of snarling, hundred-pound, ravenous, supremely irritated polar bear cubs.

In stunned amazement, Subcommander Zero watched house after house in Serenity's exclusive Founders Estates neighborhood collapse into a lengthening chain of sink-holes, with water from the noticeably higher lake quickly pouring in. In Portofino Harbor, five thousand Serenity residents and tens of thousands of tourists ran amok, as Whipple officials and deputies desperately tried to assure everyone that the situation was fully under control.

Beside him, emerged from under his tarp, a similarly slack-jawed Walt Littlefield suddenly pointed to the Jumbotron set up on the bandshell stage. There, rather than the syrupy, condensed History of the World that ranked Waldo Whipple World on a par with China's Great Wall and Giza's Pyramids, there played now instead the Serenity Underground's home video, documenting the cut corners and shoddy materials of Serenity's home-building pro-gram.

Zero checked his watch, realized he'd missed his cue, but that amid all the commotion, Veintiuno's strike force had taken the trailer without need of a diversion.

Another roar went up as rumbling preceded the col-lapse of Town Hall. A genuine stream flooded in from the lake to fill the newest sinkhole, which led to a sponta-neous exodus among the gathered Jubilee-goers away from the harbor toward higher ground.

"Look!"

Zero turned in the direction of Nueve's outstretched finger, blinked, then squinted toward the north end of the lake. "Is that what I think it is?"

The crowd on shore also noticed it, and started point-ing out at the water. Then the pool cameraman on the media platform noticed it, too, until there on the Jumbotron, larger than life, appeared the fantastic image of two ice floes floating on Lake Serenity—a $75,000 German automobile on each, and on the nearer floe, a pair of polar bear cubs assaulting the car in obvious hopes of getting at its two terrified occupants.

Zero alternately squinted out at the lake, then at the video monitor, then suddenly gripped Nueve's shoulder: "In that car! It's that reporter, Ernie Warner!"

On the Jumbotron, one of the bears finally smashed the windshield, with the tempered glass holding together, at least temporarily, in a sort of flexible shield.

Zero quickly glanced around, pointed Nueve toward the bow as he pressed the ignition switch and bent to slip the stern lines. "Get the anchor up! We've got to help them!"

Within moments, *Gone Fishin'* was chugging toward the floe, Zero at the helm and Nueve at the bow, binoculars raised.

Zero winced as one bear cub threw himself at the windshield, then stood on the hood on his hind legs in frustration. "*Dammit,* we're not going to make it! If only we could get them away from the car. . . ."

His eyes wandered around the boat, lingered on the gas grill, the cooler, the pitching machine. He throttled the engine up toward the red line, shouted at Nueve: "Crank up the generator and get the pitching machine going! I've got an idea!"

Ernie and Emma clung to each other in the back seat as one bear, Snoball, they thought, attacked the broken windshield while the other, Igloo, they believed, slammed on the driver-side front door. It was only a matter of time, Ernie realized, before the windshield popped out of its frame.

He squeezed her tight one final time, then drew away. "Okay, here's what I'm gonna do: On the count of three,

I'll open my door and run for the edge of the floe. As soon as the bears follow, you get out your door, dive into the lake, and swim for shore—"

"No, no," Emma cut in as Snoball took another swipe at the windshield. "I'll distract them, and *you* swim for it."

"Forget it! *You're* the high school freestyle champion, not me. You actually have a shot at making it—"

Emma shrieked as Snoball lunged once more at the windshield, this time poking a paw through the antiglare film as it finally gave way. The cub pushed his snout through the hole, then put an eye to it to peer inside, then stood on the hood to roar.

Which was when the first frankfurter plunked on the roof.

Ernie and Emma looked at each other, then at the bears. The noise had come from smack on top of the roof, where neither animal was. The next flying wiener hit the hood, then bounced off onto the ice. Both bears scrambled after it, wrestling with each other over who would eat it until— *plop*—another one landed a few yards away. Snoball pounced on it and swallowed it whole, while Igloo, still chewing the last one, scrambled after the next hot dog that fell from the sky.

"What the . . ." Ernie craned his neck out the back window, saw a pontoon boat with two men aboard, one of them feeding uncooked Ball Park Franks into a baseball pitching machine. "It's Zero and Nueve! How about that!"

The hot dogs fell farther and farther downfloe as the boat approached, until finally they began splashing into the water. Snoball and Igloo dove in after them, swimming and eating, and the franks kept falling farther away, until the first one landed on the other ice floe.

Igloo clambered out first and immediately noticed two, far more substantial hunks of food standing beside a cream-colored metal box. Igloo stood and roared, then began ambling toward the convertible. Snoball climbed onto the ice, shook the water off his coat, then loped after his brother.

•  •  •

Eyes wide, Jack Leahy pushed the button on the dash repeatedly as the motor swung the canvas top forward slowly, ever-so-agonizingly slowly, until Leahy could stand it no more and reached up to pull the latches down by hand.

Lew Peters paused digging through Ferret Albright's duffel bag long enough to flash Leahy a look of disdain. "What the hell point is there to that? You moron!"

"It'll at least slow them down!" Leahy looked over Lew Peter's shoulder at the charging bears. "What are you *doing*? Why don't you just shoot them?"

Lew Peters looked up from the duffel in disgust. "I can't believe Albright didn't pack a tranquilizer gun. The idiot."

"A *tranquilizer*? For Christ's sake, Mr. Peters, just shoot them!" He watched as Lew Peters appraised the approaching carnivores with narrowed eyes. "*Please,* Mr. Peters, whatever they cost, I'll personally reimburse you!"

Peters peered into the duffel again. "We may have no choice. Where's that .45? I know I saw one in here. . . ."

Snoball reached the car, bounded onto the hood, then slapped at the windshield before noticing how easily his claws could tear the roof. With a roar of excitement he began slashing at the convertible top with both paws. Leahy screamed, grabbed at the duffel with both hands, in so doing dumping its contents all over the floor.

"Moron!" Peters snapped. "Look what you've done!"

But Leahy didn't have time to look. With an awkward lunge, Snoball dove over the windshield and through the torn canvas top, knocking the breath out of Jack Leahy's lungs as he set upon him with open jaws.

Lew Peters winced at the sight, right then decided to give up on the .45 and take his chances on the ice. He opened his door—and ran smack into Igloo's waiting arms.

"Aw, fuck," Lew Peters said.

*"Rarrarraaarghhhh!"* Igloo said, and then dug into his first decent meal in days.

Nueve pushed away from the ice floe and hopped onto the bow as Zero backed *Gone Fishin'* off a few boat lengths, then swung her around back toward shore.

Under the canopy, Emma buried her head in Ernie's shoulder and shuddered when, from a hundred yards away and over the noise of the pontoon boat's Evinrude, came the still-impressive roar of a polar bear mauling its prey.

"I can't look," she said. "What's happening?"

Ernie watched the carnage with a mixture of fascination and revulsion. On the one hand, it was awful. On the other, they were getting exactly what they deserved—and getting it with supremely poetic justice, too. Wild Dominion? Untamed Arctic? Here it was. Wild and untamed, both.

"Well, Snoball is eating Peters. And Igloo is eating Leahy. Either that or *Igloo* is eating Peters and . . . you know what I mean."

She shuddered again, then opened her eyes and finally saw the mayhem at Portofino Harbor.

"Look!" she gasped.

Ernie turned away from the spectacle on the ice floe, noticed for the first time the spectacle on shore. Nearly every waterfront building was gone, either washed away or partially collapsed. The banners and streamers hung to commemorate the Jubilee now littered the water, the orange and aqua flotsam thickening as they neared shore.

Thousands of Serenity residents watched their wrecked community from the concrete wall fronting the Whipple Institute, as hundreds more crowded the bandshell stage to escape the rising lake water that had flooded the picnic grounds. They stood transfixed by the video image on the giant-screen television: once-cute, now ferocious polar bear cubs standing atop a broken Mercedes roadster, their snouts blood red and their paws raised in triumph.

Finally, someone in the control room cut away from the picture and replaced it instead with a giant chiron that filled the Jumbotron from edge to edge: WWWS?

# epilogue

**...**

🌴 The Billy Baboon–themed gondola car lifted past one tower, then another, then approached and passed high above the rebuilt, multispired awning sheltering the ticket booths.

Ernie Warner, for the first time in his life, sat at ease, ninety feet up in the air and climbing toward the majestic, plaster Mont Blanc still a good mile away. He stared down at the canvas that had broken his fall just a week earlier, how it didn't seem nearly as far down anymore.

"I could almost do it again," he said. "Just for fun."

Emma stretched back against the side of the car, laid her legs across Ernie's lap. "Really? I could build a bungee-jump tower for you."

"Yeah, I guess you could, couldn't you?" He grinned. "Miss CEO and Chairman of the Board."

"Chair*woman*," she corrected. "And interim at that. Until we can find someone qualified. The day-to-day decisions are more than enough for me, thank you."

After the globally televised Jubilee debacle, the Whipple board had hastily convened a meeting at which the handful of pre-Peters members moved that an actual Whipple be brought in to once again run Whipple Corporation. Without a dissenting vote, Emerson Whipple had instantly taken command of her great-uncle's empire.

Ernie surveyed the parks, stretching off toward the horizon in every direction. "So this is all yours now."

"Not really. Whipple's still a public company. It's going to take me four, five, maybe even six years to buy up enough stock to take it private again. But you know what? It'll be worth it. Wall Street's expectations are ridiculous. I'm dumping Whitney Pharmaceuticals, Fontaine Auto Auctions, the tobacco company, even the record company. Everything except the theme parks and the movie studio. There's going to be some changes there, too. No more R-rated pictures. And we're going to free all the healthy animals in the Dominion and turn it into a rehab center for sick and injured exotic species. Whipple Corporation worked best as a family-oriented family business, and that's what we're going to be." Her speech over, she looked up with a grin. "There. How did that sound?"

"Great." Ernie nodded, then smiled at her gratefully. "Thanks, by the way, personally and professionally."

One of her first official actions as CEO was to revoke the purchase of Schylle Newspapers, with the exception of the *Orlando Advocate,* which she had kept. The next day, she named Ernie the new executive editor and announced a stock-purchase arrangement in which employees' profit-sharing money would be used over a period of ten years to buy full ownership of their paper.

"Don't mention it." She playfully pinched his leg between her toes. "Anytime I can wrench a boyfriend of mine's newspaper away from a blood-sucking chain, I feel a moral obligation to do it."

Ernie stroked her feet and sighed. "Well, *this* boyfriend, for one, is forever in your debt." He stroked her feet some more, pulled his head back to study them. "You know, you really do have beautiful feet. No wonder Sheriff Albright had the hots for them."

"Don't even . . ." She shuddered, shook her head. "Just the thought of all that . . ."

Ernie sat quietly a moment, letting her reflect. The governor, faced with Ernie and Emma's press conference explaining all that had happened, had had no choice but to issue an executive order initiating an outside investigation. A sweep of the Serenity cloverleaf retention pond had turned up five additional cars, including Tony Armstrong's Crown Vic. A subsequent forensic exam of the debris basket at the sewage treatment plant had found a good dozen possible artifacts, mainly bits of dental fillings but including at least one piece of jewelry.

Serenity the town, Emma had decided, was better off gone. The cost of modifying the landscape back the way it was, and then rebuilding, was many times what it would take just to buy out all the homeowners with a generous settlement. Not to mention the psychological toll the Jubilee flooding had taken. Even the most ardent Whippophiles had indicated that they would just as soon live elsewhere, thank you very much, even if Serenity were somehow restored to everything that had been promised in the sales brochures.

Ultimately, despite Uncle Waldo's original dream, Emma had determined that it would be best to let the new, deeper, longer Lake Serenity—or Lake Weechkatuknee, as it would once more be known—remain. She even decided to go ahead and launch the *Dixie Princess* there, but only as a scenic ride. No gambling.

Emma returned from her reverie and slid herself closer to Ernie so she could wrap her arms around him. "Well, enough of that. So. What are you doing later?"

He caressed her hair, then her neck. "Oh, not much, really. But I'm an important guy, you know. Run my own newspaper. Got a nice house. Drive a Mercedes. It's in the shop right now, but I can show you pictures. Impressed yet?"

"Absolutely." She gave him a peck on the cheek. "So

what, you want I should come over, look at your record collection or something?"

Ernie glanced around the horizon, saw Prince Charming's Palace approaching on their left. He smiled and nodded at the castle. "Actually, now that I'm not afraid of heights anymore . . . how about we check out the view from up there?"

"Become charter members of the *New* Top of the World Club? Maybe while we're watching the fireworks? Maybe make some of our own?" Emma bit her lip and leaned closer. "You're on."

They were still kissing when the gondola slid into Mont Blanc Station. The ride attendants didn't say a word as the car swung around, past the row of bemused passengers, and right back out again.

Turn the page
for an exciting preview of

# BLACK SUNSHINE

by S. V. Date

# Prologue

**...**

To the west, over the Seven Seas Resort's red-tiled condos on the shore, the squall line assumed an ominous, purplish-green cast as it advanced seaward. A leading edge of wispy cirrus eclipsed the late afternoon sun, instantly robbing the water of its sapphire brilliance.

It would not be long, Spencer Tolliver knew, before the dark thunderheads themselves blocked out the sun, turning blue sky and bluer ocean into a uniform slate color, and the first, cold breath of air came blasting out ahead of the storm. It would be at that moment, he promised himself, that he would abandon the enormous fish on his line and point the boat back in toward the inlet.

Which meant, he estimated, looking over his polarized Ray-Bans at the western sky, he had about ten minutes to tire and boat a monster he had been fighting now for more than an hour. Tolliver gave his rod a yank, got a tug in return that reeled off a few yards more line, and then settled back to wait another minute before going all out.

It was a grouper. That or a snapper. Big bottom fish, darting in and out of a maze of hidey-holes along the coral-and-rock seabed some fifty feet down. He had three feet of wire leader at the end of the line. Three feet of margin. If he let the fish go any deeper into a hole than that, it would simply shake its head a few times until the nylon line snagged and parted with a snap.

Tolliver sighed. This fish had no doubt escaped more than one angler that way in its lifetime, and it was looking more and more like it would escape yet another.

Well, that was fine. There was no dishonor in losing to a smart old fish. And certainly the old saw was still true— a bad day's fishing was indeed better than a good day's work, which in his case was being the Comptroller of Florida, and was many times better than a good day's campaign fundraising, which was what he was scheduled to do later that evening.

There was, in fact, little he disliked more than fundraising—going around the room, shaking hands, grinning like a fool, thank you, thank you, thank you ever so much. Occasionally the donor would whip out a checkbook right in front of his eyes, post-date it, put pen to paper, then look up to ask him: how much?.

Spencer Tolliver always struggled to contain the smart-ass reply: Whatever you think owning a piece of the next Governor of Florida is worth.

Technically, with his campaign still unofficial and below the radar, he was collecting commitments, not actual money. It made little difference. Owning a piece of the next governor was what nearly every one of his potential contributors was thinking, particularly those who attended the swanky, black-tie optional, quail eggs-and-caviar events that netted the big, six-figure IOUs. It hadn't been as bad during the campaign for Comptroller, but that was only because, (1) few people had even heard of the office, and (2) even fewer thought he had a chance of winning.

There he'd been, a cranky, old retired Marine general and one-time POW, whiling away his golden years on a Panhandle beach, fishing at sunup and sundown and writing cranky, old op-ed pieces to the local newspaper in the afternoon about corruption in Tallahassee, particularly in the office of the Comptroller, the so-called watchdog of the rest of state government. Finally the local party boss had suggested he put his money where his mouth was and run against the guy. No one, not even Tolliver, thought it possible he might actually win. The incumbent was going on his fourth term, with a big, fat campaign war chest for a race that few voters paid any attention to. Tolliver decided to run because he believed *somebody* should.

Then, out of nowhere, the FBI and U.S. Attorney swooped down and indicted the guy, and political first-timer Tolliver walked into the office with sixty-two percent of the vote, putting him in charge of regulating Florida banks and brokerage houses, giving him oversight over all state finances, and, most important, giving him a seat on the Florida Cabinet, one of six votes equal to that of the governor in state executive branch matters.

And it was in that capacity—as a free-thinking Republican on the Cabinet, who could not be bought by the special interests, as staunch a defender of Florida's remaining wilderness as the environmental lobby could hope to see—that Tolliver began catching the eye of good-government purists, who began a whisper campaign to persuade him to run for governor.

Tolliver had thought about it long and hard. There was a lot about public life that he was not crazy about. Particularly following his experience in the military where his orders were carried out without discussion, the endless wheedling by the moneyed interests on issues where the Right Thing to Do was as obvious as a flashing neon sign, sometimes drove him to distraction. At least once or twice a week, to regroup, he would need the long drive from Tallahassee out to his beach house in Cape San Blas for a soothing hour of surf-casting for blues and jacks.

On the other hand, Tolliver had realized, he was facing a rare political opportunity. The incumbent Democrat was retiring after his second term. His lieutenant governor, a decent enough fellow, was nonetheless a bad candidate, and beatable. Meanwhile, among Republicans, only he had successfully run a statewide campaign before. A former congressman, two state senators and the political novice Billings brothers were also interested in running, with the state party chairman openly supporting the Billings boys, on the theory that their father's name would make either of them the strongest candidate in the field.

Tolliver had almost bought that argument before his contrariness had gotten the better of him: *He* was the one on the Cabinet, by God, not Percy or Bub Billings. And if party boss Farber LaGrange didn't want him, it was because the electric utilities and Big Oil and Big Sugar and Big Everyone Else didn't want him. And that right there was reason enough to run. Besides, he was a widower whose children were grown. What else did he have to do?

Three weeks earlier, he had told LaGrange his decision, that he intended to announce his run for Florida Governor on June 1, and if that meant the party had to endure a primary in September, then so be it. That's what democracy was all about. To his credit, LaGrange accepted it and told him he would do all he could to get the party behind him. He'd arranged a series of unpublicized meet-and-greet sessions with the big-money set in Sarasota, Naples and Palm Beach, had even arranged for Tolliver to use his fishing boat for a little R&R before his event at Jupiter's swanky Seven Seas Resort.

And a nice little boat it was, Tolliver thought again as he eyed the craft up and down. A 26-foot Robolo with a 225-hp Mercury. He personally would have picked an Evinrude, but what the hell. Beggars could not be choosers. Plus the man had been generous enough to point out his favorite fishing hole. Tolliver knew he had little grounds for complaint.

The water around him suddenly lost its remaining color, and Tolliver took off the polarized sunglasses and put them in his pocket. They would not do him much good, particularly once the rain started. He eyed the tall thunderheads approaching from shore with a twinge of nervous energy. It would get wild, once the wind started blowing and the waves started frothing. Wild, he knew, but not particularly dangerous. He was only a few miles offshore. Not enough room for the waves to build quickly. Besides, the big Merc would let him cover that distance in ten minutes, tops. Then, if the wind was still blowing too hard once he made the inlet, he'd drop the hook in the Intracoastal for a while before tucking back into Seven Seas's marina.

Tolliver eased back the rod a bit, preparing for his final attempt to land his fish. He had the butt of the pole resting in its receptacle in the leather harness he was wearing, with the pin pushed through the base to keep the pole from flying overboard. When the time came and he still hadn't caught the fish, he would simply tighten the drag wheel and walk back a few steps until the ten-pound line snapped, and then turn his attention to getting the boat back in ahead of the worst of the storm.

He'd go to his room, shower and order a room service sandwich before dressing for the gala that evening. He'd spend the night and maybe get in a half day of fishing in the morning before hitting the road for an Orlando gig the following evening—his twenty-first event in twenty-nine days, bringing him close to the million-dollar commitment mark that would help cement his lead among potential GOP candidates and, with any luck, keep the rest of them from even filing papers.

Then, with all that grubby money locked in early, he could spend the remainder of the summer and early fall doing what he liked best: the town hall meetings where he'd mingle with regular Floridians, one-on-one, and explain why they should not only vote for him for governor, but also pester their legislative candidates into supporting his broad, campaign-financing proposal to take big money out of Florida politics once and for all. Like fishing, he thought with a grin, he could happily talk about campaign finance reform for hours on end.

Perhaps, he realized, he could even do both. . . . After all, the vast majority of the state's population lived within twenty miles of a coast. He could park the RV each night at a nearby beach for a couple hours of daybreak surf casting to start out each morning. He smiled at the prospect, gave another gentle tug at the rod perched on his still-flat belly and, without warning, felt himself nearly knocked over by the blast of frigid air barreling ahead of the squall line. Landward, the resort's tiled roofs had nearly disappeared in sheets of rain, and Tolliver wondered if he'd perhaps underestimated the storm's strength.

Well, no matter. He'd run through spring squalls before, and he'd do so again. There was nothing like driving a boat under a purple sky, wind roaring, lightning flashing all around, icy rain coming more straight at you than down. It re-invigorated the life force, reminded him what it meant to be alive.

He couldn't help the beginnings of a grin as he cranked down the drag on the vintage Penn reel, tightening as hard as it would go. Then, a mere tug on the handle would make the rod bend over and the line sing for a moment before it snapped, like so. . . .

But the line didn't snap.

He tugged, then tugged harder, then stepped back from the transom, but the monofilament showed absolutely no sign of strain. His brow narrowed and his lips thinned as he stared at the reel, then tried pulling the line out by hand.

Nothing.

The drag was indeed set, but for some reason the ten-pound test simply refused to break, no matter how much force he applied. He reached for his belt for his wire cutters, realized they weren't there, saw them on the port bait well and began moving toward them when the fish hit again and again, bigger than it had all afternoon, yanking

Tolliver bodily toward the starboard gunwale, slamming him hard against the rail.

Over and over, it hit, now actually pulling the Robolo through the water, and Tolliver struggled to work the pin free from the base of the rod handle, realized he couldn't against the strain of the fish, tried instead to undo the buckles of the harness attaching him to the fishing pole—which is when he felt the unmistakable tightness of electricity surging through his body, contracting every muscle, locking the breath in his lungs, stopping his heart. . . .

And with Spencer Tolliver's ears unable to hear the roaring wind and the exposed skin on his neck barely registering the first cold drops of rain, the fish pulled yet again and yanked him clean over the side and down into the wind-roiled black water.

# one

# ...

The port cap rail was about half scrubbed when the state car pulled into the gravel parking lot beside the single-wide trailer that served as the marina office.

Murphy Moran knew even before the plain yellow tag with the official lettering came into view that it was a state car, and stood with one hand on the starboard shroud to watch. Like most boat docks in Florida, Blastoff View Marina was on sovereign waters, with the submerged land leased to the boatyard. A code enforcement officer had been by a couple times previously in recent weeks, once even coming on Columbus Day, a state holiday, and Murphy looked forward to the distraction a confrontation between humorless bureaucrat and humorless scofflaw would bring when he noticed the erect carriage of the silver-haired gentleman who emerged from the passenger seat.

Ramsey, he realized with a wide smile. Only Ramsey.

Of all the high-ranking politicos he had ever known, Ramsey MacLeod was the only one who refused to treat his Highway Patrol driver like a chauffeur and insisted on riding in the front seat beside him.

Quickly, Murphy appraised himself, set the plastic bristle brush in his hand on the cabin top, grabbed a torn T-shirt off the dorade vent and ran stained fingers through his hair before returning Ramsey MacLeod's wave.

"Mr. Lieutenant Governor!" Murphy called out, moving quickly to the bow.

MacLeod was already walking quickly down the worn dock, agilely avoiding the spots with the missing planks before reaching out to pump Murphy's hand. "Permission to come aboard, Captain!"

Murphy helped him over the pulpit and Ramsey MacLeod grabbed him by both shoulders and squeezed, gray eyes twinkling merrily, then bent to slip off his loafers. "I know how you yachtsmen are about scuff marks." He glanced around the boat, at the squalid trailer on shore, then affected mock concern. "I don't mean to sound unkind, man, but I thought you were a *Republican* consultant. How come you're living like a Democrat? I thought you had a big boat." He nodded at the half-scrubbed teak rail. "And I figured Republicans had *people* to do that sort of thing."

Murphy shrugged. "I did the math. I didn't have money to quit *and* keep *Dark Horse*." *Dark Horse* had been his Hinckley Sou'wester 54, the dream boat he had rarely sailed in the years he'd owned her. He shrugged again. "You wanna retire at forty, you gotta make sacrifices. With *Mudslinger*, I can pay my running costs and living expenses off the interest, never touch the principal."

Ramsey MacLeod took off his blazer and slung it over his shoulder. "Spoken like a true Scotsman."

"I'm Irish," Murphy said.

"Well, we all got our shortcomings," Ramsey said with a wry smile. "Anyway, I admire your fiscal discipline. And you gotta love the name: *Mudslinger*." He pursed his thin lips a moment. "Actually, it was on that matter I came to see you."

Murphy nodded toward the stern and led his guest down

the narrow side deck, into the cockpit, then down the companionway into the main salon. MacLeod admired varnished cherry bulkheads, hunched over the chart table and dinette, poked his head over the stainless-steel stove and sink, then ran his fingers over weathered bronze portholes.

"Well, this is cozy," he announced.

"The smaller the boat, the less there is to maintain," Murphy said, with more than a twinge of defensiveness.

"She ain't that small," Ramsey MacLeod said.

"Yeah, she is. Southern Cross 31. Nine-and-a-half foot beam. Canoe stern. She's small." He pounded the bulkhead, and it gave a solid thunk. "But she's built like a tank. Oversized, redundant rigging. Hand-laid glass in the hull. Anywhere I want to go, she'll get me there."

Ramsey MacLeod nodded, impressed. "And once you get there, will you be able to watch videos?"

He reached into his blazer pocket for a VHS cassette and handed it to Murphy, who opened a cabinet over the starboard settee and popped the tape into a compact, combination TV/VCR. It turned on automatically and showed a home video of a boisterous campaign rally, the camera panning over hundreds of people clapping to bass-and-keyboards Eurotech rock music.

"In case you haven't been following, this is one of my *opponent's* events," Ramsey MacLeod narrated. "Mine don't attract quite as many folks. They got better stuff to do, like rearrangin' their sock drawers."

The camera settled on the stage, where a dozen stuffy, Republican-looking community and business leaders stood clapping and stomping their feet at random intervals, when suddenly the crowd went berserk as a short, curly-haired guy in a golf shirt and khakis came strutting onto the stage, his head doing its own strut, like a hen's, and stood at the microphone with arms outstretched and thumbs up.

"That's my opponent," Ramsey MacLeod said. "Bub Billings."

Bub mouthed "thank you" about a dozen times, then,

with head still bobbing, he launched into his remarks and got as far as *My fellow Floridians* before the crowd erupted again and the candidate had to say "thank you" another dozen times. Finally he began again: *My fella Floridians, I am humbled and honored by your energy. If I could bottle it and sell it, shoot, I bet I could give ol' Bill Gates a run for his money!*

Another round of insane cheering, with Bub once again flashing thumbs up, before he settled into his.speech: *When I founded Bub's Fine Lawn Furniture in my garage five years ago, I didn't have but two nickels to rub together. But I invested both of them in the business, and you know why? Because I believed that in America, you CAN make a difference. Now my payroll's fifty-seven fine people. Fifty-seven TAXPAYIN' folks like you an' me! Because in America the business of America is business! And that's an ethic, a . . .* Bub squinted just off-camera for a long second . . . what the heck . . . *what?* oh: *para-*dime. Yeah. Great. Teach me for usin' speechwriters that use fifty-cent words. Alright: *A para-*dime *that we gotta have instead of the somethin'-for-nothin' culture that encourages the economically disadvantaged to pass their values on to the next generation.*

"Amazing, isn't it?" Ramsey MacLeod said. "Guy can't read a Tele-Prompter. Turns it into an applause line."

*We CAN take this back, folks. For eight long years, the liberal-media-elite's' been runnin' things in Tallahassee, and look what they've given us: the highest unemployment in twenty years, and three-dollar-a-gallon gas. Anyone here like payin' three dollars a gallon for gas?* A resounding "nooooooo!" from the crowd. *Me neither! It's time the regular folk got a chance! Or my name ain't Bub Billings!* Bub smiled and pointed out into the crowd until the applause died down. *Three and half more weeks, everybody! So keep your eye on the brass ring and get ready to grab the prize, and on November the 5th, we the people are gonna win! Thank you very much!*

Bub ran off the stage, thumbs held high, as the music thumped. Rammsey MacLeod reached around the folding dinette table to hit the STOP button.

"And Elvis leaves the building." Ramsey removed the tape and slapped his palm with it a few times. "He does five of those rallies a day. Half the folks in the audience are bused from one to the next like cattle. We suspect they're gettin' paid, but can't prove it. He and his handlers ride in one luxury bus. All the press rides in the other. The buses have satellite TV and catered food. After five, the press bus has an open bar. On my campaign, the press has to squeeze into a rented mini-van. They eat McDonald's. Sonny's Barbecue on a good day. Guess which campaign the reporters like covering better?"

Murphy Moran said nothing, kept his arms folded across his chest. He had a feeling where this was headed.

"Pretty much the same story on the fund-raising side. They're raising and spending five dollars to every one of ours. Now, I've been a Democrat all my life. I'm used to getting outspent. But five to one? That's a bit hard to take. Especially from a guy and a campaign like this: Had it been Spencer Tolliver beating the pants off me? I wouldn't have minded so much."

Murphy nodded. "I heard that rumor, too. That he was starting to raise some money. It's a damned shame about what happened."

"Even Percy Billings wouldn't have been so bad. Sure he's an arrogant son-of-a-bitch, but there's no doubt he's worked his butt off his whole life. But I suppose he doesn't poll as well as Bub, and we all know how important *that* is in the World According to Farber." Ramsey shook his head. "I can't tell you how depressing losing to this one is. Shoot, he didn't take his own life seriously until a couple years ago. He hasn't put forward a single policy objective. His entire campaign is high energy and flashy production. That and three-dollar gas. Like that's somehow my fault."

Murphy shuffled his bare feet on the cabin sole. Like

most boats, it was dark teak interspersed with strips of white holly. Like most boats too poor to afford paid-crew, it was badly scuffed, in need of stripping down to bare wood and re-varnishing.

"You been paying much attention to the race?" MacLeod asked.

Murphy shook his head. "I've been trying to get *Mudslinger* ready to go down island this winter. Finally. You can imagine how it is: a million things to do, fewer and fewer days left to get them done. Like right now, I'm waiting on a part to fix the VHF, haven't even started to install the SSB. Haven't even taken it out of the box yet—"

"They dragged out 'Mother,'" MacLeod said.

Murphy winced, then let out a long, deep sigh. "Mother" had been Murphy's brainchild four years earlier, when MacLeod and his boss, Governor Bolling Waites, had run for re-election against a punk real-estate developer from Miami. Murphy had worked for the punk, and "Mother" had been a masterpiece of below-the-belt campaigning, a thirty-second television ad shot in grainy black and white, flashing between the image of an old lady lying in a hospital bed with tubes running in and out of her nose and stark white lettering explaining how she had developed bed sores and lesions and, ultimately, a fatal infection while negligent nursing home attendants had failed to notice—all on the Waites-MacLeod watch. The only sound was the beeping of a heart monitor that, by commercial's end, became the steady flat tone signifying death. Left out of the spot, naturally, was even a hint of how it had been the Republican-dominated legislature, not Waites and MacLeod, who had refused to fund even a token number of nursing home inspectors as a sop to the industry that, coincidentally enough, had provided millions for their campaigns.

The ad had been as effective as it was unfair, and had given Murphy's man a solid lead in the polls that Waites had been able to overcome only with a stunning performance in the final debate and a blitz of tens of thousands of last-minute "scare" calls to elderly voters accusing the Republicans of wanting to repeal Social Security.

"How bad is it?" Murphy asked finally.

"Twenty-one days to the election, and I'm a solid eleven down in the polls. Before gas prices went nuts, I was actually ahead. Gas got to two-fifty a gallon, and I was four points behind. Three bucks a gallon, and I fell to eight points. Now they started running your ad, and suddenly I'm down eleven."

"Their poll? Or yours?"

"Mine," MacLeod said to Murphy's groan. "Exactly. So it's probably more like thirteen, what with pollsters always shading it on the side of whoever's writing the check."

Murphy stared at the grease- and paint-stained to-do list on the navigation table. More than half the items on it still did not have a check mark against them, and he was quickly running out of weather window. If he wasn't in Georgetown by mid-November, he could kiss the Caribbean goodbye for yet another winter.

Still and all, it was *his* brutal handiwork that was continuing its ruthless destruction long after he'd left the scene: like an abandoned gill net in the middle of the ocean, indiscriminately killing every swimming thing even after the fishermen had forgotten they had lost it.

"Now I know I ain't the most charismatic candidate to come down the pike. Far from it. But I know state government, and I know how to make it work better," Ramsey MacLeod said. "I suppose that's not near as sexy as making fun of it and running against it. But there it is. That's who I am."

"You don't have to apologize for being decent, Ramsey," Murphy said, with a sigh. "I'll do it. I owe you."

MacLeod shook his head. "You *don't* owe me, Murph. Not after how you came around and helped Bolling in the tobacco fight like you did."

"That wasn't to help Bolling. That was because it was the right thing to do. I still owe you."

Ramsey nodded slowly, then cracked a grin. "I guess I can't pretend I wasn't hoping you'd see it that way. All right then. I thank you. I don't mean to drag you out of retirement or anything. I just need a mind like yours to come up with a fresh idea. You know, something. . . ."

"Devious?" Murphy offered.

Ramsey grinned again. "Just whatever you can manage. I won't destroy your reputation by paying you or anything. It's not like I can afford your rates, anyway. I'm a Democrat, you remember. Just . . . a new concept, is what I'm looking for." He gathered up his blazer and started to climb the companionway ladder. "I've got a few ideas you could work with. About a dozen different things he's said on the campaign trail—"

"We haven't got time for that. That would take a solid two months, minimum, to build a strategy based on contradictory statements. We've got less than three weeks." Murphy followed MacLeod up into the cockpit, felt the boat list to port slightly as they walked forward along the port side deck. "This late in the game, we need a sucker punch."

MacLeod put his shoes on and swung one leg over the stainless tubing of the bow pulpit. "You were thinking. . . ."

Murphy thought for a second, opened his mouth to answer before closing it again. "You probably don't want to know."

Ramsey MacLeod stood on the dock and waved at his driver. "You're probably right. But I can tell from that gleam in your eye that whatever it is, it ain't gonna be pretty. Okay then. Bolling warned me it might come to this. So be it. *Alia iacta est*. Go for it. Get me something I can use to kick the snot out the little twerp." MacLeod took a deep breath, blew it out. "You got yourself a cabin wench yet? For this world cruise of yours? Hey, weren't you seeing that lobbyist for Bell South Wireless?"

Murphy winced, shook his head. "Don't go there, please."

Ramsey MacLeod raised a sympathetic eyebrow. "Sore subject? That's all right. I'm sure the wench issue will take care of itself when you get to one of those islands where the women all go topless. You are planning on visiting some of those islands, aren't you? Well, of course you are." He thought about that and nodded slowly. "Well, I think I'll shut up now, before I talk you out of helping me. Take care, and thanks again."

And with a broad grin, MacLeod turned and walked up the dock to the car, where he carefully hung his blazer in the back seat before climbing in beside his driver.

Murphy watched from the bow as the Crown Victoria bumped down the gravel road ahead of a cloud of dust, then turned to gather up and stow his teak-scrubbing gear before heading to the marina bathroom for a shower.

Clyde Bruno cracked his knuckles impatiently as Grant carefully copied the question off the printed page and onto the back of his hand. Behind him hung a giant banner, "Floridians Meet Bub!" over the Coral Reef Ballroom, and Clyde was starting to get nervous that the candidate would at any moment stroll on through and start the bull session, leaving Grant and his big yellow name tag that said "Regular Floridian Grant" out in the lobby, still copying.

Clyde said, "Hurry it up," and got a grunt in reply.

He stood, walked to the front window, and saw the candidate on a stage set up in the parking lot raising his thumbs skyward. triumphantly, the crowd going wild on cue. He turned and walked back to the vinyl seat, sniffed with wrinkled nose at the mildew that managed to overpower both salt air and disinfectant.

There had been a time when such a smell would not even have registered with him, so accustomed was he to the rank mess that was his own trailer park home. Stale beer, cigarette smoke and mildew were a constant, interrupted only during the occasional tropical-storm-induced flood that left instead a month-long stench of non-specific organic decomposition.

That, though, had been before he'd caught the eye of Petron North America chief Link Thresher during a labor dispute. The boss happened to be in town and took notice of refinery hand Bruno and how he'd sided with the foreman against the rabble with enthusiastic violence, resulting in three concussions, a broken nose and a shattered kneecap. The end result was that the unionizing effort failed, and Thresher had started him on a chain of rapid promotions that quickly put him in the rarefied air of the executive suite with the title: Special Assistant to the President.

Now it was strictly first-class for Clyde Bruno. Company house, company housekeeper, company cook, company car. On the road, it was a room next door to Mr. Thresher at five- and, in extremely rare instances, four-star hotels. No more Holiday Inns, no more Waffle House dinners, no more *mildew*.

Except now, he allowed grudgingly, for the sake of getting the job done to Mr. Thresher's satisfaction. Once again he growled, "Hurry it up," and this time leaned over Grant's shoulder to check his progress. The goober was clutching the pen in his hand like a carving knife and copying each letter individually in all capitals, and Clyde rolled his eyes and shifted his weight from leg to leg.

Whether Grant was a first or last name he had no idea. The man had simply introduced himself as Grant from the Party. Clyde knew he was on the Party's Goon Squad, the thick-browed gents who were dispatched as the GOP's "observers" during election disputes. He personally wouldn't have chosen Grant for this particular task, but there apparently was not a whole lot of choice. They needed someone whom the candidate absolutely had not met before, which ruled out pretty much everybody at party headquarters. Grant happened to have been out on assignment during Bub's visit and therefore met the main criterion. Others, like the ability to read and speak . . . well, Clyde had had to make do.

"Got it, boss," Grant proclaimed, handing the pen back.

Clyde Bruno read Grant's hand and nodded his assent. "Okay. Good. Now, you know how this works?"

"I'm a Regular Floridian with an important question," Grant recited. "Mr. Billings—"

"Bub," Clyde Bruno corrected. "He likes to be called Bub. Everyone else will call him Bub. Don't draw attention to yourself."

"Okay, Bub. Bub will ask me if I have a question for him, and I read this."

Clyde Bruno heard a roar outside and saw the candidate bounding down the steps off the stage toward the hotel entrance as rally organizers began shepherding the dozen or so other yellow-name-tagged Regular Floridians in the lounge into the Coral Reef Ballroom. Clyde Bruno reached into the inside pocket of Grant's too-small houndstooth blazer, pulled out the Sony microcassette recorder and pushed the record and play buttons simultaneously, then dropped the recorder back in and patted Grant's jacket.

"You're ready to rock and roll, sport." Then he grabbed the larger man's lapel and caught him with a steely gaze. "Don't fuck this up."

Clyde Bruno turned Grant to face the Coral Reef Ball room and gave a gentle nudge to get him moving before he ducked into a hallway to avoid the approaching entourage.

In the penthouse suite of the Floridians for a Better Future, the Politics Channel blared on from the corner about the latest national poll numbers from the various congressional races that were expected to be close.

Percy Billings paid it no mind, instead furrowed his still-youthful brow as he dug into the raw data of a different poll, one commissioned by the party five months earlier following the sudden death of its top potential candidate for governor at the time.

In broad numbers, it showed that likely voters regarded Percy Billings most highly among the remaining field for his intellect, his depth of knowledge and his experience for the job. And yet, just as convincingly, it showed his brother as the most likable candidate and the one they thought would win with the biggest margin in a head-to-head election against Ramsey MacLeod.

Percy swore inwardly at the data, shaking his head in disgust but not, he allowed, disbelief. It had been this way all his life. No matter how hard he worked, how much he learned, how sincere he was, he would still be measured against his brother and come out poorly in the comparison.

It had baffled him since their youth. Percy had been the straight "A" student in prep school. Byron made C's. Percy had gone out west to Stanford and earned a masters and bachelors together in just four years. Byron had gone to Florida State, had dropped out to "find himself," and eventually finished his single degree with night courses at Central Florida.

After college, Percy joined Southwest Florida's largest commercial developer and had ultimately worked his way up to senior vice president while at the same time serving on a number of volunteer boards. Byron worked the line in an Alaskan cannery, drove semis over-the road, then did two stints as a roustabout on a Gulf oil rig before "settling down" to a series of failed businesses in Brevard County until, at age 42, he had finally hit upon his one success: a lawn furniture company.

In politics, Percy had served as a county committeeman, then county chairman, then state committeeman and, finally, RNC delegate.

Byron had done nothing. Nada. Zero.

And yet, Percy was reminded with each hourly update, it was his brother, not he, who was cruising toward an easy win as Governor of Florida in less than three weeks, in so doing becoming the first son of a governor to himself reach that position.

Percy still blamed the obviously defective polling data relied upon by state party chair Farber LaGrange. What else could it be? He flipped through the pages to see the numbers for Brevard County again and shook his head: In these tables had to be the proof of the poll's fatal flaw.

How else to explain it? The people of Brevard County knew his brother better than anyone else in the state. They had seen his Launch Café fall flat and his Nerds-on-the-Go Dry Cleaning close after a single month. Bub's Computer Repair had folded even before the grand opening because, by then, even the greenest graduates coming out of Florida Tech were wise to him and would not take a job with a known loser. At one point, Byron had even incorporated as Billings' Space Services to bid on NASA's multi-billion dollar Shuttle Processing Contract. The agency had refused even to respond to his application.

Yet somehow, according to the party's poll, the public even in Titusville, Cocoa Beach and Melbourne—towns with among the highest education levels in the state—had been snowed by Byron's cute dimple and aw-shucks manners, rating him fifteen point higher in likability, twelve points higher in trustworthiness and seven points higher in competence, than Percy.

Percy read that last bit again and stood to walk over to the plate-glass picture window overlooking downtown Marco Island and, beyond it, the green Gulf of Mexico. A pair of charter fishing boats were heading in toward the cut, coming down off plane as they approached the jetties. Percy sniffed angrily as he stood, hands thrust in the pockets of his khakis, as the boats tied up at the fuel dock and the charter parties disembarked, floppy white hats shining in the sun.

He turned away from the window and stared absently at the television. Higher even in competence. Amazing. Ab-

solutely amazing. It proved again his long-held suspicion
that no one ever got elected overestimating the intelligence
of the voting public. He snorted again at the poll numbers.
Likability: sure, Bryon was more likable. Like a big, dumb
Labrador was likable. Trustworthiness: okay, fine. Boy
Scouts were trustworthy, too: But competence? On what
planet?

In front of the focus group Farber had assembled, Percy
had presented a well-reasoned, fully documented, Twelve
Point Plan for Florida, dealing with everything from the
lousy public schools to out-of-control Medicaid costs.
What had Byron presented? Nothing. Instead he'd just
shown up, talked about integrity and honoring the memory
of their daddy and some such other nonsense . . . and the
idiots had fallen for it!

Given the focus group, given the polling backing it up,
there really wasn't much of a choice, Farber had explained.
At the time Percy had sucked it up and taken the news like
a man and a brother. After all, what else could he do, other
than give Byron a big clap on the shoulder and wish him
good luck?

But then, over the months, it had started to rankle inside
him, how this wasn't some minor delay, some temporary
setback. This was the real deal. The people of Florida were
never going to elect *both* of Lamont Billings' sons to the
Governor's Mansion. Only one of them would reach that
level. If it was Byron, it would never be Percy.

In other words, it would be the same as always. *He* had
always been the more dutiful, the more loyal, in short, the
better son, but Byron had always been Father's favorite.
*He* had always been better-looking, but Byron had dated
prettier girls. *He* had always been smarter and worked
harder, but now Byron was going to get to be governor.

The whole thing had pushed him to distraction, to the
point where it was noticeably affecting his work. He had,
inexplicably, missed a buying opportunity for a prime,
forty-six-acre tract on the edge of some wetlands outside

Fort Myers. A perfect spot for a new strip mall, anchored with maybe a Walgreen's, filled in with the usual mix of tanning salon, Laundromat and payday loan outlet, and Percy somehow had let it slip away to their arch-competitor from Naples.

It was even, Percy had realized one morning, affecting his golf game. It had been months since he had shot below eighty. One recent Sunday, he had actually been on a pace not to break a hundred when it thankfully began to rain and thunder.

He became conscious that he was hearing the name "Billings," and brought his gaze back from deep space to the television set. The Politics Channel had turned its attention to Florida's gubernatorial race, where political novice Bub Billings was incredibly heading into the final stretch with a double-digit lead over the sitting lieutenant governor Ramsey MacLeod, for eight years the right-hand man of popular incumbent Bolling Waites.

The TV showed a clip of Bub wading through an affectionate crowd, shaking hands, tousling children's hair, pointing at recognized friends, while the reporter's voice-over filled in Bub's back story, the black-sheep-son-made-good of legendary Florida governor Lamont Billings, the man who'd dragged a redneck legislature into the civil rights era and racial integration, a stance that had cost him his job after a single term. Political observers around the state, the reporter noted, had fully expected another Billings to make a run at the Governor's Mansion someday. Interestingly, nearly all of them had assumed it would be Percy Billings, a Marco Island real-estate developer who for years had worked his way up the Republican Party totem pole.

The blood in Percy's ears hissed, his eyes narrowed and his hands clenched, but he was unable to tear himself away from the set. The reporter continued with the tale of Bub Billings' meteoric rise from small businessman—Florida's Lawn Furniture King—to a mere step away from chief executive of the nation's fourth-largest state, while his brother, in all likelihood, was doomed to fade into political obscurity. . . .

The hiss had become a full-blown roar, darkening Percy's vision, when the phone rang. Percy hunted for the remote, hit the mute button, then grabbed the handset off his desk.

"What," he snapped. But then he heard who it was and his brow relaxed a bit. "How did it go?"

He listened, and his face began to brighten. *"Really . . .* and the tape is clear? Let me hear it."

Percy listened to the phone some more, and a smile began spreading across his face: "Okay, listen: Dub it and keep a copy safe. Got it? Good. . . . Let me know how it goes."

He hung up, then turned with an amused glance at the television set, where his brother silently mouthed malapropisms to a packed high-school gym. Percy picked up the remote and switched the set off completely, then moved to the plate glass window. He took a deep breath, let his face assume a posture of equal parts sorrow and sincerity, and addressed a shrimp boat heading out the cut into the sparkling Gulf:

"My fellow Floridians. . . . These are indeed the times that try men's souls."


With one ear listening to Farber LaGrange's latest tirade in his office, Florida Republican Party Finance Director Antoinette Johnson sorted through folders until she came to the one marked "Donors—100k—3Q" and cleared some space on her crowded desk.

It was a nearly an inch thick, testament to her success at getting the state's richest individuals and businesses to put their money where their mouths were and fork over substantial sums to put a Republican in the Governor's Mansion after twenty years on the outs. Week after week, she went through reams of donations, inputting them into the database so they could be reported the Friday before election day to the state Division of Elections, while simultaneously writing personal thank-you notes to those donors who had given more than $100,000.

This election, she had noticed, that latter task had started to give her writer's cramp. At one point, she had run a query and was honestly shocked to learn that the six-figure donors now accounted for ninety-four percent of every dollar the party collected, up from seventy-three percent when she'd taken the job a decade earlier.

The official line to the media and the watchdog groups was that this was a wonderful thing: The more money the Party collected, the more the free speech rights of Florida's populace were being expressed, the more joy and happiness would spread across the land.

The only one who could manage that explanation with a straight face was Farber. Of course, the only one who could manage a lot of explanations with a straight face was Farber—everything from solemn attacks on the other party's masculinity to a spirited defense of a Republican Miami city commissioner caught embezzling.

As for Toni, she had a while back concluded that the big money she helped collect was the single most corrosive factor in politics. The big checks came in, and a few weeks or a few months later, the contributors would call for help arranging a meeting with their beneficiaries, who were by then elected officials. Toni would always try to discourage such attempts, but would eventually pass the calls along to Farber, who would quickly and without fail set up the requested meetings. And, a few days or weeks later, a particular person would get appointed to a particular job, or a certain state contract would get awarded to a certain vendor, or an obscure rule or regulation would get waived in an equally obscure permit application.

Toni was fairly certain that these exceptions and shortcuts were not advancing the public good. Being a part of the system that generated them had in recent years worn on her soul—to the point where she had taken to making the occasional photocopy to let a newspaper know about a particularly egregious situation.

The treasonous leaks in the name of good government had at first salved her conscience, particularly in those rare instances when a bad actor wound up losing a contract or, even better, going to jail. Ultimately, though, she had come to accept how little real effect the public disclosures had on the system. It wasn't the extreme cases that made the system corrupt, she had realized, but the everyday acceptance of the little ones: the Insurance Commissioner who returned phone calls from the insurance company executives but not from the consumers who'd gotten screwed on a policy. The museum grants awarded by the Secretary of State that happened to correlate with the largest fundraisers in her last election. The no-bid contracts let by the Department of Agriculture that went to relatives of the citrus baron whose jet the Agriculture Commissioner had used on the campaign trail.

It was time, she had told herself that summer, to get out. One last campaign cycle and she would leave politics and Tallahassee for good. Maybe move down to the islands. Find an oceanography lab somewhere that needed a CPA or even an office helper or even, frankly, a janitor. Something that would get her back to the sea again. Something that would let her enjoy life for a while, give her a chance to figure out what she wanted to do when she grew up. She'd always been good with numbers, so accounting had been a natural choice. Politics, though, had not been, particularly not Republican politics, and it was time she found something she could make a life out of.

A throat cleared beside her, and she returned from her reverie to a perky little blonde holding out a stack of new mail. Her name was Britney. Or maybe Meghan. She always got the two of them confused.

Toni eyed her up and down, over the skimpy blue sundress and sandals, and with a smile accepted the packet from the girl. Toni checked her tongue as Britney or Meghan sashayed away, casually touching the male employees of the office as she walked and generally creating a stir. Farber called them Victory Hostesses, but Toni thought of the dozen, fresh Florida State graduates and non-graduates more as honey bees, the way they flitted around, alluring yet dangerous.

During their first week on the job, she had tried to suggest a professional dress code to Farber: closed-toed shoes and business-length skirts, for starters. Farber had come back with one of his vulgar southernisms that, roughly translated, wondered why in the hell he'd go out of his way to hire a gaggle of sex pots and then make them dress up like old ladies.

Toni had stood steaming in a rage for a long minute before stalking out. There was no reasoning with Farber when he was being an asshole. Besides, the girls' presence in the office was minimal. They'd been hired, as their name suggested, as arm candy for fund-raising events, to meet and greet donors, serve them drinks, help with the set-up and clean up.

Or at least that was what Toni continued to tell herself, despite the rumors of what was actually going on aboard Farber's big sailing yacht, the *Soft Money* . . . that the Victory Hostesses had become more like comfort girls, starting each event wearing little more than a bikini and losing coverage from there. Toni didn't know details and she didn't want to know. That despite the number and size of checks that poured in from *Soft Money* events, every single one of them written by a male.

Well, it just wasn't her problem. All the girls were of legal age, old enough, if they wanted, to perform in pornographic movies or take jobs at the Mustang Ranch. She sure as hell wasn't about to take it upon herself to become their mother hen and try to protect them from sexual harassment—particularly given the attitude they displayed to every other female who worked at party headquarters.

The whole Victory Hostess thing, though, added to her rising discontent with Farber in particular and the state party in general. Back when she'd taken the job, the Democrats controlled both chambers of the legislature as well as the Governor's Mansion and five of six seats on the Cabinet. They ran the state like a fiefdom. She personally had little political ideology beyond good government, and had signed up with the Republicans because anything was better than the way things were.

A decade later, thanks to Farber's organizational skill and her financial knack, the situation was nearly reversed: Four of six Cabinet seats were Republican, as were both House and Senate, and the old, popular governor, the Granddaddy Gator of Florida politics, was retiring after two terms.

Yet even before the election that would realize Farber's dream, Toni could sense that Floridians were getting a state government every bit as bad as the one they had methodically voted out of office over ten years. And it was Farber's single-minded drive, she realized, that had brought it about. Instead of winning to make things better, he had become consumed with winning for the sake of winning.

It was an attitude that trickled down from the top, so that freshmen Republican legislators, flush with victory, would at once forget the constituents who had actually voted for them and instead start sucking up to the special interests that paid their way. Farber saw nothing wrong with it. Toni couldn't find the words to adequately express her disgust.

She sighed and pushed her frustration aside. In less than three weeks, it would all be over. Farber would have gotten what he wanted, and Toni could submit her resignation letter, take her weeks of accumulated leave and sell all her belongings at a yard sale. Then she'd fly down to, say, St. Barts, and start from there. Maybe find a waterfront bar that needed help with its books. Maybe use her off-hours to find a beat-up thirty-footer she could restore, down in the tropics, away from politics. . . .

Twenty-one more days, she thought, then realized she was once again chewing her thumbnail and made a conscious effort to pull her hand away. One of the Hostesses, Tiffany she thought it was, had been so kind as to inform her that chewed fingernails were *not* sexy. The last thing she needed was another grooming lecture from a twenty-year-old bimbo.

With a sigh, she removed the rubber band from the fat file folder representing the week's hundred-thousand-and-up donations, then began filling in her database and deposit slips for the party's checking account.

She studied a cover letter, entered bank number and $500,000 for the amount, flipped a page, entered bank number and $450,000, flipped another page, entered bank number and $575,000. . . . She stopped, looked at the column for bank number, and realized the three entries were the same. Three checks totaling one and a half million dollars from three different corporations, all coming from the same bank. . . .

She blinked, quickly skimmed through the rest of the folder, found three more big checks from the same commercial bank in Miami from three more contributors. She leaned away from her computer, thought a long moment, then brushed a strand of dark hair behind an ear and moved to the query field and typed in the name of the bank.

Within seconds, the screen filled with a list of twenty-four donations over the past five months, all from the same Miami bank, but every one from a different corporate account. She blinked again, thought for another minute, then toggled over to her web browser, where she brought up the state Division of Corporations and looked up the first name on the list.

She noted the result, then looked up the next and, with a sigh and a nod, looked up third and fourth and fifth. Then she flipped to an open page of her notebook and wrote down names and addresses and drew arrows between them. For a good hour she zipped back and forth across first the Corporations, then the Securities and Exchange Commission and finally the Dunn and Bradstreet web sites. Finally she uncrossed her legs, slipped her feet back into the beige pumps beneath her desk, and walked over to her boss's office.

She knocked twice and entered at the grunt to find Farber LaGrange seated at his massive desk scribbling on a yellow pad. She watched the bald spot on the exact top of his big head, where Grecian Formula black strands crossed at regular intervals, waiting for him to finish writing. On the wall behind him were photos of him playing golf with Gerald Ford, welcoming Ronald Reagan at the bottom of Air Force One, fishing with George Bush in Islamorada. On the credenza to the side were assorted saltwater fishing trophies, at least a dozen of them, with the largest one a good four feet tall and topped with a gold-plated sailfish in leaping splendor. Fishing and politics, and Farber played both to win.

"You rang?"

Farber's tanned, leathery jowls reflected his age and time on the water, but the steely blue eyes that stared across the desk were as steady and sharp as a bird of prey's. A hawk's. Or in Farber's case, Toni thought, an osprey's, diving out of the sky at full tilt to snatch up an unsuspecting fish.

She glanced down at her notebook and cleared her throat. "Northstar Consulting of Jacksonville, Harris & Beauchamp of Naples, Interlink Transport of Tampa, Rancourt and Associates in Orlando, Southeast Marine of Fort Pierce, Ronadet Service Corp. in Miami and Island Graphics of Palm Beach. You want to guess what they all have in common?"

Farber LaGrange put on the poker face that Toni knew

meant he was about to lie: "I ain't got the foggiest idea," he said, pronouncing it *eye-dee*.

Toni continued to play it straight, glanced back down at her notebook. "Well, as it turns out, they have two things in common. One, they all have given our party between $400,000 and $600,000 since May."

Farber said, "You want I should write personal thank-you's to 'em?"

"And two, they all list as their registered agent somebody in Apalachicola called Goodkind and Sams. Sounds like a law firm, right? Well, that's what I thought, too. But I checked in the Bar Journal, and there's no such law firm in all of Florida. So I ran it through corporate records, and Goodkind and Sams has a registered agent named Clyde Bruno. Isn't that something? You remember Clyde, don't you?"

Farber said nothing.

"He's your fishing buddy Link Thresher's, uh, how should we call him . . . executive assistant? Fixer? Kneecap-smasher? Whatever. It's kind of interesting that ol' Clyde would have the time, given his day job, to manage the affairs of so *many* unrelated companies." She watched for a response, got none, continued. "Except, of course, I suppose it's not particularly hard, seeing as how none of those companies actually *does* anything. No record with the SEC, nothing in D&B. Not even a phone number."

Now Farber cleared his throat, played with the fountain pen in his hands, balancing it on the tip of his forefinger. "I'm just curious here, Toni, if any part of what you've described is in any way against the law—"

"Of course, those aren't the only companies for whom Clyde is the named agent. There are, via three other inter-mediary firms, fourteen more, for a total of twenty-four companies around the state, whose sole business seems to consist of giving us an average $500,000 to elect a Repub-lican governor."

Farber nodded and smiled, now. "I'll ask you again,

Toni: What Florida statute or Division of Elections rule is either Clyde Bruno or his various companies or the Florida Republican Party violating with these donations?"

Toni tucked the notebook against her chest and crossed her arms. "The whole point of the campaign finance code is to let the public know who gave and who got. We're breaking the spirit of these laws."

"That's why we got all them high-falutin' law*yers*, Toni," Farber laughed. "To find ways to break the spirit of laws without messin' with the letter of 'em. Ain't that right? Now you seem to be concerned that Clyde Bruno, and, I presume by extension, Link Thresher and Petron Oil is given' all this money to us. Correct me here if I'm wrong, but this is all *soft* money, ain't it? Which means, if he wanted, ol' Link coulda written out a check on a Petron account for the *en*tire twelve mil in one shot and it woulda been perfectly legal. Am I not correct?"

Toni stood her ground. "So why didn't he?"

Farber threw his arms up in mock surprise. "Fuck should I know? Ask *him*!" He began stacking his appointment book, a Palm Pilot and other items from his drawers onto his desktop blotter. "Look, maybe he thinks it's to his strategic advantage for everyone not to know he supports our side."

"That's my point," Toni said. "The law was designed so everyone could know exactly that. He's making that impossible."

Farber straightened, narrowed his eyes. "Not *completely* impossible. You figured it out. Now, Toni, I always said you're a smart gal. It's why I hired you. But seriously, you're not suggesting that there ain't nobody in the entire Democrat party, in all the media, who can't connect the dots like you just did? Christ almighty, Toni, it's what they get *paid* to do." He grabbed his briefcase from the floor and started packing the things on his desk. "Now if you'll excuse me, I gotta get a move on. Flyin' back out to Titusville tonight. Got fundraisers on *Soft Money* the rest of the week." He glanced up with a smile. "You might even get a couple more checks from Clyde Bruno companies, if you're lucky."

Toni sighed again, thought of one last protest, when the phone buzzed on Farber's desk. He hit a button and the speakerphone's static filled the room.

"What now?" Farber bellowed.

"Thought you'd wanna know," a voice crackled. "MacLeod ducked away from his campaign this morning. Guess who he visited."

"The Pope. I ain't got time for games, Buckin'ham. Just tell me."

"Murphy Moran."

"Hah!" Farber laughed, then shot a wink at Toni. "Ain't heard that name in a coupla years. Thought he slinked away with his tail 'tween his legs after the tobacca fight. Well, too bad for Ramsey. Not even ol' Murph's gonna be able to save his bacon this time. Becky, hold on just one second." Farber nodded at Toni: "We finished?"

Toni Johnson shrugged, then remembered three other transactions that had caught her eye. "Not unless you can tell me anything about the Clean Gulf Trust."

"Ain't got the foggiest," Farber said, then turned back to his phone. "Bucky, you still there?"

Toni blew out an exasperated breath and headed back toward her desk, shaking her head as she walked. It was a giant game to him, that's all. He knew as well as she did that the chances of anyone catching on to the trick with all those checks in the days left before the election were negligible. It was only because the name Clyde Bruno rang a bell with her that she had been able to figure it out.

As Toni walked, though, resignation rekindled into anger. She had no idea what exactly Petron wanted, but could only assume from their desire to remain anonymous that it wasn't good. She should tell someone, is what she should do . . . is what she *would* do, she decided.

She paged through the corporate search printouts in her

notebook, tried to think of who. . . . It was probably too late to get them to anyone in the press. Plus, it was a crap-shoot, getting them into the hands of a reporter who had both the ability to do the necessary digging as well as fifteen free minutes at the moment he or she opened the envelope to realize the significance of the documents rather than simply pitching them in the waste bin. And sending it to the Democrats was pointless; anything they said this late in the campaign would be viewed as last-minute desperation. If only there were somebody else, somebody not associated with the Democratic Party, somebody with the savvy to—

And then a wide smile broke across her face as she walked right past her desk to the rear window that overlooked tree-lined Meridian Street, to the high-speed photocopier just beside the window, and pushed the green button to let it start warming up.

Enormous gas turbine engines emitting a low thrum and giant screws churning the Gulf into a swatch of whitewater behind her, the oil tanker *City of Galveston* slid steadily west-northwest toward New Orleans.

Seven-hundred feet of black hull streaked with rust stains, she carried a Panamanian ensign on her stern rail and sixty thousand tons of Bahrain crude in her holds. Like most commercial freighters, she was staffed with a bare skeleton crew, with nearly half of the ship's complement unfilled. Like most tramp freighters, the crew that was aboard rarely paid much attention.

On most hours of most days, the six-foot radar antenna that spun atop her superstructure was purely ornamental, collecting data for an empty radio room. Neither radar operator nor radio man made a distinction between on- and off-watch hours, typically spending both in the rec room playing cards and drinking whiskey or in their bunks sleeping it off.

All of which had made the wet-suited man's mission that much easier.

Eighteen hours earlier, as the vessel plowed west through the Florida Straits, hugging the hundred-fathom line to avoid the worst of the Gulf Stream current setting the opposite direction, he had climbed aboard easily, finding no one at the forward lookout station.

The one thing that had worried him the most, that during the daylight hours the aft lookout might notice the thin Kevlar rope he had tied to a fitting near the stern, also never came to pass. On the *City of Galveston*, no one kept watch at all—forward, aft, or any other direction.

His first six hours aboard, the wet-suited man conducted a thorough reconnaissance of the vessel, finding a total of eight people aboard as he drew himself a schematic of the engine rooms. Less than twelve hours after he'd come over the rail, the wet-suited man was finished and waiting in one of the tarpaulin-covered lifeboats that hung from davits as a red, mid-October sun sank into the Gulf off the port beam.

He lifted his head as the moment grew near, risking detection to watch the final seconds of sunset. Alas, the fiery ball dropped uneventfully into the sea—no green flash—and the wet-suited man ducked back into his bivouac and closed his eyes for some sleep.

Hours later, his dive watch beeped softly six times, and he was instantly awake. He checked forward and aft along the deck, and with two steps was over the rail. He clung to the metal bulwark with one hand, undid a knot and retied it around his waist with the other, and then tossed a waterproof, buoyant tool bag into the darkness before following it in with a dive so clean it barely made a splash.

Twenty minutes later, six small explosions occurred simultaneously in the *City of Galveston*'s transmission and engine rooms. Had anyone been monitoring the systems panels, he might have seen and heard the oil pressure alarms. As it was, the chief engineer and his mates were placing bets on one of two Hialeah-bred, Mexican-trained roosters in the main lounge, and it was only a few minutes later, after moving parts in both of the ship's propulsion systems had fused into much larger, non-moving parts, that anyone noticed all the smoke pouring out of the engine room hatches.

Ten minutes after that, the wet-suited man finished pulling himself along two thousand meters of line back to a 22-foot Ranger flats boat, stripped of her poling platform and painted black and midnight blue and therefore invisible in the moonless night. There he hooked up one of a dozen, twenty-gallon fuel tanks arranged in two rows to the big Evinrude on the stern, then sat on the equipment locker forward of the driver's console sipping from a Thermos of hot coffee he'd swiped from the *City of Galveston*'s galley.

He put a hand-bearing compass to his eye every few minutes to check the tanker's progress. Then, when the coffee was gone and he was satisfied that *City of Galveston* was dead in the water, he pulled a rope on the outboard to start it, keyed his destination coordinates into the GPS navigation unit and got the black-and-blue skiff up on a plane and pointed toward Flamingo.